BERLIN
BREAKDOWN

Bill Rapp

SterlingHouse Publisher, Inc.   Pittsburgh, PA

BERLIN
BREAKDOWN

Retrothrillers

ISBN-10: 1-56315-418-8
ISBN-13: 978-1-56-315418-8
Trade Paperback
© Copyright 2008 Bill Rapp
All Rights Reserved
Library of Congress #2008924349

Requests for information should be addressed to:
SterlingHouse Publisher, Inc.
7436 Washington Avenue
Pittsburgh, PA 15218
info@sterlinghousepublisher.com
www.sterlinghousepublisher.com

Pero Thrillers
is an imprint of SterlingHouse Publisher, Inc.

SterlingHouse Publisher, Inc. is a company
of the Cyntomedia Corporation

Cover Design: Brandon M. Bittner
Interior Design: Kathleen M. Gall

Printed in U.S.A.

ACKNOWLEDGEMENTS

There are many people to thank for their help on and support for this book, not the least of whom is my wife, Cynthia. She experienced these momentous events in Berlin with me, carried much of the joy and most of the burden of raising our first daughter and gave birth to our second during our time there. It was she who kept pushing me out the door to see, "what was going on." There are also my wonderful colleagues in the U.S. Mission and the U.S. Embassy Office in the city, with whom I shared the honor and privilege of representing our country during these tumultuous days, not to mention the sheer professional wonder of working in the middle of it all. Finally, there are the people of Berlin—East and West—and the thousands of East Europeans who took to the streets to protest against the dictatorships imposed by the Soviet Union. They are the true heroes of this seminal period. They are the ones who overthrew communism and brought an end to the Cold War. It is to their memory that I dedicate this book.

PROLOGUE

The train crept toward the Dresden *Hauptbahnhof*, as brief bursts of sunlight danced along a giant web of silver rails. Hans Kroehler leaned forward through an autumn air crisp with anticipation. Voices buzzed as the train rounded the corner. The extraordinary cargo of people and emotion looked ready to spill across the rails, with heads and shoulders surging from the windows and eyes squinting against the cold breeze and gritty air that swept the cars. Arms reached out, fanning the air in collective triumph.

Hans marvelled at how so many had crammed themselves into every available inch of space. Their journeys had begun days, even weeks ago in lands further east, and they had endured weeks of privation and fear, camped on the grounds of the West German embassy in Prague, desperate to reach the West.

But today there had to be room for one more.

Hans tucked his head deeper into the padded collar of his nylon jacket and studied the crowd around him. Thousands more had joined him, surging through the police cordon at Lenin Platz outside the station. Never having been in a riot before, he was not prepared for the desperation of the mob and viciousness of the police in the streets circling the station. Hans heard bones crack and skin rip as the police had swung at the crowd in a frenzy of anger and frustration. The Stasi had been there, too, their black leather jackets a poor disguise. One had even chased him through the high-rise apartments along Prager Strasse, as though there hadn't been hundreds of others he could have arrested.

Hans stamped his feet to keep them warm underneath the overcast sky, his loose blue jeans shaking with an uneven rhythm. East German jeans. Not a bad fit, but still not the real thing. Soon he would be able to afford Levis. Denim shirts, too.

The crowd surged forward. Hans fought back with his elbows and shoulders, his fists and teeth clenched, determined to protect his place at the front. Nervous words swirled in the air above.

"Get ready! It's almost here!"

Hans cocked his wrist and raised his forearm. Four p.m. The fifth of October, 1989. In a few hours it would all be over. Another wave pushed from behind, and Hans shook his shoulders with all the force he could muster. Bodies slammed against his back.

"Out of my way, damn you!"

More voices swore, their desperate strains echoing through the awnings of steel and concrete.

"Stand back!"

"There won't be enough room!"

Hans probed the inside of his jacket. The packet of papers was still tucked into a narrow tube taped just inside the felt lining between his chest and arm. He struggled to pick whole sentences from the blur of words. "Stop...not enough room...can't lose you now."

The train inched through the station, the engine taking on an image that was almost superhuman, a macabre, demonic power screened behind a face of metal and glass. But this demon would deliver him from his tormentors and provide a measure of revenge.

It was only 50 meters away. Hans steadied himself at the edge of the platform, bracing his legs to jump. His fingers rolled themselves into a ball, then stretched out again, poised to grab the sides of the car as it passed. He would ride on the roof if necessary.

Then he felt it. Two powerful hands seized his arms and spun him around. Muscled fingers curled around the lapels of his jacket, then probed inside along his ribs. His breath, his muscles, his whole body froze. The face from Prager Strasse. Then the hands released his jacket and shoved.

Hans tumbled onto the track and heard his own voice echo against a sky suddenly empty and ominous. He jerked his head back toward the other voices, grabbing for the hands of strangers stretched out to him.

But then the hands disappeared, and a bed of stone and steel spread beneath him. Hans wondered about the hard, chiselled face of the man he had fought in the streets, the one who had tossed him from the platform. The eyes were impenetrable, lost behind dark sunglasses.

A smile of recognition and triumph broke across the stranger's thick, rugged lips. Rounded, muscular shoulders shrugged under the padded black leather. "You thought you could buy your freedom, comrade. Well, now you'll have it." The smile widened. "But precious little else."

In that instant, Hans knew that this man had marked him for death days before. His whole plan of escape and revenge had been futile from the start.

"*Auf Wiedersehen*, Hansi. You were too close. I doubt they'd believe you over there anyway."

The hard, square face glanced up at the intermittent clouds sweeping in from the east as a darkening sky announced the approach of night. "Now it's time to take care of your friends."

Those final words sailed past the ears of Hans Kroehler, lost in the futile, desperate screeching of the crowd and the train's thundering mass of metal.

CHAPTER 1

*'Auf, Auf,' Sprach der Fuchs zum Hasen
'Hoerst du nicht den Jaeger blasen?'*
Austrian proverb

Erich Jens, a short, compact man, leaned against the wall as he struggled to follow a fading alley of light along the dark, silent corridor. Rounding another intersection, he halted, alarmed. A door slammed, and footsteps followed, then more silence. The only noise came from the crowd outside as it surged toward the Wall, open now for the first time since it went up 28 years ago.

Jens thrust his hand backward at eye level as far as he could reach. He hoped Lamprecht would recognize it in the darkness and stop before he made too much noise. His old friend and fellow dissident had never been able to guide those long lanky limbs with any sort of grace or stealth. Hermann's awkwardness had plagued him even during their grammar school days and only seemed to get worse as he grew older.

They had been in the headquarters of the *Staatssicherheits-dienst*, or 'Stasi,' on Normannenstrasse for half an hour, and Jens was beginning to worry. They should have found something by now. Files, cabinets. Something. The directions had not been precise, but they had given Jens a general idea of where to look.

Besides, both men had been there before, arrested for their political activism by the Stasi. Jens never thought he would regret not having gotten beyond the interrogation quarters in the basement. But he did tonight.

Lamprecht bumped into Jens's arm. "What's wrong?" he

grumbled, pushing his friend's hands away. "Did you hear something?"

"Didn't you?" Jens muttered. He pressed the palms of both hands against his friend's chest.

"It's probably just a janitor." Lamprecht leaned forward to muffle the sound of his own voice. His breath stank from the early evening beer. He claimed it gave him the courage he needed.

"Well, just the same, it's someone who could sound an alarm."

"I doubt it. Just about everyone in this city is at the Wall, including the assholes that work here. That's why we chose tonight, remember?"

"We can't be so sure."

"Maybe it's one of the others."

Jens slid into the next room, motioning for Lamprecht to follow. Through the windows on the far wall he measured the steady flow of cars and pedestrians moving west toward the Berlin Wall, wave after wave of eager humanity, spreading like a river that had overflowed its banks and now rushed wherever its momentum would carry it.

"Look at them. Jesus, it's only the second night." Lamprecht sounded despondent. "How many do you think will be back?" He joined Jens by the window and rested his forehead against the glass. His breath left a small circle of mist. A scent of disinfectant lingered at the base of the windowsill.

"Most of them," Jens guessed. "There's no reason not to, now that the regime has lifted the travel restrictions."

"They'll be easily spoiled, though, once they've gotten a taste of all that western prosperity."

"God, I hope not. There's so much to do back here."

Lamprecht reached over and grabbed Jens's arm. "Let's go. We're wasting time. We need to find those files and then get the hell out of here. Besides, I've got to pee."

"Why do you think the Stasi will destroy them? Those guys are data freaks."

"Because they've got to start erasing the evidence sometime."

"How can you be so sure? And how are we to know which ones Hans copied?"

"I know the lists we need, Erich. We just have to find the right room."

Jens turned toward the door. "How can you be so sure?" He resented his friend's confidence and self-assurance. He was always this way when they dealt with the Stasi.

"Trust me, Erich. Those pricks were behind Hans's death. It was no accident. Not with what he knew." He glanced at his friend. "He told me too much." Lamprecht's gaze returned to the window and the world outside. Then he spat on the glass. White specks of saliva clung to the window, outlined against the dark urban night. "I just wonder who else he told."

"But look at what's happened, Hermann. Honecker is gone and soon there'll be free elections." Jens balled his fist in front of his friend's face. "I mean really free, Hermann."

Lamprecht pushed the hand away. "Don't be so naive. You can't be so certain. Who knows what will happen in Moscow?"

Jens did not answer. He turned his head from Lamprecht's voice to track the crowd below, hoping to read his friend's thoughts in the mass of pilgrims surging west.

"Let's find a quicker way then. We can't search every room. Not together."

"How then?" Lamprecht asked, angling his bulk against the wall to face his companion.

"We'll work the floors alternately. You finish this one, and I'll start on the one above. After that we just keep alternating."

"But what about Schmidt and Joanna? What do we do about them?"

"If they ever get the hell out of the basement, they can join each of us on a separate floor." Jens peered around Lamprecht's broad chest and the brown sweater that hung over Lamprecht's frame like a curtain blocking his view of the door. "What do you suppose they're doing down there?"

"Fucking for freedom, for all I care. Which is fine with me. It's better to work alone on something like this. Schmidt's the one who claimed the files would be on the third floor. I never should have listened to him."

"Why?"

"I don't trust him." Lamprecht pressed his thumb against the wall. "He asks too damn many questions. He gave me a real grilling last month when he saw me writing notes after a meeting at the *Marienkirche*."

Jens turned his head back toward the window. "He's just nervous."

"Well, he makes *me* nervous." Lamprecht surveyed the room. "Let's get going. This place gives me the creeps."

"Wait." Jens held his hand up. "Did you hear anything?"

Lamprecht waved his hand toward the window and the world outside. "Relax. Whoever it was, he's probably on his way to a shopping spree on the Ku'damm." He strolled through the door and into the hallway.

Jens left his friend and ran to the fifth floor, skipping every other step. He wasted 20 minutes in a series of conference rooms before reaching one where the file cabinets were unlocked.

The drawers were empty. A lone file card on the bottom of the top drawer had markings associated with the HVA, the Stasi's foreign activities arm. Jens slipped the card into his coat pocket with his right hand, the left one slamming the cabinet door shut. He flinched at his own carelessness.

The next room was tougher. Jens had to jimmy the lock open, working slower than he liked to avoid making too much noise. Inside he spied about two dozen boxes stacked along the wall opposite the windows. He ran over, pushed the cardboard flaps apart and plunged his hands inside.

These were full of 9" x 12" manila envelopes and brown cardboard folders.

He skimmed through them. Several sheets fell to the floor, then an entire file. He scooped the pile up and stuffed the papers back into the box on top. He grabbed another folder and held the bound pages in the slim notebook over his head, trying to catch the light from the street outside. After a minute of cursory reading, Jens crammed the sheets back into their box.

This was too good to be true. Jens ran to get Lamprecht, leaping the stairs two and three steps at a bound. He wanted to laugh out loud. The Stasi must be getting careless, panicked perhaps, over the sudden changes. Maybe they had given up. Maybe they were all at the Wall after all. And maybe he had just saved these files from tomorrow's shredder. He slid to a stop on the landing when a figure shot up in front of him.

"Schmidt, where have you been?"

"Running in circles, like you."

"Help me find Lamprecht. I think I've stumbled onto some important stuff here."

"I haven't seen him since we got in." Schmidt moved quickly to follow Jens, who was already trotting through the hall. "Tell me what you've found."

Jens worked to catch his breath and get the words out at the same time. "I think it has something to do with the Stasi and the Church. And that was just one folder. Another one had some financial stuff." He turned to face Schmidt, skipping backwards down the hall in his eagerness to reach Lamprecht. "It could tell us a lot about Hans' death." He stopped. "And perhaps what else may be going on."

"How can you be so sure?"

"Well, it's as good a place as any to start."

"Then let's go get the stuff now. Something might happen to it while we're looking for Lamprecht."

Jens ignored him. He turned and scampered through the darkened passages. Behind him, the sharp, purposeful footsteps of Schmidt worked to keep pace.

Whispering Lamprecht's name, Jens glanced in each of the rooms as he passed. Halfway down the hall a door stood partly open, a thin shaft of light jutting out into the tile hallway and linoleum floor of dark beige and pea green. The light created a double line of shadows in the shape of elongated triangles along each wall, reminding Jens of the night he had snuck back into his high school, hoping to steal a teacher's report of some disloyal jokes he had recited in the schoolyard. Jens wondered why Lamprecht had been so careless to leave the light on and take the chance of attracting attention.

Near the door Jens came to a sudden, reflexive stop. His eyes caught the lower half of Lamprecht's legs, the black soles of his shoes staring up at Jens like holes in a skull. Jens refused to move any further into the room, hoping to block out what he already knew lay waiting just seconds ahead.

"Hermann, is that you?" Jens could barely hear his own voice. It sounded as though it had been separated from his body and cast into the room from some dark, distant corner. Siberia perhaps.

When he stepped closer, Jens could see that the back of his friend's head was a mixture of brown and red, a blend of hair and blood. The floor around the body was covered with blood, a darker pool already beginning to congeal. The room stank of death and disinfectant. A spray of light from the window cut the body in half at the waist. Jens felt his own limbs turn stiff and sore. A cold, churning nausea began to rise from the pit of his stomach.

Jens bent over Lamprecht and instinctively picked up his friend's wrist to feel for a pulse. He let the arm drop to the floor and knelt beside the body, trying to collect his thoughts. What about Schmidt? Where was he now? And Joanna? Was she safe?

Jens rose. His knees seemed to melt. He turned to say something but heard himself stuttering. He shook his head and started over.

Before he could get anything out, a sharp stab of pain burst at the back of his neck. It sent a dull, throbbing shudder through his temples and crown, then down his entire body. He reached to rub the pain away. But an overpowering numbness swept over him as the room went dark. He fell toward the floor, his body tumbling into the litter of empty boxes and cabinets, his message trapped in his throat.

Down the hall, Schmidt's frightened legs stumbled toward the stairway. Beads of sweat collected on his forehead and wrists. He thought of removing his sweater, a heavy woolen carpet of blue, but the terror of what had just happened would not let him stop. He had to find the files Jens had told him about.

He stopped to catch his breath and rest his back against the wall. Schmidt struggled to remember what Jens had said. It had sounded like a single word. A name. The American diplomat in West Berlin. Rosman. Great. Now that nosy American bastard was involved. Someone would have to find out how much he knew, and what could be done about it.

CHAPTER 2

The phone would not stop ringing. Night shone on the other side of his bedroom window like black ice, but the damn telephone just kept on ringing. If there was one thing he hated, it was waking up when it was still dark outside. John Rosman was not a morning person.

"What?" he grumbled at the telephone on his nightstand. "Do you realize what time it is?"

"Mr. Rosman?" The words sounded so soft. "John?"

Not only was it a woman's voice, but it sounded like the stunning blonde he had met several months ago in Kreuzberg. It was the same evening he met Erich Jens and several other East German dissidents. He had seen Jens several times since then, but she was the one he remembered best. She had been sitting directly across from Rosman throughout that evening of beer, wine and cigarette smoke, and it had taken him nearly the entire evening to learn her name.

The group had gathered under the watchful eye of Gunther Sussmann, a member of the Alternative List, West Berlin's left-wing environmentalists, known elsewhere in Germany as the Greens. Fortunately, Sussmann did not appear to share the visceral anti-Americanism of so many of his colleagues. Rosman had met Sussmann at a lecture at West Berlin's Free University on NATO and American Imperialism in Postwar Europe. Rosman had been ever so grateful to have the shaggy German with the long blond hair and patchy beard rescue him from some coed's harangue on American genocide in Vietnam, for which she appeared to hold Rosman personally responsible. Later, Rosman had challenged his new contact to introduce him to some like-minded colleagues in

East Berlin, and Sussmann had dragged him along to the rendezvous in Kreuzberg. After that, Rosman had plunged on his own into the turmoil sweeping the country on the other side of the Wall.

"Joanna?"

She stammered in a mixture of halting German and bad English, and it was all Rosman could do to pull himself into consciousness and make sense of the hurried words and static sifting through the poor telephone connection that linked East and West Berlin.

"I'm sorry, but there's been an accident," she finally explained,

"What's happened?" He sat up in bed and stared at the alarm clock. The time emerged in a blur of yellow numbers. 2:35. Rosman blinked, but the numbers stayed the same. His head fell back against the pillow.

"It's Erich. He's been beaten. He's at the Charite over here in the east." Rosman sat up, suddenly alert and fully awake. "He's been asking to see you."

Rosman leaned toward the table, grabbed a pen and slip of paper, then jotted down the address. "I'll be right there." He tried to sound reassuring but found himself wondering what he could do to help. He doubted intervention by an American diplomat would do much in the city's eastern half, but at least he could visit his friend and see if anything could be done.

Rosman hung up, fell out of bed, and stumbled toward his bathroom. He leaned heavily on the white porcelain sink and splashed some cold water on his face, dragged a comb through his hair, then pulled on a pair of blue jeans and white socks to go with his tennis shoes. Rosman nearly tripped as he navigated the stairs while tugging on a forest green cotton sweater.

During the ride to East Berlin Rosman struggled to weave his used brown Mercedes 280SL through streets overflowing with a mob of East and West Berliners that had come together on the second day of the city's new-found freedom and precarious unity. It was as though the buildings had emptied themselves onto the streets in a spasm of joy and reunion. It was not so bad in Zehlendorf and Dahlem, the neighborhoods where Rosman lived at the western edge of town. But as he drew closer to the city center, rolling along the Hohenzollerndamm toward Wittenbergplatz, the crowds grew thicker and the streets more confused. The Kurfuerstendamm was closed to traffic entirely, throwing even more cars onto the avenues that paralleled it. Rosman cursed himself for not taking the subway, until he heard over the car radio that the West Berlin system had been overwhelmed by East Germans pouring through the new openings in the Wall to ride the transit system for free. Some lines had been shut down entirely.

By the time he got to Checkpoint Charlie, Rosman could see rows of West Berliners pouring *Sekt*, the German champagne, and tossing bouquets onto the squat, puttering Trabants, twin-cylindered boxes of press board that passed for automobiles in East Germany. The people looked at him like he was a lunatic, wondering why a westerner would be going east tonight.

Rosman fought his way across traffic to the Charite, a collection of squat red brick buildings that reminded him of a run-down college campus. In its middle stood a tall modern structure that hovered like a beacon of socialist health, overwhelming its smaller neighbors in a panorama of glass and steel. To his left, spotlights and jubilant Berliners swept the Brandenburg Gate in waves of light and emotion. Just to his front and across the River Spree stood the *Reichstag*, outlined against the night sky by a glare of camera lights and history. Between them, of course, loomed the Wall. But tonight it was gathering place, not an obstacle. Rosman slipped his car into an open spot along the curb.

Once inside, Rosman hesitated for a moment at the elevators. He would never forget getting stuck in one at the apartments on Leipzigerstrasse, where several of the Americans assigned to East Berlin lived. The worst of it was that he had had to wait nearly half an hour for the lift to move, his only companion an overweight Bulgarian, who smelled like he had just returned from a Balkan sweatshop and garlic factory. But he was not about to walk up. Jens was being held on the ninth floor, and in Germany you started counting *after* the ground floor.

The elevator ascended without difficulty. Rosman let his breath out, hopped off the car, then trotted over to the nursing station to ask for the room number.

"Herr Jens is no longer here." A thin, officious face studied him with narrow, indecipherable eyes framed by a cap of starched white cotton.

Typical Prussian, he thought. "What do you mean? Has he been released already?"

"Of course not. His injuries are far too serious." Her stiff, tired face continued to stare at Rosman as though he were a visitor from another universe. "He's been moved to the seventh floor. This"—her hand swept the air above the floor at her feet—"is for patients under intensive care."

Rosman thanked her, then jogged down the two floors and located Jens after about five minutes of searching. He shared a large room with perhaps 20 patients and lay in a bed at the far end of the ward. Rows of ceiling fixtures bathed the room in a rich, white glow. Pale and indistinct behind white linens and a languid skin, Jens looked lost amidst his sea of sheets. His bed sat in a corner by a window, and his view, appropriately enough, opened out to the west, to the Wall and the *Reichstag*. His face brightened with a splash of color when he saw Rosman.

"John? Thank God! Who told you I was here?"

Rosman moved a chair from one of the tables by the door to the bedside and dropped into it.

"I believe it was the blonde who attended our session in Kreuzberg. Her name's Joanna, isn't it? She sounded pretty worried."

"Tell me what it's like out there. It sounds glorious."

Rosman peered out the window. "Oh Christ, Erich, it's crazy. The people are lined up by the hundreds at all the crossing points. I even heard on the radio that they expect your side of the German border to have people backed up for 50 kilometers by mid-morning."

Jens let his head fall back against the pillow. "My God. I never imagined...."

"But more to the point, Erich, how do you feel?"

"Well, my head hurts like hell." Jens patted his scalp and leaned forward. "Who did you say called?"

"Joanna." Rosman smiled and arched his eyebrows to signal his interest.

Jens sank back into his pillow. "That was good of her. I remember asking about you, but I don't remember who was here."
His hand rose to cover eyes squinting against the glare.

"What's wrong?"

Jens turned his head and murmured something in the direction of the window in the heavy Berlin dialect that Rosman still
could follow with only the greatest difficulty. "They won't give me
anything for the pain. It has something to do with some tests or
other medication."

"What did they say is wrong with you?"

"I believe it's some kind of concussion. The worst of it is I'm
not sure how long I'll be in here." Jens massaged his temples.
"God, I can't wait to catch up with the bastard that did this."

"Do you have any idea what happened?" Other visitors kept a
steady hum of murmured conversation in the background. Rosman glanced over his shoulder, then leaned in closer to Jens.
"Joanna said you were found in a gutter on Unter den Linden.
You don't seem like the type who would pass out after too much
champagne."

Jens glanced about the room. His eyes narrowed, and his lips
barely moved. The words seemed to slip out the corners of his
mouth. "John, we were in the Stasi headquarters. We were looking for some files...." His eyes grew moist as Jens stared out the
window. "Hermann is dead. Someone crushed his skull."

"What the hell...?" Rosman's body jerked and his spine stiffened, his eyes widening with disbelief. "Are you guys crazy? The
Stasi building? And now Hermann is dead?"

Jens put a finger to his lips and glanced toward the door. Rosman sank back in his chair and stared out the window, while Jens
stammered on about what he had seen from his quick glance at
the files.

"Wait a minute, Erich. How the hell did you get in?" Rosman
asked. "They must have some incredible security at that place."

"Schmidt arranged it. A door was left open at the back, and
a couple of security guards were bribed to keep the floors clear
and then head for the Wall like everyone else in Berlin. Man, there
were pages and pages of reports on meetings with all kinds of

church officials. And with dissidents. If someone could just get his hands on those files...."

Rosman stared in disbelief. "Erich, what possessed you to go searching for that kind of stuff in the Stasi headquarters? I mean, you'd have to have a death wish or something."

"About a month ago a friend of ours, Hans Kroehler, was killed in Dresden. He was on his way west, to your people."

"Why?"

"He had something very damaging, very important. He wanted your people to have it."

Rosman shook his head and sat back in his chair again. He glanced out the window. "This is moving a little too fast for me. Why was the Stasi involved?"

"Hansi wasn't with us that night in Kreuzberg. He was always afraid to travel to the West."

"So why now, and why would the Stasi kill him?"

"I'm not sure why. Hermann said he knew, but that he needed proof."

"And you guys think you found something that explains this at Stasi headquarters."

Jens forced out another smile. "Yes. And perhaps more. This is where you come in."

"Wait a _____ man threw his hands up toward Jens, palms out, _____ was coming. "Just a damn mir_____ This does not sound

"You _____
I'm laid _____

"Lik _____

"Y _____

"Y _____

short _____

they l _____

ger. _____

hea _____

ex

man would be tough."

"Forget the damn translations. Just finding the stuff will be next to impossible." Rosman looked toward the floor, shaking his head in disbelief. "And why me?"

"Why not? You have the German, and I know I can trust you."

Rosman studied Jens's pale and haggard face. Despite the smile and the eagerness in those eyes, Rosman saw only mysteries from a world that was still new to him. "You only think you can trust me."

"No, I'm fairly certain of it."

"Erich, you hardly know me. And I never knew this Hans Kroehler at all. Lamprecht just a little better. Why should I let myself get pulled into this?"

"John, I need someone untainted, someone I know has had no contact with the Stasi. Someone they won't be following, like your colleagues over here. I also know you well enough to know that you will want to find out as much as possible about this business."

"You sound pretty sure of yourself, Erich."

"Oh, I am. Have you ever read *Faust?*"

"The long poem by Goethe?"

"Yes." Jens leaned forward. "You have what we Germans refer to as *Wissensdrang*. The 'urge to know'. Faust had it. It's what drove him."

"Yeah, and didn't he get himself into all kinds of trouble?"

"Yes, but that's because he made a pact with the devil." Jens laughed and let his head sink back among the pillows. "I'm sure you can avoid that."

"Let's hope so," Rosman said.

Rosman shifted his gaze toward the window again. Crowds surged through the crossing at Invalidenstrasse, and thin beams from headlights danced among the dark figures spilling over the streets. Thousands had assembled behind the *Reichstag* and up beyond the Brandenburg Gate, many of them pressing forward to climb aboard the flat slabs that topped the Wall in front of the Gate. Here and there West German flags fluttered among waving champagne bottles. A hazy mirage of red and black and yellow surged across the night air against a backdrop of painted concrete and a night sky lit by searchlights and song. A joyous city had finally found a reason to keep itself happy.

"You've always wanted to find out more about the revolutions here behind the Iron Curtain."

"I can read the newspapers."

"No, John, this is your chance to find out what is really happening." Jens smiled. His face shone with the discovery of a new idea. "Maybe Joanna can help you. You'd probably like that. It would give you a chance to impress her."

Rosman sat in silence for a moment. "Or embarrass myself. Did you see anything with Lamprecht's body?"

"I'm not sure. All I can remember is empty boxes, rifled cabinets, overturned chairs. Stuff like that." Pools formed at the edges of his eyes. Jens wiped the tears away with the sleeve of his hospital gown, and his blue eyes hardened.

"One thing I can't figure out is Schmidt's part in this."

"Schmidt? You mean the guy who was so silent that night in Kreuzberg? The one with the straight brown hair?"

"Yes, that's the one. He may have seen something."

"He went there with you?"

"Yeah. As I said, he knew one of the guards and got us in. But I checked, and he isn't here. So he must be all right." Jens propped himself up on one elbow. His eyes narrowed as they zeroed in on Rosman's. "We need to find him and learn what he knows."

"Anyone else? What about Joanna?"

"What about her?"

"She said she found you in the gutter. But she was there with you, wasn't she?"

"That's okay. She probably wanted to avoid giving herself away in case the phone line was tapped." Jens' eyes shifted in the direction of the window. He seemed to gaze right through the panels of glass streaked by dust and streetlamps. He turned back to Rosman. "There is one other thing."

"You mean besides the files?"

"Yes. It may help you locate them, or at least give some clues as to what we're looking for. I need you to go to Lamprecht's apartment. If his sister is there, tell her you're picking something up for me. It would mean a great deal if you would hold on to it for a while. You can give it to me later."

"Shit, Erich, this gets deeper and deeper."

Jens reached for Rosman's arm. "Please, John. You're the only one I can turn to right now."

Rosman surveyed the room, then focused on Jens's tired, frightened eyes. "Oh, Hell. I'll see what I can do."

A nurse appeared at the front of the bed and barked orders about a bedpan to an orderly. Rosman almost snapped to attention. "But try to get some rest. You look terrible. And for God's sake, be careful."

"I'll be all right." Jens spoke in a raspy whisper, his gaze locked upon the scenery unfolding outside. "We've had a revolution here, John, a true *Wende*. There's no turning back now."

Rosman got up to leave. The Germans had adopted *Wende* as the label for the events of the past fall, a 'change' to signify that East Germany had "turned" an important corner. *I wish I believed that*, Rosman told himself, *then maybe I wouldn't be so worried.*

As he left the ward, Rosman ignored the people milling about in the hallway and headed straight for the elevator. He folded and pocketed the slip of paper on which Jens had written Lamprecht's address. Rosman did not have the faintest idea where it was. Apparently, his night was far from over.

Back in his car, Rosman grabbed the flashlight he kept for emergencies from his glove compartment and tried to plot his route. First, he located the address in a distant neighborhood called Marzahn. Then he traced several paths through the warren of streets that would keep him from going beyond the city limits. After several minutes he gave up. With so little prior experience in this part of the city, he opted for public transportation, which in East Berlin meant the historic *S-Bahn*. He folded the map and returned the flashlight to the glove compartment. Only then did Rosman realize that he had forgotten to ask Jens what it was he was supposed to pick up from Lamprecht's sister. Christ, he'd make an awful courier, he thought.

Rosman drove his car to the parking lot across from the U.S. Embassy on Neustaedtische Kirchstrasse and parked in the street next to the lot. Hopefully, if anyone got curious, they would see the American military plates and assume he was on some sort of official business. It took only a minute to hustle to the main terminal at Friedrichstrasse, three short blocks away.

The black steel and dirty red bricks underneath the high arched dome of soiled glass seemed to transport Rosman back in time to a Berlin long gone. The ride was an excursion through a tired city marked by coal dust, diesel exhaust and decay. He sat stiffly on the hard wooden seats, and his feet slid along the smooth plank floors as the train pitched along tracks running past shops and apartment buildings hiding behind dirty windows and peeling paint, all of them leaning on one another for support. Maintenance did not appear to be part of the five-year plan, Rosman noted. It was as though this half of the city had been living on distant memories and a worn-out ideology, and nothing memorable had emerged to replace the faded glory and old ideals of ancient political battles.

When the train arrived in Marzahn, Rosman's heart sank further. Once a broad meadow on the outskirts of Berlin, Marzahn was to have been a monument to the new socialist regime, to the achievements of Germany's first—and last—workers' and farmers' state. Instead, Rosman found huge rectangular, concrete eyesores that passed for communist urban planning, massive high-rises set haphazardly on a barren moonscape of intermittent grass and periodic shrubbery.

He strolled past walls swimming with bright graffiti, much of it neo-Nazi. Rosman had heard that these newer living accommodations were supposed to be rewards for party functionaries, loyalists of the regime, and other exemplary communists. Those with the right connections. This made the juvenile splashings of some minor fascists all the more surprising. Was it youthful rebellion, East German style? he wondered.

It took only 15 minutes to find Lamprecht's building, planted three rows deep in the maze of cement and glass. It looked like all the rest: a 10-story collection of apartments that resembled a patchwork of square concrete blocks, each with a small window in the center. Every unit also had its own patio, a small thin rectangle about three feet by ten feet with sheet metal and iron gridwork for a railing.

Lamprecht's name was next to a mailbox with the number 206. The elevator would not be an issue this time. Rosman strode through the unguarded doors, ran up the two flights of stairs, and knocked on the door.

Nobody answered. Rosman tried the door. To his surprise, it was open.

Rosman paused, considering his next step, his hand on the doorknob. He glanced down the hall in both directions, then pushed the door back about a foot and slipped inside.

The apartment was almost completely dark, just a shade shy of pitch black. He waited in the foyer for his eyes to adjust, listening for a sound or sign of life. Slowly, the room came into focus. A few pieces of furniture, a picture window at the center, some wall-hangings. He could make out a row of bookcases along a far wall, stuffed with hardcovers and a handful of paperbacks, plus the knickknacks one picks up at vacation spots. As his eyes searched the apartment, Rosman noticed a young woman seated in a rocking chair at the far end of the room.

"Can I help you?" The question slipped from a weak, nearly silent voice.

His heart leaped inside his chest. "I…I'm sorry. I…I didn't mean anything. I just…." Rosman felt the sweat on his wrists and forehead. The eerie pitch in the evening's darkness reinforced a sense of unease that now bordered on fear.

"Miss Lamprecht?"

She nodded.

"I wanted to say how sorry I am about your brother. Erich Jens gave me this address. I didn't know Hermann well, but I did want to express my sorrow at his tragic death."

"You are American? From the Embassy?"

"Yes…no." Great. This was bound to confuse her even further. "Actually, I'm from the American Mission in West Berlin. I've just spoken with Erich Jens. May I come in?"

She did not answer, but the movement of her head as she looked away resembled a sign of assent. Or perhaps it was resignation. "May I turn on a light?"

He moved carefully toward a wall that looked like it led into a kitchen and groped for a light switch. He swept his right hand across rough wallpaper until his fingers hit what felt like a switch and flipped it toward the ceiling.

Through the dim light of a single bulb that hung just over his head Rosman could see living room furniture made of teak and pine. They had the basic pieces: a sofa, two armchairs, the rocking chair Lamprecht's sister occupied, a coffee table and two bookshelves. The bric-a-brac represented souvenir items from various East European capitals and Black Sea resorts. Rosman recognized one from the island of Ruegen on East Germany's northern coast. Behind him, someone had spread an assortment of small framed photographs across a dining room table, all with Hermann Lamprecht in some happy pose.

Rosman felt lost. "Have the authorities found anyone yet?" he finally asked.

"How could they? Someone just disappeared back into the mob."

"Haven't they checked the list of officers who were working there that night?"

The woman's face registered nothing except for the vacant eyes rimmed by red from the crying that resumed as Rosman spoke. Her light skin seemed to have been stretched taut across a thin frame, the bones of her cheeks and chin etched sharply against the dim light. She was wearing a large shawl that covered most of her body as it rocked lightly back and forth.

"What are you trying to say?" Her words gathered more force. "The police told me Hermann was beaten by someone in the crowd this evening. They said there is a great deal of that sort of criminal behavior going on."

"But that wasn't what happened. Don't you realize...?" Rosman stopped. This was unfamiliar territory, a place where the rules were different from those he knew in the west. He felt dizzy and thrust out his hand to steady himself against the wall. "I'm...I'm sorry. Perhaps I shouldn't have come."

Rosman backed toward the door. Then he halted and cast a long, anxious look at Lamprecht's sister. "But please," he began, "be careful. Your brother did not die in the crowd or at the Wall tonight."

Cold narrow eyes held Rosman. The woman seemed to be staring right through him. He turned to leave.

"Wait." Rosman froze at the door. "Were you there?"

"No. But Erich was. He told me what happened. The police, I mean, the Stasi killed Hermann."

Her eyes closed for a moment, as though she had finally resigned herself to what she had suspected. "I was afraid of that. I always warned him."

She placed her hands on the arms of the chair and pushed herself up. "Please." She wavered, then extended a hand. "Just a moment."

She disappeared into the bedroom and returned a few minutes later carrying a small package, neatly wrapped in brown packing paper. "Here, some notebooks of my brother's. I found them this morning. Perhaps you can pass them to Erich."

She hesitated a moment, her right hand pressing against her forehead, as though trying to remember something. The left hand held the shawl tightly around her chest and shoulders. "A couple came by earlier asking if there was anything my brother had left for his friends. An older man and a younger woman. I considered giving these papers to them, but I'm sure Hermann would want Erich to have them. They were so close."

"Thank you," Rosman mumbled. "I promise I'll get these to him."

Out in the hallway, he stopped to unwrap the package, then glanced at the contents. He quickly lost himself in a maze of letters and numbers scattered across lined, white pages of notebook paper. *Great*, he thought, *a code.*

The wrapping paper fluttered to the floor. Rosman stuck the notes inside his jacket, jogged down the stairs and out the building. A cold November air grabbed the breath from his lungs like a highway bandit. Something moved in the shadows. Rosmann halted, searching the darkness. But he found only more cold air.

He stepped away quietly, wanting to get back to the west as quickly as possible. If he were stopped, he had no plausible excuse for being here. He would have to think fast, keep his wits intact.

Stopping to suck in a lungful of air, Rosman hugged the package close to his ribs. He noted how little more than a day had passed since the Wall had opened, but somehow he knew that his days in Berlin, and probably the rest of his life, would never be the same.

As the *S-Bahn* retraced the path back to Friedrichstrasse, Rosman glanced at the other passengers. Four shared his car. Two appeared to be a young married couple or lovers, their hands entwined and eyes searching the street for sights to share. Had they been to the west? Rosman wondered. A third was a middle-aged woman, whose sensible clothes suggested she was on her way to or from work. The fourth, a man sitting in the back row, made a point of avoiding Rosman's eyes.

Rosman felt a quick rush of adrenaline. He stood up and walked toward the door as the train pulled into the station at Warschau Strasse, just five stops from the end. He let his hand rest on the handle of the door. As soon as the car halted, Rosman jumped out and began to walk as rapidly as he could toward the exit. Running would be a mistake. He didn't want to draw any unnecessary attention. When he heard the announcement that the train was about to proceed, Rosman jumped back on board. His heart felt like it would burst. Once the train was clear of the station, Rosman turned his head as casually as he could to see if he still had company. The familiar face with the shifting eyes now occupied a bench in the next car back.

Not the smoothest move, admittedly, but he now had the distance he needed. He folded the pages from Lamprecht into small squares and pressed them all together. As the train pulled into the terminal at Friedrichstrasse, Rosman stuffed the wad of paper into the hollow at the small of his back.

The trick now was to get to his car as quickly as possible. Rosman hustled out of the station, using the side door that led directly to the park between the station and the Embassy. He walked with a slight limp, the bundle in his pants cutting into the skin of his back and pressing against his lower spine. But he did not dare stop.

Just another hundred yards.

Footsteps accelerated behind him.

Rosman quickened his own pace. The absence of any lighting in the park heightened his sense of vulnerability. The stinging pain in his back increased, each step sending a sharp jab along his hips.

When he reached the street, Rosman broke into a light trot. The footsteps kept pace. But they did not close.

Rosman released his breath in a sigh of triumph when he felt his hand grip the hard metal of his door handle. Fortunately, he had forgotten to lock it. A hand tapped his shoulder. A heavy voice asked for a cigarette.

"No, I don't smoke," Rosman said as he turned. A fist that seemed to reach out of nowhere dove deep into his stomach. He blew a breath full of saliva across the blacktop and doubled over, his arms grabbing at his midsection. Pain shot through his stomach and up toward his lungs. Rosman struggled to suck air into his body. Another fist delivered a thunderclap to the top of his spine, just below the neck.

Rosman reached out to steady himself, but he found only air. His knees buckled, and he dropped to the ground. He rolled over, coughing and gasping for air. His lips puckered enough to spit another mouthful of saliva onto the asphalt at someone's feet, leaving a trail of speckled foam across scuffed brown leather.

Rosman pushed himself up against the car door, trying to get a bearing on his attackers. One of them stood squarely to the front, legs planted apart in the shape of a woolen triangle. Without even thinking, driven by adrenaline, Rosman drove his fist up into the man's groin. The phantom figure howled as it doubled over.

That's one at least, Rosman thought. He straightened himself against the door of his car. Then another blow burst against the side of his face, square on the cheekbone. A needle of pain shot across his face. Powerful hands grabbed Rosman's shoulders and spun him around, slamming his face against the roof of his Mercedes. Another fist threw a rabbit punch at his ribs.

A swelling lip pressed against his teeth, and blood ran from his nose onto his chin. Blinking through the tears, Rosman felt his wallet slip from his back pants pocket. Cards and notes fell to the ground. Strong stubby fingers pushed his face against the car. Another hand probed his ribs and the insides of his arms, then slipped down along his legs. The scent of beer and schnapps oozed from behind his neck. He heard the wallet smack onto the hood of the car.

Footsteps retreated across the street, and Rosman inched his hand forward to his wallet. The cash, about two hundred West German Marks and fifty U.S. dollars, was gone. He thrust the billfold back into his pants and leaned against the driver-side door, while he turned in the direction his assailants had fled. Rosman could see two men shuffling toward a gray Lada parked on Clara Zetkin Strasse across from the Hotel Metropol, just around the corner from the American Embassy. Between them, they dragged a third individual, doubled over, his arms draped over their shoulders. His legs were not moving.

When they reached the street, a middling sized man with dirty blond hair combed straight back behind a receding hairline turned in Rosman's direction. His long gray raincoat marched to within a block of Rosman before it stopped. The strange figure stood for a minute observing Rosman, a rough and confident smile on his face. Then he waved.

"Thanks for the cash, Ami," he said, in accented English. "It's nice to know you're all so rich. But it's still best for your kind to stay where they belong. Hopefully, we won't have to meet again."

Hugging his ribs to ease the pain, Rosman watched the figure saunter away. He hoped so, too. But he doubted it. He had no intention of staying away. Not now.

CHAPTER 3

Tucking his Allied pass into his shirt pocket, Rosman swung his Mercedes through Checkpoint Charlie and around the corner of Kochstrasse. He steered toward the shell of the old Anhalter station. Only the broken rubble of its bombed-out facade still stood at the head of the rusted tracks overgrown with weeds. A sagging chain link fence enclosed its vacant lot. Rosmann edged ahead cautiously, searching through a blur of pain for the road ahead.

West Berlin's streets thinned as the night faded into morning. Rosman encountered only stragglers from the celebrations or the odd pair of lovers. Empty *Sekt* bottles littered the gutters, holding vigil for broken flowers and streams of paper. Occasionally, a cop rested against a doorframe or a storefront, his broad shoulders packed into a light green jacket. Streetlights pushed streaks of white across the blacktop that lined the pathways of modern Berlin. Windows yellow with light cast bright squares against the roving grey of early morning. It was the closest this city would come to sleep.

Rosman considered stopping at the U.S. Army Hospital in Dahlem just to make sure no real damage had been done, but there would be time enough for that. What he really wanted was a beer and a bath.

He left his Mercedes standing in a diagonal bisecting his driveway, marched through the front door and straight to the refrigerator. He grabbed a large green bottle of Jever, a bitter northern German beer, something with an edge to match his anger. Rosman moved his hands carefully over his ribs and around his jaw. Nothing had been broken, but his face had probably been banged up pretty well. A glance in a mirror confirmed that the bleeding had stopped, so at least he would not need stitches.

He walked upstairs gripping the thin green neck of his Jever and limped into the bedroom. He just hoped the bruises wouldn't be too noticeable. Stabs of pain forced him to peel off his clothes one piece at a time.

Rosman dropped onto the edge of his bed, surveying his room. The mess at his feet reinforced the throbbing pain in his head. Two weeks worth of laundry lay scattered around the floor, and books on German history and literature—always study a country's background, he had been told—lay piled at odd intersections of the room. He had never been this sloppy before. Then again, he asked himself, how often did one live through a revolution?

With a loud sigh, Rosman walked into his bathroom and drew the water for his bath. After about 20 seconds, steam rose toward the patches of peeling paint along his ceiling. He finished undressing and tossed the pants and socks toward a laundry hamper that was already overflowing. Sitting on the edge of the tub, Rosman saw the pages of Lamprecht's notebook spread across the tile floor. He scooped them up and began to read.

Or at least he tried to read. He leafed through pages marked with series of notations, listings of letters, usually matched to dates, and locations. There were also pages with numbers, figures matched in sets of seven or eight, these too with locations. Occasionally, a full name appeared, but never one Rosman recognized.

To hell with it, he thought. Tonight was not the time to read, and this tub was not the place to try. Besides, the link to Hans's disappearance and Lamprecht's death was Jens's problem. He would just keep it all safe until he could get the entire collection back to his friend, where it belonged.

Rosman rose, hid the pages in the bottom drawer of the dresser in the spare bedroom, then returned to his bath. He slid into the tub with his Jever, the warm water rising to his neck.

Seconds later, the doorbell rang.

"Shit." He leaned from the tub to glance at the clock on his nightstand. 6:15. "Now, who in the hell...?"

He towelled himself off, threw on a pair of blue jeans and a robe, then plodded down the stairs. To his surprise, Joanna Beierlich, the East German who had called earlier, greeted him as he opened the door, her face glowing under the porch light like a blond goddess from some ancient German legend.

"May I come in?" she asked. "I've been watching your door for about half an hour. It took me a while to work up the courage to ring your bell."

"Of course. You must be cold." Rosman stumbled backwards, holding the door open. "Can I get you something to drink? Perhaps a brandy or a coffee." He tried not to sound too eager.

"Yes, thank you. A brandy would be wonderful. I haven't been to bed yet, and I think I may have caught a chill waiting in the cold." She stepped inside. "I didn't get by to see Erich before the hospital closed, so I came here to find out how he is doing. I've been too worried to go home."

"He seemed all right, although I'll bet his head hurts like hell." Rosman walked toward the kitchen, looking back to be certain that she was following.

"Is there anything you can do to help him?" Joanna halted in the middle of the foyer. She seemed to notice his clothes for the first time. "Oh, excuse me. You were in bed."

"Actually, I was taking a bath. It's okay, though."

She looked remarkably like she did that evening in Kreuzberg, her medium length blond hair falling just shy of her shoulders, the smooth pink skin covering the straight lines of her face and her small rounded chin. Deep hazel eyes stood out against the light complexion, drawing him in like a snare. He made no effort to escape.

"Oh yes. I've heard that you Americans are fanatics about bathing, and that you may actually bathe too often." She strolled into the kitchen.

And you Germans not enough, he thought to himself. But when he looked at that face and that body, Rosman didn't care if she ever washed. In the room's full light Rosman could see her study his bloodied and bruised face for the first time. Her eyes clouded, and her voice assumed a tone of concern.

"You've been in a fight. Are you all right?"

She stepped closer to inspect the damage. Her body moved with a fluid grace, as her hand rose and touched his face.

Rosman jerked his head away, surprised that it still hurt so much. "I was jumped just beyond the park near the Friedrichstrasse station tonight." He winced. "On my way home from Marzahn. I had been to Lamprecht's place."

Her eyes widened with surprise. "Yes, I heard. But, good Lord, why did you go there?"

Rosman sank into a chair at the table. "I suppose it was a stupid move on my part, since I didn't have the faintest idea what I was doing. But Erich asked me to. Then some guys jumped me when I got back to my car."

Joanna shook her head. "What did they want?"

He paused, scratching the side of his head. "Money, naturally. One of them even thanked me." He let out a short hard laugh. "I got in a good shot at one, though, and he'll be singing in falsetto for a while." He leaned forward. "How did you know?"

"I think I'd rather have one of those beers?" She moved over and stood by the sink. Rosman brought her his last Jever. She reached for the bottle, and a shy smile spread across soft, pink lips. "I heard it from Regina Lamprecht that you had been by when I called. She told me that she had initially been afraid of you. She suspected you were from the Stasi. Then she came to believe you were an American. No Stasi officer would be so uncomfortable. Or so awkward."

Rosman fell back into his seat and watched her take a long sip from the Jever. "I'm sorry. Would you like a glass?" He stood up again.

She shook her head and waved a hand. "I'm fine. Thank you."

Rosman sank back down. "There is something I need to ask you, though." He thought he read concern, maybe even pity, in her eyes as he braced his arms against the tabletop. "Jens told me you might be able to help. Do you know where I can find Schmidt?"

Joanna stared at him, a look of disbelief breaking through soft laughter. "Don't you ever quit? Are you ready for the next round already?" She walked slowly around the kitchen, as though she was taking an inventory of Rosman's belongings.

He frowned. "Joanna, I am touched by your concern."

"It's not concern," she said, the words trailing over her shoulder.

Rosman took in every move of her body. She strolled the length of the kitchen, then stopped just a foot in front of him. The light from the ceiling fixture cast a soft yellow glow behind her. "You have a nice place here, from what I've seen of it."

He took a deep breath, ignoring her comment about his house. "If it's not concern, then what is it?"

The smile broke free again, and her lips curled. "Perhaps it's curiosity."

"About what?"

"You. How you live. But tell me why you want Schmidt's address."

Rosman paused for a moment, chewing his lower lip. Joanna shifted her weight from one foot to the other. "What was Schmidt doing at Normannenstrasse tonight?" he asked.

Joanna frowned. "The same as the rest. Looking for documents to steal. They think the regime is very vulnerable now."

"Why did you go?"

"Mostly to keep them out of trouble. I guess I failed."

Joanna just stared at his chest, the bruise on his face, and finally, his eyes. The silence in the room, disturbed only by the hum of his refrigerator, made him even more aware of Joanna's presence. Rosman struggled to find something to say. "I think..." the bottle of Jever rose to his lips, then sank, "...it could be important."

"What is important?"

"Schmidt's address. Perhaps he can help, perhaps he saw something."

"What about you?" she asked. "How far are you prepared to go to help us?"

"That all depends."

"On what?"

"On what happens. On what we find, and how far it takes us." He hesitated, then gulped a mouthful of beer. It flowed down his throat like soft lead. "There are a lot of people who would like to know all the Stasi has been up to."

Seconds later she stood next to Rosman, almost touching him.

He hadn't even noticed her move. She leaned against the table, her right leg stretched slightly forward toward his own. "Who would like to know? The Americans?"

"I suppose so." He shrugged. "And lots of others, especially on your side of the Wall."

Rosman looked at her slim figure, the full breasts pressing against the white linen shirt that disappeared into the waist of her black slacks. It had been one hell of a night. He was tired and sore, confused and scared even. But he focused more and more on the woman in front of him.

"I'm glad you came by," he whispered. "I've been hoping to see you ever since that evening in Kreuzberg."

Joanna reached out and touched his bruised face. Rosman took her hand, spreading it out palm down in his own. He raised it to his lips. She drew the hand away, then bent down and brushed his lips lightly with her own.

"You must be very sore and tired." Her hand moved across his chest, up around his shoulders and into the tuft of hair at the back of his neck.

His arm snaked around her waist, then slid lower along her hips. Images flooded back. The sight of Lamprecht's sister, the sneering smile of the man at his car in East Berlin. Rosman bit his lower lip and rolled his eyes toward the ceiling. "I'm sorry, but I need to be sure. Can you get me Schmidt's address?"

"Is it that important?" Her words were crisp and distant. She moved her body away from his. Her arm fell from its place behind his neck.

He nodded. Joanna grabbed a pen from the table and wrote an address on a napkin. "I'm sure Jens told you that he lives in Rostock but spends a good deal of time here in Berlin."

"Does he study here?"

"Yes. Is that also so important?"

"I'm not really sure at this point."

He tried to ease out a smile. She leaned forward to meet his lips. This one was a full kiss, and the press of her body made his knees tremble. Rosman winced as he felt the muscles in his chest pull when he straightened himself. His lips were throbbing, and his temples pounded against the insides of his skull.

Joanna peered up at him through silken eyelids. "Perhaps I'd better go. Maybe tonight is not right."

Rosman searched her face. "I have a whopping headache. And then there's this backache. And a rib ache." He studied her face. "But I could forget all that in a moment."

"No, I'm sorry," Joanna sighed. "It's better if I come back tomorrow. I would like to go see Erich with you. After that, perhaps we'll have more time together."

Rosman groaned and let his head roll to the side.

She kissed him again before pushing herself lightly away from Rosman's arms. "Be brave, John. You will need it."

He walked her to his front door, conscious of their closeness as he held onto her hand as long as possible. At the end of the hallway her fingers slid from his and brushed his cheek. Then she slipped out the door.

Rosman leaned against the heavy wooden door frame and listened to the sound of her footsteps echo across the stones of his front pathway. He thought he'd better try to get a few hours sleep before his day began. It was turning out to be a challenging—and promising—weekend.

CHAPTER 4

Johann Gracchus stood for a moment contemplating the peeling paint and chipped concrete in the building's facade. Sunlight cast a hazy, faltering glow among the crevices of the rambling apartment buildings that stretched for miles along either side of Karl Marx Strasse. Each time he returned over the years, those cracks had grown and multiplied. The buildings had been covered by large tile slabs, and when they fell unreplaced to the ground, it gave the complex the look of an increasingly sick patient, one in whom the doctors had lost all hope. The resemblance to the buildings he remembered from his childhood in Moscow was striking, the "wedding cake" style of Stalin's day still so prominent. They always brought back to him the popular saying there that the best and most durable structures were the ones built by the German prisoners after the war. It actually made him proud of his heritage, no matter how dedicated a communist he was. If we can't succeed, who can? Gracchus had often asked himself.

Sweating from the long walk up four flights, Gracchus let himself into number 413. He wondered when they would fix that damn elevator. With nearly 4,000 other safehouses in East Berlin, he knew it was poor tradecraft to use the same location so often, a particularly serious error for such an experienced and high-ranking officer in the Ministry for State Security. But he liked it here. Although the complex was falling apart, the rooms were much more spacious than those in the newer buildings.

Gracchus passed from the foyer to the living room along the dirty olive green carpet. He reached up to adjust a curtain rod that had fallen from one end of its holder and now hung at a 45-degree angle across the living room window. Unfortunately, the hook was just out of reach. He had to use one of the armchairs to finish his chore.

Wilhelm Meyer, the Lutheran pastor from Potsdam, had not yet arrived, so Gracchus looked about the apartment to see if anything else needed mending. He ignored the peeling wallpaper, having already given up trying to get it fixed. Instead, he went to the kitchen to make himself some coffee and decided to add a touch of brandy. There was still some of the Armenian bottle left. The *de la Grange* from Paris was too good to sacrifice in a cup of coffee. Gracchus began to pour tap water into the pot, then thought better of it and poured from one of the bottles he had purchased in the west. Rumors about toxic metals and bacteria in the regular water system these days were too common to ignore.

Staring at nothing in particular, Gracchus waited for the water to boil. He heard Meyer enter as the tiny bubbles began to rise to the surface. "I assume you observed the usual precautions," Gracchus shouted.

"Of course, for whatever good it does. Many of my colleagues are aware I come."

"It's still best to avoid any unpleasant surprises," Gracchus replied, aware that he had overlooked these same precautions today. He felt relatively secure. The Wall's opening hadn't changed that much in his daily life. Not yet, anyway.

Gracchus marched into the room carrying two cups of coffee and a small pot. He contemplated the tall, thin figure in the light blue suit for a moment, wondering what had brought him to continue these meetings for the past 12 years. Gracchus realized suddenly that all he really knew about Meyer, beyond the basic facts of his life, was that he liked his coffee black. He held out the tray as Meyer hung his raincoat over the armchair that stood closest to the kitchen.

"I have another request," Meyer said, taking his cup from the tray.

Gracchus rolled his eyes, an instinctive reaction that he no longer bothered to conceal. He set his own cup on the coffee table.

"Several young people arrested at the Rosa Luxembourg

demonstration last year have yet to be released. Their families have appealed to the Consistory to approach the authorities once more."

"I am tired of hearing about those little pricks," Gracchus snapped. He folded his hands and directed his eyes toward the ceiling as though in solemn prayer. "Why is it that every generation believes that it, and it alone, has discovered the Holy Grail of True Socialism?"

"I hardly think those students can be considered a threat to the state. Can't you concede to them the exuberance of youth— no matter how naive—one that matches a commitment you supposedly share?"

"How do you know that the ideals they hold are so pure?" Gracchus thrust his finger toward Meyer. "You of all people have given us enough reports on their activities to know how subversive they can be. Goddammit!" he muttered, shaking his head and leaning forward. "What makes them think they know better than us how to build socialism? Where were they when we pulled this state out of the rubble? What do they know about what it took to eradicate the roots of fascism?" Gracchus stopped. He had made this speech before, many times in fact. He leaned against the window sill, his gaze upon the carpet.

Meyer had certainly heard it. His face betrayed a knowing smile. "A little more tolerance would do us all well. Even you, Herr Gracchus, are aware, I'm sure, of Our Lord's words about what can come from the mouths of babes."

Gracchus let his body down into the beige sofa facing the window with one swift movement and rubbed his eyes with the fingertips of both hands. He knew that he would intervene for the students. "I'll see what I can do. They've probably sat long enough to learn their lessons. There will be a price, of course."

"Yes, I'm sure." Meyer stood in front of Gracchus, his right hand trolling back and forth inside the hip pocket of his sport coat. "I brought a list of recent visitors from West Germany. A delegation of Social Democrats from North Rhine Westphalia, as well as reports of their views on the possibility of closing the documentation center at Salzgitter."

"That can wait." Gracchus flipped his right wrist in Meyer's direction. "We are actually more worried about our ability to track the dissident movement after the events of the last two days. There is also the role members of your church are playing in the demonstrations in Leipzig." Gracchus looked at Meyer to be sure he understood. "You've heard the sort of thing they're chanting now, haven't you? All that crap about 'One Fatherland.' In fact, that is why I scheduled this meeting today on such short notice."

Meyer looked troubled, confused even. Hell, it was probably both, Gracchus decided. After all, 24 hours was not a lot of lead time for a slow-witted asset like Meyer.

"What do I have to do with any of that?" Meyer asked. "Besides, these demonstrations are hardly new."

"Thursday's surprise announcement opening the Wall has changed things radically. We are operating in a different environment now." Gracchus slammed his fist against his thigh. "That Schabowski is such an idiot."

"Why blame him?"

"He wasn't supposed to open the border so soon. We needed to prepare the people."

"Well, I'm afraid that genie is out now. But I'm not sure I see how it affects the marches in Leipzig. In fact, it should begin to quiet things down. The people have what they want. It should also make our business less pressing."

"I'm afraid not. In fact, it makes our relationship even more important. It is my judgment that we will have to be even more vigilant."

"But why? The relationship between the east and west is changing now. It's less tense now, isn't it? The threat of war is receding now."

"No. Now the threat to our society and our state will grow. I shall give you just one example. It will also entail some instructions for you."

Meyer did not move. He continued to stand with his back to the window, his figure backlit in a hazy afternoon glow. Tired of squinting, Gracchus walked over to the window and pulled the drapes shut. He returned to his seat and massaged his temples, trying to ward off the beginnings of another headache. Stress, he assumed. Perhaps the world was spinning out of control. He had always held such a firm belief in history's linear, dialectical development.

"Last night several dissidents, including ones you know quite well, attempted to steal something from our headquarters at Normannenstrasse. I have a pretty good idea what it was they were after. I want you to find out just what they have, where it's being held, and what they plan to do with it. Also, let me know if they plan any new adventures."

"Are you going to give me any clues? Don't you know what's missing?"

"I just want you to tell me what you find. You'll learn more if it's necessary. Check your sources within the church circles and report back to me."

"When?"

"I will send you the usual signal. And I'll want names." His head snapped toward Meyer. "All of them."

"Things must be slipping in the Stasi. How did they get into the building? One would never have assumed...."

A sharp look from Gracchus brought Meyer up short. "That is none of your affair." Gracchus climbed from the sofa, then disappeared into the kitchen. He re-emerged a minute later carrying two glasses of the good French cognac. Meyer's eyes lit up with anticipation when he raised his glass to study the color.

"How can you be so sure, Herr Gracchus, that things have not changed completely since Thursday? I would think that the Wall's opening would affect your world drastically."

Gracchus examined his cognac. "Oh, I agree, my good pastor. Things have changed, including my own work. It will be even more difficult now. But I do not intend to give up just yet. I still have a purpose to serve." He looked at Meyer. "And I will continue to rely on the cooperation of this state's citizens, willing or otherwise."

"Can you tell me how it has changed for you?"

"No."

Gracchus felt relatively certain of Meyer's loyalty. The man may have been a tad naive, but any errant ways were controllable.

It was all a matter of how you mixed the force with the persuasion. He reached inside his jacket and extracted a white envelope stuffed with 500 West German Marks.

Gracchus handed the envelope to Meyer, who nodded and tucked it away inside his own jacket. Meyer stared at nothing in particular, then tipped the glass back to drain every last drop. He saluted Gracchus with the empty container and returned his glass to the kitchen, his tongue sliding back and forth over his lips.

Gracchus cocked his head and released a smile in Meyer's direction. He held his own glass aloft. "There will be more of that for you if you have to help with the American."

Meyer froze at the door, his hand on the doorknob, the eyes wide. His mouth opened and locked, the lips about an inch apart. His tongue moved with some difficulty. "An American?"

Gracchus drained his cognac, then turned and carried his empty glass to the kitchen. Force with persuasion. And a touch of fear. He only had to find the right mixture.

Nora Meyer watched her husband park his Trabant in front of their modest two-story house in Potsdam. She kept her eyes on his tall, thin frame as he walked past the plain stucco walls that had been baked brown by the soot-filled air that came from burning the soft brown coal so abundant in the east. He continued walking past the small collection of briquettes left from last winter, a shrinking pile against the side of their house. She reminded herself to call for another delivery. Turning from the window, Nora strolled to the kitchen to lay out the slices of sausage, cheese and bread for dinner.

When her husband entered, Nora greeted him with a light kiss on the cheek, searching his face to see if the drive home had produced its usual aggravation. What under normal circumstances would have taken perhaps 30 to 40 minutes always lasted twice that long. Rather than drive through Berlin's western sectors, her husband was compelled by international politics and the Cold War to exit Berlin's eastern half and drive the highway ringing Berlin to the Potsdam exit, then through the city to his modest home on the edge of the Wannsee, the rambling lake that marked the city's southwestern boundary.

"You're home early tonight. Was traffic lighter than usual?"

"On the contrary. Nearly every inhabitant of the Peoples' Republic must be on the street tonight. And they're all heading for West Berlin."

"Was your meeting with him as long as usual?"

Meyer hung his raincoat on the rack in their small foyer just inside the front door. "No. It was actually shorter."

"Why was that? Is he worried about what happened on Thursday?"

She spread three platters across the oak table in the middle of their living room and walked back to the kitchen for two dinner plates and utensils. When she returned, Nora sat in one of the two dark green armchairs that stood on either side of the table. The evening news played softly in the background. She could never bring herself to mention the name of her husband's case officer.

"Somewhat. Gracchus tried to act as though he had things under control. He's not the sort to get flustered easily." Meyer dropped into the open armchair and set his eyes on the television while recounting the details of his conversation with Gracchus and the new assignment.

"You didn't notice any change in him?"

Meyer rotated to face his wife. "He seemed more short-tempered. Beyond that he was even cagier than usual. He wouldn't provide me with any information beyond the statement about this break-in at Stasi headquarters. It was as though he didn't trust me."

"Did he at least bring a gift this time?'"

Meyer waved his hand. "No, only the money. Perhaps they are cutting back on expenses." He shook his head and fingered the utensils. His eyes rested on the food, as though they were avoiding Nora's gaze. "He also put up much less resistance than usual to my request for the release of the protesters. Just the usual speeches."

"What will happen to them?"

"I'm not sure. Their real crime was embarrassing the regime.

That, of course, was their big mistake, so they'll probably be expelled. At the least, their university careers will be curtailed."

Meyer stabbed at his sausage, which disappeared 30 seconds later. Then he stuffed a piece of rich, brown farmer's bread into his mouth before he had finished chewing the meat. Nora poured two glasses of Radeburger beer from the half liter bottle and passed one to her husband.

"I hope they enjoy living like real workers in our workers' paradise." The words escaped from his mouth as he chewed.

"How much longer can you risk a relationship with this man?" she asked. "Haven't the events of this week given you concern? Haven't you noticed how things have escalated since the summer?"

"It's no longer up to me, if it ever was. And it goes beyond just me and Gracchus." Meyer reached for a slice of Edam cheese and placed it atop some buttered brown bread. "Who else would intervene for our church members and those who look to us for shelter?"

"Couldn't somebody else take your place?"

"I doubt it. At least not now. I've built up a certain amount of credit with Gracchus and his group."

"But what if you do decide to stop? Will he force you to go on?"

"I am not sure what would happen then."

Nora sat lost in thought, her eyes focused on a piece of sausage on the serving platter, her hands folded neatly in her lap. Periodically, she brushed back the light brown hair she kept cut short, and which came down just over the ears with an inch or so across the forehead. The bread and cheese sat untouched on her plate. "Things are changing, Wilhelm. Perhaps it would be better if you tried to make a change in this as well."

Meyer did not answer. He cut another slice of bread, avoiding his wife's eyes.

"Have you thought about how our future could look if things continue in Germany as they're going now?" She waited for some kind of response, enduring a full minute of silence. "At least be careful."

She decided against pressing the matter further. Not today, at any rate. Instead, she shifted away from her husband and the television and sat looking out their window at the Wannsee, just several hundred meters in the distance. When she turned to look at her husband again, he was finishing his meal, his gaze still focused on the television screen. He sat there alone with his thoughts, bent over his evening bread, strands of thinning gray hair falling over his temples. Were his motives really as noble as he made them out to be? she asked herself. How had they gotten so close to such an unpopular regime? It had all seemed so purposeful earlier, innocuous even. What would the consequences be if the *Wende* continued its course? What would it take to break their unholy bond?

CHAPTER 5

Back at Karl Marx Strasse, Gracchus paced around the apartment, removing all traces of the afternoon's meeting. He instinctively placed Meyer's list in the inside breast pocket of his jacket. It was the same general area he liked to keep his Makarov semi-automatic, near his heart and a natural reach for his right hand.

Gracchus rushed into the kitchen to wash the dishes and put the coffee and brandy away. He would have to hurry to catch Preselnikov. Although such household cleaning struck many officers as menial chores, Gracchus preferred to perform such mundane matters himself, leaving nothing to someone else's oversight.

After drying the cups and saucers with a towel, he put the dishes away in the cupboard above the sink—he had to get a kitchen chair to help him reach the second row of shelves—then turned to cast one last glance at the kitchen. Before he left, Gracchus checked to see that the stove was off and the caps to the brandy bottles tight.

At the door Gracchus pivoted abruptly and returned to the bedroom. There, he retrieved the plaque he had intended to give Meyer as a memento of their long relationship, a gesture Gracchus had forgotten in his momentary anger over the student rebels. He didn't understand them and their world. He had never had the luxury of a university student's rebellious age, not during the difficult years of his youth.

He slammed the door to the bedroom shut, the blood rushing to his head. What was with all these demonstrations? Hundreds of thousands marching every week in Leipzig, chanting 'We are the People' and 'We are One People'. What bullshit. As he turned the key in the lock, Gracchus suddenly realized how disappointing this autumn, normally his favorite time of year, had been.

Five minutes later Gracchus sat on a bench directly across from the Red Army monument in Treptower Park. He shrank back into the shadow of this imposing structure and hoped that Preselnikov would not be too late. Working his way through the broiled bratwurst from one of the stands that dotted the park, Gracchus studied the many people occupying the shaded pathways: young mothers with baby carriages; couples arm in arm, or just holding hands. A few stopped to kiss. But mostly there were older people, either alone or in pairs, probably pensioners seeking an afternoon's escape from their small, cramped apartments.

The tall Russian trotted into view, his black overcoat flapping open in the breeze. Gracchus stood to greet him, patting the slope of his own mid-section with his free hand.

"You're still looking good. A little too good, comrade."

"Yes, after 30 years I'm finally gaining on you, Johann," Preselnikov answered. "Even the years together in Rome could not help me to catch up with your heft."

"You mean, my strength."

"Whatever. But age and bad politics are finally doing it."

They embraced, rocking each other back and forth.

"I see you're as punctual as ever," Gracchus scolded. "What sort of example is that for the KGB chief in Berlin?"

"What do you expect from someone who has to perform countless daily tasks for an idiot?" Preselnikov shrugged his shoulders. "Unfortunately, this idiot just happens to be my superior."

"Your real one?"

"No," Preselnikov assured him, "not my real boss." He cupped his hands to shield a flaming match while he lit a cigarette. "I just can't get accustomed to these press releases we have to give out these days. Things are so confused and tedious now. Moscow is completely at a loss. Yet we still have to coordinate everything we release with those clowns for fear of adding to all the speculation in the West."

"Not to mention the speculation here."

"Yes, not to mention here. Meanwhile, they keep screaming

for more information, but I doubt they read what we do send in."

"All the more reason for us to carry on, comrade," Gracchus stated. "Someone has to act, be prepared for the future."

Gracchus wiped the small drops of mustard from his fingers on a torn white handkerchief. The two men strolled away from the statue of a Soviet soldier rescuing a young child caught in a cross-fire with SS troops during the final days of the battle for Berlin. Legend had it that he was killed for his efforts when the SS fanatics refused to stop firing. Appropriately enough, his sword loomed over a shattered swastika.

Preselnikov's gaze remained with the soldier for several steps, his forehead wrinkled and lips pursed. Probably irritated by all the pigeon droppings on the statue, Gracchus thought. Preselnikov shook his head in disgust and shifted his gaze to a young blond woman in a short black skirt and black stockings. Gracchus glanced over when he saw his friend staring. Probably a westerner.

"Moscow is extremely unhappy with the way things have gone here. First that fiasco surrounding the fortieth anniversary celebrations in October. And now this thing with the Wall."

Gracchus walked along in silence.

"Honecker was embarrassing, but he did serve a purpose. At least until recently," Preselnikov continued. "I'm not sure the same can be said for Krenz and his crowd." He emitted a short laugh. "It seems that all of the leaders we help install tend to outlive their usefulness eventually. Some even become dangerous."

"Is that Moscow's official assessment of the Krenz government? Or just your personal observation?"

"I'm not certain what anyone thinks back there anymore, officially or otherwise. But the ninth of November is not going to win Krenz many friends in Moscow. Or anywhere else in the east, for that matter." Preselnikov chuckled. "Well, maybe in Warsaw."

Gracchus sighed. "It seems that when we need forceful and insightful leadership most, we get little of either. I just hope you haven't given up on the rest of us here."

Preselnikov frowned. "I still trust your judgment, Johann. But there are others in Moscow who question the wisdom of our operation. Things look much shakier now."

"I don't recall hearing any other plans from all those naysayers a month ago. Unusual times call for exceptional measures, Sergei. That's still true."

"Do you think I'm not aware of that?" Preselnikov slowed, shaking his head in disbelief. "That's what I told Moscow in October, and I am prepared to continue arguing that we have no other choice."

"Then you agree that we should move into the second stage?" Preselnikov did not answer right away. "How certain are you of your sources? Hasn't Mielke outlawed the dissident groups? You can't very well ignore your own Minister for State Security."

"If you give me the backing I need, I will take care of Mielke."

"Are we in for any more surprises?"

Gracchus paused to look at Preselnikov. "Do you mean like Friday's break in?"

"Yes. I'm sure you were expecting that. A trap of some sort?"

"Yes and no."

It was Preselnikov's turn to stare. "What do you mean? Are you telling me there are more complications now?" Another pause. "Your service must be falling apart, Johann. You were always so proud. The best we had, according to you."

"We were and still are." Gracchus thrust his chin toward the Russian and stuffed his hands deep into the pockets of his gray raincoat.

Preselnikov waited. He shook his shoulders to ward off the cold air and buttoned his overcoat. "Go on."

Gracchus looked back in the direction of the Soviet monument before catching his friend's eyes. "We may have overextended ourselves. There's an American involved."

"Dammit, Johann." Preselnikov sighed, shaking his head. "How deeply?"

"I'm not sure. It's something I'll have to look into."

Gracchus shivered as the wind blew through his unlined coat. In his haste he had forgotten to put on a sweater. "Can I be sure of your support?"

Preselnikov used his right foot to rearrange some dirt along the edge of the path. Finally, he spoke. "Yes." Another pause. "But we also need to think about cleaning up any tracks we may be leaving." The Russian's eyes swept the city's gray skyline. "In case we need to pull out."

Gracchus did not move. He studied his friend. Preselnikov's answer had lacked the ringing affirmation Gracchus wanted. For the first time that Gracchus could remember, his Russian friend avoided his eyes.

"I always clean up after myself." Gracchus's voice was firm, the words carefully chosen. "As long as you give me the assistance I need, we won't need to pull out of anything."

"I know, Johann. You've always been a thorough man. It's one of your strengths." Preselnikov studied Gracchus's face closely. "But be careful. Too much is happening around us."

The two men shook hands and, after a slight pause, embraced. Then Preselnikov turned and walked toward Puschki-nallee running along the edge of the park. Without glancing back, he climbed into the car that would take him back to his office.

"You and comrade Gracchus go back in time together, eh, Comrade Colonel?" Preselnikov studied his driver. This man was competent, but nosy. Too nosey for someone of his rank.

"Our families met in Moscow during the war."

"Has he changed?"

He was also persistent. "Why do you ask?"

"You looked worried when you came back to the car. And he looked tired."

"He's no longer as young as he once was, of course." Preselnikov laughed to himself. "His hair is almost as gray as mine. I always wondered how he had been able to retain his dark blond coloring for so long."

"Sort of like the natural order of things, comrade? He still looks to be in excellent shape. Very strong. Even more so than you, Comrade Colonel, if I may say so."

"Of course, comrade. Truth is always best. Not to mention scientific." Preselnikov smirked. The driver would have to learn not to be too obsequious. It made things obvious.

"I hope you're not too worried about whatever you're working on, comrade," the driver continued.

This really was going too far. But Preselnikov had to admit that for the first time he did wonder if his friend's judgment was sound.

"Comrade Gracchus remains one of the most dedicated and capable men I have ever known," Preselnikov answered. The driver stared straight ahead.

As they crossed the Spree, Preselnikov could see the long thin lines of Trabants and Wartburgs blocking the streets ahead. And they were still several kilometers from the nearest crossing point. That would be Heinrich Heine Strasse. No, that was for pedestrians only. All these people must be waiting to drive through Checkpoint Charlie. Those fucking Americans always seemed to find a way to be at the center of everything.

Preselnikov shifted his weight in the back seat and leaned forward. "Can you find a quicker way back?" he ordered.

"But Comrade Colonel...." The driver simply shrugged and pointed to the cars to their front.

Preselnikov leaned back in his seat and rested his forehead against the window. The sidewalk was packed with hundreds of East German pedestrians. Several pointed at his solid black Zhakia, a stark alien presence on streets that had suddenly grown oppressively German.

To hell with them, Preselnikov thought. The interior of his modest Russian sedan had the refreshing smell of newly washed upholstery. He, at least, was warm and comfortable.

Preselnikov lit another cigarette, a Marlboro from the carton he had picked up at the American shopping center in Dahlem near the U.S. Mission. He lowered the window a crack to let the smoke escape. Even in their own town, these Germans looked oddly out of place in their polyester pants, nylon jackets and fur caps. Most were carrying a plastic shopping bag in each hand, filled, no doubt, with products from the consumers' paradise in the west, all of them unquestionably paid for with the 100 West Marks in welcoming money the Bonn government so obligingly provided. They all looked so smug and content with their little satchels.

"You'd be nowhere without Gorbachev, or the Poles, my good comrades," he said out loud through the window. The driver glanced back through the rear view mirror. Preselnikov continued. "Or the Hungarians. Those bastards are the ones that really set it off."

He tossed his cigarette out the window and leaned back in his seat. Preselnikov wondered if the West Germans were still lined up on the other side, showering their eastern cousins with champagne and flowers as they drove through. How much longer would this national camaraderie, this insanity, last? It was Saturday afternoon, November 11. The Wall had been open for nearly three days.

CHAPTER 6

Rosman pulled the bedding over his head to block the morning light pouring through his bedroom window, then let loose a groan. His chin and lip were throbbing, and the sharp pain in his ribs stabbed at his chest. He must have slept awkwardly. Fortunately, it was Saturday. He looked at the clothes strewn about his bedroom and noticed that his curtain covered only half the window. This much of his life, at least, had not changed.

He thought of Joanna, swung his legs out of the bed and fell back on his side from the pain. Rosman counted to 100 before fighting his way out of bed and shuffling over to the window to close the drapes. He hesitated, caught by the morning frost, a soft glistening surface blanketing the world outside.

The morning shower felt especially good. The hard heat of the water massaged his sore body and wrapped Rosman in a protective shroud from the images of frost outside. After drying off with the towel still damp from the night before, he searched his pile of clothes for something clean and color-coordinated. The brown corduroys and burgundy sweater would have to do. Then he hobbled downstairs to get some coffee on before she arrived.

By 10:30 Joanna was at his door, her smooth, white skin and light green eyes outlined against the cool damp air of an autumn morning in northern Germany. She too was wearing corduroys, white ones, but her fit was much tighter than his. The loose yellow sweater also failed to hide her figure. Only her hair, ruffled by the wind, suggested a hint of imperfection.

Rosman bowed in welcome and held out his hand to lead the way to a kitchen table set with coffee for two, some fruit, a loaf a bread, strawberry jam, honey, and several slices of Gouda cheese.

Just in case, he also set out two boxes of cereal: Sugar Frosted Flakes and Honey Nut Cheerios.

"This all looks so nice," Joanna said, clasping her hands together.

Rosman nodded in awkward appreciation and poured two cups of coffee. He offered Joanna her choice of utensils and a plate.

"There's so much I'd like to know about you. But I feel very awkward." He shrugged his shoulders and shook his head.

"I thought you Americans were supposed to be so forward." Joanna cocked her head again and smiled. "Why don't you just ask me about myself? I promise to answer."

Rosman took a seat next to her at the table. "Okay. Do you study theology as well? Is that how you came to know Jens and Lamprecht? And where does your family come from?" The knife in his hand swung back and forth over a piece of toast resting in the other.

"Wait. One question at a time." She laughed. "No, I study history, but I came to know them as members of a Church protest group."

"How did you meet them?" Rosman bit into the piece of toast he had lathered with sweet, syrupy honey. He watched Joanna's fingers toy with the handle of her coffee cup.

"We attended many of the same meetings. I guess I was attracted by their sincerity, and by the fact that they seemed like nice guys. With the right political inclinations, of course."

"And your family?"

"We're from Berlin."

"What about Jens?"

"Erich and Hermann are from Halle. They attended the Martin Luther University there, and I decided to look for some like-minded compatriots outside of Berlin to avoid being too easily identified by the Stasi."

"Did it work?"

"I suppose so. At least I haven't been bothered."

"Perhaps you're lucky."

"Or not important enough. I think that's more likely."

Rosman eased himself back into his chair with a smile and offered her more coffee. He saw then that she hadn't drunk any yet.

"Thanks, but it's still a little hot. And what about you?" she asked. "Where does your family come from?"

"Here, actually."

"You're a Berliner?"

"No, not here here. My parents are from Germany. They fled to America before the war?"

"Are you Jewish?"

"No, Catholic. But religion wasn't the problem. They were Social Democrats and active in the Resistance. Most of our family was lost during the Third Reich."

"I'm sorry. Where in Germany did they come from?"

"Near Stuttgart."

Joanna sat back in her chair and crossed her legs. She cradled the cup of coffee close to her face, the steam rising several inches to mask her eyes. Rosman put down his knife and fork and reached for an apple.

"Shouldn't we be leaving?" Joanna asked after another moment of silence.

"Yes, I suppose so. But only if you're sure you're not hungry. You haven't eaten much." Rosman pointed to the food. "In fact, you haven't eaten anything."

"I'm sorry. I'm sure it's all very good, but aside from a cup or two of coffee, I usually don't eat breakfast."

Rosman finished his fruit, and Joanna helped carry the dishes over to the sink. He rinsed them off but hesitated before finally dropping them in the sink.

He turned to find her standing close behind him. She set her eyes upon his and stood close enough for him to catch the scent of perfume that lingered on her body. He wondered if this was common in the east. Then he decided he didn't care.

He grabbed her arm and pulled her closer so that their bodies fit tight against one another. Joanna brought her lips up to his, and Rosman slid his arms around her shoulders. She locked hers around his waist. He felt her breasts and legs press against his own and leaned hard against her, letting himself melt into the warm softness of her body. After about 10 seconds, she pulled away.

"There will be time enough later. We really should go see Erich."

Rosman suppressed a growl as Joanna pushed herself lightly away from him and walked toward his door. He did not move, but stood leaning against his sink, trying to catch his breath. His fingers gripped the edge of the counter.

"Goddammit," he muttered. He turned off the coffee maker.

"We should drive to the hospital separately," Joanna said when he came outside. "It would not be safe to leave my car at your house. You never know who may be watching."

Rosman laughed and glanced at Joanna, uncertain if she was joking and half expecting to see her smile. But she looked deadly serious.

The streets downtown seemed just as crowded as last night, perhaps more so. It was as though East Berlin had emptied itself into the city's western half, and it took Rosman nearly an hour to drive to the hospital. Joanna was already waiting when he arrived. He found a parking space just a block from hers, and trotted over to Joanna.

"What took you so long? I was beginning to worry." She hugged her bag.

"The guard at Checkpoint Charlie was unusually slow," Rosman explained.

"How was that? Why would they be slower today? Was the crossing crowded again?"

"That wouldn't matter, not for Allied personnel."

"I don't get it. What makes you so special?"

"Well, for starters, we get to skip past the mob of mere mortals." Joanna did not look amused. "We go to the head of the line in the lane on the far left reserved for Allied diplomats and military types. Haven't you ever noticed?"

"Not really. I've never crossed there. I come through Invalidenstrasse, by the Lehrter Bahnhof."

"Well, anyway, the crossing for us has evolved into a diplomatic ritual to allow both sides to maintain their own interpretation of political and legal realities here in Berlin. The procedure is well established and pretty much a formality at this point."

Joanna dropped the bag into her right hand and held out her left for Rosman to take. "This is starting to sound pretty complicated."

"Now bear with me," Rosman said. "Let me see if I've learned my lessons. Once I'm in the lane—I've already registered with the American on duty at our little hut in the middle of Friedrichstrasse. Then one of East Germany's finest studies my Allied pass through a rolled up window, jots down something or other, and then waves me through."

"Why the rolled up window?"

"Because I'm not supposed to exchange any words or papers with your people. Otherwise your side can claim it is controlling access to its capital, a sign of the sovereignty we do not recognize."

"So, what was the problem today?"

"I'm not sure. Maybe I got someone unhappy with the way things have been going. Or maybe I just got some prick. But he took forever."

They entered the hospital still holding hands. Although the crowded elevator moved at a glacial pace—typical East German engineering, he told himself—Rosman enjoyed every second of the ride. He held Joanna close at his side, trying to insulate them both from the pressed mass of Teutonic flesh. She leaned against him, as though eager for support. He caught her eyes and smiled. She mouthed a kiss, and Rosman noted how her eyes moved to an old matron in a starched white uniform.

"Maybe she took care of the Kaiser," he whispered.

"Or Frederick the Great."

Without warning, she nuzzled his ear, then kissed his cheek. The other passengers pretended not to notice.

As soon as the elevator doors opened at the seventh floor, they strolled down the hallway to Jens' room. Rosman's feet skidded on the newly waxed linoleum when he came to an abrupt stop in the doorway. His eyes were frozen to the corner where Jens was supposed to be lying.

The bed was empty. Next to it stood a nurse changing the sheets, blissfully unaware that anything could be wrong, fluffing pillows into the right shape and form.

"What…what happened to the patient who was here?" Rosman stammered, speaking in English before repeating himself in German.

The nurse hesitated, her eyes darting around the room, as though searching for support. "He was moved during the night."

"Why?"

"How should I know?" Her eyes continued their dance.

"Where is he now? Where can I find him?"

"You'll have to ask at the nurses station in the hall." Her Prussian formality had returned, along with her official sense of composure that came with any job involving a uniform.

Joanna had been waiting patiently behind Rosman, letting him handle this stage of the inquiries. As soon as the nurse finished speaking, she hurried back down the hall and continued past the station. She disappeared behind a double door. One of the nurses at the station rose to intercept her, but Joanna brushed her aside with a few words Rosman could not hear.

Rosman walked to a set of chairs at the end of the corridor and sat down. The fear and anxiety from the night before suddenly returned. He looked to the doors through which Joanna had vanished, struggling to catch his breath, the muscles of his ribcage straining with each gulp of air. His temples throbbed. A powerful, nauseating scent of antiseptic filled the hallway, and the small white cards pinned to the bulletin board behind the nurses' station swam in place along the wall.

Several minutes later Joanna reappeared, searching the crowded hall for Rosman's face. When she saw him, she ran to his side, her eyes wide and her hands shaking.

"They say he's disappeared. Late last night, when the nurse came to administer a sedative for his sleep, his bed was empty. He has not been released."

"Where was the nurse on duty? What about his doctor?"

"They've gone home."

She looked at Rosman. Long, thin creases cast her face in a

stark, oval outline. Suddenly, she looked much older. "This is not at all normal. Not for this system, not for Erich. I'm afraid, John." Rosman felt dizzy. He gasped for oxygen. He had to leave somehow, to get out of the building. He wanted desperately to get back on the other side of the Wall.

He walked to the stairway, his mind shutting out the buzz of distant human conversation and the rustle of starched, white hospital linens. Instead, he sought the sensation of movement. He needed to keep his body active. He knew he did not want to wait for and then ride in another one of their goddamn elevators, or any other inferior technical invention in this goddamn country. Or half-country.

Rosman turned to look at Joanna, who trailed several steps behind him, lost in her own thoughts. He wondered what to do next. Surely Joanna would know. After all, she knew these people better than he did. If anyone knew what to do next, she would. They descended the stairs in silence. The cold bright tiles lining the stairwells froze the air in a brittle shroud.

When they got to the street, Joanna reached for Rosman's hand. He looked into her soft sad eyes, their green color sheathed behind a curtain of tears. He held her close, assuming the worst. She cried softly, and Rosman's fears grew as he listened to her soft, confused voice speak as though from some distant corner of the city.

"I don't know what's happening, John. It's all moving so fast."

CHAPTER 7

"What the hell happened to you?"

Bill Harding stood in the hallway of the U.S. Mission just outside the door of Rosman's office, his chest and shoulders bunched together under a blue and white striped shirt and red polka-dot tie. He bent forward. Harding's eyes were wide with a look Rosman had seen only once before: when the gay punk contingent took to the streets in Berlin's infamous May Day parade.

"I ran into a wall...sort of." Rosman tried to bark out a gruff laugh, but it hurt too much.

"It must have been a big fucking wall." Harding's legs uprooted themselves as he backed up to let Rosman emerge from his office.

"Well, it's getting smaller."

Harding's eyes narrowed, and his head shook slowly. He was a big, imposing man, well over six feet tall.

Rosman blew out his breath and started to walk through the hall. "I'll explain it later. Right now I need to see the boss."

"Sure." A broad smile broke across Harding's freckled face. "You devil, Rosman, you're talking about the Wall. Don't tell me you were back down there this weekend?"

Rosman looked back over his shoulder and shrugged. "Kinda looks that way."

"And it looks like a lot more. I'm actually worried about you."

The door to the office of Jack Friedlander, the chief of the Political Section and Rosman's boss, was open. His tastes shaped by over 20 years in the Foreign Service, Friedlander wore the bottom half of a blue, pin-striped suit, a white shirt, and red paisley tie. Rosman felt underdressed in his brushed cotton slacks, plaid shirt and red knit tie. His feet resting carelessly on top of his desk, Fried-lander waved Rosman in.

Dorothy Sutton, the Political Section's senior officer, sat parked in one of the two armchairs facing Friedlander's desk, a smile framing her ubiquitous cigarette. She stood to leave and brushed a few scattered ashes from her navy blue sweater vest.

"He's all yours," she cooed on her way out, leaving behind a trail of stale odor from her Winston. Rosman tried to wave the smell into the upper corners of the office.

"Thanks. I think." He turned to his boss.

"Ouch." Friedlander stroked his cheek and chin as he stud-ied Rosman's face. "What can I do for you? Besides get you to a doctor."

"Oh, I'm okay. Just a little accident."

"You'll have to make it quick then. I've got an appointment in half an hour with my Russian double to discuss last week's glori-ous events."

"What for?" Rosman eased himself into the armchair left vacant by Sutton's departure.

"Well, it seems their East German allies forgot to advise the Soviets of the plans to remove all travel restrictions and open up that Wall they built." Friedlander tossed the cable he was reading on the desk. "The Soviets have gotten this crazy notion that Thurs-day's developments could somehow affect the status of this city."

"That's pretty insightful."

"No shit. But I doubt the East Germans have given it much thought. I also doubt they're in control of things."

"How so?"

"Did they look to be in control of things during your trips to the Wall, John?" Harding interrupted. He was angled like a fence post against Friedlander's doorframe.

"Not really," Rosman admitted. He did a half-turn in the chair to check on his friend.

"Same here," Friedlander said. "My wife and I were having dinner with the Sidlowskis in Kreuzberg at some chic new Italian place when we heard all this commotion a couple of blocks away. We strolled over and were amazed at the crowds and the chaos.

People were pressing on the *Vopos* to let them through, shouting about Schabowski's announcement on TV removing all travel restrictions." He laughed. "The friendly *Vopos* didn't know what to do."

"That must have been a first," Harding broke in.

"Yeah. Well, finally one of them—a lieutenant, I believe— came out of the guardhouse and just threw his hands in the air. Then they started to let everyone through. I guess the East Germans were supposed to have some sort of documentation to stamp, but the people were just shoving anything they had at the *Vopos*. Passports, driver's licenses, student i.d.'s. You name it, it got stamped." He laughed again.

"What's so funny?" Rosman asked.

"Well, who should I see there in the midst of all that chaos but Kramer."

"Rick Kramer, our friend from military intelligence?" Rosman edged forward in the chair.

"One and the same." Friedlander's feet swung to the floor.

"That could have been a very touchy situation for an American military officer." Harding eased himself further into Friedlander's office. "Any idea what he was doing there?"

"Beats me. But he was in civies. He sure knows how to find his way into the middle of things." Friedlander sat forward, and his forearms came to rest on the desk. "But you didn't come over here to reminisce about last Thursday, did you, John?"

"No. Not exactly. I was wondering how you might feel if I spent more time in the east, now that things are more open."

"Any reasons for this?"

Rosman shrugged. "There'll be a lot going on now. It would help, I think, if I expanded my contacts and did some additional reporting on this. I thought I might be able to use some of the contacts I've made on both sides of the Wall to look into the movement of ideas and people between east and west."

"How do you plan to handle our colleagues in East Berlin?"

"I figured as long as it involved the city of Berlin itself, I'd be safe."

"How so?"

"Well, I'd still be on U.S. Mission turf."

"Technically yes. But that's not what I meant by my question. According to your evaluation, you didn't get to do any political reporting in New Delhi, right? Your work was entirely consular."

"That's right."

"Don't you think the political scene in West Berlin is enough for you now?"

"Not anymore, Jack. The Wall's opening has changed our jobs. The story is no longer just West Berlin politics. Now it's the whole damn city, or how it might become a whole damn city. Besides, there are a host of new issues out there for us to explore."

"You couldn't do that from here?"

"Wait a minute, Jack," Harding interjected. "Hear him out." He grabbed a seat in the armchair next to Rosman. "Berlin has often acted as a cutting edge in Kraut politics. And now that the Wall is falling, every Heinz and Brunhilda will want to get into the act."

"How so?" Friedlander frowned at Harding, then shifted his gaze back to Rosman.

"For one thing," Rosman interjected, "the Social Democrats have always prided themselves on being in the forefront of any attempt to bridge the east-west divide." Rosman found his hands thrusting in the air as he warmed to the topic. This was familiar and welcome territory. "This is where it all started, Jack. Ostpolitik, I mean."

Friedlander picked up a rubber band from his desk.

"And you can bet the other parties will be jumping aboard this particular bandwagon," Harding interrupted. "You should see the *Rathaus*. It's a madhouse right now. Those conservative Christian Democrats are ready to wet their pants. They even think reunification is no longer out of the question."

Friedlander scowled for about a minute while his hands spun the rubber band around his two index fingers. "Sure." He dropped the rubber band and waved his hand at Nixon and Rosman. "I'll concede your points about inspired Germans and what that usually means for the rest of the world. But that's not the issue here."

"Than what is?" Rosman pressed.

Friedlander turned to face him. "Well, your beat-up face, for one thing." Rosman frowned. "John, I'm responsible for your safety and your career while you're in Berlin. Tell me, why haven't you reported this incident to the RSO?"

"I didn't have time. I only got to work this morning."

"Bullshit. Tell me how you got your face punched the other night."

"It's not that serious. And I don't see why I should bother the security officer with every petty detail of my private life."

"I'll decide if it's petty."

Rosman shifted in his chair. "I was out on a date on the Ku'damm Saturday night, and I got jumped. That's all. The greatest damage was actually to my ego." He smiled weakly.

"What were they after? Money?"

"What else?"

"Will the police have a record of the assault?"

"No. A cop came by, but I told him to forget it."

"So, how many were there?"

"Three."

"And you couldn't handle them?" Harding smiled at his friend. Rosman waved him off.

"East Germans?" Friedlander pressed.

"I think they were. Only one spoke. But he had one of those old Berliner accents. I still don't see the problem," he insisted.

"It means we have a new security problem here in Berlin. I'm sure that a good many of those East Germans flooding our half of the city are not attracted by a love of freedom alone. And once you go east, you compound that danger by interfering in a whole host of things unfolding even as we speak. Things you can't begin to grapple with, John. Not at this stage of your career."

Rosman leaned back in his chair, crossed his legs, and stared out the window. There was a moment of silence.

Friedlander leaned back in turn and sighed. "John, I don't mean to sound old and cynical." Friedlander held up his hands. "If I was in your position I'd be doing the same thing. But I'm not sure you're prepared to handle the kinds of things you might find over there right now."

Rosman turned to Harding, his hands outstretched. "Help me, Bill."

"Actually, you do look pretty bad."

Friedlander continued. "There's a great deal going on in this city. Hell, in Europe right now."

"Exactly." Rosman thrust himself forward.

"But we have to be circumspect in what we, as State Department officers, choose to pursue," Friedlander continued.

No one spoke for what seemed like a full minute. The clock over the door filled the vacuum with sharp monotonous clicks. Finally, Friedlander spoke again. "What exactly did you have in mind?"

"Well, it's still in the exploratory stage, but I thought of something along the lines of what the parties over here will be doing to help their new friends and colleagues in the east."

"Where will you start?"

"There's an old Social Democrat, retired now, but I think he still has some ties and insights into what's up over there."

"His name?" Friedlander pressed.

"Hermann Buechler."

Friedlander pushed himself up from his desk and walked over to the coat rack next to the door to retrieve his jacket. Rosman thought the double-breasted suit would make a fashionable impression on his Soviet counterpart. For one thing, it helped hide the ever-growing belly that betrayed Friedlander's affection for the heavy German diet of starch and beer.

"I'm sorry, John, but there's going to be too much to do. We're about to be swamped by visitors. I can't stop you from pursuing something in your free time, but there will be precious little of that in the weeks ahead. And the minute I hear a complaint from the Embassy in the east, or you show up for work with one more bruise, I'm going to jerk your chain so hard you'll be happy just to copy recipes for the rest of your tour."

"Anything you say, Jack."

"And whatever you do, there is one more thing I want you to keep in mind." Friedlander nodded in the direction of Rosman's bruised face.

"What's that?"

Friedlander stood in his doorway for several seconds. "Don't let your moxie get the better of you. It's a tricky, dangerous place, even in normal times. And these are anything but normal."

Rosman was no longer listening. He nodded and wandered into the hallway, his imagination running with the crowds dancing in front of the Brandenburg Gate.

"Yo, John. Wait up."

Harding hustled through the corridor outside the Political Section at the U.S. Mission.

Rosman pulled up short of his office, turned and waited. "What's up?"

Harding halted at Rosman's door and leaned against the wall, his face buried in the afternoon shadows. "You gonna tell me what's going on? I tried to take your side back there, you know."

Rosman held out his hand. "I know, Bill. And thanks. I appreciate it. I really do." They shook. "I seem to have stumbled into something this weekend, and I'd like to play it close to my chest. At least for a little while."

Harding's face emerged from the shadow. "It almost sounds like you don't trust me. Or maybe you don't think you need any help."

Rosman's hands rose, then fell back to his sides. "For Chrissakes, Bill. Give me a little time to sort through everything. You'll get all the gory details." Rosman smiled. "As soon as I figure out what they are myself."

"Have it your way. Just do me one favor."

"What's that?"

"See Rick Kramer for a quick lesson in self-defense. He likes you, and I'm sure he'd be willing to help."

"You think so?"

Nixon nodded. "Yeah. And from the looks of your face, you could use at least that kind of help."

Not a bad idea, Rosman thought. He brushed his chin and fingered his lower lip. He strolled into his office, opened the top drawer in his desk, then rummaged through pens, paper clips, and unused envelopes for some Tylenol. On top of the pile he found the photo of his parents when they first arrived in America. His thoughts wandered back to his childhood outside Chcago and those difficult years of transition and remembrance for his parents.

He could almost see the steam escape from the solid metal coils that stood together like an old car wreck under the dining room window, filling the room with a barricade of warmth against the bitter wind howling outside. His gloves rested on top of the radiator, a drying ritual as much a part of winter as the snow storms that brought drifts to the Midwest high enough to bury a man. Along the lower edge of the window, a thin layer of ice always formed when the moisture rose from the wet cotton to the cold glass, freezing at the touch. Patterns spread along the glass like roads on a map. If it was thick enough, he would write his name, or secret messages to spies trapped on the other side.

The heated coils had provided warmth and welcome at the end of a bitter bike ride through the early morning of a Chicago winter. Rosman had hated delivering papers on those days when the cold, polar wind descended upon the city. He had barely been able to catch his breath through the scarf covering his face, matted with perspiration and saliva, his gloves almost frozen to the grip of the handlebars on his bike.

From his nest in front of the radiator, Rosman had watched his parents and his aunt and uncle from Germany seated at the slim oak table set into the breakfast nook at the back of the kitchen. Between them sat the dirty lunch dishes and the bottle of wine his relatives had brought from the Kaiserstuhl region outside Freiburg, near the Black Forest. To Rosman, the name meant only fairy tales and cuckoo clocks.

"It's nice to have something to drink besides Liebfraumilch," his father had said. His eyes glowed with memories as he pondered the glass of liquid gold.

"They don't know anything about German wine over here," his heavy uncle protested in a thick Swabian accent. His hand reached out from a fluffed black and white sweater and never seemed to leave the glass that was always moving to his face. Why did it never get empty? This time they had opened a bottle of Sylvaner, and it was the good stuff. *Trockenbeerenauslese*. From the

grapes that had hung on the vine so long they turned to raisins.
"Ach, Helmut. Why don't you ever return? Even if it's only for
a short while," his uncle implored. "A great deal has changed."
"But has it?" Rosman's father demanded. "Things like that,
an insanity that grips a people, it cannot be just wiped away."
"Perhaps after a few more years," his mother added. "Right
now the pain is still too great." Rosman had seen the tears pool in
her eyes.
"But it's been so long already. You'll never get past it sitting
here in America. That's probably why it's lasted this long. You force
yourselves to live in the past." His uncle studied Rosman's father
for a moment, as though he were weighing the consequences of
continuing. "Do you think Johann would have wanted it this way?"
"Besides, it's so hard to see one another when you're this far
from home," Aunt Hannelore claimed. "And what about the
money?"
"No! We don't need that blood money. We don't want it." His
mother nearly spat the words at the table.
"Chicago is our home now. It has been that way for 20 years,"
his father had announced, his fist pounding the table. The discussion was over.
Rosman was certainly happy to stay in Chicago. His friends
had been there. So were his football and baseball teams. What
did he care for that old country, with all its old battles and old
wounds? It had always been this way when one of the relatives
came to visit. First the wine and the reminiscing. Then the pain.
And the sorrow that brought the tears.
His mind drifted back to the present, and Rosman glanced
down at his desk. His eyes stayed fixed for a moment longer on
the posters of German wine regions that someone had hung in
the hallway just outside his door. One of them advertised the wines
of Baden, especially those of the Kaiserstuhl. "Spoiled by the sun,"
the words said. He picked up the telephone and dialed Rick
Kramer's number.

CHAPTER 8

Captain Rick Kramer shook his head, his hands resting on his hips. "I just hope it was worth it, Rosman."

"It's too early to tell."

"I also hope you look better than the other guy." His head still shook. It reminded Rosman of those bobbleheads people had put on the dashboards of their cars years ago. "I'd say this lesson is long overdue."

Kramer had agreed to join Rosman that same afternoon at the gym just to the side of Truman Plaza, the American military's shopping center. The two had met at a diplomatic reception at the Minister's house several months ago, hitting it off almost at once and even becoming occasional handball partners.

"It can't look that bad. It happened a couple days ago," Rosman protested. Kramer led the way from the locker room to a large red mat set in one corner of the gym, just to the side of the basketball hoops.

"What the hell were you doing over there anyway? Doesn't that belong to the embassy in East Berlin?"

"Not exactly, Rosman explained. "We still have responsibility for the entire city of Berlin."

Kramer glanced at Rosman suspiciously. "Whatever you say." He extended his legs to stretch the hamstrings.

"Actually, it was a private matter."

Kramer's eyebrows arched. "Aren't you the mysterious one. So, this is not a professional request?"

"Not really. And it's not really very dangerous. At least it shouldn't be." Rosman lay down and tried to imitate Kramer's stretching exercises. His fingers stopped about two inches short of his toes. "But it did bring my path across some toughs near the Friedrichstrasse train station." Rosman winced at the sudden pain in his side, the tender muscles pulling at his rib cage. His hamstrings were also tighter than he realized.

"I just hope you weren't trying to play James Bond. That's not something you State weenies are cut out for."

Rosman said nothing as he brought his knees up to his chin.

"Seriously, though, John, you should be more careful over there." Kramer jumped up. "I don't know what you're up to. But from the looks of your face, you got in over your head the other night. Did you report the incident to the Regional Security Officer?"

"Jesus, everybody's so damn concerned about the RSO. What's he going to do about it anyway?" A scowl broke across Kramer's face. "Look, it's okay, really. I just want a little insurance in case I run into trouble again." Rosman climbed off the floor. "Now, can we get started?"

The two men stood for a moment, staring at each other, their hands on their hips. Then Kramer laughed. "Okay, okay." He circled the outer rim of the mat, then moved into the center next to Rosman. "My first piece of advice would be to stay home."

"Forget it."

"That's what I figured. Since that doesn't look like it's about to happen, you should play dumb and innocent." Kramer hesitated, motioning toward his head with the tips of his fingers. "Let them think you're just some jerk fumbling around. Don't push things to the point where you pose a threat. That's when you'll get in trouble."

"Well, that shouldn't be much of a problem. I really am just fumbling around."

"Okay, the next time some goon comes at you, try giving him the flat of your hand, down by the heel where the muscle is." Kramer jabbed at the middle of Rosman's face with the palm of his hand. "Straight to his nose. It will hurt like hell, cause a shitload of bleeding, and, more importantly, give you a chance to get the fuck out of there." He shoved the open face of his hand toward Rosman's nose once more in a swift motion that sent his palm toward Rosman like a projectile.

"Or come down hard with the side of your hand on his shoulder, up near the neck. Like this." Kramer tapped Rosman to show where he should deliver the blow, probing Rosman's shoulder blade with the muscled edge of his hand.

"What's wrong with a real punch?"

"A 'real punch,' as you put it, will probably break some knuckles and fingers. This isn't television. It will be a lot better if your opponent can't hit back because of his broken collarbone. Are all you State guys so street dumb?"

Kramer moved in closer, his eyes intent on Rosmann. "You sure this isn't related to some big adventure? Harding told me about the showdown with your boss. What did Friedlander say?"

Rosman rolled his eyes toward the ceiling. "I'm not on any fucking adventure, Kramer. I told Jack I'd like to do so reporting on changing east-west relations in the city, but that has nothing to do with this." Rosman pointed at his face. "Believe me."

"That should be interesting." Kramer cocked his head and squinted at Rosman. "As well as provide you with some useful cover."

"I don't need any cover." Rosman shrugged and looked toward the mat, then looked up at Kramer, whose face had broken out in a broad smile.

"Oh, but you do need some karate." Kramer wagged a heavy finger. "There's something you're not telling me, buddy boy."

Rosman let a faint smile escape. "Maybe some day."

"Okay, if you won't say anything about that, tell me what you think of Dorothy Sutton."

"What for?"

"Because I think she and Harding are getting it on. And I'm not sure I trust her."

Rosman's mouth fell open. "Why not?"

Kramer shrugged. "She impresses me as one of those shopworn 60's radicals. You know, pampered Ivy League upbringing, anti-war demonstrations."

"She went to Amherst."

"Same thing." Kramer shook his head. "I still have a thing about college grads that marched against the troops in Vietnam while they enjoyed their deferments. It pisses me off."

"They weren't marching against the troops, Rick, just the policy."

Kramer studied the mat for a second. "Aw, fuck it." Then he grabbed both Rosman's shoulders. "If the guy's facing you, try to slip your leg behind his calf real quick like, then give a twist and a shove. Like this."

Rosman tumbled backwards and pitched to the side, slamming hard onto the mat with Kramer on top of him.

"The problem, of course, is that he might grab you, giving you absolutely no time to get away." His weight shifted off Rosman's back as Kramer rose and rested on one knee. Then he stood up. "Here, try it on me."

Rosman found it much more difficult to throw Kramer to the floor. "It's okay," Kramer reassured him. "I'm trying to make it a little more difficult for you. I know what's coming. Your opponent won't."

He also demonstrated an over-the-head body toss that reminded Rosman of the kind of self-defence moves he saw advertised on television. It was still shy of the Bruce Lee thing, though.

"Look," Kramer repeated, his chest rising and falling after 20 minutes of exercise, "the smartest thing for you to do is to stay out of harm's way. Why don't you let me look into a few things?"

"No, that's okay," Rosman answered, wiping the sweat from his forehead with the forearm of his sweatshirt. "There shouldn't be any more trouble. I have no plans to play the hero. In the meantime, you keep your eyes on Harding and Sutton."

"I think your story is going to be more interesting."

"Thanks for the lesson." Rosman limped toward the door "And the warning."

"What warning?" Kramer shouted. "I'm just curious."

CHAPTER 9

Hermann Buechler had told Rosman to meet him at a bar called the *Zeughaus*, or "Armory." When he walked out the front exit of the Schlesisches Tor *S-Bahn* station, Rossman saw the pub sitting where three streets met to form an urban triangle. The elevated train station stood directly opposite the point. A small park across from one corner offered little more than the shade of a tree and the comfort of a bench. A block away, the River Spree drifted through the middle of the city. East Berlin loomed on the opposite shore, outlined by the thin gray line of its crumbling Wall, the *Oberbaumbruecke* spanning the water and decades of division. Rosman watched a steady flow of dark shapes moving in both directions. Constructed near the end of the last century as a rail line to connect that part of Berlin with the city's center, the bridge had served since 1961 as one of several pedestrian crossing points between east and west.

He was in the middle of Kreuzberg. Rosman's eyes and imagination took in the neighborhood, so typically Berlin. During the ride out, this sector's vitality had spread before him like a newsreel. The buildings, dissected by the train, presented a collage of styles, timelines and politics, their open cement sides billboards for any cause that spray paint could carry. A few of the buildings dated back at least a century; others were more recent, probably from the *Bauhaus* period. Most, however, stemmed from the post-war years, their straight lines and square shoulders testimony to the Germans' hurry to rebuild and the necessity of sacrificing taste to utility. The present occupants tried to compensate by splashing an assortment of colors, slogans and mosaics along the walls. Rosman wasn't sure it always worked, but you knew you were in

Kreuzberg: a haven of hippies, dropouts, Turks and anarchists, a Central European blend of Soho, Haight-Ashbury and Greenwich Village. An artists' and left-wingers' milieu, in which May Day parades—and riots—were a matter of pride.

Once inside the Armory, it took Rosman a minute or so to adjust to the murky light and the dense curtain of cigarette smoke. He searched the sea of tables for Buechler but saw only a mob of young people in baggy sweaters and patched blue jeans, black leather jackets and black leather pants. Both sexes wore some kind of facial jewelry, while the men tended toward long, shaggy locks and facial hair. The woman inclined toward closely cropped coifs that dropped an inch or two of bangs over the forehead but kept the ears in full view. The heavy beat of German rock pulsated above the stale scene of spilled beer. *Jesus*, he thought, *what the hell was Buechler thinking?* He longed for some Bruce Springsteen or Grateful Dead to kill the time and alienation.

A waiter approached. His dirty blond hair hung loose down to the shoulders of an ill-fitting red woolen sweater. Only his tray distinguished him from the customers. Together they slid sideways through the throng toward the back, where Rosman found Buechler planted at a table, a fresh *Schultheiss* at his fingertips. The foam stood undisturbed at the rim of the thin crystal glass.

"Where the hell did you find this place?" Rosman shouted.

"My neighbor's son recommended it," Buechler bellowed in return. He extended a hand to the chair facing his.

"Well, I'm not sure we're the kind of Berliners who normally come in here. And I doubt we'll be discussing this crowd's kind of politics."

"Don't worry, Herr Rosman. None of these people care about us. We can discuss our affairs in relative privacy here. Besides...." Buechler's finger circled the air above his head. "The noise helps."

The waiter brought Rosman a *Schultheiss*, then added another crooked blue line to the coaster at the center of the table. As soon as he left, Buechler leaned forward, his blue eyes dancing around the room.

"So, Herr Rosman, I have been asking myself when I was going to hear from you again. How long has it been?"

"You have to admit, things have been rather busy this month."

"Yes, I can certainly understand that."

The initial conversation covered a host of topics so essential to the political life of contemporary Berlin but of little consequence to most Americans, or even most Germans. Over time, the relationship between West Berlin and West Germany, as well as the Allied presence in the city, had evolved into an arcane political theology akin to medieval scholasticism.

During a pause in their exchange over the limited voting rights of West Berliners Buechler shrugged and sucked down about a third of his beer. Rosman had liked Hermann Buechler from the start. His open and almost cheery pro-Americanism came as a welcome change to someone who spent too many days hearing lectures from German leftists on the shortcomings of American political culture in general, and post-war foreign policy in particular.

The man did not look well, though. Rosman hoped the red rims around his eyes were only the product of the room's smoky air. But his heavy frame failed to hide the pale skin and deep-chested cough that periodically wracked the older German's body.

Rosman's gaze wandered around the room while he let the rich, refreshing liquid run down his throat. God, he loved German beer. "Actually, I really wanted to talk about the recent developments in the east, and what sort of impact you think it might have on the city."

"What specifically did you have in mind?" Buechler finished his beer in two more gulps before holding up his hand for the waiter with two fingers extended.

"You have an extensive personal history over there, don't you?" Rosman asked. "As I recall, you had to flee from the Communist regime."

"Yes, but it goes back further than that. Politics actually began for me during the Third Reich. At the age of 16 I joined a Social Democratic resistance call."

"You fought against the Nazis?"

Buechler shrugged and studied his beer. "Nothing that glamorous, I'm afraid. I was just a courier. Nobody suspected a young fellow like me. After the war, I resumed my work with the SPD, helping to rebuild the party's organization after the Nazis had destroyed it." Buechler glanced toward the bar, where he studied the row of patrons leaning against a thick brass railing. A ten second coughing spell intervened before he could continue. "That was difficult work in the Soviet Zone, though, because the Russians naturally favored the KPD, the Communists."

"Did you find your work with the resistance useful?"

"Useful for what?"

"For life after the war. In the east, I mean."

"Yes, I did," Buechler responded. "Particularly after the forced merger of our party with the Communists. Those of us who tried to maintain our ties to the SPD in the west were labelled 'Schuhmacher Agenten' and arrested."

The waiter delivered their beers with a light thud. The interruption appeared to settle Buechler, who leaned back in his chair, his fingers playing with the glass, rotating it on the table's smooth wooden surface.

"So...." Rosman continued, "....the Social Democrats built their own intelligence organization in the east, didn't they? The Schuhmacher part I get. That's a reference to the SPD leader Kurt Schuhmacher from the 1950s."

"Yes, and he had the party maintain a network of agents to report on the Soviet Zone. He was an ardent anti-Communist, Herr Rosman."

"What happened to you?"

"I was arrested and spent seven years in the prison at Bautzen before Bonn purchased my freedom and that of several others." Buechler smiled. "You're aware, I'm sure, that the West German government purchased the freedom of many political prisoners from East Germany."

"Yeah, but it sounds a bit like white slavery."

Buechler shrugged. "East Berlin quickly recognized a source of hard currency when it saw one. Anyway, I came to West Berlin, where I found work restoring bombed out buildings and monuments. Finally, the party got me a job in the local office of the Inner-German Ministry so I could use my knowledge and contacts in the east. That seemed like the best place to do it. I stayed there, directing the prisoner buy-outs, until I retired three years ago."

Hearing all this, Rosman examined Buechler's face more closely. Deep furrowed lines set off a prominent chin and nose, and the heavy eyebrows and receding gray hairline outlined a face with hard, chiselled lines. It was the face of a man unable to escape the sweep of events that history had chosen for this city and for his lifetime. Even Buechler's large tanned hands were marked by time, the skin and bones of his fingers scarred by the passing years.

"Actually," Rosman continued, "that's why I called yesterday. You clearly have a personal interest in events over there. Some experience, too."

"Of course."

"Do you still have some contacts over there, people who could provide an insider's view of the changes underway?"

"Perhaps. Just what would you like to know?" His hand waved in the general direction of the bar. "My eardrums will not hold out forever."

"Well, it's kind of particular, maybe even dangerous."

"How particular and how dangerous?"

"Some friends of mine in the dissident movement in East Berlin have gotten themselves into trouble with the Stasi." Rosman told Buechler of the break-in at the Stasi headquarters.

Buechler was silent, his eyes studying the crowd. After a moment, his gaze returned to Rosman. "Does it have something to do with the death of the young man in Dresden?"

Rosman's glance shot toward Buechler. "How did you know about that?" Buechler said nothing. His stare made Rosman uncomfortable.

"And you think your friends are in physical danger?" Buechler asked.

Rosman nodded. The waiter appeared suddenly and dropped two new beers on the table between them. Buechler looked away from the table to study the patrons at the bar, while he coughed into his right hand. "I'm trying to find out more," Rosman continued. "That's where I was hoping you might be able to help me."

"Of course. I'll do what I can. But what exactly would you like me to do?"

"I need help finding out who to contact, how to make my way through the political minefields over there."

"Can you give me their names?" Buechler asked.

"Yes. And there's been a second death." Buechler's eyebrows arched. Knuckles whitened around the rim of his beer glass. "That's right. A dissident named Hermann Lamprecht. And another one, Erich Jens, has disappeared from the Charite."

"And the cause of this?"

"Some files, I believe. And a notebook."

"What was in these files and papers?"

Rosman relayed the gist of his conversation with Jens and his adventures at Lamprecht's apartment and afterwards.

"Where is this material now? Do you have it?"

At that moment a fight broke out near the bar, and a large, rotund body clad entirely in black leather crashed down onto their table. The glasses tumbled into the void, and Rosman reeled over on his side. Buechler disappeared on his back into a sea of blue jeans and faded corduroy.

"*Du besoffener Arschloch!*" the waiter screamed, yanking the man by his shirt to his feet. The drunk's knees stayed wobbly and drops of beer foam dripped from his thin brown beard. He smelled like he hadn't bathed in weeks.

Buechler rolled to his feet with an agility surprising for a man of his age. He yanked Rosman to his feet. Rosman brushed at his pants legs, soaked from the overturned *Schultheiss*.

"Let's get out of here," Buechler ordered, pulling Rosman's arm toward the door.

Rosman tossed a twenty Mark note at the spot where the table had stood, then turned and followed Buechler outside. They hurried toward the *S-Bahn* station, Buechler's eyes darting back toward the bar. At the curb he turned and stepped backwards until they reached the other side of the street.

"That was close."

"I know. I nearly took my second bath of the day."

"That's not what I mean."

Buechler gripped Rosman's upper arm tight enough to make him gasp. The pupils of Buechler's eyes narrowed to a fine point. "You have to learn to be more careful. That may not have been what it seemed. The man's eyes betrayed him. He had not had that much to drink. He had been hovering near our table until somebody pushed him."

Rosman stared at the pub entrance, his heart pounding so hard he was sure Buechler could hear it.

"You were probably followed. From now on we must be more careful and meet where we can be alone." Buechler wrote something on a small scrap of paper. "Here. This man may be able to help."

"How so?"

"He was my contact for the prisoner buy-outs."

"What's he doing now?"

"I believe he's retired. I haven't spoken with him in over a year. Perhaps he can tell you something about the death in Dresden. He may also be able to answer questions about the Stasi and its interest in your friends," Buechler said.

"Is he well-connected?"

Buechler shook his head. "Well-informed. It's how he's survived."

"Why would he help me?"

"That, my friend, is up to you."

Rosman climbed the steps to the *S-Bahn* platform one slow step at a time. The words on the slip of paper held the name and address of a Joachim Hetzling. Rosman wondered if he could get him to talk to an American. Was he still carrying a lot of baggage from the past, or did he want to take advantage of the new opening to the West?

When Rosman stopped at the top step, he turned to call to Buechler. But the old German stood at an awkward angle, leaning against his car at the curb that ran beside the river. One arm lay across his chest, pinned to the front of his long brown coat. The other held a white handkerchief to his lips. His chin had sunk to his chest, but Rosman saw that Buechler's eyes were focused on the door of the pub.

CHAPTER 10

Rosman had been lucky to find the pub so quickly, especially on his first trip to Rostock. The green and white sign advertising the "Wild Boar"—*Zum Wilden Schwein*—had been hidden among the drab, run-down facades that marked much of the neighborhood. The buildings dated from what the Germans call the "*Gruenderzeit*", the time of the foundation of Bismarck's Reich, which would put their origins back some one hundred years. It was astonishing luck for them to have survived five years of Allied bombing and 45 years of communist neglect.

But they had survived, and one had a bar with a restroom, which he immediately visited. It had been a three-hour drive, longer than necessary. But the dictates of Allied diplomacy required Rosman to exit Berlin through Checkpoint Bravo on the city's western edge rather than further north at Reineckendorf. This added another hour of driving and god-knows-how-many cups of coffee from his silver thermos. And spills were inevitable when you were jostled by little pissant Trabants all the way around the Berlin Ring until you finally hit the long, smooth ride along deep black asphalt to points further north. The Autobahn stretch was the newest transit route, built in the 1980s to carry traffic from Berlin to Hamburg, and it provided a better ride than the older routes to the south, highways built in Hitler's time, with precious little repair since.

Rosman zipped up his blue jeans and walked to a table by the window that fronted onto the street. He ordered a bowl of goulash, eagerly anticipating the heat of the stew on this late autumn day. It was hot, but it was also watery, and the meat fatty. At least there was plenty of it, and the place had bottled Radeburger from Dresden.

Washing the goulash down with his beer, Rosman studied the neighborhood outside. Joanna had told him that Schmidt was visiting his family's place in a high-rise apartment near the train station. He studied the street name and number on the napkin Joanna had given him, then stuffed it back into his shirt pocket. Unfortunately, Joanna had not known the apartment number, but the phone book had listed a flat in one of the buildings in the complex.

Outside the window, a monotony of steel and concrete ran along a warren of streets laid out in a criss-cross pattern, a design common to many German streets, thanks to the awesome destructive power of Allied bombing. They were nearly identical to the collection of cement blocks spread throughout East Berlin, their litany of square compartments broken at regular intervals by rusting steel balconies. *Life inside one of those must be incredibly cramped, not to mention boring,* Rosman thought. Rather than wander through the maze, he decided to wait a moment longer on the outskirts, in the tavern.

Minutes later, his patience payed off. Rosman saw his quarry leave one of the doorways that yawned like the mouth of an abandoned cave. Rosman jumped up, tossed twenty East German marks on the table and rushed for the door.

Throwing it open, he bolted down the steps and into the street, pulling on his coat and looking in all directions for Schmidt, a six-foot mirage in a dark green, woolen overcoat that ran to mid-calf. Half-way across the street, Rosman slipped on a patch of mud, slamming his body against the cold ground. Christ, he thought, now his ass would be as sore as his ribs. Forcing the pain from his mind, Rosman rolled over and jumped up. More than anything, he did not want to lose Schmidt.

After a moment's confusion, Rosman saw his quarry plunge around the corner of a high-rise and skirt the edge of a dirt pathway. He was heading for a square two-story blockhouse nestled in the middle of the development.

Rosman ran to catch up, shouting after Schmidt, whose head jerked around. His face looked puzzled as his eyes tried to focus.

"Rosman! What are you doing here? This isn't your turf."

"Schmidt, you've got to talk to me. You've got to tell me what happened the other night with Erich and Hermann."

"Who told you I was there?"

Rosman slowed to a stop, keeping a distance of about 10 feet between them. "Jens told me. He said you were with them."

Schmidt's anger turned to confusion. His lips parted, and his eyes narrowed.

"I spoke with him right after the attack," Rosman continued, "but he's disappeared. You've got to help."

Schmidt's black-gloved hands rose involuntarily and then came back to rest by his side. He looked at the ground, shook his head, and let out a long sigh. "I was afraid of this." He looked around the courtyard. "Come on. Let's go somewhere before someone sees us."

They walked back to the neighborhood pub. The bartender set down the glass he was rinsing long enough to nod at Schmidt. He also cast a big smile in Rosman's direction. Apparently, twenty marks more than covered the tab.

"If you're hungry skip the goulash," Rosman advised.

Schmidt frowned. "It could be a lot worse. At least there's meat in it." He chose a table at the back and dropped into a chair with its back to the wall, affording himself a clear view of the door. He left his coat on and signalled for the bartender to bring two beers. "I've been worried ever since that night in Kreuzberg that Jens would get you involved. He's such an impulsive bastard. You were perfect for him, the innocent young American diplomat, so eager to make the world safe for democracy."

Rosman shook his head in disbelief. What, he wondered, had he done to derserve this?

Schmidt blew out a mouthful of air, as though he were glad to be rid of it. "Don't worry. Jens isn't dead."

"How do you know?"

Schmidt settled back in his chair. "Well, I was with him, and he certainly hasn't died from anything I did. I'm the one who saved his ass."

Rosman sat forward, trying to process this new information. "What do you mean?"

"Look, first tell me why you're here."

Rosman glanced around the room as he stuffed his gloves in his coat pocket. "I'm just trying to help Erich find out what happened to Hans and Lamprecht."

Schmidt frowned. "I'm not sure I believe you. You never even knew Hans."

"Well, you'll have to. And I'm not going away." Rosman paused to study Schmidt's expression, which remained skeptical. The frown shifted to a smirk. To hell with it, he thought. In for a penny, in for a dollar. "Erich also said there were some files. Do you know anything about those?"

"Yes, I do." Schmidt's hands roamed over the tabletop as if he was trying to smooth the wood between them. "But shut up and listen for a minute." He leaned forward.

Rosman nodded and settled back into his brown wooden bench. The back formed one border of the aisle that led to the restroom, and Rosman glanced over his shoulder to check on the foot traffic behind him. The bartender set the two bottles of Radeburger on the table with a thud, the white foam running down the sides to form a puddle on the cardboard coasters.

"First of all, I do not know who killed Lamprecht. I saw him on the floor there for the first time when I entered the room with Jens. I was with Jens and Lamprecht that night searching for files too. But Erich...."

"Where is he?"

"He's safe. From you, as well as the others."

"Did you know that Lamprecht also had a notebook? Is that why he was killed?"

"I don't know why he died," Schmidt said, leaning across the table. He studied Rosman's eyes, as though trying to measure the strength of his commitment, of his character. "Where is this notebook?"

"It's safe."

Schmidt reached over to grab Rosman's forearm. "What's in it?"

Rosman shook his head. "Tell me what you know about Hans' death first."

"Jesus, Rosman, you don't waste any time."

Rosman sipped his beer while he surveyed the room. "I don't have a lot."

Schmidt sighed. "Hansi was a fool. He couldn't let things go. He always thought he moved in a higher moral plane than everyone else." Schmidt broke off his thought and drained about a quarter of his bottle. When he finished, a thin white mustache had grown along his upper lip. "That was okay, though. The Stasi can live with that. But when you try to screw them, that's when you make real trouble for yourself."

"How so?"

Schmidt laughed. "You've obviously never dealt with our friends."

"Have you?"

"We all have at one time or another."

"What was he trying to do? Why was he fleeing Dresden?"

"A lot of people were. Have you seen the pictures of that train?"

"But why was Hans trying to get out?"

Schmidt watched Rosman coolly, as though taking the measure of a potential antagonist. "Why should I tell you anything? You're just an American diplomat. If that's indeed all you are. And what can you do about it anyway?"

"More than the likes of you."

Schmidt's face turned hard, the skin and muscles cold and tense. "What do you mean?"

"I mean that you sound pretty cynical, Schmidt. Just why did you join the dissident movement?"

"I was fed up with the whole mess in our lives, if that's any of your damn business."

"It's just that you don't sound very idealistic. Not like Jens and the others. So I wondered about your motives."

Schmidt's hand slapped the table. "What the hell do you know about it? What do you know about anything in our world here? You grew up warm and safe in your Disneyland culture. You have no idea what it's like to have to survive here." Schmidt stopped abruptly, his eyes covering first the room and then Rosman. "Go fuck yourself, you self-righteous prick."

Schmidt rose to go. Rosman swore under his breath.

"Wait." Rosman grabbed his arm. "It sounds like you're in this up to your commie fucking ears, Schmidt. I'll bet you've been informing on your friends, probably for years. I'll bet you're even involved in Hans's death, too. And it wouldn't be hard to get that information and pass it along to people who would like to know. I'm sure Joanna would help, if Jens can't."

Schmidt stood at the edge of the table, scowling. He glanced toward the door and then bent over the table, speaking to Rosman in a voice just above a whisper. "You should get more information before you go making wild accusations. And you should be more careful of whom you choose for your allies. I say that as a friend."

"I don't want your friendship."

"Shut up," Schmidt commanded. "First of all, Jens is not dead yet, but he's still in danger."

"But...."

"Shut up, I said, and listen. I helped see to that by driving him away from the Charite the other night. What is important for you to know, however, is that two people are already dead, in part because of that search the other night at the Stasi headquarters and something that happened earlier this year. So, if you do have a notebook of Lamprecht's, you'd better get rid of it, especially since you don't know what it is you've stumbled onto. You don't want to be number three."

Schmidt paused for a moment, looked away from Rosman, and then turned his gaze upon the American once more. "And it would be better for all of us if you'd mind your own damn business. Stay in the west. You don't know what it's like over here. You can't help us."

"Do you know who the killer is?"

"No, and I doubt it was any one person. But I think I know why those people died. And it scares the hell out of me."

"Did you know this before or after you went to the Stasi headquarters?"

"After. And I didn't help myself by being there, if that's what you're wondering."

"Are you in danger?"

"I am now. Thanks, in part, to you. And you probably are, too."

"What do you think I should do?"

"Go home. And don't follow me here ever again."

With that warning, Schmidt pulled away from the table and darted for the door.

Heeding the call of Nature, Rosman ambled to the back of the pub to lose some of the Radeburger. When he returned, Rosman laid a ten Mark note on the table next to his empty bottle. The bartender grunted and shook his head.

Outside, Rosman pulled his coat tighter together and hustled to cover the two blocks to his car. In a few hours he needed to be back in Berlin for a reception. As he reached for the door, Rosman thought he noticed a familiar figure. And then he heard the words. "Gracchus, come on."

That was it, just those three words.

The sound came from two men who climbed inside a brown Trabant and sped off toward the train station about a mile in the distance. Rosman froze for several seconds, struck by a sudden, frightening realization as he coughed through the sickly blue smoke left behind by the Trabant.

That name had appeared several times in Lamprecht's journal. And the man called Gracchus was the shadowy face that had thanked Rosman for his cash that night near the Friedrichstrasse station.

As he approached the Autobahn, Rosman reminded himself to fill his gas tank. He could not recall seeing a station on the road between Berlin and Rostock. And he did not want to find himself stranded on this highway, not today, not with the image of the man called Gracchus stuck inside his head.

CHAPTER 11

Darkness was already descending over the city like a heavy woolen cloak when Rosman walked out onto the front steps of the Polish Embassy in East Berlin. It was just a few minutes shy of six o'clock. He had found this reception as boring as all the others, mostly idle chitchat with the occasional East Bloc diplomat and intelligence officers. He could never be sure which was which. Rosman stuffed canapés of bread and cheese and ham between his lips during the rare intervals when he did not have to think of polite conversation.

He did, however, hook up with two overweight West Berlin politicians engaged in the round table discussions with representatives from East Berlin, Potsdam, and Frankfurt an der Oder, negotiating how to combine their municipal services. Friedlander had been hounding him for a cable on budding east-west ties in the city, and this would provide valuable material. He should have something to send his boss in a week or so. Inner-German ties and negotiations were taking on the momentum of an international steamroller.

After about an hour and a half of eating and drinking, he passed a nearly plausible excuse to Harding and Sutton and then left the reception. Rosman pulled the collar of his dark green Lodenmantel tighter around his neck, tucking his chin in behind the collar to shield his face from the bitter evening air. Hetzling's apartment was not far, probably about a 10-minute walk from the Embassy building on Schadowstrasse. Emboldened by the two glasses of vodka, he trotted down the stairs and jogged across Unter den Linden.

The streets of East Berlin hummed with an activity that had

not been visible last year. The sidewalks carried a steady parade of consumers, most of them packing colorful, plastic shopping bags from West Berlin stores. Rosman had to weave a passage through the throngs of strollers, his hands buried deep in the pockets of his coat and his shoulders hunched forward to ward off the cold and the bumps of unwary stragglers.

Plenty of West Berliners were evident. You could tell them by their Scandinavian furs and Italian boots, an easy contrast to the bright polyester jackets and fur caps of the Easterners. This made Rosman even more cautious. The Westerners were the more dangerous pedestrians, pushy and aggressive.

When he reached the complex that ran along Mauerstrasse, Rosman stood for a minute, studying the buildings nestled against the stretch of no-man's land that ran along the Wall from the Brandenburg Gate to Potsdamer Platz. From a distance, the buildings looked surprisingly tasteful, an attempt to blend older German architectural styles—Gothic and Rococo mostly—with more modern Bauhaus lines. They were still too heavy on the concrete, though. He had seen the style elsewhere in the city, probably the product of some architectural five-year plan.

The buildings also looked incomplete, especially inside. Rosman entered the foyer and saw none of the finishing touches in the hallways, stairwells, and entrance foyers normally found in western apartment buildings. The walls lacked any woodwork and they had no wallpaper. In fact, Rosman could find no decorative coloring at all. Just caverns of gray stucco and plaster.

Rosman located Hetzling's name on one of the mailboxes. Apartment 360. He eyed the elevator. After a minute's indecision, he decided to climb the three flights of stairs.

The ascent was more arduous than he had calculated, and Rosman had to lean against the doorframe of the exit to Hetzling's floor. He wiped a thin line of sweat from his brow and wondered what else had been in those vodka bottles besides buffalo grass.

Halfway down the hall, Rosman halted and knocked. Twenty, maybe thirty seconds passed. He was ready to knock again, but the door creaked open about six inches. A gold-colored chain bridged the distance from door to frame.

"Who are you and what do you want?"

"My name is John Rosman." He studied the edge of a small, earnest face that peeked around the edge of the door. This had to be Hetzling. "I'm from the American Mission in West Berlin. I was wondering if I could ask you a few questions."

"Like what?" The door and face did not move.

"I'd like to talk about the events over here this fall, if that's all right. I'm trying to help some friends."

"I've already said everything I'm prepared to say to the journalists. Do you read *Der Spiegel?*" Hetzling asked.

Rosman nodded, although he couldn't recall any article that had mentioned this man lately.

"Well, you'll find it all in there," he continued. "For now, that is."

Hetzling started to shut the door, but Rosman thrust his foot in the way. It must be the vodka, he told himself. The heavy metal door pinched his toes against the doorframe.

"I'm not that concerned about November 9th. I'm really more interested in the events leading up to that."

"Like what?"

"Actually, it's several days in October that I care about most."

"Which days are those?"

"The days when something happened in Dresden. An accident with a train."

The little round eyes shrunk further. The opening in the doorway widened by about a foot. "You can come in for a few minutes. I have to leave shortly for a friend's house."

Rosman passed through the foyer and made his way to a sofa that faced a window looking out toward the west. The apartment, though small by American standards, was well furnished. In fact, the place seemed almost luxurious for East Berlin. The living room held four armchairs grouped around two end tables across from the sofa, and four sets of bookshelves, all arrayed with a large collection of photographs. Rosman recognized none of the portraits but assumed they were figures from East Germany's brief history. Around the corner he could see a china cabinet and a large table of dark wood with eight chairs spaced evenly around it.

The best Rosman could do was compliment Hetzling's taste in art, which seemed to span the centuries from Gothic to Cubism. Hanging just outside the kitchen was a reproduction of Delacroix's "Liberty Leading the People," a paean to the 1830 Revolution in France. The irony of it all left Rosman momentarily speechless.

"First," Hetzling began, "tell me if you're from the American press or the CIA. I don't want to play games anymore."

He sat in a large leather chair, his small figure almost lost among the cushions and shadows collecting in the corner of the living room as the sun set. His physical presence was well short of imposing. In fact, it was almost forgettable, with his round drooping shoulders, wisp of gray hair, and short legs. Rosman noted how Hetzling's tan pants rose several inches above the ankles when he sat down, exposing inches of white skin and leg hair above the black socks that had fallen around his ankles. He wondered why Buechler had set him on to this particular man. At first glance, he possessed only the stature of a quintessential bureaucrat, a small, rather pathetic figure that drew his authority from a position within a well-defined hierarchy.

Rosman pulled out his diplomatic passport and waved it at Hetzling. "I assure you I am what I say. I'm simply trying to put some pieces of a puzzle together. I'd like to help some friends in this half of the city, and I was told you might have some information."

"Who told you to talk to me?"

"A friend in the West, Hermann Buechler. He told me he used to work with you on occasion."

Hetzling shot forward, his fingers kneading the arms of his chair. "Buechler? Is he still at it?" Hetzling threw his head back and laughed. "Why should I help him? Or you?"

"No real reason. But I thought you might be able to throw some light on a death in the early part of October."

"And which death is that?"

"The one in Dresden. October fifth. A young dissident was pushed in front of a train."

"Earlier you said it was an accident."

"I think we both know better."

A knowing smile broke across Hetzling's face, while his head shook back and forth. "If you're so sure, try the police. Tell your friends to talk to them, Mr. American Diplomat."

"The name is Rosman."

"I don't care." Hetzling waved his hand in Rosman's direction. The smile evaporated, and Hetzling's face turned into a solid mask, as though etched in some of the concrete the East Germans had used to cover the better part of their state.

Rosman spoke cautiously, considering his words as he would the moves of a chess match. "Was the Stasi involved?"

"Why do you ask that? I thought you were so sure." Hetzling had produced a cigar from a small silver box resting on the table next to his chair. He twirled it in front of his nose, his eyes shut. He did not offer one to Rosman.

"I've formed a theory," Rosman continued.

Hetzling's eyes remained shut. "Oh, please. I'd like to hear it."

"I believe it had something to do with the Stasi's infiltration of the dissident movement."

"You are young, Mr. American Diplomat." Hetzling's eyes opened. He struck a match against the side of its box, then held the flame for about 10 seconds at the tip of the cigar, puffing heavily. The room filled with clouds of heavy, rancid smoke. "Excuse me. I meant to say, Mr. Rosman."

Rosman ignored the insult. "But if I'm correct, the purpose of that infiltration had to be obvious. To gather information and undermine the movement. Correct?"

"Go on."

"But then I have to wonder how extensive it was. Who directed the infiltration? And why didn't the Stasi put a stop to the movement? And why did someone have to die just then, on October fifth?"

"Those are several questions. There are several possible answers. Perhaps they tried, but couldn't stop. There was a lot going on then."

"I know. The GDR's fortieth anniversary celebrations, Honecker's removal, the Leipzig demonstrations and the threat of a real crackdown. Could the death have had something to do with any of those?"

Hetzling leaned further back into his chair, almost disappearing from view. "Just whose death in Dresden are we talking about?" Hetzling did not wait for an answer. "Never mind. I guess everyone is wiser with hindsight. Even me. Buechler, too."

More silence ensued for what seemed like several minutes while Hetzling puffed on his cigar with obvious delight. "If you really want to know more about the Stasi and its movements, you should talk to someone else." Hetzling blew a half dozen smoke rings through the air between them. "I never worked for that Ministry. Talk to someone involved in the discussions with Moscow."

"Moscow? What did that have to do with any of this?"

Hetzling waved Rosman's words away in a cloud of smoke. "There were some who even made trips there."

"Trips to Moscow?" Rosman leaned forward "Who? Why?"

Hetzling was silent again, and when he did speak the sound came from deep within the cushions of his armchair. "I'm not going to tell you anymore. You'll have to get whatever there is from the others. That is, if they're willing to talk to you."

"Others? Like who?"

Hetzling laughed briefly. "I doubt, though, that they will just answer the door like me. Some need to be more cautious. You can try, of course. Wolf, for example, lives nearby in the *Nikolaiviertel*. Do you know where that is?" Rosman nodded. "Do you know who he is? Or, more to the point, was?"

Rosman did not respond. He had heard of Markus Wolf, reputed to be East Germany's master spy. He had even heard Wolf speak at the large rally on November 4, when the man had been heckled into silence by the disapproving crowd. He knew little of the man's career and personal history. But Rosman was not about to admit this to Hetzling.

Instead, he stared out the window. He studied the long patch of light brown earth that extended for several hundred yards until it reached the Wall, empty of any sign of life although it was in the heart of one of Europe's great cities. Only barbed wire, steel fragments and cement blocks marked Hetzling's view of the west, the direction so many of his countrymen had chosen to flee.

Rosman turned his face toward Hetzling. A large bookcase

covering most of the wall stood behind Hetzling, the obligatory volumes by Marx and Lenin lining the lower shelves. His gaze stumbled across several titles by dissident East German writers, principally Christa Wulf and Stefan Heym. Those, at least, were the names he recognized. There was also a collection from the Mann brothers and other assorted German classics. Interspersed among these and the photographs was an array of souvenir ashtrays, soccer club pennants, and the bric-a-brac that Rosman had always associated with households of the petit bourgeoisie.

"Let me ask you a question." Hetzling did not wait for an answer. "Why do you wish to know? Is it only to help your friends?"

"Does it have to be anything more? You believe in friendship over here, don't you?"

Hetzling smiled and nodded. "Oh, yes. And so much more. But I have to wonder what an American could be after over here, and at such an exciting time."

"Perhaps I'm after justice."

"Oh, I'm sure you are," Hetzling laughed. "And probably much more."

"I'm only trying to help some friends. I'm not answering to anyone on this but myself."

Hetzling emerged from the cushions. "Then you have a lot of work ahead of you. I don't see much point in you're returning until you've learned more on your own. Remember my words about Moscow. We'll see if you're up to playing the game."

Rosman rose from the sofa, his face red with anger. "Goddammit, this is more than a game."

Hetzling's smile returned. "Of course it is, you young fool. But just like a game, there are rules, and there are winners and losers. Which will you be?"

"But don't you have any sympathy for the changes underway? Didn't you help people leave for the West? Don't you want to help my friends? They didn't do anything wrong. They're in trouble, but only for some political activities that wouldn't be a crime in the west."

"Of course I sympathize with the changes that have come. Everyone does now." Hetzling's speech held its defensive edge.

His feet remained planted in front of his chair. "And what I did earlier is probably best left for the history books. It doesn't make any difference now. You can tell that to your friend Buechler. And you can tell him to leave it be. And you should understand this. If your friends are in trouble with the Stasi, it may be for more than you realize. And I doubt I or you can help them."

"Is that why you mentioned Moscow? Are there Russians I need to see?" Hetzling just stared, like some Teutonic sphinx. "Who else can I talk to? Do you have any names?"

Hetzling stuck the cigar in his mouth. A smile curved around the brown stub. "Keep at it, Mr. Rosman, and they'll find you." He strode over to the door and opened it. "Now, good-bye."

Rosman shuffled past his host, avoiding Hetzling's vapid eyes, small brown dots that looked like orbs pressed from the soft coal skimmed off the surface of his part of Europe. Then he marched through the bare hallway and down the stairs. Out on the sidewalk, he tried to determine why Buechler had thought this man might be useful. He had been uncooperative, abrasive. Hell, he was downright rude.

And yet there had been hints of something more. The forbidding image of the Stasi still loomed. And now something about Moscow. That was when Hetzling had withdrawn into himself. Had he sensed a need for caution?

Rosman slammed a fist against his thigh. He wished he knew more about this man and the others who had lived and worked here.

The streets continued to fill with East Germans returning from a day's shopping in the west. Walking in the direction of Checkpoint Charlie, Rosman remembered to check the street for any sign of a tail. Fortunately, the brown Trabant from Rostock was nowhere in sight.

On the other side of Checkpoint Charlie, Rosman strolled to the Café Adler, a trendy pub habituated by Berlin's peculiar brand of German intellectuals: prosperous anarchists and radical left-wing environmentalists mostly. He broke a ten Mark bill for change, then dialled Joanna's number. More than anything else right now, Rosman wanted to see her again. And right away. But there was no answer.

When he got home Joanna's beige Trabant was nowhere in sight. The only East German car around was a deep yellow Wartburg, parked about a block up Vogelsang, near the corner with Spechtstrasse and just beyond the pet store. He decided to try calling again, all night long if necessary. Rosman inserted his key and cracked the lock on his front door. He pushed it open.

Soft, white hands reached around his waist and grabbed his belt buckle. Two thin arms rose along his sides, and the hands locked across his chest. Rosman felt himself pulled back against a set of firm breasts, the rounded flesh spreading along the muscles of his back. He flipped the switch to the ceiling light in the hall foyer.

"Where did you come from?"

"I was just around the corner." She pecked at his cheek. "You must be more careful, John."

She was wearing blue jeans and a white oxford dress shirt. She had the shirt unbuttoned as far as a multi-colored vest, accentuating the milky-white cleavage that disappeared beneath the folds of her clothes.

"Where's your car?" Rosman tugged at the top of the vest to pull her closer. "And how did you get in?" He slid his arms around her shoulders.

"I took the *S-Bahn*. The city is open now. Remember?" She kissed his chin. "I was waiting for you to come home, and your door was open."

"No, it wasn't. I had to use my key."

"I locked it so no one else could sneak in."

"Thanks. Hungry? I probably have something we can fix here."

He led Joanna into the kitchen, where she grabbed a seat at his kitchen table. Rosman held the refrigerator door open and peered inside. He needed little after the reception, and he knew that Joanna was a light eater. Some cheese, sausage, and bread would do. Fruit for desert.

"There's not a whole hell of a lot in here," he apologized.

"I'm not very hungry."

"We should have met at your place, since I was already in the east." He set out some slices of Swiss cheese and *Bauernwurst* on a rectangular wooden cutting board.

"Oh, I much prefer coming here." She waved her hand at him. "Your house is so big and comfortable compared to my little flat in Prenslauer Berg."

"Speaking of which, when am I going to get to see your place over there? What is Prenslauer Berg like? I hear it's an artists' and workers' community of sorts."

"You'd probably find it boring. It's not as interesting as Kreuzberg."

Rosman started to slice the brown, granular *Bauernbrot*. "How could it be boring if you're there?"

"I'm sorry, but you can only be so romantic in the workers' and peasants' capital of the German Democratic Republic." Joanna rolled her eyes and sat down at the kitchen table. "This place is so much nicer."

She crossed her legs, then buttered her bread before spearing a slice of cheese with a fork. "Do you have any plates?"

"Of course. I'm sorry." Rosman took down two plates from the cupboard just to the side of the sink. "Would you like a beer? Or a glass of wine?"

"Some white wine would be nice, thank you."

Rosman poured her a glass of fume blanc, holding the California label for Joanna to see before returning it to the refrigerator. "See? We do make wine on our side of the Atlantic."

Rosman could understand her attraction to his house in Dahlem. He loved it too. Although more modest than most on his street, its two stories, three bedrooms and full basement offered more space than he would ever use. And it came fully furnished, including a cabinet stocked with fine china and crystal. All of this was normally well beyond a junior officer's salary. But since the Germans were picking up the costs of the Allied occupation in Berlin, Rosman could afford to live like a minor potentate. He even hoped to talk his parents into using his place for a visit to the old *Heimat*.

And, like most of Berlin, his street had its own particular history. Hjalmar Schacht, the financial wizard who restored Germany's monetary stability during the Weimar Republic and then financed Hitler's rearmament programs in the 1930s, had lived kitty-corner from this house. Admiral Canaris, the head of German military intelligence in World War II, who was later executed for his involvement in the plot to kill Hitler, had kept his residence just a block away in a modern, square-shaped structure of white stucco and glass.

"So, what did you do in the east?" Joanna sipped her wine. "Not bad...for an American wine."

"I called on someone named Hetzling. And that," he pointed to the glass, "is damn good."

Joanna nearly choked on her mouthful of wine. "You talked to Hetzling?" She spat the words out between coughs. "For God's sake, why?"

"A friend over here recommended him." Rosman frowned. "He thought the guy might have some information."

She stood up and began to pace around the kitchen. "But John....he's one of them. He had to be."

"What do you mean? One of who?"

"John, Hetzling was one of the men running the buy-out program here in Berlin. He had to be connected to the Stasi. They're not going to let something like that go on without having a say in who gets to go west."

"But then why would Buechler send me to him?"

"Who?"

"Hermann Buechler. He's a contact of mine over here. And he's well connected in the east."

"Apparently. But we'll have to be very careful. Especially now."

"How so?"

"Who knows whom Hetzling will speak to."

Rosman fell into the chair Joanna had occupied. "Jesus, that complicates things even more."

"There's another reason we need to be especially careful." Joanna leaned against the refrigerator door, her arms folded across her chest. "It's also why I wanted to come by to see you tonight. I heard from Schmidt this afternoon."

"Schmidt? What did that asshole want?"

"He wants to set up a meeting with Jens as quickly as possible."

"So, is Erich okay?"

She nodded. "I think so. I haven't seen him."

"Has Schmidt changed his mind about me? When I saw him he told me I should mind my own business."

Joanna slid across the kitchen tiles to stand directly in front of Rosman. She ran her hands through his hair. Then, she turned to the side, picked up a piece of bread and bit into it. "What happened when you two spoke?"

"He thinks I'm only going to bring more trouble into all our lives."

She finished chewing. "That fits. He thinks it would be best to let you meet with Jens, pass back the notes, then get you out of the picture."

"I'll let Erich decide that." Rosman stood up and took the plates to the sink. "Do you think we can trust Schmidt?"

Joanna laid her knife and fork on the table. "John, do you know much about Schmidt's past, about his family?"

"I just know I don't like the son of a bitch."

"His mother left him at an early age. She filed for emigration back in the 70s, and she had to divorce his father before she was allowed to leave for the Federal Republic. He was raised by his father, a petty bureaucrat, the sort our system has bred so well over the years. But he was a committed communist, and Thomas was raised as one too."

Rosman stared at Joanna, her lower lip quivering. She tossed the brown piece of crust on the table. "Then why did he join the dissident movement?" he asked.

"Ask yourself that question. Perhaps he was disenchanted. A disappointed true believer, the most dedicated kind of convert."

"I'm not sure I see what this has to do with his role in this whole affair."

"Perhaps people are more complicated than you realize, John. Perhaps there are motives at work you cannot understand. Not yet anyway."

"That's not fair," Rosman responded.

"Who ever said any of this would be fair?"

He stared at Joanna to see if she was serious. She picked an apple from a basket at the middle of the table and began to chew her way around the core. Her green eyes studied his face.

"When is the meeting supposed to happen?" he asked.

"Tomorrow at lunch time. In front of the KaDeWe. That part of town is usually packed. The crowd of shoppers will give you plenty of cover."

She took off her vest, draped it over the back of another chair, then slid down slowly onto Rosman's lap, her weight pressing against his crotch. "I don't want to talk about Schmidt or Erich or any of this anymore."

Rosman nodded in agreement, unbuttoning her shirt. He slipped his hands inside the soft, cotton material, then ran them along her waist and up the small of her back. Her skin felt like fine silk. "But we haven't done the dishes yet."

"Who cares?" She kissed his lips, grabbing the side of his head in both hands.

"How unGerman of you," Rosman accused.

Joanna frowned. "I thought you Americans just did whatever you wanted."

"Sometimes we do."

Rosman stood up and led her by the hand toward the stairs. When he passed the living room window, Rosman stopped to glance outside. The yellow Wartburg was still there. It was too dark to see if anyone was inside.

CHAPTER 12

Gracchus caught the scent of burning paper the minute he turned down the street leading to the GRU headquarters in Karlshorst. The smoke had been visible for about a mile before that, a gray cloud drifting lazily above the square blocks of two-story homes and occasional shops that lined the streets of this northern suburb. Once aloft, the smoke blended with an overcast sky before floating off toward the west, driven, Gracchus hoped, by a stiff breeze from the Russian plains. A gift for the Allies, he sniffed.

Gracchus pulled his yellow Wartburg into the parking lot beside the main building in the Soviet military complex, leaving it in one of the spots reserved for visitors. He rammed the emergency brake into place, slammed the door shut, and spat on the dark black asphalt when he realized he had parked in a "visitors" slot at an army headquarters in his own country.

He did not bother to register at the main building, whose drab concrete blocks had turned the color of charcoal in the 40-odd years since the liberating Red Army had seized it. Instead, he marched around to the side, where a gate and a guard awaited him. Gracchus showed his pass, then hustled over to his friend Preselnikov.

The Russian was watching two Soviet enlisted men maneuver a flamethrower toward a pile of boxes in the middle of a courtyard safely encircled by a 12-foot fence. A thick roll of razor wire topped the enclosure. They were standing a good hundred yards from the nearest building.

"Do KGB jackets now come with a special lining?" Gracchus asked, smiling and slapping his friend in the middle of the back. "Or is the extra weight protecting you?" Gracchus rubbed the lapel of Preselnikov's navy blue jacket and then prodded his mid-section. He had never known his friend to brave the damp cold of northern Germany without an overcoat. The enlisted men, on the other hand, wore canvas overcoats and thick asbestos-line gloves. Shivering slightly, Gracchus envied them. His own overcoat was in the Wartburg. He stepped closer to the burning trash.

"I wish it were the first." Preselnikov then yelled something in Russian to the enlisted men. They carefully shut down the flamethrowers.

"So, why did you ask me to meet you here?" Gracchus asked. "Are you running out of matches?"

"Actually, it's not unrelated to all this." Preselnikov tossed his head toward the glowing heap of cardboard and paper.

"Sergei, I realize drastic changes are underway in Europe, but this seems a bit dramatic." Uncertain where the conversation was leading, Gracchus tried to smile again and kicked a small rock that lay at his feet toward the fire.

"Yes, I suppose it does look that way. But this," Preselnikov gestured towards the fire, "is on orders from Moscow."

"It looks almost as bad as when the Americans had to flee Saigon." Gracchus considered the sky. "You need some helicopters, though."

"It's not that bad. At least not yet. But Moscow has ordered everything of importance sent back to the Soviet Union for safe-keeping, and to destroy the rest. What you see there," Preselnikov said, again motioning with his head toward the smoldering heap, "is the rest."

Gracchus watched the flames in silence. His tongue darted out to wet his lips. After a minute, he spoke. "Is there anything of concern to me in there?"

"Yes. I'm leaving nothing to chance. I'm destroying all my records." Preselnikov turned his eyes on Gracchus. "All of them."

"What does this mean for our plans?"

"I have not received anything concerning those. But it does not look like Krenz will last another week, and God knows what will come after him. So caution does seem appropriate."

When Gracchus motioned as though to protest, Preselnikov

raised his hand and peered into Gracchus' eyes. "I know. One could also argue that forward movement is more important than ever."

"That would be my advice." Gracchus pulled out a pack of Lords cigarettes. "Have you got a light?"

Preselnikov handed him a box of matches. "You don't want to use that?" He gestured with his other hand toward the flamethrower.

"No. I'm not that desperate."

"Since when do you smoke a western brand?"

"Whenever I can nowadays. I got these on surveillance in Dahlem."

"The American?"

Gracchus nodded as he cupped his hand to protect the flame.

"Tell me," Preselnikov asked, as he took his matches back and lit a Marlboro, "is it true that Kessler was forced to resign as Defense Minister because he wanted to call out the troops last month?"

"That's not far off. I believe he wanted them held in readiness to restore order."

Preselnikov laughed. "What order?" He looked over at his own soldiers holding the flamethrower. "Do you think your troops would fire on their own citizens?"

Gracchus was silent again as he turned his head to study the Soviet enlisted men. "No," he said, finally, "not anymore. But they shouldn't have to." He shook his head and looked out toward the parking lot. "Christ, Sergei, even the Felix Dzerzhinskiy brigade has begun to unravel."

"Who will man the Wall?"

Gracchus studied his friend, surprised at his seriousness. "I'm not sure we'll have to bother much longer."

"That could make things even easier, now that I think about it."

Gracchus nodded. "My sentiments exactly. I've already begun to lay the groundwork."

"What about the American?"

"I'm going to make him useful."

Preselnikov's eyebrows arched. "How so?" He blew out his smoke in the direction of the enlisted men.

"He will lead us to what we need."

"Exploiting his inexperience?"

"That, and his eagerness. It's all a matter of how we bait our hook."

Preselnikov dropped his cigarette to the ground, then rubbed it out under the toe of his right shoe. He raised his hand to interrupt Gracchus. "I would also recommend that you get your papers in order. Remove as much as you can. Do not leave any trails, if at all possible. You would have been smart to do this," he said, gesturing toward the fire, "instead of your last operation."

"That's the least of my worries right now."

The lines running from Preselnikov's cheeks to his chin betrayed his pain. He shook his head in disbelief. "Have you given any thought to your network? Can you protect them if we fail?"

Gracchus shrugged and tossed his half-smoked cigarette toward the fire. "I'll find something else for them to do."

Preselnikov continued. "Perhaps I don't need to say even this much, but I think it best not to take anything for granted. Not in these times. Are you sure you can still trust them?"

"Did you have anyone in particular in mind?" Preselnikov just stared. Gracchus studied his friend. "Have you had any trouble from any of our people?"

"Yes and no," Preselnikov answered. "For the most part, your colleagues continue to be as professional as one can expect under the circumstances." Preselnikov extracted another cigarette and returned the pack to the side pocket of his sport coat. He held it between his second and third fingers without lighting it. "The locals have been different. One of our sentries was stoned to death the other night."

Gracchus hissed. His eyes narrowed when he glanced at Preselnikov. "Did you find the people involved?"

"No. But the word here"—Preselnikov poked his finger at the ground—"is that some dissidents are responsible."

Gracchus thought of the "visitors" parking spaces. "Are you sure?"

Preselnikov shrugged. "It should tell you something that this explanation is so readily believed by our authorities. You can see how concerned we are by conditions here. And some in Moscow are pressing for a response."

"How sure are you of your co-workers here?"

Preselnikov laughed. "I'm not even sure I can trust my own chauffeur anymore."

Gracchus said nothing. He frowned and thrust his hands deep into the pockets of his charcoal gray slacks. Preselnikov said something to the enlisted men, and they resumed their assault on the remains of the dossiers.

Gracchus turned and began to walk toward the gate. "I have to get back to the city. I'll be in touch," he shouted as he strolled out into the parking lot, looking right through the guard's salute.

"Just be careful," Preselnikov shouted at his back. "That's more important than anything else at this point." Then he turned to watch the last of the files disappear in flame and smoke.

Rosman lay in bed and shivered from the cold air. He hoped he hadn't caught a cold or the flu from all this running around. A thin layer of frost lined the outer space between the glass and the window frame, and crisp layers of morning air escaped from the hard wooden floor. It looked like it would be a cold winter, he told himself. He needed more carpets. And he wondered if it was wise to have arranged a meeting with Buechler on the Wannsee for later, just before his meeting with Jens.

Rosman thrust his hand toward the radiator and was gratified by the thin stream of hot air reaching out from the coils. He rolled off the edge of his mattress, skipped to the radiator, then twisted the dial another thirty degrees to warm the bedroom some more.

He walked to the window and gazed outside. The early morning traffic had yet to disturb the thin layer of frost that covered the earth or the mist encircling the rows of birch trees in the tiny park across the street. It was as though a sea of white shadows were drifting just beyond his front steps.

Rosman turned to contemplate Joanna. She lay asleep under

the dark green woolen blanket he had thrown over them in the middle of the night. They had both felt the chill despite their heat and sweat in the sweet aftermath of sex. He pulled another blanket—a multi-colored quilt—up along the length of the bed until it covered her shoulders. He was surprised at how much he looked forward to spending the rest of the day with her. He even wondered if that was the principal reason he had gotten involved in the search for Jens and the missing files in the first place.

He pulled on his terry cloth robe, swung through the guest bedroom to retrieve Lamprecht's notes, then strolled down to the kitchen, where he tossed the papers onto his kitchen table. Rosman put on some coffee, settled into a chair, reached for the notes, and began to read.

But what the hell was he to make of the letters and dates that covered the pages of the notebook? Midway through, Lamprecht had added some kind of numerical code, often coupled with place names. Rosman recognized some. Wittenberg and Dessau were easy enough. So were Wenigerode and Halberstadt, historical towns in the Harz. But Greifswald and Stendahl? Cottbus and Plauen? Rosman tucked the notes under his arm and poured two mugs of coffee.

When he came back upstairs, Rosman walked first to the guest bedroom. He set the mugs down, then slid the papers into the top dresser drawer underneath a set of prints he had purchased on a weekend outing to the medieval town of Goslar. Then he returned to his own room, where he set one mug of hot coffee on the night table beside Joanna. She rolled over slowly, squinting to escape the morning sun. Her right arm slid from underneath the covers, her hand rising up and across her forehead to shelter her eyes. After a moment, she sat up and leaned against the pillows propped against the back of the bed. "Oh, thank you," she cooed.

Her eyes studied Rosman as he strolled around the bed to the other side. She reached for the mug, whose warmth she cradled against her belly. "Tell me more about yourself, John."

"What would you like to know?"

"Your family. Your home. You already know something of me."

Not much, he thought. "I believe I've already mentioned that I grew up in Chicago."

"But what about your parents?"

Rosman told her of his parents' academic and political careers, his father working at Loyola University and mother for the Democratic Party in Chicago. He found himself enjoying this moment, opening up his past to Joanna and wanting to promote her interest.

"Why didn't you follow in your father's path?"

"I started to. After I graduated from the University of Illinois I began working on a doctorate in European history."

"What happened?"

"I got my master's and finished the course work for the doctorate, but then feared that a professor's life would be too sedate for me."

"Yes, I can see why."

"Well, none of this particular business was foreseen. But there was something else. Because of my German background I felt drawn to Berlin. I called in a few favors and extended some others after my New Delhi posting to get this one."

Joanna smiled from behind her coffee. "Welcome home."

Rosman reached over and stroked her thick blonde hair. He ran his fingers along the rim of her thin, pointed nose, then down to her full, round lips. She kissed the tip of the finger. "It's not really home anymore. But thanks anyway," he said. Rosman studied her face and the unmoving eyes with their shifting hazel light for a moment or so. "Now it's your turn. Tell me more about your family."

She frowned. "There isn't much to tell. Mine was not a very happy childhood. My mother died when I was still very young, and I barely knew my father."

"What sort of man was he?"

"Very warm, when he wanted to be. But he was also very dedicated to his work. He was one of our many bureaucrats. But a committed communist."

Rosman slid closer to her under the covers. "I'm sorry things weren't better for you."

Joanna set her coffee on the night table, then rolled over as the sheet fell to her waist. "Sometimes I wish the revolution had never happened." She leaned back against the pillows, her head sinking into the foam.

"Excuse me? Did I hear you right?" Rosman stared hard at this woman sharing his bed and realized how little he knew of her background, her plans for the future, and how all that may have been affected by the events of the last week. "Are you serious?"

"Yes, but I didn't mean it like you think. I'm happy for all the political changes." She grabbed her mug. "I've always wanted the right to travel and vote as much as anyone. But there has been a lot of sadness, too. I didn't know Hans very well, but Hermann was my friend."

"Of course. I'm sorry."

"And now there's Erich." Joanna sipped her coffee.

"What do you think he's up to?" Rosman asked.

"I'm not really sure. But I'm afraid for him."

Rosman reached for his coffee, took a sip, then set it back on the floor. He turned on his side to face Joanna. "But what did you mean by wishing all this hadn't ever happened? What if we had never met?"

"No, not that. That's not what I mean." Joanna smiled. "I think we would have met somehow." She pushed his hand away from her hip. "Just imagine. What if I had seen you at the Wall one day and made some daring escape to be with you? I would be like some character in a Le Carre novel."

"Oh, really? And how is it you know about him?"

She smiled, batting her eyes. "A girl can't give away all her secrets, John."

"I think those years behind the Iron Curtain made you fantasize a bit too much."

"Perhaps. But then we wouldn't be tangled up in this mess. We could just be lovers."

"But that's what we are. We're lovers, and the rest of this is just a temporary diversion." Rosman looked out the window. "At least for this morning."

She sighed, while her eyes took on a distant look. "Of course we are," she said.

Joanna finished her coffee and looked past Rosman to the patches of frost along the window's lower rim. "How long do you plan to pursue this business with Erich?"

"I'm not sure. He asked for my help, and if I can help find the killers, I will."

"And will you talk to this Hetzling again?"

"Perhaps. If it helps catch the killers."

"And after that?"

"I don't know." He ran his fingers through his hair and sighed. "It seems every time I turn around, I find there's more we don't know. I mean, there could be a Moscow angle. And I'm wondering if there isn't more to the Stasi thing that goes way past Hans and Hermann."

"What do you mean?"

"I'm not really sure. Not yet, anyway. But I'm afraid Hans and Hermann were on to something pretty dangerous."

"What do you plan to do about it? Can you bring in your American friends? The CIA perhaps?"

"I'm afraid it's not that easy." He drained the coffee. "I'm sort of playing this day-by-day right now."

Joanna stroked his arm and chest. "Please be careful." She turned toward Rosman. "I worry about you. I fear that something awful might happen. I find that I'm troubled more and more about your part in this and about how it might affect us."

He watched as she rolled onto her side and kicked her legs free of the covers in one swift movement. Rosman bent to kiss her smooth, white skin, his lips moving along her side then resting on the hard brown ridge of her nipple. Joanna moaned. He moved his lips lower, running them down her front and past the navel. She ran all ten fingers through his hair. He rolled over on top of her as she opened herself to him. *Finally*, he thought, *finally I have you. And you belong here with me.*

The cabin cruiser pulled away from the dock, leaving in its wake the ancient brown pilings that lined the newly painted pier.

From the deck, Rosman studied the cultivated patchwork of garden and shrubbery that ran down the steep slope of lawn until it met the panelled wharf and white boathouse. An expansive, three-story house of white stucco sat like a throne atop the lakeside property belonging to the U.S. Mission, reminding Rosman of an American country club. There was no golf course, though. The house disappeared behind the rise and would not come back into view until the boat was near the middle of the *Wannsee*.

The waves, no more than a foot high, broke from the side of the boat before disappearing on the vast expanse of dark green water. He lumbered down the steps at the boat's stern to a small cabin that could seat perhaps eight people.

"This is impressive, Herr Rosman. How were you able to arrange it?" Buechler asked.

He unsnapped his raincoat, revealing a yellow sweater over a brown sport shirt, buttoned at the neck. Buechler pulled off his plaid Cambridge cap, coughed into his fist, and shivered slightly. Rosman appreciated his dark green turtleneck and black corduroys all the more.

"It's the Ambassador's boat. For his use whenever he's in Berlin," Rosman explained. He angled toward the bar to pour two cups of coffee.

"You are not the Ambassador."

"But I know the person who manages his affairs here. We have an ambassador's aide in Berlin as well. His name's Bill Harding. And at this time of year, naturally, he seldom gets the urge for a cruise on the lake."

"Who pays for a morning's outing like this?"

"Not the American taxpayer. Black?"

Rosman handed a mug of coffee to Buechler. Colorful boating pennants against a field of white covered the sides of the mug. Steam rose from the rim and curled toward the panelled ceiling.

"Yes, thank you." Buechler leaned back against the foam padding that lined the bench along the back side of the wooden table.

Rosman climbed to the deck to see that the pilot was still in his cabin at the helm. When he went below again, Rosman shut the door at the top of the stairs. "Nothing like a little privacy."

"Yes, this will be fine." Buechler sipped his coffee, his lips barely touching the cup. "The coffee too." He reached into the side pocket of his sweater and extracted a small bottle of long white pills. He spilled two into his palm, tossed his head back and threw them into his mouth.

Rosman propped himself atop one of the barstools. He took a cautious sip from his own mug.

Buechler cradled his cup in his hands and leaned forward, his blue eyes dancing. "Have you heard? The Stasi headquarters in Erfurt and Leipzig have been raided. In several other cities as well."

"By whom?"

"New Forum and other dissident groups. It was probably a matter of revenge." Buechler took another sip of coffee. "And prevention."

"The files?"

Buechler smiled. "Exactly."

"But wouldn't the government try to prevent their destruction? I thought the good guys were in control."

"What makes you think it is all over?"

"But the reformers are in charge now."

Buechler frowned. "A government run by a man who was party chief in Dresden? The party chief knows perfectly well what goes on in all branches of the government. *All* branches of government, Herr Rosman."

Rosman shrugged and glanced out the porthole to his right. The *Pfaueninsel*, or "Peacock Island," rolled past.

Buechler caught the direction of Rosman's eyes. "Amazing, isn't it, how European monarchs have indulged themselves?" He nodded toward the porthole. "To create a home for peacocks in the middle of a lake in Berlin. Expensive delusions seem to have been a characteristic of so many. We Europeans would have been better off, I believe, if we had deposed our monarchs years ago, like you Americans."

"But Germany did. Over 70 years ago."

"Not really. In many ways only the labels changed. Have you ever been on the island?"

"Not yet. Is it worth a visit?"

"Very much so. At any rate, the attacks at their headquarters have probably made the Stasi very defensive. They're probably 'circling the wagons', as you say."

"Do you think those other raids by the dissident groups had anything to do with the deaths of Hans and Lamprecht?"

"That's hard to tell. At least no one was hurt in these other raids. But I think your friends' presence in Normanenstrasse that night was for other business."

"Why do you say that?"

"It had all the marks of a private operation. Otherwise, why did they sneak in all alone?"

Buechler turned to the side, hoisting his right leg onto the bench. He glanced out the porthole over his right shoulder, two bellowing coughs erupting from somewhere deep in his chest. "What time is it?"

"Ten o'clock. Why?"

"Because the sky is turning quite dark for such an early hour." He glanced at his wrist watch.

Rosman stepped to the table, then leaned over to peek out the porthole. An army of dark, bulging clouds had moved in from the east. They appeared to be several miles off, but with the moderate wind blowing, they would probably glide over the lake in less than an hour.

"It looks like a cold front is coming in. I'll go tell the helmsman to return to the dock."

"He'll know enough to turn around," Buechler reassured him. "If he doesn't, we're in trouble anyway."

He tipped the coffee mug back and swallowed a mouthful. "How did it go with Hetzling the other day?"

Rosman sat on the edge of the bench. "Not very well. He wasn't very forthcoming."

Buechler's forehead wrinkled, and his eyes narrowed. "What did he say?"

"Not much, other than to tell me Moscow might be involved. But he refused to elaborate. I'm wondering if he really knows anything."

"If you're going to find out more about what it is you're after, you need to think of why those friends of yours were in the Stasi headquarters that night and what they encountered that was so dangerous." Buechler studied Rosman. "You also need to find out why they haven't told you more themselves."

Rosman thought of Joanna and if he was letting his feelings for her cloud his own judgement. "Perhaps. But more to the point right now, I can't see why Hetzling would say much. He's got to be concerned for his own well-being, like the rest of the Stasi."

"Hetzling was never a Stasi officer. At least, not that I know of."

Rosman tried to read Buechler's face, but the eyes had gone blank, as though they were shrouded by the cold, damp air coming off the lake. "That's not what I hear. How closely did you work with him on the prisoner buy-outs?"

"He was my principal contact with the East Berlin government. He always acted honorably, as far as I could tell."

Rosman shook his head. He gulped his coffee. It was too much and burned his upper palate. "That's not how I would characterize his behavior."

"He may also have been afraid, Herr Rosman. These are very uncertain times."

"Afraid? Of me?"

Buechler laughed lightly. "No, of course not. But he may have been afraid that what he told you would find its way back to the wrong people in the east, or even in the west."

Rosman fell back against the bench, stunned. "What are you trying to say?"

"Perhaps he's worried about a mole in your Mission."

"Where did you hear that?"

"I didn't. But it's something you always have to consider."

"But what would make Hetzling vulnerable?'

Buechler smiled. "His vulnerabilities are the same as those of everyone else right now. His past may well affect his future, Herr Rosman."

Rosman ran his right hand through his hair. "Let me ask you a direct question, Herr Buechler. Why do you trust this man?"

The smile returned. "I'm not sure I do. Or if it's even necessary. But I believe he is the best source for the information you need. The rest is up to you."

Rosman nodded. "Okay. Then Hetzling aside, do you think the two deaths are linked?"

Buechler shrugged. "Isn't that what your friends believe? It's certainly a strong possibility. And how likely is such a coincidence? Two deaths among the same group of dissidents, and in such similar circumstances?"

"Which are?"

"Searching for information linked to the Stasi, or possibly a specific operation."

"What do you believe?"

Buechler paused, considered his coffee mug, then spoke to the window at Rosman's left. "Yes, I think they are connected."

"You sound pretty certain."

"I know the kind of people involved."

"And Hetzling is linked to these people?"

"He probably knows who they are, and how they operate."

"Hetzling also said something about Moscow. He hinted at some connection."

"That does not surprise me. Not with someone like Gracchus involved."

Rosman slid off the stool. "Gracchus? You...you know him?"

Buechler leaned back against the cushions. "Yes, very well. I've always suspected he was involved. It makes sense, especially if Moscow is in this." He looked at Rosman. "It's probably why Hetzling was so hesitant."

Rosman turned to the window and stared at the waters of the lake for about 10 seconds. "It's more than just these two killings, isn't it?"

Buechler stared at Rosman. His silence was answer enough.

"I mean, it looks more and more like Hans and Lamprecht were on to something that's gotten the Stasi worried. Possibly the KGB. It's no longer a matter of simply finding a guilty individual or two, is it? Some rogue criminal."

Buechler rubbed his hands together. "You know, Herr Rosman, we Germans did rather poorly after the war in making sure that those responsible for the Nazis and their crimes did not come to positions of power again. In the East and the West."

Rosman leaned forward. "What are you talking about? What about Nuremburg and all the other trials?"

"But there were so many more. It's a problem we Germans have. We become too attached to our leaders. We try to preserve all of them in some way, like the peacocks on the island, or make them more useful. We don't seem to be able to act on our own."

"What does this have to do with the killings?"

"My point is that I believe you were correct. It goes beyond these two killings. They had a purpose, and the perpetrators a goal."

"Which was?"

"I have only an idea at this point. And I'm far from certain."

"Does it touch on something from your past?"

Buechler let a knowing smile escape. Rosman read years of history in that face, experience that spread beyond the life of one man.

"Everything in this city seems to touch my past, Herr Rosman, and the pasts of so many others."

Rosman stepped toward the table. "You know, I have a history in this country, too, Herr Buechler. At least my family does. But this is already well beyond me."

The old German waved his hands in front of him. "No, no, John. That's not so. I see so much more in you. You will be ready, like the others."

"What others?"

Buechler shook his head. "Hetzling can help you, if you know how to approach him."

Rosman swirled the coffee left in his mug. "I'm not so sure."

"For God's sake, don't appeal to his sense of justice. Remember, he helped preserve the leadership over there. And he is looking at an uncertain future, like everyone else. You need to find the vulnerabilities. They are there. Do you have anyone else right now?"

Rosman shook his head. "Do you?"

Buechler studied the sky. "No one you can handle yet."

Rosman stood up and paced the cabin floor. After a minute he climbed out onto the deck and took a post along the railing on the starboard side. He placed his hands on the iron railing, but quickly tucked them back into his pants pocket. It was too damn cold. He had left his gray, wool herringbone sports coat draped over a stool below. He thought of retrieving it.

By now they had reached the Glienicke Bridge, and the driver arced the boat in a wide, slow turn to the left to return to the Mission dock. Rosman observed the colored columns of East and West German cars lined up in mile-long queues at either end of the bridge. In the middle, underneath the elaborate iron grillwork that rose from either side of the bridge, the East German guards were examining everyone's documentation, as though they still found it necessary to prove how indispensable they were. Several hundred pedestrians were also strolling in either direction across the bridge, hustling through the thin blue clouds of Trabi exhaust that hung in the air above the scene, a testimony to the East's unwillingness to pass from this stage of history so easily. Rosman noticed that someone had covered the sign stating in four languages that you were now leaving the American sector with bright red letters asking, *"Fuer wie lange?"* How long indeed?

"The clouds are closing in. I hope your helmsman has not miscalculated." Rosman turned to find Buechler standing next to him at the railing. "It could become very dangerous in the next hour or so," Buechler warned.

"Yes," Rosman agreed. "The winds are already making the water churn."

On the bridge above, Rosman saw two East German *Volkspolizei* pointing toward their boat. They were leaning against the iron railing at the East German side of the bridge, outlined against the dark, billowing clouds. One of them raised a camera with a long telephoto lens, aiming it toward the water. Rosman glanced about and saw that he and Buechler were the only ones foolish enough to have come out on the *Wannsee* today.

"Yes, it could become very dangerous very quickly," Rosman repeated, thinking of his meeting with Jens. He shuddered before scrambling below to get his jacket.

After he reached the shore, Buechler strolled along the stone pathway that ran from the elegant Glienicke hunting castle near the bridge and just inside West Berlin on through the park and along the *Wannsee*. He cocked his wrist to check the time. Another 30 minutes before he could take his medication. If only it wasn't so wet. He could stand the cold.

His cell at Bautzen had been damp too. Constantly. The bronchial disease that came of it had worn him down, eaten at his lungs. Just as it had with so many others. The young American would never understand that. Even his family could not teach him what it had been like in those days.

Buechler nodded to himself, grinning. He tossed scraps of stale bread at the small red squirrels that scampered between the footpath and the trees. They ate better then he had. But not better than his second cell mate. The dampness never seemed to bother him. After a week, Buechler knew why this one's face stayed pink, his cheeks rounded and flush.

He fell into a seat on the bench at the top of a round hill that looked down into the water below. Buechler studied the steel pilings that rose from the water, marking the demarcation line between the Germans in this corner of Europe.

"There will be time enough for revenge," he told no one in particular. Buechler felt his cheeks flush against the cold air. He wondered if that was wrong, immoral even, to carry the burden of his past and all he had lost for so many years while it festered inside him like the virus in his lungs.

He stood. Many had told him to leave it all behind, to move on. There was never anything you could do anyway.

Buechler spoke out loud to no one in particular, but he wished that Joachim Hetzling and others were there now. "You're wrong. You were wrong then, and you're wrong now." He pushed aside the flap of his coat and reached into his sweater pocket for his pills. "Just in case," he murmured. It hadn't been 30 minutes yet, but Buechler reminded himself that he had waited long enough.

The army of shoppers migrated from one consumer palace to another, a constant stream of well-dressed Germans flush with cash and eager to spend it. It was just two o'clock; the crowd would only get thicker. Rosman peered at the *U-Bahn* station at Wittenbergplatz, directly across from the KaDeWe, or *Kaufhaus des Westens*, as it disgorged one regiment after another, adding to the swarm and chaos overwhelming this square of Berlin. He wondered how he would ever be able to pick Jens from among this sea of faces.

The KaDeWe was Berlin's premier department sore, a rival to London's Harrods'. As such, it had become a favorite destination for East Berliners, who loved to stroll through its impressive array of consumer goods, gawking at the wonder of it all. But they rarely purchased anything. Most just came to look before heading off to Woolworths, or Herties, or someplace else to make a more economical investment. In fact, the West Berliners often complained that the damn Easterners were taking up too much space, crowding out the more serious shoppers.

Rosman hoisted his watch to eye-level, cocking his wrist. He felt a tug on his sleeve and turned to see Erich Jens smiling triumphantly, very much alive and not looking a whole lot worse for the wear. Rosman embraced his friend. "My God, it's good to see you. Joanna and I had almost given you up for lost."

"Oh, I won't go as easily as that. You should know me better by now."

Jens had been right. The crowd was perfect cover. His lined yellow nylon jacket and fur cap marked him as one of the many East Berliners mingling at this consumer paradise.

"How did you get out of the Charite without anyone knowing you were gone?"

Jens smiled and motioned for Rosman to follow him as he walked down Lietzenburgerstrasse, away from the 'KaDeWe' and Wittenbergplatz. "Schmidt helped me get out."

Straining to hear, Rosman had to dodge an older German couple laden with packages. "I don't get it. What's in it for him?" Rosman countered.

"You haven't figured him out either?"

"Not yet. But I do have one thought. I think he's afraid I'll gum up something he's got planned. I don't think his interests are the same as yours."

Jens smiled. "Perhaps. But I believe he thinks you're another complication. Someone we don't really need. He's probably afraid you'll give us away. Did you bring the notes?"

"Of course. But why are they so important?"

Jens shrugged. "I'm not sure myself. Hermann told me he was keeping a diary of sorts and a list that I should read if anything ever happened to him. And Schmidt thinks there could be some important clues to something the Stasi was working on."

"How would Hermann have known?"

Jens smiled. "My old friend was more resourceful than you realize."

"And how has Schmidt helped?" Rosman checked for more shoppers ahead. The crisp air of late autumn breezed past. Sunlight danced in the middle of the street, dodging the moving shadows on the sidewalk.

"Well, for one thing, he saved my life. I was trying to get to sleep after you left and wondering whether it was safe to remain in the Charite overnight."

"Why wouldn't if be?"

"Because, John, that place is riddled with Stasi agents."

"Jesus! Is there any place over there they missed?"

Jens did not answer. "The nurse working the night shift told me I was being moved to another room, and I was waiting for her return when Schmidt arrived. At first, I didn't know what to make of his presence. I actually expected the police to enter right behind him. He tried to be reassuring, telling me that he had panicked in Normannenstrasse when he saw Lamprecht's body and the files. His first thought had been to get the papers out of there."

"But did he say what happened to you?"

Jens shook his head. "No. He said he found me on the floor.

Unconscious."

"Is that it?"

"He claims I was gone when he returned."

"It sounds a little too convenient."

"He also said he thought I was still in danger, and that he had a car waiting outside."

"So, what did you do?"

"I just stared at him like he was crazy. But he warned me that we did not have much time if we hoped to escape unnoticed."

Rosman looked up and down the block, searching the crowd for familiar faces. Jens smiled at him.

They had reached the Kurfuerstendamm by now. Jens turned to continue strolling down the Kudamm, back toward the KaDeWe. "Has anyone else tried to get the notes from you?"

"I was jumped the very first night, but they didn't do much of a search. I think they only wanted to warn me. They must not have realized what I had."

"You were lucky. We were lucky."

"Well, the sooner I get this stuff in your hands, the better. How do you want to do this?"

"Inside the store. We can pass it more safely in one of the aisles than out here in the open."

Rosman nodded. "Sounds good to me. Let's go."

"Just a moment." Jens removed his bare hands from the jacket pockets and brushed the hair from his forehead. He rubbed them together before jamming them back into his pockets. "I also wanted to warn you about something. That night at the Stasi headquarters I had picked up a card from some HVA file."

Rosman leaned toward his friend. "What kind of files?"

"HVA. It's the part of the Ministry for State Security that deals with foreign espionage. Sort of like your CIA." Rosman began to protest, but Jens waved his hand to cut the American off. "I'm afraid that people like me have come to distrust all intelligence organizations, no matter what system they work in. At any rate, the card has disappeared."

"But that's not what you were looking for, right?"

Jens nodded. "True enough. But it looked like they had been

moving things, that the files were being transported. So I decided to grab what I could and sort it out later."

"How did you lose it?" Rosman grabbed Jens' arm. There seemed to be no end to the complications.

"It was taken from me in the hospital."

Rosman stopped in the middle of the sidewalk, exchanging an angry glance with a Berliner who had swerved to avoid a collision. Rosman flicked his wrist at the man, then ran through more pedestrians to catch up to Jens.

"That card has probably raised the stakes," Jens continued. "The Stasi may suspect that the CIA is involved. It may be what got them interested in Lamprecht's notes and made them more intent on recovering them to see if there is a connection with the Stasi's foreign operations."

"And you think there is?" Rosman asked.

"I believe so," Jens responded. "That's one reason I want to see them."

"But what about the missing files?"

Jens rolled his eyes. "I'm still trying to locate those."

"What's in them that makes them so important?"

"From what little I saw they contain information on Stasi assets, some in the east, but also in the west." He nodded again and sighed. "I know, not what we originally wanted. But who knows anymore how these things fit together?"

Rosman looked at his friend with a new sense of awe. "Jesus, Erich." He thought for a moment of his beating in East Berlin that night and the words of Schmidt and Buechler, and where all this might lead him. "This is beginning to fit together in a strange way. But what about you? Where are you staying?"

"It's better that I not tell you. It's much easier for me, you see, if fewer people know." Jens motioned with his head back in the direction of Wittenbergplatz. "That's why I was late. I wanted to have some time to observe the square and see if either of us was followed."

They halted in front of the KaDeWe. The shoppers were pouring into the street, as though some giant temple of consumerism was sending forth a new wave of converts after its weekend mass.

"Good. I timed it correctly," Jens observed. "The lunch time crowd will help me disappear on my way home." Jens started toward the store. "Let's do this quickly."

But Rosman found that his feet would not move. Instead, he grabbed Jens by the wrist, pulling him back. Rosman's eyes narrowed as he tried to focus through the waves of moving faces.

"What's wrong?" Jens asked.

"A man by the postcard stand. It's someone I recognize. There." Rosman jabbed his finger through the air. "The one in the black leather jacket and white turtleneck. He looks like one of the guys who jumped me the other night after I returned from Lamprecht's apartment."

Jens bit his lower lip and glanced around the square. "Is he alone?"

"I'm not sure. Come on. Maybe we can lose him in the store."

Rosman rushed into the KaDeWe. He pushed ahead, shouldering customers aside and glancing back to be sure Jens was following.

When he stopped to take their bearings, Rosman saw Black Jacket hurry through the doors, his head scanning the crowd to find his quarry. Rosman and Jens hurtled past a cosmetics display and down a set of stairs, bent low. They ran past the Panasonics, Grundigs and Phillips, all of them breezing by in a whirl. Then they leaped aboard the escalator, jumping the steps two and three at a time over the protests of Germans bearing a multitude of gifts, shocked at the alien display of ill manners.

Rosman spotted the back entrance to Tauentzienstrasse. An escape route. He pulled Jens in his wake.

But Black Jacket was waiting for them behind a stall of men's underwear and socks. Rosman felt a surge of blood and energy rush to his head when he saw the features of the man who had pinned his chin against the hard metal of his own car. He led Jens through aisles of shirts and slacks. The double glass doors loomed just ahead.

But the stranger had guessed right. He cut behind a row of overcoats while he moved to overtake them. Then he reached inside his jacket.

Without thinking, Rosman lowered his head and rammed straight ahead, knocking the man against a stand of Alpine chocolates. An older, gray-haired woman in a light blue overcoat shrieked as her packages scattered over the floor. She knelt on the floor to pick up her parcels and shot Rosman a look of disgust.

Jens jumped on their pursuer from behind, his fists driving at the man's face. Rosman seized their antagonist by the collar and threw him against the wall. Black Jacket slammed full into the hard concrete, and the force lifted his feet a good foot off the ground.

Rosman did not have much time to enjoy the sight. A heavy blow to the back of his neck sent him sprawling across the linoleum floor. He rolled to the side and under a rack of cookies just as a heavy-soled black boot stomped the ground next to his head.

Rosman reached up, grabbed a shelf of cookies and sent it crashing toward this new assailant, sweeping his foot at the back of a leg covered in denim. He felt the knee buckle and heard a guttural curse. Then he leaped up and grabbed a handful of marzipan and buried the man's head in it while aiming his own foot at the bastard's ribs.

Rosman glanced at the door just in time to see Jens disappear in a sea of shocked faces and plastic shopping bags.

"Erich, wait!"

But Jens was already gone. Rosman bolted for the door, hoping to catch his friend. But Jens was nowhere in sight. So Rosman aimed for the Kurfuerstendamm, where he hoped to lose himself amidst the crowds before the police arrived. "Now what?" he mumbled to himself as he stumbled down the steps of a subway station.

He did not have an answer when the train arrived. Settling himself into a seat, Rosman patted the role of notebook paper tucked against his chest. *Just what did you compose here, Hermann,* he thought, *and what have you and your friends gotten me into?*

The entire way home Rosman searched the weekend crowds

for familiar faces and possible threats. It took most of the ride for his heart to slow and his breathing to ease into a regular rhythm

The anxiety from the fight was bad enough, but it got worse. When he arrived home, Rosman realized that Joanna had left without a trace. No word of parting, not a hint that she wouldn't be there when he returned, not even a note. He needed her. Instead, he felt utterly alone.

CHAPTER 13

"Would you like some company at the Brandenburg Gate tomorrow?"

Rosman looked up from the folder of cables on his desk to find Bill Harding standing in his doorway. Rosman closed the folder and pushed it away from him. It had been two miserable days since the fight at the KaDeWe and since he had heard from Joanna. She had finally called that morning with a message from Jens. Her voice had been reassuring as well, telling him how much she had missed him.

"I'm sorry, Bill. What did you say?"

"I wondered if you were looking for company tomorrow at the Gate. I heard that Friedlander asked you to write a cable on the reopening of the Gate to pedestrian traffic, and I thought we could head down there together."

"Geez, Bill, I feel kind of awkward. Joanna and I will be taking in the festivities together."

"Who?" Harding pulled a chair next to Rosman's desk and sat down.

"The woman I've been seeing."

Harding ran his red plaid tie through the fingers of his right hand before pressing it flat against his blue cotton shirt. He squinted against the sun pouring in through Rosman's window.

"Should I close the drapes?"

"No, that's all right." Harding hesitated before continuing. "Who exactly is this Joanna?"

"A woman from East Berlin."

"I take it you've been seeing a lot of this East German woman. It would explain your recent absence."

"Well…yeah," Rosman answered. He sat uneasily in his chair. "Kind of like you and Dorothy. Who all knows about that?"

Harding shook his head. "I'm not trying to hide anything, John."

"I'm not either, Bill. I just don't see the need to broadcast it."

"Me either. Look, don't get me wrong, John. I don't care one way or another about your love life. In fact, I'm glad to see you actually have one."

"Thanks, big guy."

"But have you discussed her with the Regional Security Officer? There are still regulations about contact with East Bloc nationals, you know."

"What are you trying to say, Bill?"

"That maybe you need to be a little careful. Why not have Kramer run a search on her name? I'm sure he'd be happy to do it. Hell, he's said as much."

"And how is it, my friend, that he even knows about her?"

"Shit, John, anyone can put two and two together. You're obviously lovesick. And he probably figured it had a lot to do with your interest in things on the other side of town."

"And why should Kramer be so friendly these days?"

"The guy likes you. Hell, he likes everything German."

"Except this particular woman."

Harding's face had the pained look it sometimes got when Rosman beat him at handball. "That's not it at all. We just don't want to see you get in trouble."

"Are you suggesting she's a security risk?"

"That's not my point. I just want to be sure you play by the rules, John. That's all. You need to keep your ass covered. We all do these days."

Rosman picked up the folder, paged through it absent-mindedly, then closed it again and pushed at the corner closest to him.

"If our positions were reversed, you'd be saying the same thing to me," Harding continued. "I'd probably be pissed too, but I hope I'd see it for the friendly gesture it's meant to be."

Rosman smiled. "I suppose you're right. I'm just a bit touchy these days."

Harding leaned forward and poked Rosman's arm. "Jesus, you must be in love."

Rosman bit his lower lip. He studied the green cardboard folder, then the yellow glare against his window. "Maybe. I have to be honest, Bill, but I don't know that I've ever felt this way before."

"So, when do we get to meet her?"

Rosman leaned back, a smile crossing his face. "Who's we, Kemosabe?"

Harding sat upright, averting his eyes. "Dorothy. Kramer. Anyone else who's interested. It might even help thaw some of the ice that's grown between you and Friedlander."

"Eh?" Rosman grunted.

"Yeah, maybe he'd understand why you haven't been all that focused on your work lately."

"You'll all meet her. Eventually. But things have been pretty hectic recently, and I'm afraid we haven't been very social."

Harding picked up his tie again and let it drop. "Just don't get yourself beat up again," he said with a slight laugh.

Rosman stroked his jaw. "I certainly don't plan to."

Harding stood up and ambled toward the door with his head turned back in Rosman's direction. "Maybe I'll see you both down there. I plan to drop by the ceremony anyway."

"Sure. I'll keep my eyes open."

"What did you say her name was again?" Harding asked, still squinting from the sun.

"Joanna."

"Joanna what? She does have a last name, doesn't she?"

"Yes, she does," Rosman responded. The two stared at each for several seconds. "Beierlich," he said finally. "Her full name is Joanna Beierlich."

It was his favorite work of art, Casper David Friedrich's painting of the cliffs on Ruegen, the small East German island in the Baltic sea. Perhaps it was because he had spent so many pleasant summer weeks there in the resort reserved for officers in the Ministry for State Security. The summer breeze that swept over the mound of forest and chalk never failed to refresh his spirit. Even more so than when he had opened the refrigerator door at their apartment in Havana. His wife and daughter had always enjoyed Ruegen, with its swimming and its bike riding. That all seemed like ancient history now.

Maybe Gracchus liked the picture because he was a romantic at heart. He had always entertained an interest in the early years of the nineteenth century, when German nationalism had burst forth in full poetic bloom.

Whatever the reason, no other piece of art adorned the walls of Gracchus's office. Elsewhere, the space was occupied by framed awards from his own democratic republic and its socialist allies, a mirror, portraits of Marx, Engels, Ferdinand Lasalle, Lenin, and Felix Dzerzhinskiy, and a hat rack that was hardly ever used. Styles had long since changed, even here. One day, Gracchus was sure, he would replace that stand with something else. Maybe an umbrella holder. After all, it rained enough in Berlin.

Gracchus unfolded his copy of West Berlin's leading daily, the *Tagesspiegel*. The single strip of white paper was taped to the fourth page, where the local news began. The drop had gone smoothly, as all things do when they're kept simple, without the fancy paraphernalia and secret hiding places of western spy novels. The were certainly not needed to meet assets in West Berlin. It was so damn easy over there.

Gracchus peeled the tape back, stripping away several columns of newsprint. He had already read his own copy, now in the hands of his asset. Gracchus tossed the newspaper into the waste basket next to his desk.

Horst Lueber knocked and, without hesitating, walked into Gracchus's office. The pipe extending from his lower lip left a trail of foul-smelling smoke in the doorway that led to a small cloud over his head. He came to a halt in front of Gracchus' desk. Gracchus wrinkled his long, thin nose.

"Have you seen my report, comrade?"

"Yes, I have," Gracchus responded, looking up from the paper. "How in Heaven's name could you lose that little prick Jens the other day?"

He stared at the floor. "I'm sorry, comrade, but it was very crowded with all those damn shoppers in the west."

"What sort of amateurs did you assign to the surveillance? They actually chased them through the store?"

"You wanted us to put pressure on the pair. And the American responded out of character for a diplomat. Are you sure he's had no intelligence training?"

Gracchus massaged his cheeks and forehead. "If he had, he wouldn't have done something to draw so much attention to himself." Gracchus waved his hand at Lueber. "And we still don't know where Jens is hiding."

"What about our inside sources?"

"Apparently, Jens is playing it very coy." Gracchus looked away from Lueber to the window. "And very smart. Almost like a professional." He picked up the report from his asset in West Berlin. "But then again, I believe our luck is about to change."

"Oh, yes, I almost forgot. I ran into Hauptmann again. He keeps asking about those files you removed."

Gracchus was becoming uncomfortably warm in his sweater. They always turned the heat on too damn high in this building. He should have worn a shirt and tie, like Lueber. But Lueber was so damn eager to please, he would probably wear a shirt and tie to his own reception in hell. He had a predictable, if limited, future. "Fuck the files," Gracchus spat.

Lueber studied the crumbled newspaper in Gracchus's waste basket as he struggled to relight his pipe and avoid his superior's eyes. Gracchus stomped over to the window and flung it open. The flow of fresh air felt good. It reminded him of Ruegen. He lumbered back to his desk and pulled open the middle drawer on the right hand side. Gracchus enjoyed the look of surprise on Lueber's face when he dropped three of the missing files in front of him. Gracchus let out a short laugh.

"Take these to Hauptmann for me. Tell him I was studying those before I go to my meeting this afternoon."

Lueber prodded the folder with his fingertips. Thin lines of smoke snaked from the corner of his mouth. "These aren't very many, comrade. What about all the others?"

"I'll need to keep those for a little while yet."

"Some day, comrade, you'll get yourself in trouble. Does Records know you have these?"

Gracchus thought for a moment. "Probably not. I never told those jerks I had them."

"Of course you didn't. That's why Hauptmann keeps bugging me." Lueber jabbed his chest with the pipe stem. "He's afraid of you, of course."

"Let's keep it that way." Gracchus winked at the younger man.

Lueber started to leave, but he turned suddenly, his face lit by a new thought. "Oh, I forgot to tell you. We picked out a West German face on Tuesday at the KaDeWe."

"Anyone we know?"

"I'm not sure. I took his picture and the guys in Registry traced it for me."

"And?" Sometimes, Gracchus wasn't so sure Lueber would make it. He was strong and loyal, but not very quick.

"It seems his name is Buechler. Hermann Buechler."

Gracchus waved his hand at Lueber and took a cigarette from the pack of Lords on his desk. "Yes, I know."

Lueber pulled his pipe from his mouth and slapped his forehead. "Oh, Jesus. Your Russian friend called. He wants to meet you two hours earlier, at 12 o'clock instead of 2."

This guy Krueger is an idiot, Gracchus thought. They could never put him in the field. "Did he say anything about the place? Was that also changed?"

"No, he didn't say. I'm sorry, comrade. I got so worried about these missing files."

"Like I said, Horst...."

"Yes, I know. Fuck 'em."

Gracchus grabbed his overcoat as he ran out of the office, a sheepish-looking Lueber still standing in the middle of the room. If he hurried Gracchus could still make it to the meeting with Preselnikov.

Twenty minutes later he rushed into the small pub across from the *Nikolaikirche*, the church built on the site of the first chapel in Berlin. It sat at the center of the historic district, or *Nikolaiviertel*, which the East German regime had renovated just two years earlier. The pub itself supposedly dated from sometime in the fifteenth century, but, like everything else here, had been rebuilt from the rubble of 1945. Still, it was comfortable enough. Its spartan menu, hard wooden booths, and low vaulted ceilings reminded Gracchus of a working man's pub. Today, those booths were packed with down-home types, if not actual proletarians, probably drawn by the lentil soup and blood sausage.

Standing at the front door, Gracchus strained to inspect the different booths. Preselnikov waved his left hand, his right busy scooping out the last bits of goulash from his bowl of blue and gray pottery. He lit a Marlboro as Gracchus slid into the bench opposite his own.

"Noon is the worst possible time to meet here, Sergei."

"Is that why you're late? It looks like it's the turn of the punctual German to keep the disorganized Slav waiting."

Gracchus motioned to the bartender for a beer. "I'm sorry about that. My colleague Lueber forgot to tell me about your call." A short, blond waitress danced over to his table in her blue smock and white cotton shirt and took his order for a large bowl of soup.

"Ah yes, Lueber. Maybe he'll defect and join the West Germans."

"That's not funny," Gracchus snapped. "Not any more."

"Well, in any case, it looks like you will no longer have a communist party in a few weeks," Preselnikov added. He leaned back and placed his foot on the bench. Smoke drifted from his nostrils toward the ceiling. Shafts of sunlight fought their way through the windows lining the wall at Preselnikov's back. The waitress set the beer and bowl of lentil soup on the table in front of Gracchus. "Not only are they renouncing their Stalinist past—whatever the hell that is—but they'll probably opt for one of those innocuous names about Social Democracy."

"You needn't remind me."

"Do you think they'll fool anyone?"

"I don't give a damn." Gracchus dipped his spoon into the soup and lowered his head to enjoy the steam and smell of the food. It was something they still knew how to cook over here. He had grown weary of the usual ration of pork cutlets and cabbage since his return from Rome. "I have more immediate problems right now."

"The files?"

Gracchus nodded. "There are still three missing."

"Names?"

"And more. Pseudos, too. Addresses."

"And you plan to recover them soon?"

"Sergei, I'm surprised you need to ask."

Preselnikov snuffed out his cigarette and ordered another beer from the bartender. "It seems our waitress is not the quickest one in town. Probably a good socialist. Anyway, I ask because there are plenty of people in Moscow who ask me."

"Such as?"

"Such as the people I work for. And they have become extremely interested in how this little operation of ours will end."

Gracchus shrugged between spoonfuls of soup.

Preselnikov pressed on. His eyes rested on Gracchus while his right hand crushed the stub of his cigarette in the clay ashtray. "How do you plan to obtain the missing materials?"

Gracchus shook his head and pulled his beer closer.

"And what about the American?"

"Which one?"

"Rosman."

"That will all be taken care of soon enough."

"How so?" Preselnikov lit another cigarette.

Gracchus winked at the Russian. His tongue flicked at the green flecks of soup at the corners of his mouth. "I'm planning a surprise tomorrow for the American." He ordered another beer as he wiped his face clean. After the waitress left, Gracchus ripped his slice of brown bread in half and bit off about a third of the first slice.

"Good," Preselnikov said.

"How are things from your end?"

"Well, like I said, there are an awful lot of people in Moscow following this thing."

"They won't interfere, will they?"

"Our base here is still officially cooperating in the operation. But we can afford to wait only a little longer." Preselnikov put out his cigarette, although it had only burned about halfway down. "Moscow is really chaotic these days, Johann. You wouldn't recognize it."

"Worse than in Stalin's time?"

"It's a different sort of uncertainty," Preselnikov said. "People are not gripped by the same kind of fear. It's more an uncertainty as to where history is taking us." He stopped to reflect, his gaze directed out the window. Gracchus sipped his beer, waiting for the Russian to finish. "I'm not sure what it all means. Or where we'll end up."

"Who? Us?"

"Yes, us. And our countries, our movement."

"Are you having second thoughts about the operation?"

"No, dammit. Well, yes, a bit about the operation, but primarily about the world we thought we knew."

"I know." Gracchus watched his friend fish in his empty pack of Marlboros for another cigarette. After about 10 seconds of futility, Preselnikov crumpled the empty wrapper and threw it on the floor. "Just don't screw things up tomorrow. We need to get this all back on track."

"I won't," Gracchus answered. "And see that *you* don't."

CHAPTER 14

Rosman shifted his weight from one foot to the other and shivered inside his jacket. He should have worn something heavier. After all, December was nearly here. If that wasn't bad enough, his loafers offered little protection against the damp ground and thousands of shuffling feet around the Brandenburg Gate. Why the hell hadn't he put on warmer socks that morning, or boots even? That's what he really needed.

He was supposed to meet Joanna, but there had to be 10,000 people clustered in front of the Brandenburg Gate, all of them crammed into the open spaces that ran between the two wings of the Tiergarten like a long open rectangle. He worried that so much could go wrong with this kind of crowd. His hand groped for the money belt stuffed with the pages of Lamprecht's notebook. All he could see was wave upon wave of bobbing heads and weaving shoulders, spread like a blanket along the western side of the Wall. Straight ahead, just beyond the mammoth cranes hoisting television cameras into the air, stood the thick, classical pillars of the Gate. Above, the winged Goddess of Victory sat aboard her chariot with four mighty steeds and pointed toward the East, where liberation awaited. And like a vision from the past, the four-cornered pillars of the Reichstag gazed upon the unfolding scene from the trees above the Tiergarten.

Rosman strained to pick out the American stations among the mobile vans and camera platforms. In this respect at least, little had changed since October. All were there—ABC, NBC, CBS, and CNN—ready to record yet another in the historic chain of events unfolding in this city: the opening of the Brandenburg Gate to pedestrian traffic between east and west for the first time since Erich

Honecker's construction brigades had sealed the city shut in those tense August days of 1961. Huge gaps on either side of the Gate yawned at the crowd, swaths cut overnight where the pedestrians would transit between East and West in an orderly Prussian manner.

Rosman snaked through the crowd, trying to get closer to the Gate and the ceremony. He felt a tug at his sleeve.

"Hey, John. Wait up."

Bill Harding had his hands buried deep in the pockets of a red down jacket that matched the color of his cheeks. Next to him stood Dorothy Sutton, her camel-colored coat buttoned all the way to the neck, a blue knit cap pulled tight over her ears. She extracted her hand from a pocket and gave Rosman a quick wave and smile.

"Well, fancy meeting you two in this crowd."

Harding peeked in several directions. "So, where's your girl-friend?"

"Probably on the other side. She left a message last night to meet her here. I was hoping to get some anecdotes from her about the easterners' reaction to this thing."

When he looked back toward the stage set up in front of the Gate, Rosman saw the three Allied Commandants, all present to lend their governments' approval to the ceremony.

"Where's the Soviet Commander?" Sutton asked.

"I'm not sure. Maybe he isn't here yet," Harding guessed.

Rosman shook his head. "Perhaps the Soviets are showing their disapproval by staying away."

Harding shrugged. "To hell with 'em. We'll leave 'em in the dustbin of history."

"Sure, Leon. I don't see anyone trying to chisel off pieces of the Wall today," Rosman stated.

"There's too many Vopos around," Sutton replied. "Not that it does much good these days. As soon as they move on, you can hear the hammering start up again."

Harding laughed. "I was down here last weekend and this old lady from East Berlin was scolding some young souvenir hunters for breaking off chunks of the Wall. 'We built it and paid for it,' she kept yelling."

All three laughed. Rosman shivered and pulled his coat tighter. "So, where's Kramer?" he asked. "I thought you said he was coming."

"He rode down here with us," Sutton explained, "but we lost him in the crowd."

Rosman felt Harding tug at his sleeve again. He was pointing toward a small space of about 10 square feet ringed by police in front of one of the openings. Helmut Kohl, large and avuncular, accompanied by his foreign minister, Hans Dietrich Genscher, and West Berlin's mayor, Walter Momper, walked through the Wall to greet the East German premier, Hans Modrow, and the mayor of East Berlin, Ernst Krack. All five men stood grouped together in Pariser Platz, just to the eastern side of the Gate. Rosman was surprised at first that the Mission had not tried to block Krack's appearance, since the United States did not recognize his office or his authority. But, then again, why quibble over such points on a day like today?

Without warning, the crowd surged toward the Wall. Harding and Sutton pressed their bodies diagonally against the moving mass until they were free of the crowd.

Harding waved to Rosman, his hand held above the crowd. "John, this way."

Rosman did not respond. Instead, he let himself be carried through the opening, and, in clear contradiction to Allied policy to cross only at Checkpoint Charlie, into East Berlin. He could always say he had had no choice. His feet just shuffled along with a will of their own, as shoulders, chests, and arms propelled him through the opening to the right of the Gate. He trailed along the back of the crowd and into the no-man's land on the eastern side of the Wall. About a hundred meters further, Mauerstrasse ran its brief route parallel to the Wall. Rosman wondered if Hetzling was watching.

He stood on his tiptoes to watch the assembled dignitaries. Each politician spoke briefly to the crowd and then hurried from the microphone, the words lost in the crisp December air. Rosman found it all irreverent—and funny—how little the crowd noticed, or seemed to care about, the dignity of the moment. The people surged forward, following their own agenda, their own sense of timing.

Modrow, the East German premier, was the first to go, pushed along by the rush of humanity, each spectator eager to take the historic passage. Kohl saw an opening and broke for his limousine, surrounded by security guards. Momper let himself be carried along in Modrow's wake, using the opportunity to mingle with fellow Berliners and potential voters. The idle metal barricades surrounding the stage were kicked aside as the people reclaimed the section of the Wall in front of the Gate, seizing the sovereignty of the moment, just as they had been doing since October.

Rosman snuck around the back of the crowd, then walked as fast as he could through the narrow park of linden trees that split Berlin's most famous boulevard. Once one of Europe's premier promenades, Unter den Linden was now little more than a long, ugly avenue of plate glass and steel. He did not stop until he came to the State Opera House, a pale rococo structure originally built by Frederick the Great and then rebuilt by the Ulbricht regime after its destruction by Allied bombers. In spite of its small size, the building stood out like a beacon.

He doubled back to Oberwallstrasse to be sure he wasn't being followed. At Werderstrasse, Rosman turned toward the west again and continued until he found Joanna's Trabant parked behind the broad, squat dome of St. Hedwig's, the heart of East Berlin's minuscule Catholic community.

"Quickly," Joanna yelled from the car. She looked harried to Rosman, her hair unbrushed and half of her white shirt collar stuck inside the light blue sweater.

"Good God, I hope we never have to make a quick escape in this thing." He struggled to cram his six-foot frame into the passenger side of her car. "I'd hate to get into a chase in one of these converted lawnmowers."

Joanna pulled away from the curb, her right hand racing through the gears as she sliced through the heavy afternoon traffic. "We can't afford to keep Erich waiting." She punched the steering wheel with her fist. "He's on the run, you know."

"Well, I got here as soon as I could." Rosman kicked his feet against the floor to warm them, then checked to be sure he hadn't left a dent.

"I know," Joanna apologized. "I'm just so nervous." She flicked a nervous smile at Rosman. "You look cold."

"I am." Rosman was silent a minute before he spoke again. "Where are we going?"

"To Prenzlauer Berg."

"I'll actually get to see your place?"

"No, somewhere else." Joanna pulled her eyes off the traffic and tossed a nervous glance at Rosman. "Better you don't know. Schmidt claims it's an old Stasi safehouse. He thought it would be safer to meet where they would least expect it."

"Right under their noses? Or has Schmidt betrayed us?"

Another nervous glance. "I don't think he has."

"Why not?" Rosman was facing her, the back of his head leaning against the window. "I mean, how does he know it was a safehouse?"

"If you live here long enough, John, those kinds of things become an open secret." She shrugged and tossed her hair back. "In any case, we don't really have a choice at this point."

He shook his head and swore under his breath. This sort of fatalism made him uneasy. "I'm still not sure about Schmidt. I still haven't figured out his agenda, what motivates him."

He studied the streets and landmarks as Joanna drove past Alexanderplatz, crossing Karl Marx Strasse. Rosman gaped at the massive apartment complexes lining either side of the broad boulevard. She then made several quick turns onto Greifwalderstrasse and Dimitroffstrasse. When she swung back toward the city center, Rosman caught sight of a synagogue and Jewish cemetery near Kaethe Kollwitz Platz. Nearby were some well preserved, or probably restored, turn-of-the-century buildings.

As the streets shrank in size, however, so did the signs. There was Bonhoefferstrasse, which struck him as odd if it was named for the Lutheran pastor made famous for his resistance to the Nazis. The old regime generally ignored the conservative and religious elements of the German Resistance to prevent them from overshadowing the allegedly more heroic struggle of the German communists.

Rosman was completely lost by the time Joanna stopped in front of a crumbling apartment block. Most of the buildings were covered with a light brown stucco, their contours lost behind a patchwork of peeling cement and plaster that exposed the brickwork underneath, like an old snake trying to lose its skin. Rusted drain pipes flowed down crevices that marked the property lines. Empty flower boxes hung from several window frames.

Joanna pulled in parallel to the curb. Without looking at Rosman, she hopped out of the car, then ran to an entrance in the middle of the block. She rang the bell to one of the apartments, shifting her feet and glancing up and down the street. She leaned her right hand against the front door, which was set into a larger gate. It looked like a garage door. She checked her watch and mumbled something under her breath. Then Joanna pushed the door open and walked across what looked like an old carriage house to a set of stairs on the left. She broke her stride to confirm that Rosman was following, then trotted up the stairs to the third floor.

Rosman turned the corner just as she knocked at the apartment. The numbers 262 appeared in small gray metallic numerals screwed to the door. After several seconds, she knocked again, only louder. Again, no response. Rosman stood behind her, ready to laugh, expecting to see Jens fling the door open, his face projecting the same sense of triumph he wore outside the KaDeWe.

Joanna bit her lower lip and glanced at Rosman. "Come on," she said. Then she called out Erich's name softly. She knocked once more. Still no sound. She grabbed the doorknob. It moved inward, moaning in suspicion and revealing a long, dark hallway that led to a silent and even darker series of rooms on the other side.

Joanna looked at Rosman, who now stood at her side. Her mouth was half open, her eyes dilated with alarm. He motioned for her to wait, then slid inside, pausing with each step to search the space around him. He blinked, trying to adjust his eyes to the darkness. *This shit would have to end*, he told himself. He was weary of entering strange, dark apartments in this part of town. Nothing good seemed to come of it. And this one had that sickly damp smell that came of too much moisture and too little use. It reminded Rosman of abandoned farmhouses he had encountered in the American Midwest.

When he reached the end of the foyer, there was enough light to make out the odd shapes in the room. Rosman realized why it had taken so long to get his bearings. The entire place looked as though it had been swept by a cyclone. Two chairs and a sofa lay on their sides in the middle of the room, and a side table had been pushed back by the window. Next to it lay a lamp and an ashtray that had split in two. Drawers to the cabinet along the wall were open, their contents dumped in a heap on the floor. A curtain had been pulled from its place above the window by the kitchen and now lay spread across the middle of what was probably the living room. The other two windows along the back wall were also bare. Light from the alley at the back filtered in through the uncovered glass.

Rosman froze. He peered through the shadows to examine the pattern of the material. Then his eyes caught a small stain divided evenly between the hard wooden floor and the corner of the beige rug.

Someone bumped Rosman from behind. His own blood rushed to his head, driven by an icy charge of adrenaline.

It was Joanna. He sighed, then motioned for her to wait. Instead, she tip-toed to the puddle on the floor.

"My God!" Joanna shrieked. "It's blood."

Rosman stepped to the stain, bent down, and ran his fingers along its edge. The thick, brownish liquid stuck to his fingers, and two round drops fell to the wooden floor. He rose, opened a window to let the musty smell escape, then joined Joanna as she examined a bedroom. They found additional signs of a struggle there and in the kitchen, but no clues as to what had become of Jens. No note, no pieces of ripped clothing, nothing. A wave of fear crested and crashed inside Rosman and his heartbeat accelerated again. He knelt by the blood and leaned back on his heels, pondering their next move. He had never found himself with unidentified blood in a strange apartment before. Call the police? Hardly.

He studied Joanna's silhouette for several seconds. Surely, she would know what to do. This was, after all, her side of town.

"Shit," she muttered.

The word startled Rosman. He had expected something more profound. He struggled with the image of his lovely maiden picking up her vocabulary in a barnyard or a loading dock.

She followed this outburst by spitting out, *"Verdammt dochmal,"* and then, once again, *"Aber Scheisse."* He was hearing profanities from her for the first time. They revealed a different, rougher side, one that he had never associated with her.

"Do you think it's Erich's?" he asked.

"Who else?"

Suddenly, they both turned heads, drawn by the sound of footsteps drifting into the apartment from the hallway. They came to a halt by the door of the apartment.

"Was denn?" asked an ominous heavy voice. The speaker entered the flat with careful, measured footsteps, evidently making his way down the narrow corridor that led to this complex of small rooms. Hopefully, the stranger would start out just as blind.

Rosman huddled with Joanna behind the overturned table on the far wall by the window near the bedroom. His hands felt wet and sticky. He hoped it was nervous sweat and not the innocent blood of Erich Jens. He reached for Joanna's hand and realized that hers were just as moist.

The newcomer struggled to find his way about the room. It sounded as if he were advancing cautiously, groping at the wall of the hallway. Rosman avoided looking over the table for fear of exposing himself. Then the intermittent sounds of movement stopped altogether.

"Scheisse!" That word again.

The stranger must have seen the blood. His voice sounded as though it had stopped just a foot or two from the table. He exhaled heavily, then fumbled in his pocket. *"Scheisse!"* A match lit the room and his face, outlining for a brief second the rough features of a large, middle-aged man. Unfortunately, the match went out before Rosman could get an impression of his height and build.

Joanna tugged at his sleeve. She was pointing to the window, which led to a fire escape. Freedom beckoned just a few feet away.

Rosman searched the floor for something he could use as a weapon. His fingers touched the slim metal lamp, which he retrieved as silently as possible. When he finally had it at his side, Rosman showed it to Joanna. She shot back a look of alarm, shaking her head.

Fortunately, the stranger had not moved. He was still within striking distance. Rising, Rosman felt himself pulled backwards as Joanna grabbed his arm. The commotion warned the intruder, whose body was slightly heavier but no taller than Rosman's.

The man backed away, just enough for Rosman's blow to miss its target at the back of the skull. Instead, he hit the side of the head, glanced off an ear, then thudded on the shoulder below. The stranger stumbled backwards, tripping over one of the over-turned chairs.

Rosman and Joanna bolted for the window.

A wounded voice called out, "Horst!"

Another voice rang from the hallway. *"Was aber…? Wo bist du, Hans?"*

Rosman and Joanna sprinted down the fire escape, their steps on the metal rungs echoing across the alley. Reaching the end of the pull-down ladder, they leaped the last four feet to the ground below.

When they reached the street, Rosman glanced back to the window above and saw a man leaning out, searching the alleyway. They turned the corner into the street. An arm shot out, pointing in their direction. The hand held a pistol. Two shots barked at Rosman's back. He felt something tug at his forearm and swing it around in front of his body.

They raced to Joanna's Trabant. Rosman stumbled from the curb to the car, bumping his head on the doorframe as he tried to hustle himself into the cramped passenger space. The blow brought forth all the frustration, anger, and grief that had been collecting inside him in one sudden outburst.

"Goddammit, Joanna. Goddammit," he yelled, rubbing his scalp.

Only then did Rosman feel the pain above his wrist. He gaped at the mottled red liquid spreading over the sleeve of his jacket.

"What the fuck is going on?" He dabbed at the blood with his handkerchief. "I thought you said it was safe. And look at this, for Chrissakes! I've been shot!"

"Oh, John." Joanna glanced at Rosman's arm.

"And who were those fucking gorillas?"

"I don't know." She pulled a first aid kit from underneath the driver's seat and handed it to Rosman. "Here. Use this to bandage yourself."

"Geez, this is convenient."

"We have to carry them. It's the law."

He rolled back the sleeve. "And, goddamn it, where the hell is Schmidt? I am going to kill that bastard!"

"John, please. We don't know it was Schmidt. We don't know anything yet."

"We know Jens may be one very dead motherfucker. And now I've been shot." Rosman wrapped a piece of gauze and a stretch of tape around his forearm. "Jesus, this stings. And stop apologizing for that asshole Schmidt. How is it that every meeting with Erich keeps getting interrupted?"

Joanna drove quickly, frantically, shifting through all four gears within the space of a single block. "I don't like this either John," she burst out, ramming the stick into fourth. "I don't understand this." She shook her head. "I just don't understand it."

Rosman looked over and saw how nervous and frightened she was. He no longer tried to remember street names, looking only to the rear, desperately searching for a tail. Thank God she was heading straight for Alexanderplatz, the quickest route to the west.

Then she turned down Wilhelm Pieck Strasse. Where the hell was she going? He knew enough about East Berlin to know that this was not the right direction to return to the west. *Hopefully, not the Charite. He could never be wounded that seriously.* Before long, she swung down Friedrichstrasse, heading in the direction of Checkpoint Charlie.

"You don't need to worry. No one has followed us." The gears of the Trabant ground harshly, Joanna grimacing as she missed on her shift.

Just blocks shy of Checkpoint Charlie, Joanna pulled the car over to the curb and stopped. She kept the engine running.

Rosman turned toward her in surprise. "You're not coming with me?"

"No. I can't. I must try to find out what happened." She took his hand and examined his arm. "Do you think it's serious?"

"No. I think the shot only grazed my arm." Rosman clenched his fist. "It doesn't feel like anything is broken."

"Have someone look at that right away, John. Please."

"Let me help," he protested. "You can't do this alone."

"No." She shook her head and turned her face away from Rosman's. "It's better for me to work this thing out alone. I know this place, this system."

Rosman climbed out of Joanna's car directly in front of what had once been Hermann Goering's Air Ministry. When he turned to walk the three blocks to Checkpoint Charlie, Rosman saw the Bulgarian Embassy across the street. *Perfect*, he thought. *Surrounded by assholes from the past and the present. And on tonight of all nights.*

He shrugged with resignation, grabbed his arm, then walked up to the border guard standing at the eastern approach to Charlie. The *Vopo* held out his hand for Rosman's diplomatic passport.

His lower arm was throbbing, but Rosman kept it buried deep within the pocket of his coat. The guard looked behind Rosman for a car, his face betraying his confusion. Screw him. He couldn't do anything about it. Rosman whispered, "Brandenburg Gate."

A cold, hard hatred for this regime and its representatives ebbed inside Rosman. The pain in his arm made it worse. His forehead began to throb. He walked as calmly as he could along the sidewalk and past the guardhouse, not stopping until he reached the Kochstrasse *U-Bahn* station across the street from Charlie. His legs felt weak, and Rosman stumbled down the stairs and collapsed onto a bench next to the track. After a few minutes, the roar of the train brought a welcome sense of relief.

The subway ride passed without incident, Rosman searching

each passenger for the slightest sign of interest. Rosman felt the sweat break out along his forehead and run down his cheeks. When he changed trains at Hallesches Tor and at Wittenbergplatz, complete strangers seemed to be staring at him. But no one followed.

When he got home, Rosman stood at his front door for a full minute, inspecting his yard, the street, his door and the exterior of his house, searching for anything unusual. The throbbing inside his head had grown worse. His right arm felt like someone was pounding on it with a hammer. His hair was matted to his forehead. The sleeves of his coat were damp with blood and the perspiration he had wiped from his brow.

Once inside, he slowly, almost absent-mindedly, removed the money belt in which he had folded and placed each page of Lamprecht's notes. They were even in the proper order, as far as he could tell. He walked to the kitchen and washed down a pair of extra strength Tylenol with two large glasses of cool, refreshing tap water.

Then he collapsed into one of the two wing chairs set against the wall in the back corner of his living room. A window allowed Rosman to look from the living room into the back yard. It was his favorite chair for reading. He watched the evening descend with a thin, gray veil. He sat silent and still in the darkness, alert to the slightest sound.

At that moment, all the emotion, all the fear and distress, burst upon Rosman. A minute earlier, his head had been racing in a dizzying frenzy. But now that he was home, Rosman's body shifted to another, slower gear, while his emotions raced to catch up with him. He suddenly realized how exhausted he was.

Rosman unwrapped the bandage. Thankfully, the bleeding had stopped. In a minute he would get up and wash the wound, replace the gauze. As he sat there, his hands clutching the money belt, tears began to run down his cheeks. His eyes and cheeks were still wet when he fell asleep, upright in his chair, his hands still firmly around the money belt.

CHAPTER 15

"I told you to watch out for that Rambo shit," Rick Kramer scolded, glancing around Rosman's kitchen. "You're lucky the bullet only grazed your arm. I'm not about to operate, no matter how clean your place is."

Rosman winced as Kramer rubbed an antiseptic lotion over his right forearm. "There wasn't any of that 'Rambo shit,' as you so artfully put it, Kramer. I was actually running away."

"Well, I hope you've learned your lesson, my boy." Kramer wrapped a fresh block of gauze around Rosman's arm and covered this with a long strip of white tape. Even on Sunday, he looked like the archetypical army officer in his olive green pullover and khaki slacks.

Rosman studied the bottle of antiseptic standing on the kitchen table. He rolled down the sleeve of his green and blue plaid shirt, then deposited the bottle in his shirt pocket. "Are you sure this stuff will do the trick?"

"Guaran-damn-teed. I've seen gunshot wounds plenty worse than this, John." He eyed Rosman suspiciously. "Just as long as it happened last night."

"Yes, it happened last night," Rosman sighed. He stood up and paced around his kitchen, raising and lowering his arm in a steady motion. "I never realized it hurt so much to get shot."

"The deeper the wound, the more it hurts. Consider yourself lucky. If I didn't know basic first aid from my infantry days, you'd be at the American hospital trying to explain this to the RSO and to Friedlander. The MPs would be pretty interested, too." He took a sip of coffee. "Are you going to tell me what happened?"

Rosman walked to the counter to refresh his own cup of coffee. Then he leaned against the counter top, raising his mug to salute Kramer. "No. But I would like to ask another favor."

Kramer marched to the sink. "I don't think so. This is the second time I've helped you, John, and both times it's looked like you've gone a few rounds with the Grim Reaper." Kramer raised his coffee to his lips. "You're a State Department weenie, John. This sort of thing isn't supposed to happen to you."

Rosman smiled and shrugged his shoulders. "So?"

Kramer frowned. "So, I need some information before I provide any more help."

Rosman motioned for Kramer to follow him into the living room. There, he took a seat in the same armchair that had served as his bed the night before. Kramer sat in the chair facing him. "I'm not really sure where things stand today, but I ran into the Stasi again last night."

"The same three guys?"

Rosman shook his head. "There were only two. I didn't recognize either one, but then again, I don't remember every face from that night at Friedrichstrasse."

"What the hell were you doing in East Berlin again?"

"We were trying to drop off some material with a friend in the opposition over there."

"Who the hell is 'we'?"

"Joanna and I."

"The East German broad?"

Rosman winced. "Kramer, where the hell have you been for the last two decades?" He shook his head and picked up his coffee. "If there are any 'broads' left in the world, Joanna would hardly be one of them."

"Sorry." Kramer sat back in his chair and looked out the window at the bare chestnut trees in Rosman's back yard. "I never realized you were such a sensitive guy. Look, John, I don't mean to sound brutal. But you can probably forget your contact, whoever he may be." Kramer waved his hand at Rosman to deflect any protest. "He is probably long gone. One way or another."

"That does sound pretty brutal."

"More importantly, do they—the Stasi, I mean—know who

you are? Can they follow you over here?"

"They must have a pretty good idea by now."

Kramer leaned forward. "You need help, my friend."

"I know. I want you to run some name traces for me." Rosman looked inside his mug, as though the answers he sought lay hidden under the half-inch of lukewarm brown liquid.

"Consider it done, son. I'll run 'em by the Agency folks." Kramer pulled a pen from his shirt pocket and grabbed a cocktail napkin from the end table. "Okay, shoot." He winked at Rosman. "Sorry."

Rosman raised his arm to inspect the bandage. "No problem." He studied Kramer a moment before continuing. "One is Thomas Schmidt. He's from Rostock, but I believe he studies here in Berlin at the Humboldt University."

"Good." Kramer finished writing and looked up. "Next?"

Rosman bit his lower lip and rubbed his wounded forearm. He glanced at the tall barren trees bent by a breeze from the Brandenburg plain. "The other one is Joanna. Joanna Beierlich."

"Are you sure?"

"No, I'm not. That's why I want you to run the fucking trace, Kramer."

"Okay, okay." Kramer scribbled on the napkin, avoiding Rosman's eyes.

Rosman rose and shuffled toward the kitchen. "Can I get you anymore coffee? Something to eat?"

"No, thanks. This should be enough caffeine to keep me running to the can until mid-afternoon." Kramer rose and sauntered toward the door. As he was pulling on his brown windbreaker, he shouted to the kitchen. "I'd say you definitely owe me. Again. I think a nice dinner should almost cover it, Rambo."

"Agreed." Rosman emerged from the kitchen holding an apple. "Oh, there's one more name you should trace. It's a West German. A West Berliner, actually." Rosman bit into the apple and spoke before he had swallowed. "Hermann Buechler." He spelled out the name.

"No problem." Kramer opened the door and walked into a blast of wind, forcing him to plunge his hands into his pockets and tuck his neck deep into his shoulders as he picked his way to the black BMW in Rosman's driveway.

Rosman slammed the door shut to keep as much warmth as possible inside. He pondered an odd point in Kramer's departure, then returned to the kitchen. Kramer had not bothered to write the last name down when he left. Then again, maybe he was in a hurry.

For once, he did not have to wait. Gracchus could not remember the last time Meyer had reached a meeting at Karl Marx Strasse before him. But there he was, pacing up and down the hallway in front of 413, his face frozen in a frown. His hands were buried deep in the pockets of his light gray slacks, and his arms had pinned the flaps of his overcoat behind his ribs. The solid navy blue tie hung loosely from the white collar, the top button undone. Occasionally, one hand would emerge to brush back a careless strand of graying air.

Gracchus had come to look forward to these few moments of solitude. He would wait for Meyer, drink a coffee or brandy, and use the time to blot out an uncooperative world, or think of the family he had barely known. And he needed that solitude today. The failure to intercept the American yesterday would force him to develop a new plan. He considered the Lutheran pastor for a moment. This awkward angle of a man had been a useful source of information over the years. Could he do more? Bait, perhaps?

Gracchus unlocked the door to the apartment, and Meyer marched toward him, his pace rapid. He pushed ahead of Gracchus, resumed his course through the foyer, and planted himself in front of the sofa.

A powerful smell of cleaning solution swept toward Gracchus. He aimed for the window and pushed it open despite the cold. He waited for about a minute, studying the morning traffic before pulling the window shut and returning to the center of the room.

Meyer's look had turned to anger. Gracchus started to speak. Meyer waved off the usual amenities and began to pace around the living room.

"How could you? Those two boys. What possible harm did they pose to your wonderful state?" His arm swept toward the window. "In any case, it appears to be breaking up before our very eyes."

"Just who and what are you talking about?" Gracchus employed the most casual tone of voice he could muster. He ambled away and hung his coat in the closet.

"Lamprecht and Jens, of course. Don't tell me you don't know who they are. Hermann Lamprecht and Erich Jens? The two students who disappeared after the break-in at the Stasi headquarters at Normannenstrasse a few weeks ago?"

"Our relationship does not extend to a discussion of rumors. You report to me, and I try to help your misguided friends and students."

Meyer stared at Gracchus, dumbstruck. "You really don't understand, do you? I know it was the Stasi. I know that those boys have been eliminated."

"Do you have any proof?" Gracchus strolled from the closet to the sofa.

"Not yet. But I know how you operate." Meyer aimed his index finger at Gracchus's heart like a weapon.

"I should hope you know that much with all the work you've done for us."

"But not for this sort of thing."

Gracchus did not bother to hide his contempt. "Don't be a fool." He spat the words at the gawking pastor.

Meyer set himself into a large green chair by the living room window. He stared ahead for a minute before continuing. "I know that Lamprecht was bludgeoned to death. And that Jens has disappeared, although his body has not yet been recovered."

Gracchus exhaled heavily, his own anger rising. Meyer would only learn what was absolutely necessary for him to know. That much would never change.

"Maybe Jens made a run for it," he said. "Maybe he decided to run for the West like so many of these other cowards, seduced by the illusions of wealth and comfort they see every night on western television."

"Spare me your loyalty speeches." Meyer frowned, his hands back in his pants pockets. He crossed his legs and turned his face away from Gracchus. After a minute, however, he shifted his body back toward the middle of the room. "You actually believe it, don't you?" Meyer asked. "All that propaganda, the rhetoric about a 'socialist paradise' in this godforsaken country. My God!" A moment's silence passed again. Meyer was looking down at the carpet, shaking his head in disbelief. "It doesn't matter. What does matter is that two promising young men are dead, and for no good reason."

Gracchus waved Meyer away with the back of his hand and went into the kitchen. *To hell with that self-righteous bastard*, he told himself. He filled the coffee maker, then reached for the brandy, the French stuff, to strengthen his nerves for this unexpected confrontation. Nothing seemed to work anymore. His state, his service, the structures that gave purpose to his life: all were crumbling as he watched. But he would fight the sense of helplessness that came and went these days like an emotional tide.

Gracchus waited for the coffee to finish dripping through the Melita filter and into the pot before he returned to the living room. Meyer stood at the window, staring at the street below. Gracchus walked over to the window with his cup and peered in the direction of Meyer's vision.

The pastor had been concentrating on a solitary old woman plodding along the sidewalk. On each arm she carried a large plastic shopping bag, about two-thirds full of groceries. Her gaze and pace suggested she hoped to make the intersection before the green light changed. It seemed too far.

"Do you think she'll make it?" Gracchus asked, half to himself.

"I suppose so," Meyer replied. "They always seem to."

Gracchus motioned toward his cup, and Meyer nodded in assent. When he had returned with the coffee, Gracchus saw that the old woman had moved far up the street. She was now standing on the next corner, waiting for that light to change, a full city block ahead of where he had expected to see her. Gracchus walked over to the sofa and took a seat in the corner by the end table.

"So," Meyer began, "you're not going to tell me who killed those boys? Or why?"

"No. Those events were beyond my control. Speaking morally—yes, even I have the right to speak as a moral being—I find Lamprecht's death, or both of them, if that's the case, reprehensible. They were also unnecessary and unprofessional."

"I wish I could believe you."

"I don't care if you believe me. There are more important matters now."

"Such as?" Meyer asked.

Gracchus ignored him and continued. "There are important materials, including a journal of Lamprecht's, floating out there somewhere beyond our reach."

Meyer returned to his seat in the armchair. He leaned forward, both feet on the ground, both elbows on his knees, his hands clasped. "What sort of notes? What was in them?" He paused, his eyes roaming the floor. His voice barely rose above a whisper. "Is there anything in there about our meetings?"

His righteous indignation appeared to have evaporated.

"Actually, I do believe I've seen him around here on several occasions, but I was never sure," Gracchus lied. He thought it wise to put the fear of God—or Marx and Lenin—into Meyer at this point. "It's not so important for you, though. Your cooperation has been documented elsewhere. Nonetheless, you can see why it's so important to follow up on people like Lamprecht and Jens. Their meddling causes nothing but trouble. For all of us."

"I'd give them a bit more credit than that."

"For what? What have they done to help this state and its citizens? And don't give me that crap about the heroic marches in Leipzig."

"At any rate, I doubt there is much more I can do for you now." Meyer stared at Gracchus a moment longer before continuing. "That's the real reason I came today. I want to quit, to make an end of it."

Gracchus's voice bellowed with long bursts of full-throated laughter. He continued to laugh for several minutes. "I'm afraid you won't get out of it that easily. Our meetings still serve a purpose."

"For goodness sake. How much longer will these sorts of things be necessary?"

"The Interior Minister is not moving with any sort of haste to disband our organization, regardless of what you may hear from the Round Table. He realizes that every state requires an intelligence service."

"Why?"

"Our security demands it."

Gracchus picked up his cup of coffee and raised it to his lips. His hand was shaking, though, and Gracchus splashed some of his coffee on the sofa. He dabbed at the nylon fabric with his handkerchief and then stared at Meyer for a moment before continuing.

"We will continue to meet. And we will meet as long as I say it's necessary. If you have any doubts, just think for a moment about your career and reputation if word got out that you have been meeting with me for some 12 years now."

Meyer opened his mouth to protest, but Gracchus silenced him with a shout. "Don't give me any of that crap about your colleagues being informed. I'm quite sure you've exceeded your writ on many occasions. You know our accounting is very exact, and I can prove precisely how much money we've given you over that time."

Meyer elevated his right hand, the fingers extended and shaking. Gracchus waved his protest off. "And then there are the numerous memorabilia and awards you've been given. They would look bad in whatever light they were cast."

Gracchus sat back in the sofa, triumphant, and crossed his legs. "I want your help in locating these materials."

Meyer said nothing but stared on the carpet.

"That includes the journal." Gracchus paused again to give his words greater effect. "We also must recover a set of documents and determine how much damage has been done."

"How?"

"You always wanted to visit West Berlin, talk to Americans. Here's your chance. His name is Rosman."

Gracchus smiled at the look of shock that crossed Meyer's

face. A touch of fear as well. Just a matter of finding the right mixture of threat and persuasion. Like always.

"Get to know him," Gracchus commanded. "His movements, his contacts. Become his friend, if necessary. He seems to like our brand of dissident. Pretend to be one. Your people are good at that."

"Why should I? Don't you have anyone else? Someone more qualified."

"Not at the moment. We're all very busy these days. And trust is no longer the ready commodity it used to be."

"And you?"

"I need to check on some other friends in the meantime."

"What am I supposed to do?"

"I want to know more about him. I want to know everything he knows, and you will help me. I will contact you in the usual way for our next meeting."

Contrary to their usual practice, Gracchus got up to leave first. When he reached the door, Gracchus turned to Meyer, who was now leaning against the window, his left hand pushing the curtain back so he could watch the street below. Perhaps he was looking for the old woman, who had long since passed.

"Think of this, pastor. If this country is godforsaken, ask yourself who made it that way. I, for one, never professed to believe in your god."

CHAPTER 16

The postcard carried a vivid color photograph of the Charles Bridge in Prague. Rosman turned the corner into his office after collecting his afternoon mail and strolled over to his desk. He could not take his eyes off the image of the famous bridge, the statues along its upper edge set in a stark outline against a clear blue sky.

"Who's the card from?"

Harding's familiar voice shook Rosman from his daydream. He stood in the doorway to Rosman's office, his khaki slacks and blue and white striped shirt hanging loosely over his broad-shouldered frame like a robe.

Rosman's head shot up. "I'm not sure. There's no signature."

"Feminine or masculine handwriting?" Harding dropped himself into the seat at the side of Rosman's desk.

"Why do you say that?"

"Maybe it's your girlfriend. I mean, you have been staring at that card with a lost and distant look to your eyes for the last five minutes. Or at least as long as I've been standing here."

Rosman let the card fall onto the desk. He leaned back in his chair and ran his fingers through his ruffled, brown hair. "I wish it was from her. But it looks like a man's hand. Besides, the postmark's from West Berlin."

"So what's it say?" Nixon crossed his right ankle over his left knee. Rosman studied the blue argyle socks.

"Not much. Just that she's in Prague if I want to find her."

"But you don't know who it's from?"

"Not the faintest idea"

"How long since you've seen her?"

"Three days."

"Did you guys have a fight?"

Rosman winced. "Not exactly. At least, I don't think so."

"Well, just to let you know, Friedlander has been asking what the hell you're up to." Harding gestured with his head toward Rosman's arm. "And it's a good thing he hasn't seen that."

Rosman pulled at the cuff of his blue dress shirt, trying to cover his wrist. He leaned forward. "Why? What did he say?"

"Well, for one thing, he's concerned about all these frigging congressional delegations coming through. And your turn is coming."

"Oh, sure. I'm happy to do my part squiring those clowns around. I know just where their wives can find some great shopping." Rosman smiled and let out his breath, shaking his head.

"Don't assume you're completely in the clear, though."

"Why? What else is there?"

"He knows something is up. Hell, even Sutton has been asking about your time in the East. I'm sure Jack's seen this kind of shit before."

"What kind would that be?"

"The kind where young foreign service officers get themselves into trouble over some woman."

Rosman felt the hair stand up on the back of his neck. "She's not just some woman." He tried to keep his voice from rising. "Have you been talking to Kramer?"

"John, you know I didn't mean it like that. But you haven't exactly been yourself lately."

"Get to the point."

"Alright, I will. Just what the hell happened to you the other day at the Gate? Why did you let yourself get carried away into the East? You know you broke all the rules about crossing into the Zone." He grabbed Rosman's hand. "And just what the hell is that?"

Rosman jerked his hand free. "That is my business." He exhaled and nodded toward the hallway. "Jesus, you sound like the perfect bureaucrat. Will it make the slightest difference a month or two from now where we cross?"

Harding leaned forward. "So, you're making your own rules now?"

"You haven't answered my question. Have you been talking to Kramer?"

"Yes."

"So, you know about the other night?"

Harding nodded.

"Then why the questions?"

"I wanted to see if you'd tell me any more than you told him. I thought we were friends."

"We are. And you know as much as I do. What can you tell me?"

"As far as he can tell, your girlfriend's clean."

"Excuse me?" Rosman sat upright.

"Kramer told me that the name trace on her came up blank."

"What about the others?"

"He hasn't heard anything yet. But he thought you'd want to know about Joanna."

"Thanks, Bill. I do. And I'll thank Kramer."

"One more question, John." Harding bit his lip, shook his head, then spoke. "Background checks aside, how well do you really know this woman?"

"Well enough."

"Well enough for what? Can you trust her completely?"

"Is there something else you have to say?"

"No. Not yet, anyway. But you're taking some big steps here. And I just want to be sure you're asking yourself those same questions."

Having said his piece, Harding leaned back and stared out the window. Rosman focused on the card on his desk, unwilling to speak. After a minute of silence, Rosman leaned forward again. "I may have to head down to Prague to see if Joanna's all right."

"Are you sure?" Harding's eyes shifted from the courtyard window to his friend's face. "I mean, what if she isn't even there?"

Rosman faced Harding. "That's just the point. I need to check this out."

Harding pointed at the card in Rosman's hand. "But you don't even know who sent this thing, or why he sent it."

"I can't just let this go." Rosman sighed and shook his head. "I can't do that."

Harding shifted his weight far enough forward to where his knees touched the front of Rosman's desk "John, what happened the other night?"

Rosman frowned. "We were supposed to meet someone, but we were jumped." He held up his arm. "There was a shooting."

Harding sat bolt upright. "Jesus, John. You've got to let someone else in on this. What about Kramer or the Agency folks?"

Rosman shook his head, adamant. "Kramer knows enough already. And that's as far as it goes. I've got to handle this myself. I won't be worth a shit around here until I do. And I'm not selling Joanna out by bailing on her now."

Harding looked away, shaking his head.

"Don't worry. I'll get a visa and drive through the transit route into West Germany first. Strictly by the books this time."

"How can Friedlander afford to let you take off with all this work coming in?"

"He'll have to. I've got the leave coming."

"I wouldn't be so sure of that this year. Hell, the way things have been going...."

"I'll have to take that chance."

Harding stood there for about 10 seconds before aiming for the door. Then he stopped and turned once more toward Rosman. "Do you think you'll find your answers in Prague?"

"I hope to find at least one."

"Be careful, John. No matter how close you are to some people, you still don't really know what's going on over there."

"There's been a revolution, Bill. And the good guys have won."

"It's not over yet. And we don't know what else has been happening behind curtain number one."

"If that's the case, then let me ask you a question. Do you trust Dorothy?"

Harding frowned. "What's that supposed to mean?"

"I mean, do you trust her? How well do you know her?"

"Well enough. And, yes, I trust her."

Rosman stood up and walked toward him. "Are you sure? Or is it because you're sleeping with her?"

"Fuck you, Rosman." Harding turned on his heels and stormed down the hallway.

Rosman walked back toward his desk and kicked the corner as hard as he could. He had just wanted to make a point with his friend by showing him that these suspicions can cut both ways, even if it isn't always fair. But it hadn't worked. And now his foot hurt as much as his arm.

CHAPTER 17

It took 48 hours, but he found Joanna.

He had checked every hotel and boarding house within walking distance of the old city. Finally, a woman at the front desk of a hostel just a few blocks from the medieval Jewish cemetery recognized Joanna from Rosman's description. But she had not been there the seven times he called, nor did he see her during his frequent stakeouts.

Rosman sat at a café across the street from the old city hall, his overcoat folded over the chair to his right, trying to decide what to do next. When the overweight waiter with the long white apron set his second glass of Budvar on the table, he knocked Rosman's coat to the floor. A thin, gray-haired German with a Berlin accent placed it back on the chair with a smile. *This place is loaded with Krauts*, Rosman thought.

Like the crowd outside, he was waiting for the ornate medieval clock on the wall of the old *Rathaus* to ring in the hour with a parade of dancing figures and unrecognizable melodies. Shadows hung from the gables of the colored Renaissance facades, and a bright sun splashed the dry slate cobblestones at the center with a white light. He was halfway through his beer when he saw Joanna near the edge of the crowd. At about five minutes to the hour, she squeezed through the ten or fifteen people between her and the open air and walked toward the cathedral of St. Nicholas at the opposite end of the square.

Rosman hustled between the half dozen tables that separated him from the door and leaned outside.

"Joanna. Wait."

She turned at the sound of his voice, her eyes wide and mouth open. Her dark green nylon jacket and faded blue jeans hovered in the middle of the square, her face searching the crowd.

When she saw him, Joanna appeared confused, stunned almost, and dropped her purse. She bent over to retrieve her bag, stumbled toward the café, then finally broke into a jog, her blond hair brushed back by the breeze. Rosman's heart leaped toward the broad smile and hazel eyes that shone with the same beauty and longing from their last night together.

"John. What are you doing here?"

"Looking for you. I heard you were here. I've always wanted to see Prague, and thought I might as well do it with my dear Joanna."

He took her hand and led her back to his table. The waiter, who had been hovering near the door, came over to Rosman's side.

"That sounds so romantic, chasing me down here to Prague." She looked up at the waiter. "No, I'm fine. Thank you."

Rosman motioned to the waiter for his bill. "Well, yes, it does sound romantic. Unless, of course, you came here to escape me."

Her smile faded. "No, of course not."

"Then why?"

She gnawed at her lower lip for several seconds. "I did need to get away, but it wasn't from you." She hesitated a moment, turning her eyes to watch the people walk past the café window as the crowd dispersed. The clock had just completed its performance. "So much has happened in the last few months, and I was so unprepared for it all." She pivoted toward him. "I never expected all these changes. Then the deaths of Hans and Hermann, and this strange disappearance of Erich. And meeting you. It's all come so fast."

A thin stream of tears ran down her cheek. Rosman put his hand on hers and rose from his chair, hoping to lead her out of the café. Joanna did not move but sat at the table, her hand cupped over her eyes while Rosman settled his tab. Then, she rose suddenly and rushed out the door. Rosman trailed hurriedly behind her, weaving his way among the tables, tossing apologies at the startled customers. The gray-haired Berliner looked away.

He caught up with her in front of the clock, grabbing the nape of her jacket. She was crying heavily now, her right hand covering her eyes, and her shoulders shaking lightly. Rosman wrapped his arms around her. A fresh scent of lavender rose from her head, and he kissed the sweet tuft of hair at the crown. "It's alright, darling. It's alright," he repeated.

It took her a moment to stop crying and dry her eyes. "But tell me, John, who told you I was here?"

Rosman shrugged. "I don't know. I received a mysterious card and figured it was from someone you knew."

The blood seemed to drain from her face. "No, it wasn't anyone I know. It couldn't have been."

"No matter. We'll figure it out some day."

Joanna's shoulders settled. She looked up into Rosman's eyes. "I'm sorry, John. But I doubt we ever will."

Rosman took her hands in his. "Let's walk a bit."

They turned together. Joanna followed his lead, leaving behind the bright facades of blue and yellow as they strolled toward the Charles Bridge. They walked in silence, hand in hand. The emptiness of the streets lent a surreal quality to the medieval lanes of cobbled pathways and dark stone walls that encased the narrow, winding walkways in the city's medieval heart. He had expected more tourists. It was as though the two lovers had reserved this place and time for their private use.

Finally, Rosman spoke. "How long were you planning to stay?"

"I don't know. I'm sure I'll be back in Berlin soon. I have a few more days left. I'm just trying to work a few things out in my mind."

"Why not come back with me? I'd like to take in more of the sights." Rosman motioned toward the café with his head. "And the beer."

He stopped and drew her hand to his lips. "Let's spend our own little holiday here together. We can drive back to Berlin afterwards. My boss only let me take a few days off."

"Oh John, don't you see?" Joanna looked away and then back at Rosman. "There is so much we need to sort out."

"We can work things out together." Rosman fixed his eyes on hers. "I'm sure of it."

"It's not just us. What do you plan to do about Erich and Her-mann?" They started to walk again.

"Don't you want me to follow things through?"

"Not anymore. It's too dangerous. Let the police do it."

"But I promised Erich."

Joanna halted, pulling on Rosman's arm to make him stop. "John, Erich is probably dead. What more can you do? There's no need to hold yourself to an empty promise."

"What about his memory? The things he fought for and believed in?" He looked at Joanna. "I thought you shared those."

"We shared more than that, John. We shared enemies as well. And I'm afraid they're still out there. Think about it, John. Who do you think told you I was here?" Rosman was silent. "They want you to bring me back."

Silence bridged their distance as they crossed the Moldau. The dark solemn statues that lined the sides of Prague's famous land-mark seemed to mock his seriousness. So much had passed over these cobblestones. His own turmoil seemed like just a brief moment in the history of this city.

"We'll tell the police." Joanna's sudden words snapped the cold air around them. "We can trust them."

"That won't help. You know that. It's never been just about murder." He pressed her fingers together, his eyes searching the street.

"That's what frightens me so."

They continued up the hilly streets toward the Hradcany cas-tle that loomed above the city like some granite shadow. Rosman sighed. His chest was heavy, as though he had been holding his breath since they had crossed the Charles Bridge.

They stopped walking and Rosman turned to hold her. He looked back upon the city, realizing only now that they had cov-ered half the distance from the river to the castle. They had passed into a more modern part of Prague, flush with elaborate Baroque structures of marble and plaster. Rosman looked up to find a mag-nificent church with broad rounded cupolas and rose-colored mar-ble columns. He had forgotten his guidebook, but the name didn't matter. It typified the neighborhood. From the flag he had seen when they entered the square, Rosman knew that the American Embassy was just around the corner, about a block away.

His arm moved across Joanna's shoulders and behind her neck. "Wait here. I'll be right back."

"Where are you going?"

"Inside the church. I think I'll light a candle."

He might even say a brief prayer, if he could remember something appropriate. There were motives enough, even if they were mixed: concern for Jens, sorrow for Hans and Lamprecht, confusion about his own direction. And distant echoes from his family's past, echoes he had given up hope of ever understanding, only to have them resurface here in the heart of Europe and take on a new, deeper meaning for him.

Inside, he barely noticed the ornate decorations of marble and gold, the jewel-covered skeletons of long-dead saints. He had encountered the brilliance of the Baroque epoch, the Counter-Reformation's evocation of the power and glory of the Roman Catholic Church, many times before. Like most apostates, he had always marveled at the wealth and splendor, but the theology had made little impression on him.

Rosman found a small altar with candles to the right of the portico and lit first two candles, and then, after a momentary prayer, a third. The "Hail Mary" seemed about right, a short plea for guidance and help.

And She did help. At least, Rosman thought it might be Her. The chaos and fear of the last two weeks, the sorrow and grief over unnecessary deaths, the turning point in Europe's history that beckoned from the heart of Germany's imperial capital, the history of his own family—it all came together in a sense of right and wrong, a political imperative that demanded an act of will and strength on his part. He would not just walk away.

After those few seconds on the cold hard steps, Rosman rose, rubbing his knees. He saw that Joanna had followed him inside. She was standing back at the entrance, the lines of her face showing her concern. He walked over to where she stood, stopped to inhale the cool, rarefied atmosphere of religious elegance and fervor one last time, and then moved toward the exit. As they left,

Joanna took his hand. This time, Rosman pressed hers in a desperate bid for affection and help.

Outside, she was the first to speak when they had reached the bottom of the stairs. "I didn't realize you were so religious. Was that the sign of the cross you made by the candles?"

"Oh that. I still remember some of the rituals from my upbringing. Occasionally they seem like the right thing to do."

Rosman turned to her, his eyes squinting against the sun. He raised and lowered his arms. "I'm sorry, Joanna. I can't just quit," he said. "Too much has happened. I made a promise to myself, as well as to Erich, not to walk away. That's the one I really have to keep."

Joanna leaned forward and kissed Rosman on the cheek, then on the lips, slipping her right arm behind his neck. "I'm sorry too, John. I wish I could help. But I have too much to fear now."

"Fear for whom?"

"For both of us."

"Why more so now than before?"

"Because I know what we're up against, and I know how little I can do to help you fight that."

Rosman leaned back, his hands resting on her shoulders. A deep shudder passed through his chest. A glance back toward the church revealed the tall thin German from the café. The man was unmistakable from the gray hair that had a habit of falling over his brow and onto his forehead. Rosman wondered why he didn't just get it cut, if it bothered him so much. He also wondered why he should keep crossing paths with this man. Had he been following them? Perhaps he was the one who had sent the card. When their eyes met, the stranger broke off, disappearing amidst the covered arcades and deep alleyways of time-worn Prague.

CHAPTER 18

This time, Gracchus entered through the main door of the GRU base at Karlshorst. He parked his Wartburg at the side of the building and marched to the entrance with firm, heavy steps. He had ignored the suburban surroundings as he drove in, his eyes fixed on the road and his mind searching for that precise combination of command and request he would need. As he walked to the door, another blast of cold air swept in from the east. How appropriate, he thought, for a truly cold winter to come this year. He pulled the fur collar of his thick black overcoat tighter around his neck.

Once inside, Gracchus loosened his grip and undid the leather buttons that ran down the front of his coat. He stamped his feet on the brown burlap mat just inside the door and pulled the fur cap off his head. "Bastards," he growled. It had taken him days to locate Jens. Now they would pay. Or at least be put in their place.

Frowning, he flipped his identification card toward the receptionist, a quiet, pimply teenager. He was dressed in the crisp, nearly clean uniform of a Soviet corporal. The young man snapped a salute after returning the documents, then released the security lock just inside the front hallway. *Enjoy your tour here*, Gracchus thought as he entered, *you'll never have it so good again. God knows what you're going back to.*

Gracchus raced to the second-floor office of a KGB major, one Yuri Chukovskiy, a well meaning but simplistic dolt. Gracchus pushed open the door of the office without knocking. "I'm here for the prisoner," he said without hesitation, not waiting to see if Chukovskiy was alone.

"Excuse me?" Chukovskiy replied, his dull round face, thick

eyebrows and flat nose a perfect frame for his puzzled look. He sat at the desk, immovable. His hands lay frozen to the top of a mound of papers about two inches thick.

Gracchus sighed. "The East German. Erich Jens. It seems some of your people mistakenly seized him the other night."

Chukovskiy's puzzled frown did not disappear. How Chukovskiy ever reached the rank of major, especially in such a prestigious and competitive organization, was a question Gracchus had given up trying to answer a long time ago. "He belongs to me," Gracchus explained, jabbing his chest with his thumb.

"I'm sorry, comrade. I know nothing of this. Would you like to speak with my commander?"

"Right away." Gracchus smiled, inwardly triumphant. He had pulled rank on them once in the past, and it had been a particularly unpleasant experience for Chukovskiy. The Russian had simply stared at the floor when he learned that Gracchus held a KGB rank above his own within the GRU.

Gracchus waited at the window, contemplating the trucks, maintenance depots and storage sheds at the rear of the main building. The yard was littered with engine parts and leaking oil drums. Discarded paper floated across the broad expanse of concrete beneath the window. Gracchus slammed his fist against the window ledge, scattering paint chips toward the floor.

He did not exchange another word with Chukovskiy, who had dispatched his secretary, another young corporal, to fetch Colonel Vorontsev. At least Gracchus would have someone of equal rank to deal with now.

He watched the back of Chukovskiy's oily black hair. The Russian pretended to work through the pile of papers, refusing to look up at the German intruder. Gracchus's attention shifted to the looming portraits of Red Army heroes from the last war that passed for office decoration. There were four, one for each wall, and each portrayed a great battle: the stand before Moscow, the tank battle at Kursk, the siege of Leningrad, and, of course, Stalingrad. Each one had the same thin black wooden frame, and each hung precisely in the middle of the wall. Gracchus wondered how long it had taken the corporal to get the measurements right.

After about ten minutes, Vorontsev entered, smartly attired in full uniform. Gracchus was not impressed. The uniform improved Vorontsev's bearing, but it failed to give his short, wiry frame the martial bravado it needed.

"To what do we owe the honor of your visit this morning, Comrade Gracchus?" His thin brown mustache dripped with false politeness.

"Cut the crap, Comrade Colonel. Surely you know why I'm here."

Vorontsev did not even blink.

"I have come to claim the prisoner Erich Jens in the name of my ministry. You may release him on my cognizance."

Vorontsev pivoted toward Chukovskiy. "Do you know anything about this prisoner? Has he been located on this compound?"

Chukovskiy made an exaggerated effort of sorting through the small mountain of papers. He stopped midway. "I believe there is an East German counter-revolutionary our men took into custody after he made some insulting remarks about the Soviet Union. He also threatened the officers, who felt that it was necessary to subdue him."

"I don't want your fucking history of the case. Just bring me the damn prisoner," Gracchus barked. He walked away from the window and paced across the room. "Is Preselnikov here?" It never hurt to drop names with functionaries like these.

"I have not seen Comrade Preselnikov today," Vorontsev replied. His nose tilted toward the ceiling.

"If you are unable to give me the answers I need, I demand to use your telephone."

Vorontsev strode behind the desk and bent toward Chukovskiy. The two men spoke with each other in hushed tones, their backs to Gracchus. Then Vorontsev straightened himself and turned to Gracchus. "Comrade, there is no need for us to insult each other. Please sit down."

"I'd rather stand. I don't plan to stay that long." Gracchus stopped pacing and took a cigarette from the pack in his shirt pocket.

"It seems there has been a complication in this case." Vorontsev hesitated, as though uncertain how to continue.

Gracchus straightened himself, blowing smoke toward the senior Russian. "What do you mean by 'complication'?" Gracchus knew what he meant. He had feared as much.

"It seems the prisoner continued his abusive activities while resisting interrogation. His heart was already in a weakened state, and...." Vorontsev let his words trail off.

"Do you mean to tell me you've killed the prisoner?" Gracchus sputtered, the cigarette stuck between his lips. Confirmation of what he already suspected only infuriated him more. Both Chukovskiy and Vorontsev looked impassively at Gracchus, their eyes four dead shadows.

"That is unheard of! Do you realize what you've done, how badly you've screwed things up?" Gracchus was ready to explode. The sheer stupidity of it all! He was sick and tired of cleaning up after amateurs like these. This never would have happened 10, no, five years ago. Hell, it would never have happened five *months* ago.

Gracchus stared at Vorontsev and Chukovskiy while he finished his cigarette. Then he strode over to the desk and picked up the wastebasket by the side of Chukovskiy's desk, ignoring the ashtray that stood alone next to the brown cardboard blotter. He crushed the tip of his cigarette against the side of the basket and dropped it back to the floor, where it crashed and rolled over on its side. Chukovskiy grabbed the smoking cylinder and hurriedly extinguished the smoking papers at the bottom. Coughing, Vorontsev waved the smoke away with half a dozen exaggerated sweeps of his arms.

"On whose authority did you arrest the young man?"

Vorontsev glanced at Chukovskiy, then back at Gracchus. "On our own, comrade. It was necessary to act quickly, and we received the proper authorization from our headquarters."

"You felt it necessary to intrude, you mean." Gracchus aimed a finger at the Soviet colonel. "You realize you interrupted an important operation, don't you? Was the KGB station here in Berlin aware of this?"

Vorontsev spoke in a calm, measured voice. "If you wish to

file a complaint, Comrade Gracchus, you will have to speak with your superiors. They will contact ours."

"I'll do better than that. I'm going to see that whoever is responsible for this mess is severely punished. I honestly hope that both of you will be implicated."

Gracchus wheeled around and stalked from the room. He wanted to leave as quickly as possible. He jerked his gloves from his coat pocket and slapped them against his thigh. "God-dammit!" he shrieked, slamming the banister with his fist as he rushed down the steps.

He ran to his car, ignoring the question thrown by the receptionist as he pushed open the heavy metal door at the entrance. Gracchus rammed the key to the right, and the Wartburg roared. He slammed his foot to the floor and sped from the lot, spitting patches of gravel at the receding images of Vorontsev and Chukovskiy in the second story window.

Gracchus raced downtown to Mitte. For once he felt like one of those West Germans that speed like maniacs along the highways of Europe, as though they own the roads and the rules that go with them. You'd think they had won the damn war.

He parked in a small side street near the Pergamon Museum and stood behind a group of tourists waiting to use one of the pay phones out front. Finally, he cut in front of a group of idiotic westerners and dialled a number at the Soviet Embassy. After three rings, he heard the click at the other end of the line.

"Preselnikov here."

"I need to talk to you."

"Where are you?"

Gracchus made sure no tourists were close when he spoke. "Nearby. There's been a new complication, if I may be so bold as to misuse the term."

"What is it? Can't you handle it yourself?"

"No. It involves your people this time."

"All right. Meet me at our usual spot nearby in ten minutes."

Gracchus pushed the receiver back in place and melted into

the tourists flowing toward Berlin's main thoroughfare. Preselnikov's 10 minutes actually meant five, according to their code, but even then there was no need to rush. He clutched at the black fur collar with shaking hands.

The walk took less than four minutes. Gracchus marched back and forth for about 30 seconds in the middle of Unter den Linden in front of the Polish Embassy. He finally stopped when he saw the tall, thin Slav dart between the moving lines of traffic and stroll toward the bench. Gracchus knew that back in Moscow the battle lines over *glasnost* and *perestroika* were becoming more firmly drawn. Had that been the reason behind the seizure of Jens, the sudden interference? Every instinct told him that a showdown was nearing, and Gracchus hoped he would be able to continue to rely on this friend. It suddenly dawned on Gracchus that he had never had to ask that question before. He sat down on the bench, weary, as though suddenly burdened by the giant sweep of events that threatened to overwhelm him and his country.

Smiling, Preselnikov spoke first. "So, have you given any thought to how you will vote in the coming election? It must be a new experience for you." He arched his eyebrows and emitted a short laugh.

His face frozen in a bitter frown, Gracchus ignored the question. He buried his hands in his pockets to wrap the overcoat even tighter to his body. "I'm sorry to have to call you out like this."

"Forget it. The weather's still a lot warmer here than in Moscow. Do you remember those nights when we would visit your family at the Hotel Lux?"

"Of course. How can I forget having to stand in line every night for the only toilet on our floor?"

"A real tower of Babel there, eh? All you exiles."

"That was long ago, Sergei. I've got a different problem now." Preselnikov's silence invited him to go on. "It seems some of your people have intruded into the operation, and they've bungled it badly."

"My people? What do you mean?"

"Right now I'm spending nearly all my time trying to remove the complications that have arisen, complications that are blocking my path to the information I need. And today they've come from this senseless bungling." Gracchus looked at the ground and then at his friend. "I told you I always clean up after myself."

"So, what is it? Tell me what happened, and tell me how can I help."

"Some GRU clowns in Karlshorst grabbed my bait before the trap was shut. It took me three days to locate the prisoner. And then they mishandled the interrogation. A third dissident has died."

Preselnikov's eyes narrow. "Jens?"

Gracchus nodded. His fist came down hard on the seat of the bench. "They shouldn't have even been there in the first place."

Preselnikov sighed. He looked up into the sky and then rotated his head, his eyes roaming from rooftop to rooftop.

Gracchus pushed himself up from the bench. "In so doing, they've screwed things up just when it looked like we were going to get what we needed. Now I will have to deal with the American directly."

"I don't envy you. What do you want from me?"

"Some advice and information." He paused. "And some gratification."

"I'll give what I can."

"How are things shaping up in Moscow? How are relations with Washington progressing?"

"You'll have to excuse me, but I'm slow today. What has that got to do with anything?"

"What sort of interference would I face if I have to take drastic measures against the American?"

"A dead American will not lead you anywhere. Not at this point." Preselnikov let out another sigh, his hands buried deep in the pockets of his camel-haired overcoat, his feet playing with the pebbles in front of the bench. "This never should have been allowed to happen."

"The American was lucky. That's all."

"No, all that paper. You should have taken care of it. I warned you." He looked Gracchus in the eyes. "You Germans are too obsessed with records and paperwork. You're too damn thorough."

"Perhaps you should have taken Italy instead. Or Greece."

"We tried. Remember? But don't you have any alternative? Surely you're not that desperate yet."

"I, too, prefer a more subtle approach. You know that. But I may have to begin turning up the pressure. And that does bring with it certain risks."

"Please be careful. I'm not sure I can give you the backing you'd need if anything unfortunate happens." Preselnikov paused. "What sort of information did you need?"

"The American must have had some help. Can you find out if anyone else is working with him?"

"I can try."

Gracchus cast a glance in the direction of the Brandenburg Gate. "I was thinking of someone from over there."

"German or American?"

Gracchus shrugged. "I'm not sure." He looked at Preselnikov. "I'm not sure of all my contacts over there right now. Too many are looking to the future." He laughed. "As though they can erase all the inconvenient acts of an unpleasant past."

Gracchus rose and straightened himself slowly, as though his muscles ached from the day's work. "The problem remains, Sergei. And now the American knows far too much. About October and Hans, for instance."

"Are you sure he has the missing files?"

Gracchus nodded. "Pretty sure. And some other notes as background. They could be valuable. The author was allowed to learn more than he should have. We were using him for a doubling operation. That's why we can't afford to ignore the American anymore."

"So, you're thinking of neutralizing—no, excuse me—'removing' him?"

Gracchus returned to his seat on the bench and leaned toward the Russian, his hands outstretched. "And then there's the matter of those idiots in Karlshorst."

The Russian shook his head slowly. "I'm sorry, Johann. I was not aware they were going to act so soon. I would have warned you."

"Do you know why they interfered?"

Preselnikov exhaled slowly. "I believe they're after the same information on the sources and the money."

"And they acted independently?" Preselnikov nodded, then looked away. Gracchus sat back, stunned. "Have things gone that far in Moscow?" He shook his head, not waiting for his friend to answer. "Still, we can't let that sort of thing go unpunished. It was nothing more than the work of simple thugs."

Preselnikov was silent for a moment. When he did speak, he looked back into the eyes of his friend. "I doubt I can do anything for you there. Those particular people are beyond my reach at the moment."

"Why? For goodness sake, Sergei, you are, for all intents and purposes, the head of Soviet operations in Berlin."

"There are forces at work in Moscow, powerful groups pursuing their own agenda right now. And I'm caught between them here in Berlin." Preselnikov studied the traffic flowing along Unter den Linden for a minute before continuing. "I'll see if I can help you with the American. Perhaps I can find out something useful. But other than that, I can't give you any practical help. Not right now."

"Why not?"

"My orders have changed. I'm out of it now."

Gracchus was silent. He looked away from his friend when he spoke again. "Do you remember that first night we went out in Moscow in search of women? 'Whoring' you called it."

"Vaguely. Why?"

"I was so nervous. I felt so out of place. I was still a virgin, you know."

"Yes, I remember it now. Your awkwardness."

"But you came across as so experienced, so sophisticated. I thought you knew everything, that I would be able to trust you forever."

"We've had a pretty good run of it."

"There's something else I remember from my time in Moscow, Comrade," Gracchus pressed.

"So many memories today." Preselnikov shifted his feet and glanced in the direction of his embassy. "And since when did you become so formal," Preselnikov hesitated, "Comrade?"

Gracchus ignored the question. He wasn't really listening. "I remember the cries at night of the women and children when their men were taken away by the NKVD. It was horrible, Comrade. I often cried into my pillow until I fell asleep."

"I can imagine."

"I even feared for my own family. I would have prayed, but I was afraid to."

"Why are you telling me this?" Preselnikov's eyes were glued to Gracchus. The Russian's breath came in short, subtle bursts of steam.

"Because I want you to know that I learned something in the days that followed. I learned that certain things, no matter how hard, are necessary for the revolution, for history. I learned that a service like ours is also necessary. Sometimes, Comrade, we have to do those things we abhor, things we normally avoid. I still believe that. I always will."

"I am truly sorry, my friend. As you said, that was long ago. That world we knew is gone."

Gracchus did not answer. He sat silently on the bench, watching Preselnikov walk slowly back to his embassy a few blocks away. Gracchus stared at the ground for a long time before he stood up and staggered in the opposite direction, toward Alexanderplatz.

CHAPTER 19

The ride back to Berlin had been exhausting, heavy rains and wet snow transforming a two-hour drive into a five-hour ordeal. Rosman was relieved to see the four-story apartment blocks of faded beige and yellow on either side of Huettenweg, the street that ran from the stretch of Berlin Autobahn known as the *Avus* through the Gruenewald and into Dahlem. The apartments served as family housing units for the U.S. Army and ended just shy of Clayallee, the main thoroughfare that ran past the U.S. Mission and Army headquarters. It was as close to an American village as one would find in this part of the world, with a shopping center, schools and movie theater packed into an area with a radius of two, maybe three miles.

Rosman cruised down Clayallee to his own house on Vogelsang as night fell with the last flakes of mush. He parked the car in his driveway and wrestled his bag through the gate and into his front lawn.

When he shouldered his way through the front door, Rosman dropped his suitcase at this feet. He stood open-mouthed in his foyer, stunned. The furniture in his living room had been thrown about, half of it knocked over, and the drawers of his desk pulled loose, their contents strewn on the floor.

He stumbled into the kitchen. The cupboard doors stood open, and half his dishes lined the counter top between the sink and back wall. The rest were on the floor, many of them in pieces. The refrigerator door gaped open, the compressor chugging. The bastards had eaten half the chunk of Edam he had left in there—and then put it back on the same shelf.

The tumult extended up the stairs. In each bedroom the furniture had been pushed to the center of the room, and the contents of all the drawers and armoires stacked in piles on the floor. Neatly stacked, like the result of some inescapable Prussian compulsion for orderliness in the midst of a self-induced fury.

In his own bedroom, every piece of furniture lay on its side. The intruder had flipped the bed upside down and left the mattress lying on top of it. His clothes, pulled from the drawers and standing closets, stood heaped in a corner. The rug was folded over at midpoint, its end resting against the bed.

Rosman raced downstairs and knelt by the desk drawers lying on their sides in his living room. His papers and cheque book were at the bottom of a pile next to the drawers. Only the spare cash was gone, but that amounted to no more than 60 Marks, or about 40 dollars. The TV and stereo equipment were also there, but they too were dumped in the middle of the floor. A sense of relief swept through Rosman.

The realization hit him minutes later, and the pain and doubt crept slowly back. The intruders had come for one thing only. And they had not bothered to hide their ability to enter his house at will. No window was broken, and neither the front or back door had been forced.

Rosman reclimbed the stairs to his bedroom, clenching and unclenching his fists. He blew his breath out in quick, short bursts. First a beating, then a shooting, and now this. He wasn't sure what he should feel more, fear or anger. Both were compelling. But so was a sense of futility and exhaustion, especially when he realized he would have to win this battle alone, without Joanna or Jens. So many allies had been taken away. And Lord knew how much help the others would be.

He leaned against the mattress. It tilted to one side and slid to the floor. Rosman collapsed and sprawled on top of it, staring blankly at the pile of clothes in the corner. He was so tired. More than revenge, more than anything else right now, he wanted to sleep. Rosman closed his eyes and let his mind sink back into the mattress until its soft cushion welcomed his weight into a dark familiar depth.

An image of Joanna floated above the piles of clothes and

debris. He could almost feel her presence as he extended his right hand in mid-air, palm up. He wanted to let go, get on with his life together with her.

"The old regime has fallen, John, and it's not coming back. It's already too late for that."

"But is it too late for Erich and Hermann?"

"You hardly knew them." She bent toward Rosman. "Where is the notebook? Why are you still holding it?"

He blinked, aware again of her striking beauty, watching as she hovered, the edge of her white silk shirt falling open to expose the deep, shadowed cleavage. She moved toward him slowly, revealing the elaborate pattern of thin, white lace that covered the lower half of her breasts. Rosman drew it all in, the magical and mysterious sight that gave him a diminishing sense of pain and loss.

He awoke with a start. He jumped up and brushed his sleeve against the sweat gathering along his brow. Only then did he realize that he still had his overcoat on.

He remembered seeing the tall thin German with the uncombed gray hair again that evening. He had sped off in a Trabant with Potsdam license plates. The idiot might as well have worn a sign. Just what was his game, Rosman wondered, and what, if anything, did he have to do with this?

Rosman ripped off his coat and tossed it to the floor. He shoved his arms through the debris on his floor, searching for the telephone. It took him about a minute to shove through the piles, find the phone and dial Kramer's number. He knew that he needed to start tonight if he was going to avoid the fate of all the others this thing had swallowed.

"More wine, sir?"

The waiter stood to Rosman's left, the bottle of German Sylvaner poised at a 45 degree angle, waiting for his permission to pour. Rosman glanced over at the diminutive German with his white hair and black tuxedo. The man had known, miraculously, it seemed, just when he was needed. "Yes, please," Rosman replied.

The *Forsthaus Paulsborn*, reputedly an old hunting lodge, was the first place Kramer had suggested when Rosman offered to repay his favor. It stood about half a mile from the Hohenzollern hunting castle in the Gruenewald. Both buildings lay nestled just inside the woods, a few miles from the Dahlem residential district and Rosman's house. Both also sat on the edge of a modest lake, more of a pond, actually, where locals, from what Rosman could tell, fished but never swam. Rosman periodically took his political contacts to the *Forsthaus* for lunch, or, if the season was right, coffee on the terrace. A waiter once told him the Hohenzollerns had put guests in the lodge on occasion, and that one could still rent rooms for the night. But you needed reservations well in advance.

The place was not cheap. This dinner would easily run 100 Deutsch Marks. But the tasteful blend of the rustic and the refined was always worth it. The chandeliers and most of the wall decorations were made of deer antlers, and the dark oak panelling along the walls reinforced the image of a country lodge. More importantly, the food got raves, especially their game dishes.

Tonight, however, Rosman opted for the poached trout, while Kramer selected the more traditional *Sauerbraten*.

"So, what finally got you to offer the dinner you owe me, Rosman?"

"Hey, I pay my debts." Rosman separated the meat from the bone in his fish with a series of simple, deft strokes he had learned from his mother.

"This place really is great." Kramer sipped some wine. "It's good for impressing generals."

"And captains." Rosman set his knife and fork down. "There is something else, though. I especially want to thank you for running those searches for me."

"No problem."

"And for clearing Joanna. I just wish you wouldn't discuss it with everyone."

Kramer set his fork down and sat back in his chair. "I only told Harding and Sutton. And that's because they were so damned pushy. Especially Sutton."

"Sutton?"

"Yeah, Sutton. Why is she so damn curious?"

"I don't know. Maybe she's trying to keep Friedlander off my back."

"Well, I'm not sure I trust her."

Rosman's eyes shot to Kramer, who was busy dismembering his potato dumplings. "You've mentioned that before. Any particular reason, or are you just in another one of your anti-Woodstock moods?"

Kramer shrugged, his eyes still focused on his food. "Naw, nothing in particular."

"Anything else for me?" Rosman poured more wine for Kramer.

"Yes. That guy Schmidt. Thomas, wasn't it?" Rosman nodded. "They found some information about someone with that name and the personal history you described." Kramer gave Rosman the "thumbs up" and a wink. "He's a Stasi informant."

"I thought so."

"He looks like a pretty minor figure, though."

"What do you mean?"

Kramer picked up his wine, swirling the light golden liquid as he held the glass up to the light. "Oh, mostly informing on fellow students, visitors. That sort of thing." His face took on a distant look as he tipped the wine toward his lips and then placed his glass carefully next to his plate. "Not any operations against the Allies that I could see."

"So, he wouldn't have been working under the foreign arm? What do they call it?"

"The HVA."

Rosman pushed his steamed potatoes through the butter sauce that swam over half his plate, then returned to the fish.

"I took the liberty of giving the Agency guys another name. Not one of those you gave me, but one I heard earlier."

"Who was that?" Rosman asked.

"Hermann Lamprecht."

"What did you find?"

"A history similar to Schmidt's."

Rosman swallowed a sliver of bone and grabbed a piece of bread. "You're shitting me!"

"Not at all, my boy. Fortunately for you, he too appears to have limited himself to domestic stuff."

Rosman drained his wineglass and slumped back in his chair.

Kramer continued. "His history is actually pretty interesting. I could see him going in either direction, dissident activist or Stasi informant."

"Why is that?"

"Call it generational rebellion or loyalty to the family cause. Both apply. His father was a minor party functionary, who divorced Lamprecht's mother. She remarried, but to a Soviet, whom she followed back to Mother Russia."

"Which way did it appear to be leading?"

"Well, he showed signs of discontent, and our own people, the Agency guys, I mean, even approached him at one point. I believe they thought of using him as a double."

"A good sign, no?"

"But they gave it up. Not disenchanted enough to make it worth a pitch."

Rosman's mind went blank momentarily as he maneuvered a potato remnant around his plate with his knife. "What about the last name?"

"Which one was that?"

"Hermann Buechler."

"Oh yeah. I almost forgot." Kramer tipped his wineglass over his lips, emptying the last drop into his mouth. He raised the bottle from the silver bucket by its neck. "Where did this one come from?" His forehead wrinkled as he studied the label. "Where the hell is Cochem?"

"It's on the Mosel." Rosman took the bottle to see how much was left. "Now what about Buechler?"

"There are some real gaps in that guy's past, especially after the war. I'm trying to run down some more information on him." Kramer smiled and shook his head while he surveyed the dining room.

"Thanks. It's important." Rosman divided the last of the wine between their two glasses.

"No problem. I'll call if anything more turns up."

Kramer set his knife and fork in the middle of his plate, wiped his mouth with his napkin and set it on top of his silverware. "One more thing, John."

"What is it?"

"I know you've heard this before, and you probably don't want to hear it again. But it applies now more than ever. In short, Big Boy, be careful. It looks like somebody is setting you up."

Rosman gazed over at the bartender, who was setting up a tray with a row of four champagne glasses next to a chilled bottle of German *Sekt* and four fruit bowls with lime sherbet.

"Why do you say that?"

Kramer leaned over the table. "Because there are too many people involved here with suspicious pasts, my boy. It's one of those cases where every answer throws out all sorts of new questions. Too many people have played too many sides. In fact, that's my guess about your buddy Buechler. That's the only way for people in those situations to survive."

"What do you think he did to survive?"

"Just ask yourself. How is it he ever got out of prison and was able to come west?"

"But why me? Why would they be setting me up?"

"That's a real good question, Rambo. Maybe because you're available and easy. Maybe they're using you to settle an old score. Or maybe you give them access to something they need." He waved an empty wine glass in the air. "Hard to say at this point."

"Thanks again, Kramer." *You're right, though,* Rosman thought. Too many people had been swimming on both sides of the Spree for too long. And he needed to find out what on which side Buechler had been getting his feet wet.

CHAPTER 20

The courtyard looked like so many others in Charlottenburg. The yard was clean enough, but it did not reflect the established refinement, the nineteenth-century respectability that the tall bay windows, heavy stone walls and steep tile roofs had once held. The materials looked old and worn, and even the gardening was haphazard. Crabgrass sprouted from cracks in the stone walkway, and the lawn at its center was patchy and brown, like a worn rug. A broken bicycle stood abandoned against the far wall.

Rosman studied the street for any hint of a tail. There was no sign of the gray-haired man, but Rosman could not be sure that this one, so easily sighted, was not a distraction, someone to direct his attention away from the real pursuer, the professional agent. But so far, so good. He hadn't spotted anyone more than once.

Buechler ambled down the long stairway from his apartment on the third floor, pulling the dark green coat over his blue sweater as he lumbered down the z-shaped steps and crossed the courtyard. Rosman wondered what kept this pensioner so spry and animated? You'd never guess his vitality from the pale skin and heavy look that hung on him like a German fog.

They walked the two blocks to the arm of the Spree that trickled through this part of the city, crossed the small iron bridge with its ornate grillwork, and strolled into the gardens of the Charlottenburg Palace. The long paths ran like narrow highways through the barren patches of lawn and empty shrubs at this time of year. The trees were also bare, their branches throwing a patchwork of thin black lines across the sky. When he concentrated, Rosman could pick out the scaffolding at the outer walls of Frederick the Great's private quarters on the eastern corner of the complex.

Behind that stood the yellow plaster walls and orange-tiled roofs of the palace.

During one of his visits, Rosman had learned that Allied bombing had seriously damaged the complex. The West Germans rebuilt it with deliberate, even painstaking, care, unlike their eastern brethren, who demolished the imperial palace in Berlin's historic center in 1950 rather than take the time and effort to restore a relic of Germany's evil imperialist past. And the palace had been in much better shape than the Charlottenburg complex, the old guide had assured Rosman.

The garden was empty. Rosman expected as much this close to noon. The Germans would be stuffing their heavy lunches into well-lined bellies right now. Only later would they venture forth—those that didn't have to work—for an afternoon stroll, as constitutional and regular as voting for these new democrats. Rosman and Buechler cut the corner of one square and began to circumvent the long pond that stretched away from the back of the palace.

"Herr Rosman, I'm glad you called. I've been trying to reach you, but it seems you were away."

"I was out of town."

"Looking for the girl?"

Rosman stopped, his eyes narrow and his lips tight. "The card was from you, wasn't it?"

Buechler turned to face him. "She wanted you out. She probably still does. I was afraid she'd win, and you would give it all up."

"Why do you think she wants me out?"

"She probably fears for you. She may also have other motives."

"Such as?"

"Ask yourself. You know her better than I."

"And why are you so damn eager to keep me in?"

Buechler strode to Rosman's side and took his arm. "Come, let's walk some more. You already know something of my past. Let me tell you more about my passion, why it has consumed me. It should help explain why I want to keep you in." A light laugh escaped from Buechler's chest, followed by a cough. "My wife will be in your debt if there is someone else to listen now."

"Doesn't she share this passion and your past?"

"On the contrary. But she tires of it all so easily these days."

"So where does the past leave off and the passion begin? Or are they inseparable?"

Buechler sighed. "Oh, it's very much the latter, because the one carries the consequences of the other." He looked hard at Rosman. "You haven't felt it yet, here in this city, of all places?"

"On the contrary." Rosman thought of his family, the events of the last two weeks, Joanna. "It becomes more imposing with each day."

They walked in silence for a moment. Finally Rosman spoke.

"And what about the future? Does the past weigh heavily there as well?"

Buechler nodded. "More than most imagine. But you of all people should be aware of that. For one thing, the past will determine how our country will look. Have you done much travelling in the east? I mean further east than Germany."

Rosman shook his head.

"If you had, you would see how miserable conditions are there. The Soviets are in desperate need of capital and expertise to rebuild their economy and society." Buechler paused. "No, excuse me. To build their economy and society. They never succeeded in doing so under communism." Buechler snorted. "Things are not much better in the German Democratic Republic. Have you traveled much outside Berlin?"

"No," Rosman said, simply. He'd leave out any mention of Rostock for now. Let Buechler figure it out by himself.

"If you had, you'd have seen how decrepit things are over there as well. It will take billions to rebuild what had once been a flourishing industrial landscape." Buechler shook his head. "They've done little more than remove the rubble."

"But what about the accomplishments of the east? Isn't there anything worth preserving?"

"Like what?"

His friends thought they had found some. "It seems like there's a good number of people who want to negotiate a new beginning for Germany."

Buechler smiled broadly, lifting his head to sniff the air. "Believe me, very few East Germans are as driven ideologically as those dissident intellectuals you know. Most are tired of suffering, and they just want to live as well as their western cousins."

"How do you feel about that, especially with the past you carry?"

"It makes little difference to me now. I have other things to settle. The past and future have become more personal for me."

Buechler veered off the gravel path under their feet, picking his way over a grassy slope to the pond's shoreline. He pulled a transparent plastic bag containing dry chunks of bread from his coat pocket. "I try every afternoon to bring something to my feathered neighbors here in Charlottenburg."

He broke off small bits of the bread, throwing them underhand to the dozen or so mallards and teals paddling toward them. Between pitches, Buechler glanced about the park, his eyes roaming the lawns and pathways. Rosman bent over to retrieve some crumbs that had fallen to the ground. He aimed his throw for a transplanted mandarin duck swimming at the edge of the pack. A beautiful, isolated stranger.

Buechler smiled again. "But there's more than that. At least for you. It's important to recall what you're doing."

"How so?"

"Haven't you asked yourself about the course and strength of the opposition to the changes in East Germany?"

"There doesn't appear to be any."

"Exactly. Haven't you wondered why the old regime has given up so easily? Did you follow the demonstration in Treptower Park the other night? The one protesting the fascist slogans painted on the Soviet monument there?"

"It seemed natural enough."

"Oh, come now, Herr Rosman."

"What do you mean?"

Buechler rewound the top of the bag into a tight spiral, then tied it into a knot before jamming it back into his pocket. "Just because you don't see the resistance, doesn't mean it isn't there. Think of your friends. What were their names? Jens and Lamprecht? And that fellow Hans."

"What about them?"

Buechler brushed the spare crumbs from his hands, then walked away from the pond. Rosman gazed at the mandarin for a moment, than ran to catch up with Buechler.

"Their case tells you something about the forces at work over there and the influence they have over events. It provides a window through which you can observe the changes. It's the one I use."

"Do you mean...?"

"Yes, exactly! Like their predecessors in the Gestapo, they are a group of professionals who are very good at what they do. And they had that state's entire resources at their disposal."

"Just what is your point?"

"Do you really believe the opposition to the changes underway is as feckless as it appears at the moment?" Buechler halted and turned to face the young American. "It didn't end on November ninth. I believe some in the Stasi infiltrated the dissident movement, and they tried to use it to their advantage." Buechler paused. "And they are still at it."

"Whose advantage?" Rosman felt his pulse quicken. His arm was throbbing, and his eyes darted around the palace grounds. A half dozen couples, older retired people in all probability, had joined them. "Weren't those people supposed to be in the "party's sword," like their motto?"

"Yes, they were. And I'm sure the vast majority saw it that way. But whether that means every Stasi officer had the same agenda as Herr Honecker is something else. Neither the party, nor the Ministry for State Security, were monoliths, you know. They were bureaucracies, big bureaucracies."

"So," Rosman continued, "you think there were differences in viewpoints, policies even, between party and sword?"

"Your friends stumbled across something that was valuable. Something worth killing to keep hidden."

"But how did it work? Could Mielke, the Stasi chief, have been making a power play?" Rosman pressed.

Buechler shrugged. "I doubt it. He wasn't that creative. Mielke was little more than a thug with some organizational talent."

Rosman said nothing. Instead, he looked over toward the ducks. The mandarin was swimming alone, perhaps 20 meters from the other ducks.

"Perhaps there were other loyalties," Buechler continued. "Ones that came into conflict with those we see on the surface. Something more venal, perhaps."

When Rosman looked up again, he saw the palace looming in front of them. Buechler led him up the six steps to a gravel patio that extended across the back of the building and straight to the bridge they had used earlier.

Rosman paused to peer through the full-length windows at a room that must have been 50 yards long. The walls were covered with blue silk wallpaper, with about a dozen windows on either side, each running from the floor to the ceiling. In each column between the windows stood a mirror easily as tall as Rosman, and each one was set in an elaborate gold frame. At the base of the columns stood two-legged tables encased in gold leaf. A huge crystal chandelier occupied the center of the room, suspended from the ceiling in a field of pink silk and layers of gold leaf.

"Jesus," Rosman gasped.

"Yes, it is remarkable," Buechler agreed. "See what I mean by the venality of our rulers? They have been very good at isolating themselves from the people."

"But how does that fit with all that's been going on? With these deaths?"

"It has to do with policies and agendas that are not always apparent. Is Frederick remembered for his ornate palace life or his military campaigns?"

"Both, actually."

"By whom? The historians or the people?"

"So where do you recommend we go from here?"

"Back to Hetzling."

"I doubt he'll be much use. Isn't there anyone else?"

Buechler resumed his stroll along the back of the palace and towards the Spree. "Are you aware of Hetzling's interesting background?"

"Interesting for whom?"

"For the party, and for himself." Buechler held an index finger in the air, as though he was testing the wind. "Back in the 1950s— I know, ancient history to you—an attempt was made to unseat Ulbricht, Honecker's predecessor."

"I know who Ulbricht was," Rosman snapped.

"Yes, of course. Anyway, as a young, idealistic party member, Hetzling became involved in a plot in 1956 by Manfred Hertwig and Bernhard Steinberger, who wanted to dump Ulbricht and pursue a less Stalinist, more independent path to socialism."

"What could they hope to accomplish?"

"They had important accomplices in the Politburo. They were all crushed, of course, but Hetzling was let off easy, presumably because of his youth. He was also a rather minor figure."

"That was a long time ago."

"But it doesn't stop there, Herr Rosman. Have you heard of Robert Havemann?"

"No."

"He was perhaps the most famous East German critic of his government in the 1960s and 1970s. I believe it was Hetzling who helped protect him, and was even instrumental in preserving Havemann's posting at the Humboldt University here in Berlin. You have heard of that one, I'm sure."

Buechler bent forward and projected an exaggerated, inquisitive stare at Rosman. "Hetzling also had a hand in the manifesto published in *Der Spiegel* in 1978 that appealed for a more pluralistic system in East Germany. It would remain communist, of course."

"So, that's why he mentioned *Der Spiegel* when I saw him. The reference went right over my head."

"That was his first test. That's probably why he held so much back."

"But why preserve him?"

Buechler sighed. "He made himself useful. But"—Buechler's index finger rose in the air—"he made himself useful to both sides." Buechler flicked his wrist in Rosman's direction as they passed from the garden to the sidewalk, then tugged at Rosman's sleeve when he trotted across the street. Together, they hopped the curb and walked up to a Russian restaurant that looked out across the front lawn of the palace and its rambling parking lot. Buechler held the door for Rosman as they entered.

Rosman paused to unbutton his coat, while Buechler headed straight for a table in the middle of the dining room. It was a beat shy of one o'clock, and Rosman was starving. He needed something to eat before heading back to work at the U.S. Mission.

The restaurant was nearly empty. Two elderly couples sat at tables near the rear, away from the sidewalk. Only one waiter, a tall, thin, homely lad in his mid-twenties, was working now. He hung back with the bartender, who looked to be a little older, perhaps 30. He, too, was thin, but shorter than his colleague. Both wore black slacks and vests, white shirts and no ties. They were finishing their cigarettes.

Rosman surveyed the room as he pulled off his coat and sat down. No one had followed them inside.

"The point, Herr Rosman, is that Hetzling almost certainly had protectors of his own. Either that, or he led a very charmed life."

"Maybe he was just lucky."

"I'm not aware of anyone in the east who could have had that much luck these past decades. Unless, of course, you occupied the top rungs of power. I think you'll find him very well informed on these matters, since he probably had a foot in both camps."

"That could also make him more dangerous."

"Perhaps. But he's still your best bet, as far as I can see, for learning something of the case from the inside. He's the only one likely to have the information, or parts of it, *and* still be willing to talk to you."

"And you think this case with the dissident deaths, with people like my friends, goes that high? Are you asking me to believe that they were part of some Stasi plot to bring down the East German state?"

"What you believe is not that important. You need to understand the broader history to gain some perspective. Otherwise I don't think you will understand what happened to your friends, or why the girl wants you out of it all."

The waiter sauntered over to take their orders. Buechler opted for a simple bowl of borscht, and Rosman chose the Chicken Kiev, boiled potatoes, and green salad. Buechler added an order for two glasses of Pilsner Urquell and two shots of vodka.

"Okay, I'll concede that much. But right now there are other issues as well," Rosman announced when the waiter had left.

Buechler's eyebrows arched over blue orbs that hardened to cobalt. "What do you mean?"

"Why are you telling me all this?" Rosman leaned over the table toward his companion. "Just what do you hope to accomplish?"

"Why must you ask that? I would have thought it was obvious."

"You see, that's the other aspect. I'm no longer sure whom I can trust. If anything, I've learned that I can never be sure about that. Not here, not now."

"Do you think our goals are really so different?"

"I'm not really sure anymore."

Buechler observed Rosman for several seconds before he spoke. He sat back in his chair, his legs crossed. "I can't help but compare your reaction now to the one I would have expected from your uncle."

Rosman's breath stuck in his throat. The waiter brought their drinks.

"He was a courageous man. And he was someone who did what he knew had to be done." Buechler leaned forward once more, almost touching Rosman's face. He spoke just above a whisper. "You're right, Herr Rosman. Trust is important, if difficult. You see, you missed that gentleman outside," Buechler said, gesturing with his head toward a man seated on a bench at the bus stop across the street from the restaurant. The individual was wearing a black leather jacket and pants, his head buried in the *Tagesspiegel*, a motorcycle helmet balanced on his lap.

Buechler sat back. "He's been with us since we fed the ducks. And there are other things you missed."

Rosman stared out the window, his mind running between the stranger outside and his family's history.

"It's also worth keeping in mind that there are plenty of intelligence people running around, officers and assets, many of them looking for work," Buechler continued. He drained his vodka, then leaned forward again, pointing his index finger at the middle of Rosman's forehead. "Any kind of work."

"Meaning?" Rosman asked. The smell of Buechler's breath made Rosman wince.

"Meaning lots of things. But most of all, it means you should be careful. In this town right now, you cannot be too careful about who your friends are. Or your enemies. So you are right about that."

Buechler sat back and threw his napkin on the table. "If you are going to question purpose and motive, you should begin with a man named Gracchus," Buechler hissed, "and the people he works with. There are even some over here. Probably some you know. But I am not one of them."

That name again. It nearly made his head spin, as the shadows and light mixed and faded. Rosman felt almost as if he had been transported in time and place to somewhere dangerous, someplace further east. At the same time, he struggled to understand and contain Buechler's emotional outburst.

"How do you…?"

"Yes, I know the man. I've known him for years." He paused, as though struggling to catch his breath. Buechler sipped his beer, winced, then continued. "I was wondering when it would come to this, when you, or someone like you, would finally return. And now that you're here, you've got to finish the damn thing."

Rosman swore under his breath and diverted his eyes to the bartender and waiter. He struggled to get his words out. The room was out of balance. He grabbed the edge of the table to steady himself. "What do you know of my uncle's death? Did you ever meet him? My parents?"

Buechler's eyes sparkled with memories. His lips hardly moved. "I was waiting on the other side of the border when your uncle was captured and shot by the Gestapo. He was making a run to Berlin to deliver some badly needed cash and instructions for a rendezvous with members of the Resistance inside the *Abwehr*." He nodded. "Yes, I know you're aware of who those men were. You must be if you want to live and work in this city. And if you want to become involved in matters such as these."

Rosman sat glued to his chair, his heart pounding. The room seemed to close in on him. He fought for breath. "That's all over now. My family lives in America. I'm an American, Herr Buechler. That war, that period is long gone." Even as he said it, though, Rosman knew it wasn't true.

Buechler's hands gripped the beer glass. Rosman thought it might break under the vise of the man's fingers.

"That is never over," the old German hissed. "I will never escape those years." A Mozart piano concerto drifted through the tables at the back of the restaurant. Voices buzzed in accompaniment. "And neither will you, Herr Rosman. Neither will you."

"How in the hell...?"

It was too late. Buechler had walked out the door without saying another word. His Urquell stood only half finished, its foam running down the sides of the glass to form a small puddle at its base.

CHAPTER 21

"John, could you come in here for a minute?"

Walking through the door at the U.S. Mission, Rosman changed direction and headed toward Friedlander's door. He followed his boss into his office.

"Where have you been?" Friedlander asked. "Having a long lunch with that Social Democratic contact of yours?"

"Buechler?"

"That's the one."

Rosman sat down in the sofa that lined the wall across from Friedlander's desk. His head felt light from the beer and vodka. "Yeah. I just got back. What's up?"

His boss was not alone. In twin armchairs to his left sat two unfamiliar army officers. To his right, at the table normally used for staff meetings, slumped a civilian Rosman had met only once before, at a reception at the Minister's house. His name was George Perry, the local CIA chief. Next to him was Al Fromer, the Regional Security Officer. He did not look happy.

Friedlander punched the intercom, then looked up to find his secretary hovering at the door. He told her to hold all calls.

Rosman shifted his weight on the sofa and suddenly found it difficult to swallow.

"I won't bother to introduce my other visitors, John. They already know who you are." Friedlander nodded toward the men in uniform. "George you know already."

Perry stepped to the door and tossed it shut. He raised his hand to Rosman, then sat back down.

"Is something wrong?" Rosman asked. His gaze bored through his boss.

"Actually, there is." Friedlander leaned back in his brown leather chair and glanced toward the door before returning his attention to Rosman. "These gentlemen are interested in learning about your travels in the east."

"What would they like to know?"

"How often you've traveled over there, and for how long?" This question came from an officer with oak leaves on his shoulders. So he outranked Kramer. The nameplate said Donnelson.

"Not very often. I've been over there 10, maybe 12 times. And the trips have taken place since the Wall opened. Why?"

"Could you give us the dates?" This one came from the other officer, whose nameplate said Avery. He was also a major.

"Sure." Rosman reached for a piece of paper lying on Friedlander's coffee table just in front of the sofa. He wrote down the dates of his visits to East Berlin, beginning with the trip to the Charite the night after the Wall first opened.

"And the names of the people you've been seeing, John," Perry said. Somehow his presence made it all seem official, ominous even.

"Of course." Rosman added the names Joanna Beierlich, Thomas Schmidt, and Erich Jens. He handed the sheet and pen to Avery, who glanced at the paper, then passed it to Donnelson.

"Is this all? Just to East Berlin?" Avery pressed.

Rosman rubbed his eyes. "That's right."

"What about Prague?" Fromer pressed.

"That was personal."

"Still...."

Rosman sat forward, his hands extended. "Here, I'll add those dates to the sheet. I spent the time with Ms. Beierlich."

Donnelson passed the paper to Rosman. He wrote down the time he had spent in Prague, adding the route he had taken there and back. No telling how much Harding had spilled. Then he handed the sheet back to Donnelson.

"Thanks, John," Perry interrupted.

"Sure. Anything to help."

"I'm glad you see it that way," Major Donnelson continued. He studied the sheet, which he attached to a clipboard resting on his lap. "But I have another question. Can you tell us why you never informed the RSO of your run-ins over there?"

Rosman shifted his weight once more, then straightened his tie. He pulled at the lapels of a blue blazer that was beginning to feel much too tight. "I didn't think it was necessary to bother him with every little mugging."

"Or shooting?" Perry interjected.

Rosman could feel his palms and forehead beginning to sweat. Rubbing his hands along the thighs of his pants, he looked from the officers to Perry and back again.

Friedlander had kept his eyes focused on an imaginary spot on his dark red carpet throughout the conversation. His fingers worked a rubber band around in a continuous circle. He looked up at Rosman. "Well, John?"

"There's not much to tell," Rosman began, his words catching in mid-throat. His mouth was so dry. "I tried to return some papers to a friend and I was jumped. I admit I was careless. There's a lot of that over there now. I should have insisted on a more open place to meet him."

The interrogators sat motionless. Both officers sat with their arms crossed and their backs stiff. Avery had his ankles crossed as well. Rosman wondered if there was special training for this sort of encounter, of it the posture just came naturally. Fromer's frown said he was still pissed. Perry, on the other hand, looked more relaxed, his thin frame slouched toward Rosman. Periodically, he removed his wire-rimmed glasses to rub his eyes. Even the light gray suit looked more comfortable, the unbuttoned shirt collar and loosened tie a stark contrast to the military bearing of the other two men.

"Who were you trying to give those papers to?" Perry asked.

"Erich Jens."

"And you never saw him?"

"No. And I haven't seen him since."

"What sort of papers were these, John?"

"They come from a notebook of Hermann Lamprecht. I acquired them from his sister, who asked me to pass them to Jens."

"What was on them?"

"I'm not sure. I couldn't read the writing." Rosman shrugged. "Sorry."

Donnelson interrupted in his drum-beat monotone. "Was anyone else with you?"

Rosman winced at the southern accent Donnelson had perfected, either through genetics or training. Somewhere in west Georgia or North Alabama, he guessed. "Just a woman I know."

Avery examined the piece of paper. "This Beierlich?" He peered at Rosman. "How well do you know her?"

"Well enough," Rosman answered. "She's active in the opposition movement over there. A member of New Forum, I believe."

Donnelson kept his hands busy writing everything down. "What's your best guess as to what was in these papers?"

"Personal notes, from what little I could tell."

"And there's been no one else involved?" Perry pressed.

"No," Rosman answered. His own voice sounded distant, as though he could hardly believe he was in the room.

Perry stood. "I think we have enough for now." He turned toward Rosman. "Do you still have those papers?"

"Not on me, no." Perry's eyes did not move. Their blue color had taken on a hard, steel-like edge. "But I can probably get them for you. Or at least a copy."

"When?"

"How soon do you need them?" Rosman countered.

"As soon as you can get them," Fromer returned.

"Today would be best, John. Tomorrow at the latest." Perry nodded and pivoted toward Friedlander. "Thanks, Jack."

Avery and Donnelson stood up and followed Perry out the door, rebuttoning the coats of their uniforms. They nodded to Friedlander on the way out.

Rosman leaned forward and ran his fingers through his hair. "What's this all about?"

Friedlander tossed the rubber band onto to his desk blotter. He threw his chest toward his desk until his elbows came to a rest in the middle of the blotter next to the rubber band. "It seems there's a leak somewhere in the Mission."

It took Rosman several seconds to respond. "You mean a

mole, don't you?"

The coffee cup Friedlander used to hold the pens on his desk swam before Rosman. He found his right hand massaging his chin.

"That's the look of it. It would probably be best if you stayed in West Berlin, John. At least for a few weeks."

Rosman rose from the sofa and walked over to Friedlander, who had picked up a cable and began to read. Rosman hooked his thumbs in his belt loops. "So that's it, eh?"

"What's that, John?"

"I'm suspected of being a commie spy? Shit, I'm probably the number one suspect."

Friedlander tossed his pencil on his desk and dropped the cable. "This is one of yours, John, and it's damn good."

"Which one is it?"

"The one about Berlin as the once and future capital of Germany. In fact, it's so good I have to ask myself why you're wasting time chasing chimeras on the other side of a wall." Friedlander's eyes burned through Rosman like well-aimed lasers. "And it's time it stopped, John. Right now."

Rosman straightened himself. "Am I the principal suspect?"

"Can you suggest someone more obvious?"

Friedlander picked up his pencil and returned to his paperwork. Rosman stormed out the door.

When he re-entered his office, the pictures on the wall, the items on his desk, all of it seemed lost in a haze. Rosman stumbled toward his desk. It took another 10, maybe 20, seconds before he found Bill Harding, his large frame settled at an uncomfortable angle on the edge of the desk.

"You're lucky I'm not the RSO, or one of the Marines."

"Why?" Rosman asked. He stepped behind the desk and started to rearrange his papers.

Harding tossed his head back toward the computer screen behind Rosman's desk. "You left your Wang logged on. That's a security violation. I stuck around in case anyone came by to keep you from being written up."

"Thanks, Bill." Rosman fell into his chair. "Although it looks like they're going to get me by the Wang sooner or later anyway."

"How bad is it?"

"Oh, not too bad. They just think I'm a Soviet spy."

"What? Who's 'they'?"

"The Army and the CIA. For starters. And maybe Friedlander. He's pretty tight-lipped, though."

Harding dropped into a chair next to Rosman's desk. "Do they have any proof? I mean, you're not, are you?"

Rosman frowned at his friend. "Thanks for the vote of confidence, ol' buddy. Apparently, they're intrigued by my trips to the east."

"It's a good thing you had Kramer check into your friends. Has he found anything else?"

"Yes, and the news isn't good. It seems most of them are tainted one way or another."

Harding shifted uncomfortably, then stood up. "Shit, John. That can't help much. Hopefully, Kramer can speak up for you. I'll let him know what's up."

"Hopefully," Rosman muttered, as Harding strolled out the door.

Rosman leaned back in his chair. He breathed deeply for about a minute waiting for his heart to slow. Then his right foot pulled open the bottom drawer of his desk. He bent down and fingered Lamprecht's notes and the copy he had made. Fuck Perry, he thought. He gets these when I'm ready. And I'm not ready yet.

Shoving the drawer shut, Rosman swung around to look at his computer screen. He couldn't be sure. This had been such a hectic, disturbing day. And he had so much on his mind now. But if he were a betting man, Rosman would have placed an easy five down that when he left to meet Buechler, he had logged off his computer.

CHAPTER 22

Rosman did not see anyone he recognized on his way home. No East Germans clad in black leather or polyester. Not even Mr. Motorcycle Man from the bus stop in Charlottenburg. He wondered if he should start looking for Americans as well. *This is great,* he thought, *just fucking great.*

His gaze caught an advertisement pasted to the back of the glass booth at the bus stop where Clayallee met Koenigen Louise Strasse. The poster promoted "West" cigarettes, and it had to be new. He did not remember having seen it before, and he walked this route home every night. The scene included a modish, well-dressed woman with deep cleavage and long legs extending from a set of very skimpy shorts. She stood next to a shorter, plump man dressed as a poor imitation of Elvis, jumpsuit and all. "Test the West," the ad proclaimed. Just who is testing whom, he wondered.

As he rounded the corner, Rosman saw him. He could not mistake the long, unkept gray hair, or the rhythmic hand movements the man made as he tried to brush it back into place behind his ears. Rosman walked carefully down Koenigen Louise, crossed the boulevard and turned onto Spechtstrasse, a block before his own street. He snuck past the two-story houses and high hedges along Im Dol, then cut through Wachtelstrasse. At the corner with Vogelsang, he crept past a stone gate post, then dodged among the alternate rows of birch trees that ran between the lanes of blacktop. He took up his final post at a bench in the middle of the park in front of his house, his body at an angle to the car to make recognition as difficult as possible.

Mr. Gray Hair sat alone and silent in a dirty white Trabant directly across the street from Rosman's house. He must have thought the trees would cover him from prying eyes and daylight. For 15, maybe 20 minutes, he just sat there, staring at Rosman's house. Occasionally, his head turned, searching the street ahead and behind him. Finally, he climbed out to stretch—Gray Hair was one tall son-of-a-bitch—returned to the car and started the engine. It kicked with a cough and a stutter, and then puttputted down the street.

Rosman jumped up and ran to his own battered Mercedes, parked in the driveway. Gray Hair had driven off in the direction of Clayallee, probably toward Potsdam, the quickest route to the east. Rosman raced around the corner of Koenigen Louise, but then slowed to avoid drawing attention to himself.

There it was. Not the only Trabant on the road, but the 'P' license plate rolling down Clayallee made it unmistakable. The erect figure at the wheel was another giveaway. Rosman checked the street behind him for any cars following the same route. Nothing. No one else, it appeared, was interested.

The gray head did not move to either side. Only when he got to the central square in the suburb of Zehlendorf did the thin, unruly mop check the traffic and swerve to the right before turning onto the road to Potsdam. Then the same purposeful lack of movement returned until the Trabant passed through the border control at Glienicke Bridge, now no more than a formality. After plodding for several more miles through once-prosperous neighborhoods, he pulled up in front of a dirty white, almost brown, two-story stucco house on the outskirts of Potsdam.

Rosman parked about 50 feet down the road and waited. Again, he could see no sign of anyone else. No indication that they had company.

Rosman had never known such anxiety, such indecision. He tapped his fingers on the steering wheel, and ran his hands over the upholstery. Seconds seemed to crawl past. Finally, he leaped out of the car and trotted up the pathway. His heart was thundering. His chest actually hurt from the pressure. His eyes were glassy and the numbers 1 and 6 blurry on their screw mounts on the green door. Rosman rang the bell.

Nothing.

He rang again.

"*Ja.*" It came from inside the house. "*Moment, bitte.*"

The door opened toward a tall middle-aged man, casually dressed in a light blue turtleneck and black slacks. Rosman recognized him immediately, the same gray strands falling across a forehead in deep folds of white skin.

"What do you want?"

"May I come in?" Rosman leaned against the doorframe.

"What do you want here?" The man repeated. His wide eyes betrayed his fear, their whites clear against the pale skin.

"Excuse me."

Rosman pushed past him and strode into a living room about half the size of his own. It was dominated by a television set running an evening news program. The announcer was reading a report on independence demonstrations in the Baltic states.

Rosman seized a spot in the middle of the room and turned to face his unwilling host. "I don't think it's wise for me to be left standing on your front step. Someone might be watching." Rosman enjoyed the look of fear. He enjoyed seeing uncertainty and confusion in the face of another for a change.

"I...I'm not sure."

"I won't bother to introduce myself. You know who I am." Rosman sank into an armchair in front of the television. The light green material was very comfortable, and Rosman threw one leg over the other while he leaned back.

"Interesting stuff going on over there." Rosman tossed his head in the direction of the sound bite from the anchorman.

Gray Hair glanced at the television but said nothing.

"But I don't know who you are," Rosman pressed, "nor what your part is in all this."

"I...I don't understand. My part in what?"

"Yes, you do. You understand perfectly. And stop stammering, goddammit."

Rosman jerked himself around when he heard someone enter the room from the kitchen at his back. It was a petite woman somewhere in her forties with short brown hair. She was dressed sharply in a white cardigan and navy blue shirt that matched a mid-calf, blue plaid skirt. She dried her hands with a checkered kitchen towel and eyed her husband with a glare that bordered on contempt.

"He must have followed you home. Now you must tell him. Otherwise there is no way out of this business." She nodded in the direction of the television. "For God's sake, Wilhelm, listen!"

She returned to the kitchen. Wilhelm walked with slow, uncertain steps and collapsed into a chair across from Rosman.

"My name is Wilhelm Meyer. I am a pastor at St. Luke's Evangelical Church in Potsdam." His head tilted slightly, almost imperceptibly, toward the street. A pillar of sunlight shone through the window at his back, cut across Meyer's legs, then ran to ground in front of the television set. "It's not far from here."

"Go on."

"There is no more. Nothing that I can say, nothing more for me to tell you."

"What about a man named Gracchus?"

Meyer did not answer. He had been staring at the floor, but now turned his gaze toward the kitchen.

"How well do you know him?" Rosman pressed.

His face did not move from the kitchen. "Why do you ask?"

Rosman leaned forward and tapped Meyer's knee. "Oh, stop the goddamn game. Why do you think I followed you here? Why else would you be shadowing me? I just wonder why the hell he pulled you into it."

Meyer sat motionless and silent.

"Look, your wife is correct." Rosman paused. "There's no future to Gracchus and his game. He's playing his last desperate bid. Don't let him drag you down with the rest."

The man's hands worked the arms of the chair. "I don't know what you are talking about. We are free to travel as we like now. I have many friends in Dahlem. People I have met through my work in the Consistory."

Rosman threw himself against the cushions. "Cut the crap, pastor. It's no use denying it any more. What can you tell me about the death of Hermann Lamprecht? About the death of a lad from Dresden named Hans Kroehler?"

Meyer raised his head slowly. "Do you mean the young dissidents?"

Rosman sighed and nodded.

"I'm not sure I can help you," Meyer said.

"Look, I know that the Stasi is behind all this. So, I'm assuming you're tied up with those creeps, which means you're implicated in anything that happened to the dissidents. You know damn well that you do not want that kind of mess following you into the new Germany. Not the way things are changing here."

His lip quivering, Meyer stared at Rosman. He brushed another stray lock back behind his ear.

Rosman pressed on, hissing the words between clenched teeth. "And unless you cooperate with me, I will make damn sure that the right people on my side of the Wall know about your involvement in this."

"What makes you think I won't call the police in? Right now, in fact?" Meyer countered.

The woman breezed into the room as Meyer finished speaking, carrying a tray with a pot of coffee, three cups and saucers, a sugar bowl and a pint-sized silver container of cream. Rosman was surprised to see the blue and white Meissen china, which looked out of place in a house just a few steps above a bungalow. Meyer rubbed his hands on his pants leg, then lifted a cup and saucer from the tray. The woman placed a set on the coffee table in front of Rosman and filled his cup.

"Please, gentlemen. There is no need for this sort of confrontation. We all want the same thing," she said, pronouncing her words carefully.

"Which is?" Rosman inquired.

"Freedom," she stated, simply.

"From what?" Rosman pressed.

Meyer did not say a word, apparently stunned by his wife's intervention.

"From want, from need," she answered.

Rosman sipped his coffee. The woman quickly topped off Rosman's cup. Steam poured from the open lip and drifted toward the ceiling.

"From outside forces that compel us to do things against our will," she continued. "From fear." She looked directly at her husband.

"Why did you follow me to Prague?" Rosman asked, turning toward Meyer.

Meyer moved to pick up his cup, but fumbled it, spilling what was left across the glass top of his table. "I'm sorry." He dabbed at the puddle with his napkin. "I was in Prague recently for my Consistory, but I do not recall seeing you there."

Rosman studied the mess. "Alright. I have a more important question."

"Yes?" Meyer's eyes shifted from his wife to Rosman.

"Why would the Stasi put someone like you onto me? As I said, you're clearly not a professional. You left a trail any idiot could follow. It's almost as though they wanted me to find you."

Rosman thought he saw Meyer's hand shake.

"But I'll take the chance that you're just bait. How many other ways are they using you?"

"You had better leave now." Meyer's voice was shaking as well. "There are dangerous people over here that do not care for you or your work."

Rosman started to rise from his seat, but thought better of it when he saw Meyer's wife staring at him. "Hell, Pastor, I already know that much."

Meyer refilled his cup and took a sip.

"And I know that they also see me as a threat," Rosman continued.

"Then you must determine why."

Rosman turned toward the sound of the woman's voice.

"Why what?"

"Why you are a threat." She placed her cup on the tray as she said this and sat back in her chair. Rosman felt stupid for asking. He realized now she had been observing his every movement, weighing his every word. He separated his cup from its saucer and took another slow sip.

"That's where I was hoping he could help."

"It won't do any good. It would be best for us all if you would simply withdraw from this affair," Meyer said. "Surrender what you have."

"And what do I have that's so valuable?"

"The notes, the files. You know that as well as I."

Rosman turned back toward Meyer. "Too late for that, Pastor. Too many good people have died to give up that easily." Rosman's head shook as with the breeze of a new thought. "No, wait. I've got a better idea. How would you like to work for me?"

"What are you saying?"

"Look, Pastor, I'm going to take a guess here, but I bet you've been informing on the dissidents. Probably for years. But there's two problems with that. One, if I've figured this out, how long will it take others to do the same? So you can start to help yourself by helping me."

Rosman paused to see if there was any reaction from his host. The man just sat there, his face pale and motionless. Rosman pressed on.

"Two, you should help me because you have to. You're expendable now. They don't need your kind of information and access anymore." Rosman paused, glancing out the window. Then his gaze drifted back to Meyer. "Why do you think Gracchus put you onto me? Like I said, Pastor, you're bait. That's all you're good for anymore. How much longer before they throw you away, like the others?"

"Please." Meyer's lips quivered. "Do not try to contact me again. It will end badly for both of us. I've simply tried to act out my part. I don't plan to report anything more."

Rosman stepped over to Meyer's chair and leaned forward, his hands pressing down on the soft green fabric that covered its arms.

"That's not good enough. Not anymore. You'll have to face it. We're in this together."

Rosman paused, glancing at the wife. "Besides, I've got trouble of my own, and I'm tired of being jerked around by you people. If you're going to follow me to my house and jeopardize my life and career, you're going to start giving me some of the information I need. Call your friends, and let's talk again tomorrow."

Rosman lifted himself from the chair, holding the first three fingers on his right hand in front of Meyer's face.

"I've got three questions, and I want three answers. What did Hans have that cost him his life?" The first finger dropped. "What did Lamprecht find that got him killed?" A second fell. "And what happened to Jens?"

The entire fist disappeared in Rosman's pocket. He spun around and marched to the door. The woman's voice followed at his heels.

"Where did you learn your German?"

Rosman whirled around. Her light brown eyes held a hint of mystery. "I spoke it at home."

"You are probably familiar with German literature, then. Do you know Goethe?"

"Somewhat. I studied a few of his poems at school."

She set her cup on the table. "Good. Great literature lifts one's soul. Don't you agree?"

"Sometimes," he conceded. "But it depends on how it's used these days."

"Yes, it would be nice if the world could find a more practical use for it in these troubled times," she added, following him to the doorway. "But I especially like Goethe and his epic poem *Faust*. I believe it helps us navigate our way through troubled times like these and determine the real truth from the chaos all around."

She reached around Rosman and pulled open the door. Her body carried a hint of lemon that drifted in the small foyer. When he looked at her face again, Rosman saw two sparkling eyes set above a wry smile. Without another word, or sign of movement on her small, cheerful face, Meyer's wife shut the door quietly but firmly against Rosman and the outside world.

Rosman dashed down the walk and scurried to the car, his head twisting to the right and left, searching for some sign of an unwelcome presence. Goethe? That was a helluva way to end a conversation. Was she just being polite? Or was she the real brains in the house?

As he pulled away from the curb, Rosman glanced down the street through his rear view mirror. Meyer's wife was standing at the picture window by the front door, her eyes following Rosman's old 280SL along the road to the Glienicke bridge.

Three blocks down the road, a light brown BMW slid into traffic behind him. A block later, a yellow Wartburg turned the corner and got into line behind the BMW.

Rosman slammed his fist against the dashboard. "Shit," he swore. He hadn't noticed either car earlier.

"Are you going to help him, Wilhelm?" Meyer's wife asked. She turned away from the window.

Nora ambled over to the sofa, reclaimed her seat and poured herself a fresh cup of coffee. The evening news broadcast was repeating the day's soccer scores. After that, a station editorial refuted Western charges that the East Germans had been doping their Olympic athletes.

"How can I?" he whined. "They'll kill me."

"Wilhelm," she scoffed, stirring in a spoonful of sugar. "I hardly believe you're that important. Nor is he," she motioned toward the street with her hand, "for that matter."

"Don't be so sure, dear. There are already three dead." He turned to face her. "Three that we know of."

"So then this Jens person is dead as well?" She folded her arms and sat back.

His head fell. "Yes, he died at Karlshorst some days ago."

"Oh, Wilhelm. You must do something."

Meyer picked himself out of his chair and strode to the television set. He flicked the news off, then spun to face his wife. He shuffled over to her seat, knelt before her, and took her hand. "I don't see why they'd keep the American alive. Not once they get what they wanted."

"Perhaps that's all the more reason to help him."

"To save him?"

"I wasn't thinking of him. You'll be next, you know."

Meyer rose from his chair and approached the telephone sitting on a dresser table near the entrance to the hallway. The television droned on about efforts to improve the border crossing into

Poland at Frankfurt an der Oder. Nora's eyes held her husband in a fixed stare, as though willing him to speak, to make a decision. He spun the dial and waited. His own eyes remained glued to the numbers that ringed the center of the apparatus, the receiver stuck to his ear. He stood with his back to his wife.

"Hello? Schmidt, is that you?" A pause. "It's Meyer. Wilhelm Meyer from Potsdam."

Schmidt must have been agitated, because his voice carried from the receiver to the sofa with a burst of static.

"Christ, what do you want? Why are calling me here?"

"I need your help. The American was here. He's pressing me. I need something to get him off my back."

"Leave me out of it, Pastor."

"Schmidt, please. You're the only one I can turn to now. You must help me."

Another pause. Had Schmidt hung up?

"Alright, alright. There's a demonstration planned for this evening at the Stasi headquarters downtown. Be there."

"What sort of demonstration? Schmidt, that sounds danger-ous."

"Just be there."

He had hung up. Meyer dropped the receiver, then looked at his wife. Nora's lower lip was trapped between her teeth. She nodded.

CHAPTER 23

The first stone smashed against the glass doors around five o'clock on that same evening. Others flew in quick succession. The double panel glass withstood the onslaught for a few minutes only. The crowd roared its approval, then surged forward through the entrance.

The young man beside Meyer thrust his fist into the air, and a full-throated bellow burst from his lips. "Forward, comrades." The cry echoed among his companions. Meyer was shocked to hear his own voice join the chorus, swept along toward the broken barrier by the sea of emotion and humanity.

The crowd had been gathering in numbers and noise since mid-afternoon. At first, it was primarily students and dissidents, inspired by Leipzig and Erfurt, where citizens' committees had seized control of the local Stasi headquarters. Now, others from all over East Berlin were joining. And they were ready to storm their own Bastille, the main headquarters at Normannenstrasse.

Meyer paused in the hallway just inside the main entrance. The building was apparently empty. Already, several protesters were throwing furniture against the walls and front windows. Two of the windows shattered, the glass crashing to the floor in large jagged fragments. The furniture, however, was of a sturdier make. Most of it, anyway. Meyer saw a coffee table leaning at an angle against a far wall, its four legs separated from the two halves of its top.

His head whipping back and forth, Meyer searched for a familiar face. His breathing was ragged and hurried. People were drifting off down various pathways, along darkened corridors. Off on their own missions of revenge. He was sure Schmidt would be among them. If he didn't show, there would be others. But he needed information, and he needed it quickly. Something more to help the American. Something more than what he alone could give. Perhaps together they could tell if the trap had been set.

Someone tugged at his sleeve. "This way. Quickly."

A tall, bearded fellow with bushy brown hair was waving the crowd toward a set of stairs.

Other took up the cry. "Yes! To the cellars!" Voices bellowed in a mob's chorus.

Most of the crowd followed their lead, and once again Meyer was swept along by the mob's direction and energy. He stumbled down the final three steps and saved himself from falling at the foot of the crowd by grabbing onto the railing and swinging his body to the left and up against the wall. The concrete and tile slammed against his back. Meyer momentarily lost his breath.

"Look at that!"

"Jesus, I've never seen so much wine."

"Look at the champagne. And the seafood!"

A small crowd of perhaps a dozen danced in front of the wine racks and freezers stocked with lobster, shrimp, crab, and floun-der—an array of seafood Meyer had never seen before. Items he could afford only for special occasions. Like New Year's or May Day. Or Nora's birthday.

"My God! Look at the selection of Bordeaux."

Meyer grabbed an estate-bottled red and stuffed it into an inside pocket in the lining of his beige raincoat. He rammed another down the outside pocket on the other side. At least he had balance.

"Help yourself, comrade. We've earned it."

It was the bearded Rasputin, the long brown hair falling in ringlets to his shoulders. Where had he seen this man before? Would he know where Schmidt was? The others?

"Here. Have some champagne."

The man thrust an open bottle at Meyer's chest. Several mouthfuls sloshed onto Meyer's shirtfront. The man's face was flush with an the inebriation of alcohol and triumph, the eyes wide and glowing red, the yellow teeth framed by wisps of light brown facial hair.

"Take it. I've got more."

The man held his coat open, a bottle stuck in a pocket on either side. He let go of his lapels, sweeping his arm around the room. "It's all ours now. And look over here. More delicacies!"

He led Meyer down the hall to another room away from the crowd. "There's some really valuable stuff in here."

Meyer strolled into the dark room and groped for a light switch. "I can't see a thing."

The first blow struck Meyer just behind the ear. A paralyzing pain shot through the back of his skull and out the front from temple to temple. A dull ringing sound from somewhere in the back of his brain smothered the noise drifting in from the hallway.

"Oh Jesus. Why have...?" The second stroke met Meyer straight across the back of his skull. As he fell, Meyer took another blow at the base of his neck, just above the spine.

Meyer tumbled to the floor. He wanted desperately to get back up, to flee from the room. Anything to escape this horrible pounding. His head throbbed as if it would explode.

But his arms and legs no longer responded.

He thought of Nora. He wanted her there. But the room's darkness crept into his soul and swept Meyer away.

CHAPTER 24

This had to be the coldest November he had experienced. Especially at work. Rosman had never been so uncomfortable, living in a professional quarantine where he avoided his boss and colleagues. Today's setting certainly didn't help. He sat alone outside the main execution chamber at the Ploetzensee Memorial, the site of the final chapter in the most famous of several assassination attempts against Hitler. Rosman stared at the memorial plaque next to the entrance, reading through the words line-by-line.

He had read it all before, and his parents had lectured on it so often he could probably recite the entire litany by heart. Hitler, in a fit of manic revenge, had ordered the last surviving members of the plot to assassinate him hung with piano wire and the entire scene recorded on film. To honor their memory, the West German government had turned the place of execution into a memorial to those men and all their comrades in the Resistance.

But Rosman did not enter the building. He had seen the exhibit and others like it before. He was already familiar with the long list of Nazi crimes. He did not need to be reminded. Not today. Perhaps it had something to do with his family history. Perhaps he had a weak stomach. At any rate, he needed to survey the crowd while he waited for Meyer. So he stayed on the bench.

But it was not Meyer who came. Instead, the attractive, diminutive lady he had seen at Meyer's house approached Rosman. She crept along, her upper body bent slightly forward. Then she nodded briefly, a slight tilt of the neck and forehead that Rosman almost missed.

"Hello, Mr. Rosman." She took a seat next to him.

He half-turned in her direction and studied the woman. With

her closely cropped, short brown hair, the thin, erect body hidden behind a pleated woolen skirt and bright yellow jacket, Rosman guessed she was definitely no more than fifty. Probably in her late forties. She had displayed greater certainty, greater strength at the pastor's house. Was it the unfamiliar territory?

She searched the crowd before addressing Rosman. "My name is Nora Meyer."

"Where is your husband?"

"He could not come today. But he wanted you to have this." She handed Rosman a slip of paper. "He tried to get you more...."

She stopped, tears welling at the edges of her eyes. It took her a minute to compose herself. "Perhaps it will shed new light on things and give you some of the information you requested."

She looked down at her hands as she rubbed them together before continuing. "He also said he hoped it explained some of the people you're dealing with."

Rosman opened the piece of paper that had been folded over twice to form a neat 4" x 4" square. On it was written the name of Erich Jens, a date, a place, and a few lines of German poetry. The date was November 19, 1989. The place name was Karlshorst. Rosman recognized the verse from a passage in Goethe's epic poem, *Faust*.

> "Zwei Seele wohnen, ach! in meiner Brust,
> Die eine will sich von der andern trennen;
> Die eine haelt, in derber Liebeslust,
> Sich an die Welt mit klaemmernden Organen;
> Die andre hebt gewaltsam sich vom Dust
> Zu den Gefilden hoher Ahnen."

Rosman understood the German. He remembered the English too.

> "Alas, Two souls live within my breast,
> The one wants to separate from the other;
> The one holds, with coarse Love's lust,
> to this world with all its senses;
> The other struggles from the dust
> to the domains of high ancestry."

The lines of Goethe's poetry was followed by two words, "Vir-gib uns." Forgive us, it said. At least now he knew was pretty certain that Jens was dead. But what were the lines from Faust supposed to mean?

Rosman was surprised to see Nora Meyer still there. She had sat by his side as he read the message. The tears had returned and now ran in small streams down the sides of her face.

Rosman refolded the paper along the original creases and placed it in his breast pocket. "Was there anything else? Another message? Is there something I should see in the poetry?"

She did not answer.

"I will have to meet with your husband again. How can I contact him?" He bent down and peered into her face. "Or should it be you?"

Rosman received only a blank stare from a face that looked like it had been chiselled in ivory, the twin blue eyes looking through him like beaded jewels in tiny pools.

"Wilhelm won't be able to meet you again," she whispered.

Rosman's lips were dry, his tongue like cardboard in a mouth of sand. He tried to wet his lips. "Is something wrong?"

The blue beads softened slightly; the ivory gained some color, a touch of pink. "You don't know then, do you?"

Rosman tried to swallow. "Know what?"

The woman drew herself up to her full length, taking on strength as she spoke, her resolution returning. "My husband is dead." She stood up, towering over Rosman. "He was beaten to death at the Stasi headquarters last night."

Rosman looked away from her toward the memorial entrance. A group of tourists came out of the building, several of the women holding handkerchiefs in front of their eyes. His heart pounded against the front of his chest. Air seemed to catch in his throat. He looked at Nora Meyer. "What happened?"

"The authorities claim it was some thugs involved in the break-in." She searched the crowd milling around them, and then turned her eyes on Rosman. They burned right through him. "Do you believe that?" she asked.

Rosman studied her face, the features melting together as she began to cry. "No." He took her hand. "I'm so sorry."

She let out a heavy sigh. "Neither do I. Just remember who you are dealing with. There are others around Gracchus, but he is your main enemy. He is relentless. Think about the poem. It should explain the people involved. They have not given up. Wilhelm told me a little of what he knew last night. They have plans for after, and your material threatens those plans."

"I see."

"There is also a Russian. A man named Preselnikov."

"What does he do?"

"He's at their embassy...."

The crowd of tourists drew closer, passing directly in front of Rosman and Mrs. Meyer. She hesitated, waiting for the group to pass. One of them, an older gentleman rubbing his moist red eyes, bumped Nora Meyer. He apologized, bracing himself with one hand against her back and the other around her arm. Her eyes stayed with the man until he disappeared around the side of the museum with the others.

Nora turned and leaned heavily against Rosman. She shuddered. Then her eyelids fell shut, and her head bent forward as in sleep. Her small body seemed to weigh a ton.

"Mrs. Meyer?"

Rosman grabbed her shoulders. He set her as gently as possible against the back of the bench, then felt her wrist. The arm hung limp. He found no pulse. Rosman raised her eyelids with his thumb and saw only pale brown pupils, frozen to a distant, unseeing light.

His head jerked around. No one was paying any attention to them. They were hidden among the crowd, like two ordinary tourists. Just what Rosman had intended. He knelt down, zipped her jacket, and propped the lifeless form against the corner of the bench. Then Rosman jumped up and searched for the group of tourists that had wandered by. He found them near their bus at the edge of the parking lot. But the clumsy assassin had disappeared.

Rosman trotted toward his car. Halfway there, he broke into a run. He glanced in every direction to see if anyone was following him. When he reached the pay phone at the edge of the parking lot he was out of breath. His fingers were trembling. Coins clattered against the pavement.

"Goddammit!" He looked around. No one. "Shit, shit, shit!"

It took Rosman three tries to dial the emergency number. Then he called Hetzling.

When he got to his car, Rosman heard the scream from the direction of the memorial. The gravel rattled against his undercarriage and the sides of other cars around him as he spun his wheels and raced from the parking lot.

CHAPTER 25

Hetzling had told Rosman to meet him at the cafe "Zum Goldenen Baer." It stood at the southwest corner of the Platz der Akademie, or Gendarmenplatz, as it had been known before the war, across from the French Cathedral. The dark panelling, Victorian chandeliers, small mahogany tables and wide array of brandies, cognacs and whiskies lining the three shelves behind the bar spoke of style and sophistication. A large wall-length mirror in an elaborate bronze frame punctuated the scene. Rosman assumed that a drink here must have been well beyond the reach of the average East German.

The cafe threw Rosman into a bygone era, reminding him of those photographs he had seen of Berlin before the war, during its heyday as an imperial capital and in the effervescent years of the Weimar Republic. Picture albums from Berlin's past were very popular in the city now, and a shot of the Golden Bear's interior would fit in nicely with those period photographs. It was almost as though the bar and its patrons were searching for a sense of the city's history, a part of the Berlin and Germany that had disappeared beneath the rubble in 1945. Or even earlier, in 1933 under the debris of Nazi Germany.

The scent was newer than that, though. Rosman expected something musty, a smell from the past heavy with memories and dust, or from a history hidden somewhere among the narrow alleyways of a sterile city rebuilt on the ruins of what was once Europe's leading metropolis. Instead, a hint of wintergreen drifted into the lounge from the restroom at his back.

Rosman arrived before Hetzling and chose a table near the back. He wanted to watch the door. After about five minutes and one cup of coffee, Hetzling entered. He hesitated a moment, searching the cafe as his eyes adjusted to the dark interior. When he located Rosman in the Bear's deeper reaches, Hetzling strolled to the table and slid into a chair across from Rosman. He didn't look at all concerned about covering his own back. Hetzling slipped from his light brown overcoat, revealing a comfortable-looking red sweater and beige corduroy slacks, before settling back against the spokes of his chair.

"Shall we order more coffee?" Hetzling asked, nodding at Rosman's empty cup. "You look like you could use some more."

"How so?"

"You're as white as one of our Bavarian snows. Have you been talking to Buechler lately? He can have that kind of effect on people."

"A lot's been happening lately."

"You said you had something urgent to discuss with me. A matter of life or death." Hetzling laughed. "I could hear you panting over the telephone."

"I'd been running."

Hetzling surveyed the room. Then his gaze returned to Rosman. He leaned forward. "I have to confess that I asked myself why I should bother to come. What do you have that could possibly interest me?" He looked at Rosman's upraised arm. "Regular coffee, please."

"Thanks anyway for coming."

A smile snuck through the pale streaks of afternoon light that snaked in from the windows. "I've always been a curious man."

Rosman leaned closer. The man's eyes were a dark, opaque brown that hinted at mysteries untold. Rosman ran his fingers through his hair. He spoke just above a whisper. "So I've heard. A careful one, too. You'll need that now."

Hetzling's eyebrows arched. And then he laughed, lightly at first. A long, guttural bark followed. "I'm not in any danger. And just how could you help me, if I was?"

"If you're not aware of it, then you're a fool. Five people are already dead, Hetzling. And if you know any of them, you may be next."

"Why is that?"

"Because you're expendable. Especially now."

Hetzling's upper lip curled.

"They don't need you to cover their runs anymore." Rosman laughed. "And you probably know far too much."

Hetzling stared into his empty coffee cup. "Perhaps."

"And perhaps ten minutes of your time today will buy you a longer life, Hetzling."

"And what do you want in return?"

"Some information."

"About what?"

"Everything. The networks, how you used the buy-outs, Moscow's interest and role."

"Why should I?"

"It may save others."

"Others? Like you?"

"That's right. Me too."

"At my age I need something more immediate."

"I'll do what I can to bring you in, over to our side. We're going to win, you know." Rosman hesitated just a moment. "Hell, we have already."

Hetzling sat back in his chair, his body slanted to the side. He studied the floor. Shifting back toward Rosman, he drumrolled his fingers on the tabletop, then nodded.

"We shall see. Let's talk."

"First, tell me about your relationship with Buechler."

"Why? Don't you trust him anymore?"

"I don't trust anyone right now. What's his interest in all this?"

Hetzling's hand waved at nothing in particular. "Oh, hell. He's just an observer. Sometimes a clever, even a dangerous one. But he carries a lot of baggage. He was more idealistic than most, but not as crafty as some. You needn't have anything to fear from him."

"He said it would help if I understood the fall of your regime."

Hetzling snorted. "You should have been at the party's inquest."

"Inquest? You mean like a trial?"

"No, not a trial. But many of us who held office had to appear before an inquest to explain our actions and policies."

"What were they after?"

"Basically, they wanted to know how we could have let things deteriorate so badly. People continue to be surprised at how poorly off we are after all the propaganda about our success in building German socialism. We were supposed to be the world's tenth leading industrial power, you know."

Rosman poured coffee for both of them from the two new canisters the waitress deposited on their table with typical Berlin abruptness. Apparently, she didn't like being disturbed. "Well? What was your excuse?"

"From my vantage, the story seems so surreal."

"How so?"

"In how paralyzed the top echelons of power were in the face of so much discontent," Hetzling said.

"And why was that?"

"I think Honecker bears a great deal of blame. He refused to listen to any criticism of the state we had built, or of the regime's policies. He was a man who had gotten out of touch with reality. His frame of reference was Nazi Germany, or the Weimar Republic, not the Europe of today."

"But weren't Honecker's illusions fostered and pampered?"

Hetzling nodded as he poured his coffee. "As with so many systems, including yours, council tends to shield those in power and those closest to it."

Hetzling stopped, his forehead wrinkled as though he was trying to grasp some difficult concept. "How do you say it in your country? 'Don't rock the ship'?"

"Pretty close."

Hetzling's eyes returned to his coffee cup while he finished pouring. He replaced the canister, then looked up to see Rosman's sceptical face. Hetzling thrust his hand forward, pointing a short, stubby index finger at Rosman. "But not everyone was like that. I, for one, certainly never pampered those fools."

"Were there others like you? Were there others willing to protest, to do anything about it?"

"Of course there were. But the word never got to the top."

"So, how did Honecker fall?" Rosman asked.

Hetzling was silent. He poured, then blended the cream with slow even strokes, moving his hand first clockwise, then counter-clockwise. Finally, he stopped, put down the spoon, emitted a sigh, and took a long sip from his cup. When he replaced it on the saucer, Hetzling looked Rosman in the eye.

"Now we get to the interesting part, eh? This will make your story even more fascinating."

"Our story," Rosman corrected. Hetzling shrugged, stirring his coffee. "That was in October, wasn't it?" Rosman continued. "The eighteenth. Why did you wait so long?"

"Do you really think it's that easy to remove the head of state and party? Many of us still believed that it was necessary to have a system that entrusted that much power to one man, or, in some cases, a group of men. It's called democratic centralism."

"Yeah, I know what it's called. I know the history, too." Ros-man shook his head. "Communism in eastern Europe collapsed under the weight of its own inherent contradictions. It was the greatest Hegelian joke of all, and it was on you."

Hetzling's head shot up, his eyes blazing. His voice rose, and his lips trembled. "Don't lecture me, you little prick. My life was spent in the service of the Party and its ideals."

Rosman retreated into his chair, surveying the bar. He did not want to attract any attention. "We're getting away from our story."

Hetzling did not seem to hear. "That's how we finally worked up the courage to get rid of Honecker. We were finally able to con-vince others of the damage he was doing to our cause."

Hetzling's hands gripped the coffee mug so tightly, Rosman feared for the china. "So, when did you finally see the light? Who was in the plot to dump the old man?'

Hetzling relaxed in his chair. "Why are you so interested in that?" His eyes twinkled with mischief.

"It matters because it may lie at the heart of this story. It's con-nected to those deaths, isn't it?"

Hetzling sat quietly as he repeated his coffee pouring ritual. The lines of his face deepened with the frown that now covered his broad features. "Remind me. Just who has died? And who do you think killed them?"

"A couple of East German dissidents. Students, actually. And now a Lutheran pastor and his wife."

"Why were they killed?"

"To silence them." Rosman studied Hetzling, whose hand played with the ring on the end of his cup. "And to keep me and others from finding their secret."

"I think you're confused. Your focus is off."

"Humor me."

Hetzling sat in silence for a moment. "Well, Mielke and Stoph were in on it."

Rosman shook is head in disbelief. "But those guys were the quintessential hard-liners." He had seen a picture of Mielke recently in the newspaper. The man had been arrested and, as part of his defense, was playing the senile idiot, someone who no longer remembered the days just gone by and the power and responsibility he once carried. He cut a pathetic figure lying on his prison cot, wrapped in an old overcoat, wearing his hat, and staring numbly at the ceiling.

"Oh, they just came along at the end. The actual plotting had been going on for weeks. Push came to shove in the days leading up to the meeting on the eighteenth." He sipped. "You were right about the date, incidentally."

"Why then?"

"It was clear that Honecker could not even comprehend the popular uprising. And there were others. Lorenz, for example, was in on it."

"Who?"

"Lorenz. He was the party leader in Karl Marx Stadt."

"You mean Chemnitz, don't you?"

"*Touche.* Schabowski was in on it too. I saw to that. And Krenz, of course. But that should come as no surprise. Those guys were smart enough to see which way the wind was blowing by that time." Hetzling let a smile slip out the side of his mouth. "Particularly when the wind blows from Moscow."

"Moscow?"

"What do you think got us moving? Gorbachev had already made his disapproval apparent when he arrived for the fortieth anniversary celebrations in early October. He flatly forbade the Red Army from getting involved in any attempt to suppress the demonstrations."

"Was he thinking of the disaster of '68 in Prague?"

"Probably. Budapest, too."

"How do you know all this?"

"I provided one end of the channel." Rosman looked puzzled. "The channel that ran from the Soviet Embassy to Moscow to our government and into the west."

"Which end were you on?"

"The last one. But I also saw something of the other parts."

"Who or what did you see there?"

Hetzling smiled and wagged his index finger. "Oh, no thank you."

"Where was Gracchus?"

"He was there."

"What do you mean 'there'? In Moscow?"

Hetzling held his coffee cup to his face while he observed the room. Two middle-aged couples sat at tables across the room, near the window that looked out onto Dieckmannsstrasse. Business people, Rosman told himself, out on a break from their office routine. A younger man in a light gray business suit sat alone at the bar, cradling a brandy. He had yet to look in Rosman's direction. Was he using the mirror? Unlikely, since the angle was too sharp.

"Gracchus had just returned from Moscow. Stoph, the President, opened the Politburo meeting that day by calling for Honecker's resignation. At first Erich resisted, but when he saw Gracchus enter with his briefcase, Honecker just got up and left the room. After that, we voted Krenz in as his successor."

"But why? What made it all so easy?"

"Because at that point Honecker saw whose side Moscow was on. That's what everyone took to be the meaning of Gracchus's presence."

Rosman sat stock still for several moments, staring numbly at

Hetzling. "Is that what Hans Kroehler knew back in early October? He was killed on the fifth."

Hetzling shrugged. "Perhaps. But I doubt it. I mean, why kill somebody like that? Who would believe him? He must have stumbled onto something else."

"But what was it that Lamprecht and Jens found in Normanenstrasse? This was all over by then."

"You'll have to ask somebody else that question."

Rosman shook his head. "I don't think so. I think they found something else connected to this story, and somewhere the two lines intersect. That's the real key, isn't it, Hetzling? And you were a part of it, weren't you? Did that intersection come at the buyout program?"

Hetzling smiled. "Perhaps they intersect somewhere on your side of the Wall. Maybe your side won in ways you haven't imagined, Mr. Rosman. Ask your friend Buechler. Or perhaps your dissident friends. They may know more than you realize."

Rosman said nothing, his eyes moving from Hetzling to the bartender, a tall, broad-shouldered blond with pock-marked cheeks. He rolled a small white towel in glass after glass, and his eyes peered through Rosman's skull.

"So, where does Buechler fit in?"

Hetzling's eyes rose like ships on a wave. "Oh, hasn't he told you? He and Gracchus go back in time together. They've known each other for years."

Rosman could not move. He struggled for breath. The bottles behind the bar seemed to bob and weave in their racks in front of a mirror distorted like a fun house.

"Excuse me for a moment," Hetzling interrupted. "Perhaps when I return from the restroom we can go for a walk, and I will tell you more."

Rosman waved weakly at the waitress for the bill. She gave him a slip of paper and directed him to the bar to pay the tab. Rosman stumbled out of his chair and approached the counter. The bartender was in no hurry. He finished cleaning the glasses and then filled another order for the waitress before giving Rosman his change. It was frustrating, but the delay gave Rosman time to recover his balance.

When he returned to the table, Hetzling's coat had vanished. Rosman glanced around the room. The waitress sat on a stool over at the bar. Rosman had not paid much attention to her before. She wore a knee-length black skirt and white linen shirt with a small black apron tied at her waist in the front.

He walked over to where she sat. The woman looked coolly at Rosman, a cigarette in hand, smoke curling lazily upwards in front of an ageing face heavy with rouge and powder that tried to draw attention away from her twin row of yellow teeth. He heard her breathe softly, *"Der ist weg."* She said it before he had spoken a word, her blue eyes reflecting the afternoon's fading sunlight.

"He's gone." That was all. Then she turned away to crush her cigarette in an ashtray at her elbow. The bartender watched the scene in silence, smiling.

Rosman tumbled into the street. Looking about in all directions, he turned and ran first toward Friedrichstrasse, and then west along the route to Checkpoint Charlie. He saw no sign of his man. Rosman walked on, moving in several different directions, until he had completed a circle of several square blocks. As far as he could tell, he was still alone and unobserved. He navigated a larger loop, down toward Unter den Linden and on to Alexanderplatz, before heading back to his car. Nobody seemed to be following the same route, no one repeated their appearance. Had they called off the dogs? Had Hetzling drawn them away?

In spite of the warmth from the sun, Rosman flipped his collar up. Seconds later he noticed the remnants of a construction project on Friedrichstrasse. The back wall and one end resembled the combination of new wave and Gothic imitation so popular in East Germany over the last decade, the same style that marked Hetzling's apartment block. It probably wouldn't win any awards for aesthetics, Rosman thought, but at least it replaced the soulless granite blocks typical of so much architecture over here.

Whatever the style, though, nobody bothered to work on it anymore. The workers were now at home, maybe drunk, maybe asleep. There was no point to the effort anymore.

Rosman knew now that the same could not be said for Gracchus and his friends. They had been very busy indeed. But he still wondered just who had been playing Gracchus's game.

Back in his apartment, Hetzling smiled to himself, triumphant over his easy escape from the young American. Sitting at his window, he pondered an unfinished construction project that ran for several blocks along Friedrichstrasse, backing up against the Platz der Akadamie. Hetzling had noticed it many times before, but only today did it strike him that nobody worked there anymore. The site was nothing more than a huge hole in the ground with large concrete pillars extending several stories upward into a darkening Berlin sky.

A sudden weariness overcame Hetzling, and he leaned against the dark grey metal of the window frame. Tears formed at the corners of his eyes. The dread that he had been experiencing with greater frequency since the fall of his regime returned now with an overpowering gloom and depression.

Hetzling sighed as he pulled himself away from the window. He walked over to the telephone, where he dialled a number almost by instinct.

"He was here," Hetzling stated as soon as he heard the other side pick up the line. "The American. Buechler's friend."

"Alone? Or were any other Americans with him?"

"I wasn't aware there was more than this one."

"There are always lots of Americans. It's a big country."

"No, he was alone. I'm fairly certain."

"What did you tell him?"

"Just about all I know."

"What didn't you tell him?"

"We never got to your little project, the one in the west. But I think he knows about it already. His questions were headed in that direction."

"You never were very discreet, Hetzling. Or trustworthy, for that matter."

"I don't care anymore. It's over, as far as I'm concerned."

"You should know better than that."

"I don't want to help fight your battles anymore. I don't see why you continue."

"I'm not in the mood for a lecture, Joachim. There are new battles emerging. Some of us are positioning ourselves to win those."

"Do you really still believe it matters anymore? Or are you just desperate and fearful?"

"So many questions can make you careless, Joachim. Let's hope you don't come to regret them."

"There's already a great deal I regret."

"Where did you lead the American?"

Hetzling laughed. "I don't have to lead him anywhere. He'll find the trail on his own. Just leave the clues where he can find them. He's already found a great deal."

"Be very careful, Joachim. Several people have already been...hurt."

"That's what Rosman said."

Hetzling replaced the receiver in its cradle when he heard the other party hang up.

CHAPTER 26

Rosman pushed the key into the lock, rammed it counterclockwise, then threw his front door open. He raced through the hallway and into the living room. He lunged the last few steps and reached the telephone just in time.

"Is that you, John?"

"Kramer? Yeah, I just got in," Rosman answered.

"You sound out of breath. You need to work on your conditioning, my boy."

Rosman passed the receiver to his other ear. "Say, while I've got you on the line, what can you tell me about Avery and Donnelson?"

"I heard they had come by to see you. Don't worry about it."

"Well, it's kind of hard not to."

"Those guys are pricks. I'll see what I can do." Kramer laughed. "That is, as long as you're not a spy."

Rosman sank into his favorite chair. His free hand played with the pages of Goethe's *Faust*. "So, what's up?"

"I got the rest of the dope on that guy Buechler. I'd have to say this one is definitely a Soviet asset, John."

Rosman shot forward, his lower jaw dropping toward his chest. "How can you tell?"

"You can never be certain with this kind of thing. But he's had too much contact with Soviet and East German intelligence types. The Agency guys ran across his name too often to come to any other conclusion. I think they've got a file on him about an inch thick."

Rosman said nothing.

"John? You still there?"

"Thanks, Rick. That helps a lot."

Rosman sat staring out his window into the back yard. Several large European crows, their distinctive grey bodies and black wings outlined against a pale green background, hopped across his lawn. He was shocked out of his Audubon-like reverie by the shrill siren calling from his telephone receiver. It was off the hook. Rosman hadn't noticed that the receiver had fallen to the floor. He replaced the receiver, then walked out the door to his car. He'd have to head back downtown after all.

The Russian must have spent a lot of time in Germany. Or at least with Germans. He was so Prussian-like in his habits. Hidden among the 40 or 50 gawkers at the dozen or so tables set up on the eastern side of the Brandenburg Gate, Rosman observed Preselnikov emerge along the sidewalk on Unter den Linden in front of the Soviet Embassy. His camel-haired overcoat was buttoned to mid-chest, and a brown plaid scarf hung around his neck. Preselnikov strolled across Otto Grotewohl Strasse and then walked diagonally through the middle of Pariser Platz, ignoring the summons from the East Germans, Poles and Gypsies hawking Soviet and Warsaw Pact military souvenirs. Fur hats, belt buckles, decorations and medals, even entire uniforms, all for a handful of West German Marks or American dollars. But the Russian marched straight past the stalls. Instead, he swung around the corner table and then passed through the exit to the right of the Gate and into West Berlin.

Preselnikov would not return for 20 minutes at least. Rosman knew that occasionally he stayed away for an hour. But today would be different. There would be a break in his routine. Rosman turned to follow.

Once in the West, Preselnikov cut sharply to the left, passing in front of the Gate. He stepped onto a gravel path that flowed like a brook through the bare branches of a barren Tiergarten.

Rosman checked the light but steady stream of pedestrians for familiar faces. He was only dimly aware of the statued presence of Goethe watching over the park and its visitors when he caught up with the Russian. "Excuse me. Mr. Preselnikov?"

"Yes?" The Russian stopped to turn. Preselnikov was half-a-head taller than Rosman. "Can I help you?"

"I need to talk to you."

"You must be the American, Rosman. I was wondering when you would finally speak up."

Rosman drew in his breath. "You knew I would come?"

"It's ironic." Preselnikov nodded toward the statue. "He's my favorite poet."

"Not Pushkin? Or Tolstoy?"

The Russian selected a spot directly in front of the German poet and admired the figure. "No. They take much better care of their statues on this side."

Rosman turned to look at the large metal figure behind him, when Preselnikov tapped him on the shoulder. "Come, let's walk. You look as though you are ready to fall asleep."

"I've had a few rough nights lately," Rosman admitted.

They strolled in a westerly direction, away from what was left of the Wall and Preselnikov's old embassy building, rebuilt after the war on the site of the Tsar's embassy to Imperial Germany.

"So, what do you need to discuss that's so important?"

"I spoke with a man named Hetzling. Do you know him?"

"Yes, I do. We used to call him 'the Hetz'. Is he keeping busy?"

"I wasn't aware that you spoke my language so well."

Preselnikov shrugged off the compliment. "I've had two tours in the United States. One in Washington, D.C., and one at the U.N. in New York. You haven't answered my question."

"Hetzling? He seems bitter, and not a little confused," Rosman answered.

"He's not alone. You should see Moscow these days."

"But he was lucid enough about a string of events in October."

"Oh? And what did he tell you?"

"He helped me understand some of the events that transpired."

Preselnikov shrugged again. "That's all been reported in the press."

"Not all of it. There are gaps."

"What sort of gaps?" Preselnikov's hands swung to his pockets.

"About the part of someone named Gracchus, information I'm sure you'd like to keep confidential."

"Did he offer any proof?"

"I have that already."

"Do you have it with you?"

"Is that why you're talking to me now?"

Preselnikov stayed silent. Rosman stopped and waited for Preselnikov. The Russian turned to face him, his gaze periodically wandering among the trees. "I asked about proof."

"How about five dead East Germans for starters?"

Preselnikov sucked in his breath. "I see."

Rosman wondered just how much he knew.

"Do you have anything else?" Preselnikov asked. Rosman nodded. "And what do you expect from me?" The Russian glanced over his shoulder in the direction of Goethe's statue.

"First of all, I'd like to hear what you have to say about Honecker's departure. And Moscow's role."

"Don't you read the newspapers? I told you, it's all there."

Rosman shook his head. "I don't think so. In fact, I know there's more. I want you to confirm the details and the roles of the various actors. Then I'd like to know more about the second stage."

"Which stage? You have quite an imagination."

"I can always go to my superiors with my imagination. That..." Rosman hesitated..." and the proof I've collected."

Preselnikov spread his hands through the air in front of him. "But you ask for a great deal. And you've offered me nothing. Why should I trust you not to run to Langley or someplace else with your theories afterwards?"

"How about a copy of Lamprecht's notes?"

"Just a copy? You retain the originals?"

"Yes."

"And what about the missing files?"

Rosman shook his head. "Some other time."

"Why not now?"

Rosman shook his head. "You'll need an awful lot to trade for them."

Preselnikov's eyes measured Rosman. "But that's all I want. You can keep the notes."

"Gracchus would disagree."

"I wonder sometimes if you even have them. Perhaps you're still looking for them, just like us." Preselnikov paused. "What do you want?"

Rosman's eyes darted from the street to Preselnikov, then back to the flow of traffic. "I want to retain a record of what happened here. And I want you to call off the hounds."

Preselnikov sniffed. "A record? For the historians? That's not very gratifying."

Rosman shrugged. "It's better than what you've got now."

"And why should I call off the hounds, as you put it, especially if you keep the documents?"

"I need to hold something tangible. We all need protection these days."

"Do you think the others would be satisfied with that arrangement?"

"Are you talking about the dissidents?"

Preselnikov nodded. "Them and others. Like your countrymen."

"In spite of what you may think, I'm not doing this for any of my countrymen."

"Then for whom are you working?"

"Myself." Rosman paused, his eyes searching the pebbles at his feet. "And the others. The dead."

"What about the girl?"

Rosman's gaze rose to the Russian. He did not answer.

Preselnikov smiled and studied the young American a moment longer before resuming his walk. "How do I know I'll get the copies?"

Rosman hustled up beside the Russian. "I'll meet you here tomorrow. Same time."

"No, that's too careless. There are two Americans walking with us right now. They will follow again tomorrow."

Preselnikov nodded at two men in light brown woolen over-coats and fedoras walking toward them. Rosman did not recognize their faces. They did not really look like Americans. But then again, how was he to tell, here in the middle of Berlin? He hoped Preselnikov was bluffing.

"I'll think of something else," the Russian said. "So, what do you want to know? That people in the Kremlin were disappointed with Honecker's leadership?"

"I did get that much out of the newspapers. I also know about Gracchus' appearance at that fateful Politburo meeting. Was he acting for Mielke?"

Preselnikov actually laughed. He paused and grabbed Rosman's sleeve, pointing to the light at the street crossing, which glared red at the obedient German pedestrians. After a short interval, they moved on, strolling past the large yellow geometric shape of the Symphony Hall.

"You know," Preselnikov mused, "in all the years I've been in Berlin, I've never attended a performance of the Berliner Philharmonic. Strange, isn't it?"

"That's unfortunate. But I haven't either. Now, about my question."

"I'm sorry. What was it? Mielke?" Preselnikov chuckled once more, shaking his head. "Gracchus may have come under Mielke's nominal authority, but as far as Moscow was concerned, Gracchus did not have to answer to Mielke."

"What you are trying to say?"

Preselnikov waved his right hand in the air. "Only that I've known Gracchus for many years. And he is a superior officer. I'm proud of my friendship with that man. I am not proud to have worked with a crummy little cop killer like Mielke."

Preselnikov spoke these last words with a bitter vehemence. He lowered his right hand and spat on the sidewalk. It was a gesture that struck Rosman as distinctly out of character.

"So you two worked together here?"

"We have often worked together. Here and elsewhere." Preselnikov started walking again, and Rosman hurried to catch up. "Gracchus was an operative in the best sense of the word. I'm told

Le Carre modelled his character Karla after Markus Wolf, the head of the HVA. I've never read any of Le Carre's novels."

"Neither have I."

"But he could just as easily have chosen Gracchus. I suppose the West Germans will seek some sort of vengeance for Gracchus having made them look like fools so often." Preselnikov uttered the last words in a burst of pride, as though his side had not lost all the battles, even if it had lost the war.

"I do know that Le Carre's real name is David Cornwell. And he worked for MI-5 before becoming a writer." Rosman paused. "Like so many people, he isn't what he seems."

"Like Gracchus?" Preselnikov glanced sideways at Rosman.

"Like him. Like Hetzling. And perhaps you."

"What do you mean?"

"All loyal to their regimes, to their cause. But in the end, one was little more than a plotter, one a bag man, and one the executioner. The challenge is figuring how you all worked together to pull off your little scheme."

"My, my. You do have a vivid imagination. You must be careful, though. People don't like to have their integrity questioned."

Rosman spread his arms. "Oh, but I wasn't questioning anyone's honesty or commitment. They were all loyal. Just carrying out orders, that constant refrain one hears like an echo in this city."

Preselnikov turned suddenly. "Don't you ever compare me, or Gracchus, to those bastards," he hissed. "Our families suffered too much at their hands. Do you know how Gracchus and his family had to flee from the Nazis in the middle of the night, what it as like for them in Moscow? What my family endured during the war?"

Rosman was silent, afraid to respond. He could hear his heartbeat amid the swelling traffic on either side of the woods.

"Of course not," Preselnikov spat out.

They had walked as far as the old Italian and Japanese embassies to the Third Reich, both across the street from the outer stretches of the Tiergarten. The Italians were now using about one third of their building as a consulate, and from the looks of it, the rest was run down and vacant. The Japanese, on the other hand, had renovated their entire building, turning it into a cultural center to give an image of recovery and vitality.

Preselnikov began walking eastward again, retracing their steps back past the Symphony Hall and into the Tiergarten.

"I'm sorry for all that. My family suffered as well. But you will never get me to believe that Gracchus mounted some sort of rogue operation. You were all carrying out someone's orders."

"I don't give a damn what you believe. And I don't care what your superiors believe either. You don't have enough proof for any of these accusations. And I'm sure you won't find it either."

"And our deal?"

"We haven't settled anything yet."

They strolled in silence for a moment before Rosman spoke again. "So, what is Gracchus up to now? Is he working for someone else, now that his old employer is going out of business?"

"Don't be ridiculous." They had come to the edge of the Tiergarten, and Preselnikov continued to walk, moving ahead toward the Brandenburg Gate. Then, as if driven by an afterthought, he turned to Rosman. "Is this your first tour?"

"My second. I did consular duty in India before this."

"It shows. Gracchus is a complicated man. We all are. Even on your own side, Mr. Rosman."

"I'm learning as much. What about you?"

Preselnikov just shook his head, a smile escaping from underneath the wavy dark hair that was combed straight back. "I'm not that important a player in all this." He pointed a gloved finger at Rosman. "And you should pay no more attention to me. Do not try to follow me again."

Preselnikov started to move toward the Gate again. Rosman grabbed his shirt-sleeve to restrain him. He wanted to pose one last question. "So, who killed the East German students and the Meyers? Was it Gracchus? Or was it someone else?" Rosman paused before going on. "Someone from Moscow?"

Preselnikov looked around and studied the ground at his feet. After a minute of this, he looked up and seized Rosman with a stare. His eyes had the look of cold, hard metal, the brown pupils flat on a field of shaded white, like pennies on a sheet.

"I'm not sure I'd tell you if I knew. What I will tell you is that it's time to end this adventure of yours. Unfortunately, it's not in my power to do that. You see, I can't simply call off the dogs. They don't work for me."

He resumed his retreat to the east, walking briskly back to his embassy compound on Unter den Linden.

"So we don't really have a deal, do we?" Rosman shouted after him.

Preselnikov stopped and turned. "Did you expect some sort of contract? Take from this conversation what you like, whatever you think helps." His finger rose against the sky. "But never rely on the words of someone else in this business unless you control him entirely."

Then, just as suddenly, Preselnikov returned across the lengthening shadows of what had once been a no-man's land. It resembled the barren, brown landscape Rosman had seen in pictures of the Western Front in the First World War, the mud mottled by the tread of tire and foot and the fall of men to their death. It was a place where nothing grew. Preselnikov approached like a lone survivor from a futile assault. The Russian walked up and looked Rosman dead in the eye, uncertainty and remorse distorting the lines around his mouth and eyes, his head tilted to one side. The hardness of his eyes had melted to a dull glow of remorse.

"What if there had been movement here earlier?" he asked. "Say, two or three years earlier? The idea was a good one; it was the right policy." His hands still buried in the pockets of his long camel overcoat, Preselnikov glanced in the direction of the Reichstag. "This country, this city. They were too important to us. Something had to be done. We just waited too long. And that young man Hans Kroehler should never have interfered."

"It wouldn't have made any difference," Rosman replied after a moment of thoughtful silence. "It wasn't the timing. It was the system. You made your mistakes long ago. At Petersburg and Kronstadt. And you kept repeating them."

"I wonder if you'll still believe that a few years from now."

Rosman did not answer. Preselnikov resumed his trek back into East Berlin, and Rosman called out one last time, "But was it worth those five lives?"

"That was not the cause," Preselnikov said. "Not for all of them."

Preselnikov halted once more and spoke across the distance. "You know, you deserve to learn a little something before they swallow you, Mr. Rosman. It would be a shame for you to die so young and so ignorant. So I will tell you this much. There are two stories at play here. One follows on the other. What I ask myself now is whether you are clever enough to figure out their connection."

"Where does Hetzling fit in with Gracchus?"

"Hetzling has known Gracchus and many others. And he has served many masters. But his part in this drama began long ago, even though it belongs to the second act. I can tell you that much."

"And Buechler?"

Preselnikov's head bobbed with a light laugh. "That you will have to learn on your own. Knowing what little I do of your past, I think you will enjoy that."

Preselnikov glanced over at the Reichstag and blew out his frustration in a long stale breath of cold air. "Forget your copies and trades. Just get rid of any papers you have. Tell your friends to do the same. They won't save you, or anyone else." He halted and turned. "If you pursue this further, nothing will save you. Or the girl."

"What's happened to Joanna?"

The Russian's hand waved at the no-man's land that had once been the busy thoroughfare known as Potsdamer Platz. "She is beyond your reach."

Rosman leaned forward, listening for more. But Preselnikov kept moving. Rosman turned and started running. He could think of one last option. He just hoped he could use it to locate Gracchus and the files.

CHAPTER 27

The ride home cost Rosman about 20 minutes. Once again, he had to pull up short. It wasn't the car this time. Not the brown Trabant or a yellow Wartburg he had been looking for. No, it was another face. This one belonged to the black leather figure from the KaDeWe. And it was the same bastard that had pushed Rosman's face against the cold metal of his own car that night so long ago. He wished he had a weapon.

Rosman parked his car around the block and in front of the Japanese consulate, just to the side of the iron gate and stone posts that stood like Prussian sentries to the long circular drive. He climbed out of the car, then pushed the door shut. Bare cherry blossom trees hid behind a tall metal fence. Burying as much of his face as possible in the collar of his dark green overcoat, he snuck up behind the deep blue BMW.

Rosman threw open the door. He grabbed the startled driver by the collar, ramming the bridge of his nose into the steering wheel. The man shrieked with pain, blood spurting from his nostrils. Rosman seized his wrist and jerked the left arm around the back, hard up against the shoulder blades. Then he leaned with all his weight against the man's back to keep him pinned and immobile.

"Keep your right hand on that fucking steering wheel, you piece of East German shit!" Rosman barked. He no longer recognized his own voice. "Now, who the fuck are you?"

"Verdammt," he whined. "I think you broke my nose."

"Who are you, goddammit?" Rosman levered the left arm higher.

"Okay, okay." His face turned an inch or so toward Rosman.

Tears swam in his eyes. "My name is Gustav."

"And?"

"You don't need to know anymore."

"Why not? Who sent you?"

"I work for Gracchus." The words broke through thin pink bubbles.

"So, where the fuck is he? Why isn't he here now?"

"Ease off and I'll tell you, asshole," the East German sputtered. He was recovering his composure. "Go find him yourself, if you're so eager."

"Gladly. Just tell me where the bastard is."

"He went to Rostock."

"Rostock?" Rosman eased the pressure on his prisoner's back a bit. "What the hell for?"

"He said he had some business to settle there." His left eye darted in Rosman's direction. "Why not go after him? He'd probably love that."

Rosman reached down and jerked the key from the ignition, pressing the side of the man's face back against the steering wheel. He let up some when he heard a gasp of pain.

"Don't try to follow me."

Rosman reached inside the jacket and pulled out a small black pistol. "I think I'll take this too."

"Good luck, tough guy. Do you know how to handle a Makarov?"

Tears had collected along the lower ridges of both the man's eyes by now, and small streams trickled south. Deep blue coloring had spread from the nose out along the upper cheeks and underneath the sockets. Rosman glanced at the weapon. "It's got a trigger, doesn't it?" He shoved it into his coat pocket. "At least you won't be able to use it."

He backed out of the car slowly, his feet probing the ground behind him. When he got to the sidewalk, Rosman turned and ran to his car. He halted once, at the corner of Wachtelstrasse, to make sure Gustav was not following him. But the East German was still in his car, head tilted back, a white handkerchief under his nose to stem the bleeding.

Rosman jumped back into his car and flew north along the Autobahn. Once he reached the center of the city, Rosman parked his Mercedes around the corner from Rostock's Gothic Rathaus in a side street just to the north of Ernst Thaelmann Platz. *That's due for a change soon*, he thought. Rosman pulled the Russian pistol from his pocket and weighed it in his hand. The unfamiliar grip felt bulky and unnatural, and Rosman shoved the piece into the breast pocket inside his coat. At least there the reach would be more natural—and shorter—for his right hand.

He wandered for a few minutes in the direction of the waterfront before choosing a pub that looked out on the Warnow shipyards, a skyline of lonely cranes sprouting from long banks of concrete. The bar was called *der Blaue Stern*, or The Blue Star.

Rosman entered cautiously, his tired legs stumbling at the top step before he pushed the door open. He surveyed the dark room of panelled hardwood and small, Formica-topped tables, then strolled to the bar to exchange two West German marks for the East German variety. The smell of old tobacco and beer drifted in the air like a memory. About 20 yards ahead a telephone hung from a wall across from the restroom, flanked by two slot machines mounted on the wall.

Rosman called Schmidt, then selected a table near the window. Despite the shadow cast by the awning over the window, Rosman waited with an uncomfortable feeling of exposure and vulnerability. But he wanted to be sure he caught Schmidt as he approached the bar.

When Schmidt approached 20 minutes and two cups of coffee later, Rosman could barely believe his eyes. Schmidt skipped across the street and through the door carrying two pairs of ice skates. They looked like hockey skates, their brown and black leather scuffed and ripped, presumably from lots of use.

"Let's go," Schmidt commanded as he ambled into the room. He was wearing a navy blue cotton sweater and smoking a pipe, which Schmidt handled like he had just bought the thing. The tip hung suspended between his lips, and the stem bobbed up and down whenever he spoke.

"Where to?"

Schmidt hoisted the skates. "Outside. For a walk."

"For chrissakes, Schmidt. I'm ready to drop."

Schmidt leaned over to whisper to Rosman. He blew a cloud of smoke over the table, his breath heavy with an aromatic flavor. "Look, I think I know why you're here, and if you want to talk, it's better to do it in the open air."

Rosman didn't answer. *It could also make us a better target for someone lying in wait,* he thought.

He rose and followed Schmidt out the door and into the cold, bright Baltic air. Schmidt led the way back toward the center of town, past a row of five and nine story buildings of brick and granite that had tried to blend the monotonous rectangular style of postwar communist architecture with the red bricks and gables popular during the fifteenth and sixteenth centuries.

Schmidt threaded a path through a series of arcades running along the front of the buildings and then across Lange Strasse, the four-lane boulevard that circled the heart of the city. Only then did Schmidt speak. "This air should do you some good, Rosman. You look like hell. How long has it been since you slept well?"

"I'm not sure." Rosman rubbed the stubble sprouting along his chin. "Thanks for meeting me, anyway."

"You sounded desperate over the telephone."

"Do you have the files? It's the only thing that makes sense now."

"Why should I tell you?"

"It's in your interest, too, you know."

"How so?"

"Have you had any visitors today? From Berlin?"

Schmidt frowned, as he surveyed the urban landscape. "No. Should I expect any?"

Rosman nodded. "It sure sounds like it. I understand Gracchus is here."

"I was afraid this would happen." Schmidt took the pipe from his mouth and studied Rosman. "Did you bring him here?"

"I followed him. They've probably figured it out, too, that you're the one with their precious files."

"So, the hare is chasing the hound?"

"Perhaps."

"We'll see." Schmidt laughed and replaced the pipe between his teeth. He blew out a large cloud of smoke as though in triumph. "What do you want from me?"

"What I want from everyone. Information. That and proof about some events last fall and, even more important, what those damn files will tell me."

"Have you figured out their importance?"

"That's where you're going to help."

Schmidt stopped to study Rosman. "Do you think you have enough time for all that?"

"We'll see."

They made their way down Breite Strasse, then Schmidt turned toward the University, situated at the opposite end of the city center from the Rathaus.

"The buildings in this part of town look pretty authentic, Schmidt. What about the war?"

"This area has been completely rebuilt." He pointed to their left. "We even reconstructed the monument to General Bluecher, the hero from the Napoleonic wars."

Rosman was impressed at the obvious effort and craftsmanship, not to mention the regime's ability to resist the temptation to recast everything in the typical linear monstrosities of steel, concrete and glass. Schmidt puffed heavily on his pipe.

"You're the final piece of the puzzle, Schmidt. That's one reason I came."

"And Gracchus?"

"Just tell me your story. That will be all the help I need."

"And what's in it for me?"

"You'll need a broker, won't you, if you plan to do something with those files?"

Schmidt's brow furrowed and stayed that way for two city blocks. "Alright then, you have to understand who the actors are. Nothing makes sense without that."

"Start with yourself."

"Fair enough. I come from a communist family. My grandfather returned after the war with my father in tow. He was raised to respect the role of the Red Army in overthrowing fascism and the need to build a workers' and peasants' state on German soil. Unfortunately, my father's career here never got beyond that of a local party official. In fact, his one notable achievement was to expel a writer named Walter Kempowski. You've heard of him?"

"Vaguely."

Schmidt held a match over the bowl of his pipe until the flame touched his fingers. He threw the blackened stub on the sidewalk and cursed. "Well, he expected a more successful career from me. He was bitterly disappointed when I enrolled at the university to study theology. But he was overjoyed to hear later that I had been recruited by the Stasi." Schmidt studied Rosman's face. "You know, defending socialism against its imperialist enemies."

Rosman slipped on a patch of ice when he stepped off the curb. He grabbed Schmidt's sleeve to steady himself. "Is it always this cold here at this time of year?"

Schmidt shook his head. "No, this is unusual. But then, these are unusual times."

"How long did you work for the Stasi?"

"I began in 1985. My job was to report on the student scene, particularly foreign contacts. That's what made it seem legitimate. In 1989, however, things changed."

"How so?"

"I was given a new case officer."

"Gracchus?"

Schmidt stopped again to relight his pipe. His gaze darted up and down the street. "That's right. And I could tell he was important by the access he had." Schmidt resumed his pace, whi.e his right hand waved the burnt match up and down. "What struck me, though, was that he worked in the HVA and seemed to bypass Mielke and the other party hacks. I still reported on the student world, but Gracchus began to push me more and more into an activist role, almost the part of provocateur."

"That surprised you?"

"Of course it did. That's not why I agreed to work with them."

They passed through the archway of an old city gate. It had the same worn edges and faded orange coloring as the other remnants of a wall that at one time must have surrounded medieval Rostock.

Rosman nodded. "And you haven't seen Gracchus today?"

"Are you sure he's here?"

"Earlier today in Berlin I ran into one of his lackeys. He told me Gracchus had come to Rostock to settle some business." Schmidt was silent, puffing on his pipe. "I assumed that meant you, Schmidt. And the files."

Schmidt blew out a large ball of aromatic smoke that the wind tossed back at them. "It could. But you can't be certain. I'm not the only person in Rostock who worked for the Stasi. Besides, the guy works a lot with Moscow. It could have something to do with that." He glanced over at Rosman. The pipe hung toward the earth like a little plastic ladder to his innermost thoughts. "And now you're here in Rostock, too."

Schmidt descended a slope of lawn and continued toward two bodies of water, one a small, round pool; the other a long, thin winding mini-lake. Centuries ago, Rosman guessed, this must have been the moat. Schmidt led Rosman to the larger stretch of water and sat down on the bank. Schmidt handed Rosman a pair of skates and started to pull off his own shoes.

Rosman stared at his companion. "Are you out of your mind? I'm too fucking beat to go ice-skating. Besides, the ice can't be that thick this early in the season."

"Come on, Rosman. I was out on the ice yesterday, and the exercise will do you good." He finished lacing his own pair. "Besides, I want to get you away from the crowd." He jerked his head toward the rear.

Schmidt leaped up and tiptoed to the edge of the ice before gliding across the smooth white sheet that covered the lake. Rosman struggled to cram his feet into skates that felt like they were about a size-and-a-half too small. His toes ached for room. He stood up slowly and hobbled to the ice.

"Schmidt. Wait up," he yelled, grimacing as his feet slid with the grace of a robot across what was now a tough, uneven topping that in places looked dark and patchy. Rosman grabbed Schmidt's arm to steady himself when he caught up with the East German.

"What's your relationship with all that now?" Rosman inquired.

"I'm out of it."

"You no longer work for Gracchus? For the Stasi?"

"Not anymore. I'm self-employed now."

"Why? What happened?"

"Oh, several things. Some little, some large. In 1987, for example, I had to start spending several weekends a year working—on my own time, of course—at the Wandlitz compound. You know, where all the party and government leaders lived." Rosman nodded. "Well, it was infuriating to see how well-off those guys were. Their stores were incredibly well-stocked, and at prices that were unheard of elsewhere in the Republic."

"What were the big things?"

"Look over there."

Schmidt gave up on the match and pointed with his new briar appendage to the shipyards. "You don't see much activity out there, do you?"

Rosman peered through the afternoon haze. He tried to wiggle his toes to relieve the throbbing. The docks looked deserted. "I don't see any."

"The industry is doomed under the new German government, regardless of what it looks like, or when it comes into power. No government, in East Berlin or Bonn, can afford to subsidize a true industrial dinosaur for too long."

Schmidt broke away from Rosman and sped ahead about fifty meters and then flew easily back, twisting and turning to display his talent on the ice. "They'll probably try," he continued, "if only to avoid the thousands of unemployed. But any attempt to salvage those shipyards out there will require massive layoffs. They're already cutting back."

"What for?" Rosman inquired. He stamped the front of his skates on the ice, then slid the blades forward.

"They're losing their market. The industry was never competitive in the west, especially against those cut-throat Asian countries. The only countries who would buy their boats were communist." He gestured with his right hand toward the water before stuffing the pipe in his coat pocket. "It was a system based on incompetence, kept alive by its isolation."

"You sound bitter."

"Those shipyards explain a lot, Rosman. I've come to realize how badly our regime screwed us with its rigid nineteenth-century philosophy of class struggle and economic determinism. The dialectic was supposed to give our rulers the insight to align our society with the progressive forces of history. But it was a professor's illusion."

Schmidt laughed lightly and waved his arm in an academic's gesture. Rosman was beginning to sweat in his woolen coat.

"You sound like a disappointed true believer."

Schmidt skidded to a stop in front of Rosman. "That's exactly what I am."

They reversed direction and skated back toward their shoes, which sat undisturbed about a quarter of a mile away.

"I must admit, Rosman, I didn't like you at all when we first met. You struck me as the typically naive and meddling American, the kind that knows everything and is out to set the world straight. According to Washington's view, of course."

Rosman's eyes fluttered in momentary exhaustion. His throat burned as he sucked in the cold air. "Of course."

"I'm not sure I like you now, but the fact that you've survived this long has impressed me. And I certainly don't approve of the way Hans and the others were handled. This may surprise you, but I considered them my friends."

"You have a funny way of showing friendship."

"No, Rosman, you still don't understand." Schmidt halted, shards of ice flying across the surface. "They were my friends. I had nothing to do with those deaths. I only tried to knock Jens out that night to get those damn files away from him. Those were not the ones we were after. They would have been a death sentence for Erich."

"He died anyway, Schmidt."

Schmidt's head hung low, his eyes studying the ice. "Yes, I know. I, too, never realized how much was at stake." His head rose, the eyes on Rosman. "Things fell apart so suddenly, I think even Gracchus was taken by surprise. The files we wanted were supposed to be somewhere else. I don't know what happened."

"So, you were there on Gracchus' orders?"

"Of course I was. How do you think we got inside in the first place?" He started to skate again. "But I was there for my friends as well. I was afraid Jens would get himself into real trouble, much worse than before. We were supposed to come across some other packages. We found some, but there were others as well. That's when I decided to take matters into my own hands."

"Come again?"

Schmidt nodded vigorously. "Remember, other Stasi head-quarters had been raided already, and Gracchus sought to use that to his advantage. I arranged for some others to be available. Older ones, some fake folders and lists of internal assets he wanted to compromise."

"Why do that? Did he want to compromise the movement?"

"Yes, in part. And I did not set you people up that night in Prenzlauer Berg." Schmidt spoke these last words with emphasis, jabbing the air with his pipe. "Somebody else did that."

"So, who killed Erich?"

"I'm not sure. But I doubt it was Gracchus."

"What happened to those files?"

Schmidt smiled and shook his head. "You're not getting your hands on those."

"Where are they? Do you have them?"

Schmidt laughed. "It's not that easy, Rosman." Schmidt grinned. The pipe swivelled. "They're secure. And they'll be put to good use."

"Such as?"

"Not what they were originally intended for. They're my ticket to the new world."

Rosman considered Schmidt but said nothing for a minute. "I need more, Schmidt."

"Maybe there isn't anything else."

"I doubt it." Rosman paused. "Why hasn't Gracchus come after you?"

"Can't you see it? He doesn't realize I have the files. Gracchus thinks I still work for him."

"You've probably been deflecting his attention to me, or others."

"He does require a bone now and then." Schmidt paused for a minute, a dry sucking noise emanating from the pipe. "I told you you were in over your head, Rosman."

"Two can play at this game, Schmidt."

The East German shook his head. "I don't think so. You give me to Gracchus, and then he's got the files. You don't want that either. They really are valuable, if you know what to look for."

"Perhaps we can strike a deal."

Schmidt paused and smiled. Then they resumed skating and aimed for the shoreline where Rosman saw their shoes waiting about twenty yards from a warming shed. About thirty yards from the shore Rosman could feel his feet dragging through a thin pool of water. He glanced down and was surprised to see the ice coated with a layer of mush at this part of the lake, where the sun burned brightest in the late afternoon.

"You know, it's ironic," Schmidt continued, "but it looks like Gracchus is losing his touch. If Gracchus was on top of this operation, Jens and Lamprecht might have lived."

"Why do you say that?"

"I'm sure whoever is responsible thought that by silencing them, he was erasing the proof, covering the trail. But it only created more gaps."

"But why has Gracchus tried to do so little to me?" Rosman pressed. "Only a few beatings. And even those were not that serious." Rosman's words trailed off.

"Perhaps he was waiting for you to lead him to his quarry. Perhaps he knew what he needed to know without striking at you. The man never impressed me as bloodthirsty." Schmidt laughed, shrugging his shoulders. "Perhaps you had a friend, or protector, in high places. Or maybe you were just lucky after all. It won't hold forever, though."

"It's lasted this long."

"Maybe today's the day."

The sound of cracking ice erupted in Rosman's ears like a rifle shot. His foot slipped through a hole in the ice, and his heart leaped to his throat. Rosman fell forward, lunging at Schmidt. Freezing water surged over his calves.

"Jesus Christ, Schmidt! Help me!"

Rosman's fingers scratched at the smooth surface. His grip failed to hold. His fingernails traced a desperate trail across the ice and slush. Rosman threw his arms at the thin border of ice to his front, but his elbows broke through to the water. The pool around him spread like a lake.

He looked up through the beads of sweat building around his eyes. He could not find Schmidt anywhere. The water lapped at his thighs, locking onto his pants and skin like a wave of iron barnacles. He struggled to level his body and reach once more for the frozen white line that promised salvation. Why did he come out on this fucking ice? What an idiot. And that goddamn Schmidt.

He reached for something solid. A pair of strong arms seized his right hand. With agonizing slowness, the arms pulled Rosman forward, easing him from the water's stinging grip. He crawled to the bank and sprawled out across the frozen ground, his chest heaving. His legs were freezing, and he could no longer feel his feet. Sure hands stripped the skates from Rosman's feet and began to massage the soles and toes. Rosman gaped into a pair of worried blue eyes.

"Jesus, Schmidt! For a minute there, I thought you had done me in. Another bone for Gracchus."

Schmidt chuckled softly. He dropped the towel in Rosman's lap. "No, I won't be the one. You're no longer a threat to me. I have what I need. But you are to others. So you had better keep checking the ice. But you're on your own now, as far as I'm concerned."

Schmidt collected the skates and trotted off. It took Rosman 10 minutes to get some feeling back in his toes. Then he limped to his car at Ernst Thaelmann Platz, fired up his engine, and threw the heater switch to full blast. Rosman leaned back and propped his legs in front of the fan. He pulled the Makarov from his coat pocket, wiped it dry, then stored it in the glove compartment.

Through his windshield, Rosman spotted what looked like a circus setting up in the main square in front of the city hall. Rosman saw a clown in an enormous red wig and bright red nose in the middle of the square, handing out balloons to the passers-by. When he looked more closely, Rosman noticed that the balloons had the logo of Deutsche Bank, Germany's largest and most powerful private financial institution. *So, they're already here advertising,* he thought. *That didn't take long.*

Then Rosman realized that the clown was looking directly at him, his gaze fixed upon Rosman with a bemused stare. At that moment a cold and frightening realization overwhelmed Rosman. The image of that clown's comical look stuck with Rosman while he drove to the Autobahn. Suddenly, he felt like a fool. And now he realized why.

CHAPTER 28

He drove fast, even by West German standards. At this rate he could cut the return trip nearly in half. Rosman raced by BMWs and Porsches in a blur, surprised at his own recklessness. None could keep pace with him. None except a pale green VW Golf that pulled up on his rear, lights flashing, demanding the right to pass him just as they left Neuruppin in their wake. *Damn these Germans,* he thought. *As soon as they get behind the wheel, an aggressive instinct takes over, and they're out to conquer the world again. But this time from the comfort of their bucket seats.*

Rosman looked over to see if he could catch the driver's eye. He wanted to get a good look at the idiot's face. But the glare of the sun on the window obscured his vision, forcing Rosman to slow down and shift to the right lane. The Golf pulled even and slowed as well.

Suddenly, the driver swerved hard to his right, ramming the side of Rosman's Mercedes, hitting it just to the rear of the door on the driver's side.

The shock of the impact was paralyzing. Rosman lost control of his car, spitting gravel to the right and left as he swerved on the edge of the highway's shoulder. He eyed the dry blacktop, then jerked his wheels out into the middle of the Autobahn to keep his car from running off the side of the road and into the ditch.

His limbs stiffened with fear. Pale images of Jens and Lamprecht flashed through his mind. What had they felt when they died? How much did they suffer? Would it come to that here? Rosman shook his head hard enough to lose sight of the road. He leaned over and opened the glove compartment.

Stay on the damn highway, he kept repeating, like a mantra. *Just straighten this thing out and outrace the goddamn VW back to Berlin.* Wind whistled through the crack the collision had opened between his door and the frame.

If that doesn't work, he told himself, *blow his fucking brains out.* Rosman grabbed the Makarov from the glove compartment.

The green VW rose on his tail again. Rosman pressed the gas pedal to the floor just as the VW overtook him, ramming the side of Rosman's car, this time near the front fender. Then the bastard locked on hard and drove him off the highway. Rosman's knuckles bled white as he strangled the steering wheel, dropping the gun. The Makarov bounced off his knees and onto the floor at his feet.

The lumbering Mercedes could not hold to the shoulder. With a sickening feeling in the pit of his stomach, Rosman bit down and held hard as his car slid sideways down the embankment, tumbling over a small range of boulders and crashing to a halt in a concrete drainage ditch at the bottom of the hill.

The car came to a rest right side up, but with the weight on the passenger side. The side of the car pointed toward the sky at a forty five degree angle. Rosman climbed out, breathing fast. Both front wheels were bent inwards like a coat hanger. A pool of dark liquid was collecting under the engine. There was no way he was going to drive this thing back to Berlin. He leaned inside and retrieved the revolver from the floor.

Still trembling with shock, Rosman started to scramble up the opposite end of the ditch, away from the road. His feet slipped on the loose gravel that had been used to line the shoulder and the small gully. Jagged little rocks scraped the skin of his palms. His arm started to pound again, a throbbing streak of pain running from his wrist to his bicep. The damp pants clung to his legs. And his socks were still wet and cold.

Where was the goddamn VW? Rosman hugged the ground as he inched forward towards the ridge above. He shifted the pistol to his right hand.

"Are you all right?"

The voice was familiar, but in his haste and anxiety Rosman

could not place it. He cocked his head to the right, then the left. He saw only a broad human outline, obscured by the glare of the sun at its back. He could still nail the son of a bitch from here if necessary.

"Are you all right?" Another pause. "Don't just stand there, Rosman. Answer me."

Rosman worked his feet along the gravel, bringing his body into a crouch. Stay low, he told himself, as he climbed back up to the highway.

At the top Rosman raised his hand to shield his eyes from the sun. The movement shot a burst of pain from his shoulder to his waist. Rosman peered into a pale face slanted by squinting eyes and puffed cheeks. The face retreated when it saw the weapon in Rosman's hand. Rosman jumped to make up the distance. When he looked again, Rosman realized he was staring into the familiar brown eyes of Bill Harding.

Rosman did not hesitate. He plunged forward, driving his shoulder into Harding's stomach, both bodies tumbling forward onto the gravel and down into the ditch. Rosman swung wildly, trying to pistolwhip his colleague and friend.

Harding grabbed Rosman's arm, shaking the Makarov loose. He locked his legs around Rosman, rolled him over, and pinned Rosman's arms to the ground with his knees.

"What the fuck do you think you're doing?" Harding screamed.

"It was you, wasn't it?" Rosman spit back at him. "And now you try to run me into some shithole of a ditch!"

Rosman rolled his torso back and forth, trying to free himself.

"Dammit, John! Will you tell me what is going on? That son-of-a-bitch down there is the one who tried to run you off the road!" Harding pointed down the highway in the direction of Berlin.

Rosman lifted his head four or five inches, searching for the green VW. "I can't see a damn thing with you on top of me."

Harding let Rosman up and studied his face. Rosman's breath rolled out in long heavy gasps.

"There, dammit!" Harding thrust his arm at something about

one hundred yards down the road. A group of cars, a mixture of Trabants and Wartburgs, Mercedes and Fords, stood parked in a long row along the side of the Autobahn.

Rosman retrieved the pistol and tucked it into the waist of his pants. He slapped the front and sides of his coat to brush the dirt and gravel from the wet wool. "What a fucking day this is turning out to be." Rosman shook his head at Harding and forced out a smile. He gave up trying to get the coat clean and trotted over to the accident.

A small crowd of Germans stood clustered around two automobiles that were stuck together in the median, about 10 to 15 yards from the road. One of them was a metallic blue BMW with a Hamburg license plate. That unfortunate West German, probably on his way somewhere to cash in on the closer ties emerging between the two Germanys, had his front end buried into the side of the pale green VW Golf. The crumpled roof on the Golf looked like it had flipped over at least once before landing upright, its sides dented and scraped.

Most of the onlookers were leaning forward or to the side to get a better view. Rosman sidled closer to the wreck, edging around the side of the entangled cars to get a better look at the driver of the VW. "Der ist hin," one of the Germans muttered. He must be dead, Rosman agreed, as he examined the shattered door on the driver's side of the wreck.

When he finally got close enough, Rosman bent over to peer through the window on the passenger's side of the Golf. He saw a tall, heavy-set policeman in his light green overcoat administering mouth-to-mouth to an unconscious, middle-aged male lying on the front seat. The officer's cap lay upside down next to the body. The face of the victim was still blocked.

Rosman thrust his shoulders through the crowd of onlookers, using his weight and urgency to angle around to the front of the car. He peeked through the cracked glass of the windshield that had been shattered by the driver's head. Later, Rosman could not be sure if it was the brightness of the sunshine, his state of near exhaustion or the shock of realization that caused him to lose his bearings and stumble backwards, bumping into an overweight

big-breasted German woman behind him. The body on the seat
was that of Gracchus.

Rosman turned and ran back to his friend. "Let's go."

"Just a minute, John. Tell me what's going on."

"In the car," Rosman yelled.

He settled into the passenger seat of his friend's car, and
Harding pulled back onto the highway. Harding handed Rosman
a slip of paper. "It's your girlfriend's telephone number and
address."

Rosman crumbled the piece of paper in his hand. "Thanks.
How'd you get it?"

"Kramer." Harding paused. "So, what are you going to do
now?"

Rosman let his head rest against the seat and rubbed his forehead. His neck was beginning to stiffen, and his jaw hurt like hell.
He worked his chin back and forth to make sure it wasn't broken.
The words came to him slowly, their sound slightly garbled. "What
do you mean?"

"Where do you go from here?"

"I'm not sure."

They rode in silence for several minutes, the setting sun turning the black asphalt into an indistinct gray mass marked by white
lines and floating automobiles in their left. *He drives like an American*, Rosman thought. *An old American.*

Rosman took a deep breath. He turned to face Harding, setting his back against the door. Rosman made sure it was locked.
"Why are you here, Bill?"

Harding looked uncomfortable. He eased out a faint smile. "I
came looking for you."

"How much do you know? And how big a role have you
played?"

Harding took his eyes off the road. "What are you talking
about?"

"Are you the one?" After a moment, Rosman added, "Did you
put the MPs onto me?"

Harding laughed, a light sound slipping from his lips. He
unbuttoned his blue overcoat, revealing the yellow sweater

beneath. Harding's fingers beat against the steering wheel. Then he thrust his hand up in the air. "I drove over to your house earlier today, but you weren't around. There were a couple of German cops in front, though, and I thought you had gone off the deep end." The hand ran through his short reddish hair. "But then I saw they were talking to some guy who looked like he had been mugged." Harding shook his head. "This city has been experiencing a lot more crime since the Wall opened."

Rosman smiled at the thought. "I guess that's the price of freedom, Bill."

"So anyhow, I called Joanna."

"Joanna? What made you think of that?"

"It was Kramer's idea. She said you had probably gone to Rostock." Harding peered at Rosman, wetting his lips. He reached over and touched Rosman's sleeve. "She told me to hurry, John. She said you could be in danger."

Rosman stared at the floor. "How would she know? I haven't spoken to her since Prague," he mused. "Man, that seems like eons ago. I think I've aged half a lifetime since the Wall opened." He jerked his head up toward Harding. "What were you doing in my office the other day?"

Harding shook his head and extended one hand toward the windshield. "I saw Kramer snooping around in there. He was leaning over your desk, as though he was looking for something. I thought it would be a good idea to keep him occupied until Friedlander let you go."

"Where was he when I got back?"

"He left when he heard you coming." Harding looked at Rosman again, but then jerked his gaze back to the road. He had to swerve to bring the car back into the right lane.

"Jesus, Bill. You're going to get us killed." Rosman squinted and cocked his head at a slight angle. "Do you think he's working with Avery and Donnelson?"

"The guys who questioned you?" Rosman nodded. Harding glanced over and blew out his breath through puffed cheeks. "Yeah, I think so."

"That slimy bastard!" Rosman pounded his fist on the dashboard. "What an asshole."

"I never did trust him." Harding glanced at Rosman. "Well, at first, sure. But he was always asking about you and your visits and friends in the east."

"But you said he had a natural interest in events over there."

"Yeah, but then I found out that he's the guy who gave your name to security."

"How did you find out?"

"Friedlander told me."

Rosman stared ahead, his face set against the sun streaking across the windshield. "Jesus, what a motherfucker." He flipped the visor down against the windshield.

Harding looked over at Rosman again, throwing his arm along the top of the steering wheel. "I have to admit, John. At first, I thought it might be true."

"You thought I was a traitor?" Rosman gaped at his friend.

"Well, you're the one with the friends over there. You're the one spending so much of his time over there. And being so secretive about it."

Harding pinned his gaze on the road ahead. Seconds later, he offered Rosman his bottle of Perrier. Rosman shook his head. The guy couldn't go anywhere without his bottled water.

"Anyway, I rushed up here to Rostock to see what was up. If there was going to be trouble I wanted to be around to help."

"Thanks, Bill. I appreciate that."

"I see you were well prepared, though." Harding glanced over at Rosman's weapon. "Soviet model?"

Rosman looked at his friend. "I guess so. I'm not very familiar with this sort of thing." Rosman pulled the pistol from his belt and weighed it in his palm. "Are you?"

"Not really. But I do know a Makarov from a Browning. It might be East German. They made a bunch too."

Rosman tilted his head back against the seat, his hand covering his forehead. "Where did Kramer go?"

"Forget it, John. The guy's too much for you or me."

The Mazda slowed for the inspection at the northern border crossing in Reinickendorf. A guard waved them to a lane reserved for diplomats and saluted as they drove by and entered West Berlin.

"Times sure have changed," Harding remarked.

"They sure have," Rosman agreed. He studied the slip of paper. "Joanna knew I was in Rostock?"

"That's right. And she sounded worried."

"Take me to Prenzlauer Berg then, would you?"

Harding shot him a puzzled frown. "You sure?"

"Yeah. I need to see Joanna."

CHAPTER 29

By eight o'clock the sun had long since disappeared behind a blanket of black sky, lit intermittently by the streetlights placed at regular half-block intervals. Rosman stared absent-mindedly at the traffic running down the middle of Schoenhauser Allee. The trees were wrapped in iron gratings, softened by patches of a gray fog that had snuck in upon the city from the surrounding plain with all the warning of a fox. Every 10 minutes or so a subway train roared along the elevated tracks that ran down the middle of the street.

Joanna's apartment lay hidden among a row of beat up buildings along a side street running from Schoenhauser to Dimitroff-strasse. At street level a wide band of white stucco ran along the outer wall, separated from the chipped cement and broken brick by heavy blocks of concrete. Peeling paint barely covered the broken wood that outlined windows resembling the tired eyes in the face of an old drunk. The sidewalk was a double set of flat, uneven paving blocks set between rows of cobblestones. Beyond them stood row upon row of Trabants. A flower shop and butcher's store stood to either side of the entrance.

He turned the corner and climbed the steps to her place on the fourth floor. Rosman knocked once, and Joanna opened the door. She advanced to embrace him. Rosman hesitated a moment, then surrendered. Despite everything that had happened, he still wanted to experience the touch and feel of this woman again. He realized he probably always would.

Her wide green eyes peered deep into his. She kissed him hard on the lips. Her scent was exactly that of their first encounter that night just weeks back, when Rosman had returned sore, bitter and confused. That night now seemed like a distant, fading memory.

As beautiful as ever, she was wearing a brown leather miniskirt with a loose, white cotton pullover and suede jacket. The outfit accentuated her figure perfectly, the long legs extending from the skirt at mid-thigh, the bust outlined against the sweater and pushing the jacket apart, the loose, slightly tangled blond hair ending just shy of the shoulder.

"My God, John. I'm so relieved to see you." She pushed the door shut, then took his hands again. Her eyes stayed with his, and the lower lip disappeared between rows of even white teeth. "Is everything all right? You aren't hurt, are you?"

"No, I'm okay. I won't be long." He strolled over and sat in the middle of a sofa that lined the wall just inside her door. From here he could see across what looked like a three-room apartment, the kitchen to his left, and what was probably her bedroom to his right. The furnishings were spartan: just this sofa, an armchair and a dining room table with two wooden chairs at opposite ends. A lone lamp on the table threw an angle of light through the middle of the room. Most of her money must have gone into the Sony stereo equipment spread out along three shelves of a teak cabinet to his right. A sandy-colored carpet lay under an array of bright, colorful Oriental rugs.

Rosman stood up, pulled the pistol from inside the waist of his pants and set it carefully on top of the table. Joanna's hand shot to her mouth.

"You needed that to come see me?" Her eyes were wide with disbelief.

"It's something I found earlier today. As it turned out, I didn't need it."

"That's good to hear." She walked over and picked it up off the table. "But put it away." Her eyes surveyed the apartment. "You never know what will happen."

Rosman took the weapon and tucked it into his pants again.

"No." Her head swung back and forth while her fingers drew an imaginary line. "Where it won't show," she commanded. Her gaze darted to the bedroom, then back again. She settled herself on the sofa next to him. "Tell me what happened in Rostock. Is it over?"

"Yes, I suppose it is."

"Was it Schmidt?"

"Yeah, I had a revealing conversation with Schmidt. I was surprised at how willing he was to bare his soul."

"Why? What did he say?"

"He told me a great deal of his family's history. And his involvement with the Stasi. He also explained his role in the Lamprecht and Jens beatings. He doesn't seem too worried."

"About what?"

"Revenge, prosecution. Things like that. Claims he's innocent, anyway." Rosman shifted his weight on the sofa. "He doesn't even have to worry about Gracchus."

"Why not?"

"Well, he worked for him once."

Joanna stared out the window when Rosman did not continue. Her hands rested on the cushion between them. The soft white skin seemed out of place against the rough brown fabric. "Many have," she finally said. "And still do. It isn't easy to stop."

"I know. And he's been dogging me these last few months, most recently on the Autobahn from Rostock. That's why my car's in a ditch."

"A ditch?" Her hands dove underneath her legs.

"That's right. But you already know all about that. Or, at least the general plan, don't you?"

"What plan was that?" She averted her eyes again. Her ankles crossed, then separated.

"That I was supposed to go to Rostock. That's what Gracchus wanted. He didn't go up there to find Schmidt. It was all a set up to lure me there."

"Why would Gracchus do that?"

"You tell me. I think you know."

Joanna stood up and paced to the window opposite the couch and back again. She dropped into her seat next to Rosman, and her ankles crossed once more. She folded her arms across her breast.

"What makes you so sure?"

"Lamprecht's notes, for one thing. Most of it, you're probably aware, is a journal of your country's political opposition, a diary of the 'Wende'."

"And?"

"Well, Hermann was also using it to hide some sort of code. It was more than just an account of events. He was keeping his own record, for his own purposes."

Rosman took a pen from his shirt pocket and began to scribble on a copy of the newspaper *Der Morgen* that lay on Joanna's table. "Look here. The letter G appears quite often, but usually with a different mixture of letters after it, sometimes nothing, other times an r, or u, or s, or even a mixture of those. And those are usually set with another capital letter, or grouping."

Joanna peered over Rosman's shoulder. "But what is that supposed to mean?"

"I think he was making shorthand references to meetings between Gracchus and others, probably arranged by Gracchus. For example, couplings with a P emerge in late 1988, continuing with increasing frequency through this spring and summer."

He tossed the pen on the table and sat back against the cushions. "Later, a series of numbers begins to appear. Some of them are matched with more letters, and occasionally the name of a town. At first I was completely confused by those, but then it came to me."

"What was that?"

"They're bank accounts. I only realized it this afternoon. That's when I remembered the series of figures from my family's savings account. It was established after the war when the West German government opened it to pay my family's reparation."

Her green eyes had gone opaque. "I...I don't understand."

"We were victims of Nazism," Rosman explained.

"How much did you receive?"

"Oh. I don't know. We never took anything out. My parents referred to it as 'blood money.' But that's not important here."

"Then tell me what is."

Rosman studied Joanna to see if she was being sarcastic. Her face was frozen and distant. Rosman took a deep breath and continued.

"You know, there's one thing that has bothered me for quite some time now. What I could never figure out was why Gracchus let me linger for so long."

Joanna shrugged, tilting her head away from Rosman.

He fetched the newspaper from the table and studied his notations. "Why didn't he ever come again when he failed to find what he wanted? There was the notebook, of course. But also a set of files. According to Schmidt, Gracchus thought I had those, too."

"Does he still?"

Rosman shook his head. "I don't think so. That's why he was willing to go after me on the Autobahn today. Unfortunately, we can't ask him. He's dead."

Her breath escaped with a hiss, and her fingers gripped the pillow like a vise. "Dead?"

"That's right. On the Autobahn."

He tossed the roll of paper at Joanna and watched it slide across her legs and come to a rest on the floor at her feet. She hesitated, then picked it up.

"What's this?"

"Lamprecht's notes."

"Why are you showing these to me now?"

"Because you've wanted to see them for some time. By the way, it's entirely plausible that the H stands for Hetzling, and the S that appears represents Schmidt. Maybe not. It's a common letter. But it isn't important right now to figure out what every single letter and date mean. Probably only Lamprecht knows that. The code was amazing for its simplicity, though. I guess he just wanted something for a quick reference when he tried to piece it all together."

"What about the numbers? The bank accounts? How does that fit in?" She continued to stare at the paper, holding it so tightly that the paper crumpled in her fist.

"Oh, the bank accounts are easy. That's how Gracchus and his cronies have been laundering Stasi funds."

"Why would they do that?"

"To cash in on the late arrival of capitalism in this part of the world." Rosman thrust his index finger in the air. "Or perhaps to prepare for the next battle. That's why Hetzling was so important. He allowed them to use the buy-out program to transfer people and funds into the West. Anyway, Lamprecht must have been involved in that as well. I don't see how else he could have obtained this much information." Rosman gave a short, hard laugh. "Geez, I hope at least Jens was clean."

"But why would Hermann want to record all this?"

"I'm not sure what he planned to do. Perhaps he wanted them for when the time came to settle old scores, if that day ever does arrive. Or perhaps he hoped to pass them along to the some-one in the West."

Joanna shrugged and grimaced. "Do you think Hermann had that much foresight?"

"Yes, I do. He was trying to protect himself. Like so many oth-ers. Schmidt, for example. I think he also recorded what he knew about those behind the overthrow of Honecker."

"Like Gracchus?"

Rosman sat back and threw one leg over the other. "Oh, Gracchus for certain. And others in Moscow. The mind boggles to think of all those that might have been behind this last desperate attempt to preserve the Soviet Union's post-war empire."

Rosman sighed and shook his head. "But whatever Lamprecht may have planned to do with them, the truly sad thing is that his murder may actually have succeeded in erasing the trail. I mean, if the interlocking parts, the explanations for the clues, are only in his head, then the papers aren't much use, are they?"

"No, I guess not."

"So, the joke's on those who were so fired up to recover the damn thing."

He looked at Joanna for a moment, waiting for her to respond. Her hands were now folded in her lap. Her eyes found Rosman, then shifted to some unseen spot on the wall across from her.

"Speaking of which, I also noticed the letter J in several places, sometimes alone, but often followed with an o, or an a, or an n, sometimes a mix as well," Rosman continued. "The really puzzling part is that they're usually coupled with the G combinations."

She turned her head back to him. Wide oval eyes glistened like fine jewels, framed in tears that ran down her cheeks.

"I never had a choice." She wiped the tears from her eyes with the back of her sleeve. "I was pressured into working for them as a student, like many others. I don't think I ever truly believed in the cause."

"Then why did you do it?"

"Because I was raised in a household that did believe. I was raised to believe as well, but I just never gained the faith that others had."

Rosman did not move. He took his breaths with as little movement as possible, waiting for the bitterness to subside.

"What you don't seem to realize," she continued, "is that it doesn't matter, because there was never really any alternative for me. She leaned back in the sofa, running her hands over her face and through her hair. "How did you find out?"

"I figured that out today as well, after my talk with Schmidt. He spoke of Gracchus, his family history, and his ruthless and efficient nature. It made me wonder why a novice like me had been spared. Then Schmidt jokingly suggested that I was either very lucky, or I had a protector in high places. And it seems I did. Not real high, but high enough."

Rosman stood up and limped over to the window. He stared at the tired and beaten city outside through the gritty panes of streaked glass Then he turned to look at Joanna. Graceful lines ran from her head to her shoulders and down along her arms as she sat there. Half-hidden in the shadows drawn by the lamp, she reminded Rosman of a Rembrandt painting. He shook his head.

"You made a big mistake by staying away. You might have been able to keep my attention diverted for a while longer. As it was, my mind stayed clear long enough to put some of this together."

He studied the graceful, careless fall of her hair as it curved around the back of her neck. Her eyes seemed to swim in front of his face. Then he realized that he had tears in his as well. "Did you know that I had fallen in love with you?"

"I won't say I didn't enjoy being with you." Joanna had folded her hands and was holding them tight to her lap. She stared straight ahead. "If it makes you feel any better, they were the most pleasant days I've had in a long time. And I can honestly say that I told them only what I had to, only the minimum."

"But it was enough wasn't it? They still got what they needed, didn't they?"

"No. I had to give them something, some bits of information. But they never got the notebook."

Rosman thrust his hands through the air. "Are you going to claim credit for that?"

"I did know where it was. I found the notes the night I met you back at your place. I almost stole them, but I didn't want to hurt you that badly. I knew it would destroy you if you had lost that…and me. Now I think I would have gladly given them those damn notes if it would have ended all this."

Rosman strode over and stood in front of her. "Was that why you went to Prague?"

Her eyes blazed at Rosman. "Yes. I wanted you to stop this crusade of yours before you…we…got hurt. I just wanted to stop the running, the trickery. That's why I sent you away."

"Do you feel any remorse? What about Hans? And I thought Jens and Lamprecht were your friends. Don't you feel responsible in any way for their deaths?"

"No, absolutely not." Joanna threw her hair back, and her voice hardened. "They *were* my friends. Gracchus promised me that Jens would not be harmed if I would just cooperate."

"Then why did they die? What happened? Was the Stasi really that desperate to cover all its traces?"

Joanna stared at him in silence. Rosman thought he detected a trace of pity in her eyes. It was the first time he had seen her look at him in that way.

"There's more to it." Joanna straightened herself on the sofa and shook her head. She leaned forward, her hands thrust out.

"Don't you realize why I wanted it all to end? I wanted to convince them that you didn't have what they really needed, that you should be left alone."

"But I did. I had the notebook."

"No, no. It's not just the Stasi and some dissidents. And it's not just the notebook."

"What do you mean?"

"Oh, John." She sounded almost desperate. "The Soviets were also involved. They're probably the ones responsible for Erich's death."

"Was it the KGB?" He thought of the warnings from Hetzling and Preselnikov.

"I'm not sure. Maybe them, maybe the GRU. Maybe parts of both."

"But why would they kill Jens? What could he have known that was so dangerous?"

"You hinted at it earlier."

Rosman extended his hands toward her, palms open.

"The power struggle in Moscow over Honecker's removal. Hans was the first to go, because he was trying to warn your people about the power play that was coming."

"But Jens and Lamprecht? It was too late by then. Schmidt said they were supposed to find some files on Stasi sources among the dissidents."

"Yes, yes. But Gracchus also wanted to use them and other dissidents as a funnel and a cover. He was building a new network, and it might have worked if they hadn't got caught up in the confusion and power struggle," Joanna said.

"What confusion? What power struggle?"

"Between various Soviet factions. I'm not really sure, but it probably goes beyond the security people. And that night in Normannenstrasse, things went all wrong. The files had been moved. People were already in a panic, trying to erase the traces to their pasts."

Rosman lowered his arms and turned away.

"Order is breaking down all over in the east, John, not just in this country. And new fiefdoms are already being built."

Rosman stood at the window, his hands on his hips and his back to Joanna.

"You see, it's about more than just the past, John. Erich and Hermann stumbled onto the future as well. That's why they had to die."

Rosman wheeled around. "What about the future?"

"Gracchus was ordered by Schwanitz…."

"Who?"

"Schwanitz, Mielke's successor as head of the Stasi. He ordered Gracchus to rebuild the networks."

"What do you mean?"

"I'm not sure myself what it all means. But I know they wanted not only to derail the 'Wende'. They have other plans as well. They're not just going to fade away on a cool autumn evening, John."

She rested her head in her hands for several seconds, and then reached out toward Rosman. "That's where the files come in. The notebook was important, but on its own it's not very damaging. The real fear came from the possibility that you also had access to the files. Together, they would allow you to uncover a large part of that network. I didn't think you had the other half. That's why I tried to end all this. That way, the two would stay separated."

Rosman walked over to an armchair by the sofa and sat down.

"So that's why the Meyers had to die as well. I guess their last message does make sense."

"Who?"

"Wilhelm Meyer, a pastor from Potsdam. He worked for the Stasi too, but before he and his wife died they tried to put me on the right path. The wife probably didn't know much in the way of details, so she tried to warn me about what was coming with some lines from Goethe's *Faust*."

"*Faust?* I don't get it?"

Rosman smiled and massaged his brow with tired fingertips. "She was pretty frightened at the end, which was probably why she never came right out and told me of her suspicions. She passed me some lines from Goethe's poem, and I spent several hours trying to decipher those words for some hidden clue. Then, I thought of finding the passage in the poem itself to see what followed and preceded it."

"And?"

He leaned forward and took the pen again. Rosman studied the wall for a moment and then wrote the words at the bottom of the newspaper.

O gibt es Geister in der Luft
(If there are spirits in the air)

Die zwischen Erd und Himmel herrschend weben,
(Who rule between Earth and Heaven,)

So steiget nieder aus dem goldnen Duft
(So, climb down from the golden haze)

Und fuhrt mich weg zu neuem, buntem Leben!
(And lead me away to a new, bright Life!)

Ja, waere nur a Zaubermantel mein!
(Yes, if only a magic coat were mine!)

Und trueg er mich in fremde Laender,
(And it carried me off to strange Lands)

Mir soellt er um die koestlichsten Gewaender,
(For me, among the most precious vestments, it)

Nicht feil um einen Koenigsmantel sein.
(Would be worth more than a king's robe.)

Joanna read the passage and glanced up at Rosman. "I still don't get it."

He sat back in the chair. "I think in their own pathetic, brave way, Meyer and his wife were trying to tell me what Gracchus and his gang were up to."

Rosman leaned forward again and underlined the last four lines. "Those accounts are their magic coat. They'll carry them to new lands. They're preparing for the future with vestments more valuable than any king's garments."

Both sat quietly for several minutes, alone with their thoughts. Finally, Rosman spoke.

"Did you ever feel that strongly for me?" He paused before posing the one question he had come to ask. "Did you ever love me?"

"I don't know." She spoke slowly. "I'm not sure I know what that means, what it's supposed to feel like." She looked into Rosman's eyes. Pools of water shone in the bottom of her own. "I'm sorry."

"But why did you agree to spy on me in the first place? How could you work for a bastard like Gracchus?"

"I told you I had no choice. He's my father."

Rosman jumped from his seat and stumbled backwards. He reeled to the center of the room, as though someone had just struck him with a fist. He gasped for breath, back-pedalling to escape the room, clutching his stomach as he stumbled into the kitchen. He was desperate for something to stem the wave of nausea that was bringing his stomach up through his throat.

The cabinets seemed to swim in mid-air. Rosman groped for a glass and poured it half full with water from the kitchen tap. A stream of cool, refreshing liquid ran down his throat. He leaned against the sink and let the faucet run. Then he splashed some water on his face, turned the tap off and rubbed his cheeks and forehead dry with a dish towel.

Slowly, the pressure in his head faded and the churning in his stomach ebbed. He shuffled back into the living room and stood before the sofa. He stared at Joanna for what seemed like minutes. Her lip quivered beneath moist eyes, and her shoulders huddled together above hands clasped and suspended over her lap.

"Did he tell you to sleep with me?"

Joanna threw her head back. "Of course not. That was my own wish, not a part of the assignment. It gave me the chance to establish my own area of freedom, my own retreat."

Rosman was silent. His heart pounded in his chest, and his breath came and went in large gulps.

Joanna stared hard. "Do you think everything I did revolved around that assignment? Even if I can't say it was love, I was attracted to you. I do care for you, and I don't want to see you hurt anymore. That's why I sent your friend to Rostock. To help you. Can't you accept that much at least?"

She held her hand out to Rosman. She let it fall against the back of the sofa when he did not take it.

"I'm not sure what I can accept right now," he replied.

"This has all been very, very enlightening. Not to mention, very entertaining."

Rosman's head shot toward the sound of the new voice. He recognized it instantly. Kramer stood just outside the entrance to the bedroom, a broad smile sweeping his face. His camouflage pants, black military boots and olive green sweater made him look as though he were dressed for combat.

"Kramer! You bastard."

Rosman's gaze shot toward Joanna. She sat immobile on the sofa, her face buried in her hands. "One betrayal wasn't enough?"

She looked up at him, her eyes rimmed in red. "I didn't want him here. John, please believe me. I'm not a part of his plans."

"Oh, but you are, you lovely thing. My plans are impossible without you." Kramer turned toward Rosman. He was pointing a Browning 9mm semi-automatic at Rosman's stomach. Somehow, the smile seemed more penetrating, more evil. "You are so predictable, John. In fact, you have been exactly that throughout this little mishap."

"What do you mean?"

"When Gracchus's clever ploy on the Autobahn failed, I knew you'd come here. You'd have put enough together by now to come running to your sweetheart and try to sort out some kind of reconciliation, if you could." His lips puckered, and the gun waved in Joanna's direction. "But she surprised you, didn't she?" Kramer's shoulders shook lightly as he laughed. "You're a romantic fool, John."

"So, you were there all along. I'm surprised Harding never recognized you in Rostock."

"Oh shit. That was a tough one, fooling someone like Harding. He's even more of an amateur than you are."

"And the traces you ran?"

Kramer tapped his temple with two fingers. "Take a guess."

"You made it up, of course."

"Not exactly." Kramer brushed the fingernails of his free hand against his chest. "But I did embellish some. I can be pretty creative when I have to."

"So, what happens now?"

"Well, it looks like I'll have to kill you. You already know too much, and the set-up is perfect. I've caught you red-handed, John. Here in your lover's apartment, the woman who doubles as your handler. You resisted, we struggled, and I had to shoot you." Kramer laughed again. "Shit, man, they'll give me a medal."

"No! You bastard." Joanna stormed across the room. She surged against Kramer, slapping his face.

"Easy, bitch." Kramer grabbed her wrist. He yanked her arm down toward the floor and spun her around to face Rosman. "It looks like she still has the hots for you, John. Although what she sees in you is beyond me." He held her waist. His smile returned while he licked his lips. "Now, don't you feel badly for being so mean to her tonight?"

Rosman had not moved. His eyes were fixed on the Browning, his feet and hands refusing to budge. "It won't work, Kramer," Rosman could barely hear his own voice through the pounding in his chest. He shifted his weight and body angle to face Kramer, hands resting on his hips. "Harding knows too."

"Not as much as you. And his credibility is shit. He's your best friend. I can take care of him."

Rosman turned his face toward Joanna. "How can you work with someone like this?"

"I don't. He disgusts me," Joanna spat. Her eyes shifted toward Rosman's waist. "I tried to think of some way to warn you he was here. I was afraid to say it right out. He's too dangerous."

"Tell me, Rick. Just who do you work for?"

"I work for nobody and everybody. Just me and me alone, my boy. I am my own intelligence service. The Rick Fucking Kramer Agency."

He threw back his head and let loose a long, low laugh that rose in pitch until it reached a howl. As he did, Joanna swung her right arm straight back, catching Kramer's nose with her elbow. He stumbled backwards, blood dripping from his nostrils. Joanna pushed off from his chest and broke free.

Rosman fired three times. The first shot drilled a rough hole through the wall above Kramer's head. His face jerked back toward Rosman, the eyes a twin set of flames in red and white. He levelled the Browning.

The second shot burst into Kramer's chest. The third exploded against his stomach, throwing a gush of red across his sweater. The impact knocked his body against the wall. The pistol flew from his grip, scattering across the bright browns and yellows of Joanna's rugs.

His back pinned to the wall, Kramer slid to the floor. Blood spread beyond his chest and stomach, turning his upper body into a carpet of deep red. Rosman watched the blood run from his nostrils and the corner of his mouth.

Kramer coughed once, throwing a spray of red foam across the floor. His pupils found Rosman. "You motherfucker," he chanted. "You pissant motherfucker."

His eyes were sets of confusion, the burning hatred dimming to a dull glow of pink, then gray as his legs twitched and stilled.

Rosman turned to Joanna, who sat against the wall, pressing her forehead into the dark green plaster. "Are you all right?"

She nodded. Tears flowed down her cheeks, and her shoulders heaved.

Rosman walked over to Joanna and kissed the hair at the crown of her head. He strode without another sound out of the building and into the night.

He wandered as if in a trance, his body drained of feeling, the Makarov hanging from his hand. When he lifted his head, Rosman could see the dark, uneven skyline of East Berlin extending out over Alexanderplatz and Mitte, toward the Brandenburg Gate and into the west. More than ever, this city came to him now as an eerie, beautiful apparition. Darkened skies lay like a shroud over the city lights, and the buildings were bathed in a distant haze, a blend of fog and shadow, reality hidden in the mist of image, memory, and illusion. He told himself that what he did not know could fill volumes. He wondered if it would ever end.

Finally, Rosman found himself at the Marx-Engels Bridge that spanned the Spree along Unter den Linden. He leaned over the edge and peered across the water. The Cathedral built during the reign of Kaiser Wilhelm resembled a huge dark blur, its modern Baroque style hid by the foreboding air of a Berlin night. Only the huge dome stood out against the sky, lit by columns of light from the television tower.

To his left, the yellow walls and brown columns of the old arsenal, now a history museum, marked a welcome contrast to the Palace of the Republic, built by Honecker on the site of the Hohenzollern palace as a symbol of his state's endurance. Schinkel's statues lining the Bridge had watched centuries of human folly parade past. They whispered that the Palace was full of asbestos; it would have to come down like so much before it. Everything passed, eventually.

The black waters of the Spree swallowed the Makarov without a sound.

CHAPTER 30

He could not remember ever seeing such a bright sun in his year and a half in Berlin. But when Rosman left the staff meeting in Friedlander's office, he had to pause on the top step of the building's entrance to shield his eyes. He waved to the German civilian in a castoff Army uniform guarding the entrance to the U.S. Mission and descended the long cobblestone driveway that led to the gate on Clayallee. Rosman pulled the plaid scarf tighter around his neck and walked with a light, quick step along the uneven cobblestones. He hailed one of the taxis waiting just beyond the gate.

Twenty minutes later Rosman climbed from the cab when it pulled over to the curb. He raised his eyes to the window that marked Joanna's apartment before pulling a wad of West Marks from his pants pocket. The driver's eyes gleamed, and his hand slid from the window to take his fee. In the afternoon sun the buildings looked almost young again. Sheets of light bounced off the glass of newly cleaned windows, and traces of red and blue paint peeked from the brick walls. Rosman pulled his glove back on and walked through the front door of the building.

At the top of the stairs, Rosman turned and strolled toward Joanna's door. It stood open, and a shaft of light from the apartment split the corridor.

"At last, Herr Rosman. I wondered how long you would wait," Buechler exclaimed.

The room was empty. Buechler stood alone against the far wall in his worn brown overcoat, cambridge cap in hand.

"What happened to the furniture? The rugs?" His gaze roamed the apartment. "And Joanna?"

"They've been gone for some time now. You must be busy to stay away for so long. What has it been? Two weeks?"

Rosman strolled through the foyer and into the middle of the room. "Yes, it has. And I am busy. My final days here, actually."

Buechler shot a glance at Rosman. "What did you say?"

"The Department allowed me to resign. It just came through today. Frankly, I was lucky."

"But what will you do now?"

"I've applied for a teaching job back in the States." Rosman smiled at Buechler's look of concern. "Don't worry. I'll be all right."

"And the inquiry into the soldier's death?"

Rosman shrugged. "Unresolved. A mysterious shooting on the wrong side of town with an East European weapon and no record of his having crossed. The authorities over there looked into it but found nothing. I think our own were happy that nothing came out in public. There are internal investigations underway, of course."

Buechler smiled. "So you came to give her the news. I mean your own news, of course. It's what you uncle would have done." Buechler's face relaxed, and he approached Rosman. "It sounds like you will be busy up to the very end, though. I read about the decision to begin the 'Two-Plus-Four' negotiations. Will you have the opportunity to give Washington your ideas on how things are going, or how they should go, here in Germany?"

"I'm afraid not. It looks like most of the strategy and policy will be developed in Washington. And by people who far outrank me," Rosman explained.

"It sounds like this could be a frustrating time for you, Herr Rosman. What will you be doing during these negotiations?"

"Mostly gofer stuff."

"Excuse me?" Buechler leaned forward.

"It's an American expression. It means I'll be doing mundane things, like running errands and escorting visitors."

"That's unfortunate," Buechler said. He eyed Rosman with a mischievous grin. "In view of what you now know, you could contribute more to such important discussions."

Rosman walked over to the window. "Just how much do I know?"

"Well, you know more about Honecker's fall than your superiors in Washington."

"Gracchus and his friends in Moscow?" He stared into the alley below.

Buechler nodded. "For example."

"But we still don't know how high that goes." Rosman turned and leaned against the window sill. "Do you think it was an official KGB operation? Did Gorbachev know?"

"Do you truly think an operation of that magnitude would occur without such high-level approval?"

"Proof would be nice."

"Of course, it would," Buechler agreed.

He motioned with his cap toward the wall next to the window. The blood stains had darkened to brown in the intervening weeks. Rosman wondered if anyone had even tried to clean them.

"Did you have any proof about Kramer?" Buechler asked.

Rosman stared at the wall. "Proof enough," he whispered.

"Proof enough for what? A court of law?"

"Enough for me..." Rosman hesitated. "...and for the others."

Buechler tilted his head. "And what about the numbered bank accounts?"

"I passed that to the CIA."

"Good. All our work would have been in vain if information like this was not used. Perhaps it will even do some good. If it can be traced. That's what it's all about, Herr Rosman."

"All what?"

"What we've been doing." Buechler walked over to Rosman and tapped his left arm with a long thick index finger. "It's about information, and getting that information to the right people."

Rosman did not speak. He had been gazing at Buechler's finger and then his hands. They were thicker and more scarred than he remembered from their first afternoon together.

Rosman strode to the door and glanced into the hallway. A woman passed by, presumably on her way to work. Her eyes were hidden behind loose strands of brown hair that kept falling across her forehead and cheeks. She must be a waitress, he told himself.

The black dress and white apron that ran to her knees failed to hide her full figure, the breasts pushing the top edge of her apron out. She held a heavy blue overcoat folded over her left arm. Rosman thought of Joanna.

"And then there's the personal angle," he said.

"Excuse me?" Buechler leaned forward.

"Why is all this information, and what's done with it, so important to you?"

"Let me tell you a story, Herr Rosman. It's a story from my time in Bautzen."

"Is that where you met Gracchus?"

Buechler waved his cap in the air. "Yes. He was my cellmate for a period. About a year."

"Hence, the revenge."

"Yes. Gracchus killed a good friend of mine."

"How so?"

"His name was Heinz Schroeder. My friend smuggled information to the West. One of our 'Schuhmacher Agenten'. You remember?"

"Yes."

"He was arrested twice, and Heinz was badly mistreated. He eventually developed tuberculosis, which, untreated in those damp cells, killed him. I saw him on the last day he was alive. Schroeder told me that the individual sentenced with him, the fellow who had returned to prison with him, was actually a plant, an informer. This man had been responsible for Schroeder's second arrest. Schroeder made me swear to get even."

"Is that where you got sick?"

Buechler looked confused.

"I'm not deaf. At times I wondered if your lungs weren't about to explode."

Buechler nodded. "Yes, but that matters little now."

"What about the bigger issues?" Rosman blinked as he thought of his parents and their history. "What good is the little we've learned when set against all that?"

"Information, Herr Rosman, is power. If it is used correctly."

"And you needed me to get that information?"

"Yes. I needed your youth, your strength. Even more important, I needed your curiosity, your eagerness to know. We call it
Wissensdrang."

Rosman laughed. "More *Faust*. I wonder if I'll ever be able to
read Goethe again." Rosman looked back at Buechler, surprised
by the sly grin that had spread over his lips. "I'm not sure that what
you're describing here is really my battle."

"That's not how your uncle would see it." Buechler hesitated.
"Nor your parents."

"They're no longer here. They've chosen to stay in America."

"Yes, unfortunately. But you see, nonetheless, the battle continues."

"Not mine. And I wonder if this chapter isn't coming to an end
for my country as well."

"How can you say that?"

"Because the good guys have won. In fact, I wonder if people
like Hans and Erich weren't tilting at windmills that had already
collapsed." Rosman looked up at Buechler. "I think you've missed
an important point. As did my late friends."

"Which is?"

"It's true that the Stasi was present in the dissident movement,
and that they tried to manipulate and undermine it. But in the end
it didn't do them any good. The Stasi, I mean. They weren't powerful enough to control the people, or to resist historical forces they
never understood. In the end, justice won out in spite of the Stasi.
I just wish the others had lived to see that, and that their deaths
had not been in vain."

Buechler threw his head back and scoffed. His face wore a
knowing smile. "I guess Reinhold was right after all."

"Who's Reinhold?"

"Oh, he was one of East Germany's leading theoreticians. A
party man, of course, and one of the dogmatists. He said that the
East German state can only exist as a socialist alternative to West
Germany. Once you take away the hard orthodoxies that distin-
guish the East German experiment, it will never be able to resist
unification on western terms. That too, Herr Rosman, is what
Gracchus and his henchmen never understood."

"Fortunately, it's over."

"Not really. I doubt they understand it now. People like Gracchus don't give up that easily."

"Is that why you're here? To warn me? Or were you looking for someone else?"

Buechler shrugged and smiled.

"So," Rosman continued, "we're back to the personal agenda, back to revenge."

"Yes, that's never very far away. You see, I missed Gracchus again. So I was looking for the girl."

"I thought so. What do you expect her to do?"

"Help me locate Gracchus."

"Check the cemetary."

"I already have," Buechler answered. "There is no record of his death."

"But I saw him." Rosman frowned in disbelief.

Buechler shrugged. "We'll see." His turned to Rosman. "But I was also looking for you. And I am not alone. They think you still have valuable information. Whether Gracchus is alive or not, I still urge you to be careful."

Buechler strode over to Rosman, pausing before walking into the hallway. He placed his hand on Rosman's arm, clenching it suddenly in his strong fingers. Rosman winced.

"The girl is gone for you. You would do well to forget her."

"I'm not sure I can. Perhaps America will help."

"You've had a good bit of luck these last few weeks, Herr Rosman. For both our sakes, I hope that streak continues."

"Me too. But I don't need that luck as much as I once did."

CHAPTER 31

The trees were still in bloom, but the colors had begun to change, which made the ride home from class particularly pleasant. The drive lasted only about five minutes. Still, the seemingly endless lines of trees—oaks and maples, mostly, with a sprinkling of poplar and tulip—were a welcome break from the miles of corn and soybean prevalent in this part of Iowa. It had only been about six months, too short a time to forget the urban landscape of Berlin. Three small groups of four to five picnickers each milled around the grills the municipal authorities had installed just beyond the gravel parking lot.

Students, Rosman guessed, now that classes were over for the week. Already, his mind was at work on the lesson plan for the following Monday. He still wasn't sure how he should deliver his lecture on the French Revolution to the freshmen class in Western Civilization, to transmit how tumultuous and unpredictable epochs like those could become. It all seemed so predictable, so linear in the textbooks. Yet, he thought, revolutions have a way of devouring their children, of taking unforeseen turns.

Rosman parked in front of the turn-of-the-century Victorian, where he had a second-floor flat. The gray and blue paint was peeling after the long, hard Midwestern winter. The landlord still hadn't responded to his offer to paint the entire house in lieu of rent this summer. Summer school classes would never cover all his expenses. Not on an assistant professor's salary.

He sat in his car for several minutes, enjoying the warm sunshine on this late spring afternoon. Rosman climbed out of his used Volkswagen Cabrio and strolled to the front of his building. He wanted to relax on the long white porch that wrapped itself from the front to the side of the house. But, like most first-year faculty, Rosman was still trying to get his lectures written the day before the class. Next year would be easier, he told himself.

He lumbered up the stairs to his apartment. Rosman guessed the house had been built in the latter years of the previous century, and the reconfiguration that had gutted the inside of the building was unfortunate. But now it held four apartments, and he had been lucky to find one of them vacant on such short notice.

Rosman fumbled with the key to his apartment for several seconds before he realized that the door was unlocked. In fact, it was open. About six inches.

There was another rush of adrenaline, as sharp as the night he and Joanna had gone in search of Jens. Rosman felt his face grow hot. His fingers twitched involuntarily.

He pushed the door open, inch by inch, leaning against the frame. He peered into the room, searching for some clue, some sign of another presence.

Rosman slid past the doorframe. He froze in mid-step when he caught sight of a pair of legs extending from a leather armchair by the wall next to the bedroom. Rosman held his breath. A hard, fast beat pounded at the ribs deep inside his chest. The bastard was just sitting there with his back to the door. This guy obviously didn't give a damn about anyone returning.

Rosman glanced around the apartment, then crept toward the chair. The figure was dressed entirely in white. The shirt, slacks and jacket were all of a color, almost at one with the air. He sat motionless, his head bowed.

Slowly, ominously, the head moved upward, the face turning to Rosman. A light brown goatee framed a self-assured smile that lent a fresh wickedness to the air around it. Rosman had not felt this presence since Berlin.

"Gracchus!" Rosman dropped his briefcase and stepped backwards. "What are you doing here?"

The shadow that framed the face against the fading sun dropped away. Rosman peered intently, searching for traces of the accident on the Autobahn. He had assumed—foolishly, he now realized—that he would never see his nemesis again.

"The beard serves several purposes," Gracchus said. "It hides the scars, for one thing. Shaving had become such a burden. In general, though, the accident was not as serious as you had thought." He laughed through hands steepled in front of his face. "Certainly not serious enough to keep us from meeting again."

"What do you want with me?"

"Oh, come now. Don't you agree that there are some unresolved matters between us?"

Rosman took another step back. He studied Gracchus' face, as though he were seeing it for the first time. It was the face of a complicated man, a true enigma. Rosman tried but could not see through the deep eyes that were almost colorless in the shifting blend of shadow and haze of the late afternoon. The eyes were set under thick eyebrows and a forehead that was alternately smooth and wrinkled, as though a deceptive, intricate mechanism was at work. He realized suddenly how much he hated—and feared— this man.

Rosman had never really thought of Gracchus as human before. He had been no more than a disembodied antagonist. It was clear now that this had been a terrible mistake. Someone had warned him against underestimating Gracchus. Perhaps it had been Schmidt. Had Jens and Lamprecht made the same mistake? "Why did those five people have to die?"

"I've been expecting that." Gracchus seemed quite calm, relaxed even. He sat back in the chair, unfolding and refolding his hands in front of his chin. "Hans was necessary. He thought he could purchase his freedom by betraying our plans." Gracchus waved a hand at the air. "Unfortunately, there was no recalling him. The train was Kramer's touch."

Gracchus sighed as he broke off to glance toward the door. "Lamprecht, however, was another matter. I actually regret his death, and not only because it was unprofessional."

Rosman frowned.

"That's right," Gracchus continued. "I actually regret it. You see, it was unprofessional because we needed to find that notebook, and his death made that so much more difficult."

"Your compassion is touching."

"It was also unnecessary for that young man to die, as long as we got those notes. He had actually been a very effective officer for us."

"But he must have turned."

Hands spread outward, then refolded themselves. "Nothing that couldn't be fixed." Gracchus paused a moment before continuing. "Jens' death was more complicated. In some ways, he was a victim of circumstances. But he was also a threat."

"I find that hard to believe."

"Oh yes, Jens was actually a threat. Not a very serious one, of course. But serious enough for some to warrant killing, although, as I have said, that is not my way of handling things. The trick is to determine first what he knew, or may have known, about the HVA file, and then whether any of that had been passed on to others. One can never be entirely sure in this business. But it was an important file."

Gracchus shook his head. "Jens never should have gotten his paws on that file." He cast a sly glance at Rosman, looking up at him from underneath his eyelids. "Of course, you already know this."

Rosman said nothing.

"His refusal to cooperate only made matters worse. He struggled, or so I am told, which was a very big mistake, since he had no way of winning, particularly against those who held him. I was not there, which appears to have been one of the two mistakes I made in this affair. I should have intervened sooner, to block interference from certain Soviet colleagues."

"Do you mean you didn't know that we were on our way over there that night?"

"Oh, I knew. But the Soviet gentlemen did not. That's why they were gone when you arrived. My colleagues from the HVA, however, were supposed to be there, but they were also late." Gracchus chuckled to himself. "I guess that vaunted Prussian efficiency isn't what it used to be. In any case, Jens may or may not have passed on important information to you, but I had to assume that he did." After a moment he added, "And that's why I'm here."

He waved a rectangular white index card in the air. "Do you

remember this? I brought it along to help refresh your memory."

"Why?"

"Call it a professional courtesy. But whatever you call it, I still need that file. I know you haven't passed it to Langley. Not yet, anyway."

The situation was so absurd. Rosman laughed inwardly. The puzzle fit. Joanna's words, Buechler's warning. The cursory searches at his house, and that night at the Friedrichstrasse station. Now he realized how ironic it had all been. He had been pursued, but pointlessly.

"I've never seen it."

"I don't believe you," Gracchus replied.

Oh Jesus, he thought. *Schmidt, of all people, has won.* Rosman had heard that those things fetched a pretty penny from the German press and other services these days. At any rate, Rosman was not about to tell Gracchus.

"I hate to shock you, Gracchus, but what I've figured out about all that I got without the assistance of any HVA files."

Gracchus stared at Rosman, no trace of emotion crossing his face.

Rosman continued. "So, how many masters did you, or do you, serve?"

"That's the beauty of it. I only ever served one. Some call it 'history', others call it the 'revolution'. Whatever label you give it, it has been my cause. There was no contradiction in my working for Moscow or East Berlin, especially since I was accepted by both. My work with the dissidents and Honecker served each, and it served both together."

"So, why all this concern about the damn notebook and file? Lamprecht couldn't have been that perceptive."

"You should never underestimate the opposition. Haven't you learned that much?"

Gracchus laughed as he rose from the chair. He strolled over toward the bay window, turning his back toward Rosman as he spoke. "You see, Lamprecht actually was quite inventive. He was his own double agent, pretending to be an asset of ours, but all the while accumulating information for his own use."

"Which was?"

His eyes shut, then flashed open again. Gracchus turned toward Rosman, shaking his head. "Whatever it was, it wasn't mine. His observations could tell the right people what they might need to know about future plans we might have and the people we could use. Especially with that file. As long as he was alive, I could control him. Like any other asset." He shrugged. "But we know how that turned out. And that introduced a new element, one that was beyond my control."

Gracchus paused for a moment while he surveyed the room. "You see, that could not be allowed to continue. I have to protect my people." The arrogant smile Rosman had first noticed when he entered the apartment returned. "I still do. That's what I told Joanna."

"And she believed you?"

"Of course she did. She's not as innocent as you think. How else can you explain what she did to Lamprecht?"

Rosman took a step forward, his fists clenched. "What are you trying to say?"

"You see, you shot Kramer too soon. He never had the chance to tell you."

"Tell me what?"

"That Joanna killed Lamprecht." Gracchus pointed a short, muscular finger at Rosman. "Oh yes. She, too, knew what Lamprecht had been up to. He had threatened to expose her if she betrayed his double dealings. It was because of her mistake, her overreaction, that I made her pursue you to find the file."

Rosman's shoulders sank. "You son-of-a-bitch, Gracchus! She's too good to be your daughter." He searched the floor and reached for the arm of the chair to steady himself.

Rosman shook his head. He waited a moment for his heart beat to slow and his breath to return. His eyes never left Gracchus.

"You said you had made two mistakes. What was the other one?"

"Underestimating you. Frankly, I never thought you had the balls to shoot someone like Kramer."

In a flash, he was upon Rosman, the first blow striking Rosman on the lower lip. Gracchus's knuckles pummelled the side of his head and his ribs. Rosman tried desperately to cover himself with his arms. A fist broke through and smashed his nose, sending a sharp stab of pain to the back of his skull. Rosman noticed then the warm, salty—and frightening—taste of his own blood.

As Gracchus grabbed for his arms, Rosman worked his foot back around Gracchus' lower leg. He gave a quick push into the body. Gracchus stumbled backwards and tripped over a coffee table.

"What the fuck do you think you're doing?" Rosman sputtered through the blood running from his nose onto his lips.

Gracchus did not answer. He simply resumed his assault, leaping up and delivering another blow to Rosman's jaw and one to the ear that spun Rosman around, the side of his head now ringing, pain stabbing at the back of his skull. Gracchus grabbed him from behind and slipped his arm around Rosman's neck.

Rosman struggled for breath, his throat closing shut. He slammed his heel down hard on Gracchus' foot, forcing him to loosen his grip. Rosman turned and grabbed Gracchus by the front of his shirt. Then Rosman fell to the floor, slipping his foot into Gracchus' stomach. He pushed up and out as he fell, pulling Gracchus over in the process.

Gracchus flew heels over head above Rosman, hitting the wall at the other end of the room. Gracchus yelped in pain and rolled over.

Rosman heaved himself upright and limped over to the telephone to call the police. As he held the receiver, Rosman turned to Gracchus. His head was throbbing. He gasped for breath.

"Don't you realize it's over, you stupid shit?" Rosman screamed between gulps of air. "You've lost the whole goddamn war, and you lost our little battle in Berlin."

"You fool," Gracchus sputtered, hurling his words at Rosman. "What makes you think it is ever over? Someone from your family should know better."

Rosman lowered his arm, the receiver still in his hand. "What do you know about my family?"

Gracchus was on his knees now, holding his ribs and breathing hard. He lifted his face in a display of sudden triumph. "What do I know about your family? My own family betrayed your uncle in Prague."

Rosman dropped the receiver. Blood rushed to his head. The image of Gracchus swam before him.

Gracchus continued. "That's right. My parents passed the information about your uncle's travels and your family's presence in Prague to the Gestapo."

"But ...why?" Rosman stammered.

"The orders came directly from Moscow. Our Soviet leaders had decided it was time to work for a rapprochement with the Nazis. It was obvious that the western powers planned to sit by and watch Germany and the Soviet Union beat each other bloody. We needed to signal Berlin that our two sides could find a *modus vivendi*, even if it was only temporary."

"How temporary?"

Gracchus's breath came in short, uneven bursts. "The Nazis decimated our organization in Germany. And the Red Army was already embroiled in the next set of purges. We needed time to recover. So, when we learned of your uncle's trip to Berlin, we passed the information to the Gestapo. It was a signal. And it worked!"

Gracchus spoke these last words triumphantly, bringing himself up to his full height. He winced with pain at the effort it cost, holding on to the edge of the sofa for support. Rosman marched over to Gracchus and grabbed him by the lapels of his jacket.

"You twisted bastard." Rosman's hands tightened their grip. He shook Gracchus back and forth, then drew back his right hand. He wanted nothing more at this moment than to shatter Gracchus's face, to crush the life out of it.

Gracchus broke the hold. He threw himself at Rosman's midsection, attempting to lift him off the ground and throw him on his back. They stumbled backwards, out the open apartment door, and bounced off the hallway wall.

Rosman swung the two of them around in an effort to free himself, forcing both of them to lose their footing at the edge of the stairs. They hung in a precarious balance for a full second. Then they fell, tumbling over and over toward the landing below.

At the bottom, Rosman scrambled as quickly as he could to get up. He felt a sharp pain in his ankle when he tried to throw Gracchus off, and realized he had twisted it, or worse. He braced for another assault. But Gracchus did not move.

Rosman crawled to the top of the stairs and stared at the lifeless form. The man lay crumpled on the ground, his leg twisted underneath his body at an odd angle. A mixture of grief and anger, of relief and disgust, built inside him. Then, Rosman felt an urge to laugh. The more he fought it, the more powerful it became. Before long, he heard himself laughing at the sight of Gracchus, lying there awkward and defenseless.

The laughter soon gave way to tears. He sat on the stairs for several minutes, the body of Gracchus growing more distant and absurd when seen through a mist of tears and the peal of laughter. After about a minute he stopped. Rosman wiped the moisture from his eyes with his sleeve.

He limped inside his apartment and grabbed an extension cord from the lamp at his bedstand. At the bottom of the stairs Rosman probed Gracchus' wrist for a pulse. It took him several tries, but Rosman finally located a faint throbbing.

He rolled Gracchus over and pressed his knee into the man's chest. Gracchus lay motionless, his breathing labored. The left leg was clearly broken. *Good*, he thought, *it serves the bastard right*. Rosman tied his hands together and looped the cord around the banister.

Upstairs, Rosman sat down next to the telephone, dialed the police and reported the break-in. After a minute, Rosman stood up and paced the apartment floor, waiting for the police to arrive. How was he going to explain this strange interruption in the life of a Midwestern college town? How was he going to reassemble the pieces of his own shattered serenity?

As he stood at his front window, Rosman remembered the letter he had been writing to Buechler. He walked to his bedroom, picked it up, and started to read.

Dear Herr Buechler,

You occasionally spoke of my youth and innocence when we met in Berlin, traits you associated with my country. I have often wondered what it was that attracted you and others to me, both personally and as a representative of my country. Was it the youth that implies exuberance, vitality, and the ability to dream? Or was it the youth that betrays inexperience and ignorance, that young and intemperate strength that needs to be tamed and channelled? I'd like to think it was the first.

Whatever it was, it is clear to me now that those momentous events in the fall of 1989, and those that followed into 1990, would not have occurred without us. Here, I mean my country, of course, although I like to think that our small act was somehow an important part of the larger drama around us. I concede that final judgment must rest with the historians, but it seems inescapable that our presence and commitment brought those events to pass in November, and that our involvement helped keep them on the right course.

As I write this note, Herr Buechler, I am convinced that you agree. And that is why you came to me. You agree with Goethe that somehow we in America do have it better, that our chance to begin anew those years ago gave us a refreshing outlook and advantage, even if we don't always use them well. And you saw that same new beginning in me, something to use for your own personal campaign, which I realize now was indeed a worthy one. I sincerely hope that I did not let you down, because there were others I could not help, people whose memories I will always treasure. You taught me an important lesson in Berlin, one that I will not forget. And for that, my friend, I thank you.

Rosman folded the letter and placed it in his pocket. When the police arrived, Rosman went out into the hallway to check on Gracchus. He was sitting upright, watching the officers approach. He turned his face toward Rosman with the slow calculating movements of an animal of prey. The eyes that studied Rosman had narrowed to hard green circles with the piercing sharpness of an ice pick.

Rosman realized that his interlude in this quiet town had been an illusion, that such solitude was something he would probably never know again. He had learned that much from Gracchus. Rosman knew than that he was back in the game, and that, given his history and all he had experienced, he would probably never be out of it.

He went into the bedroom to wrap his ankle and pack for a trip to Washington. Perhaps the CIA would take him on. Before he closed his suitcase, Rosman tossed in the well-worn pages of Lamprecht's notebook.

THE END